Grandfather Zero

Anthony W. Eichenlaub

Oak Leaf Books

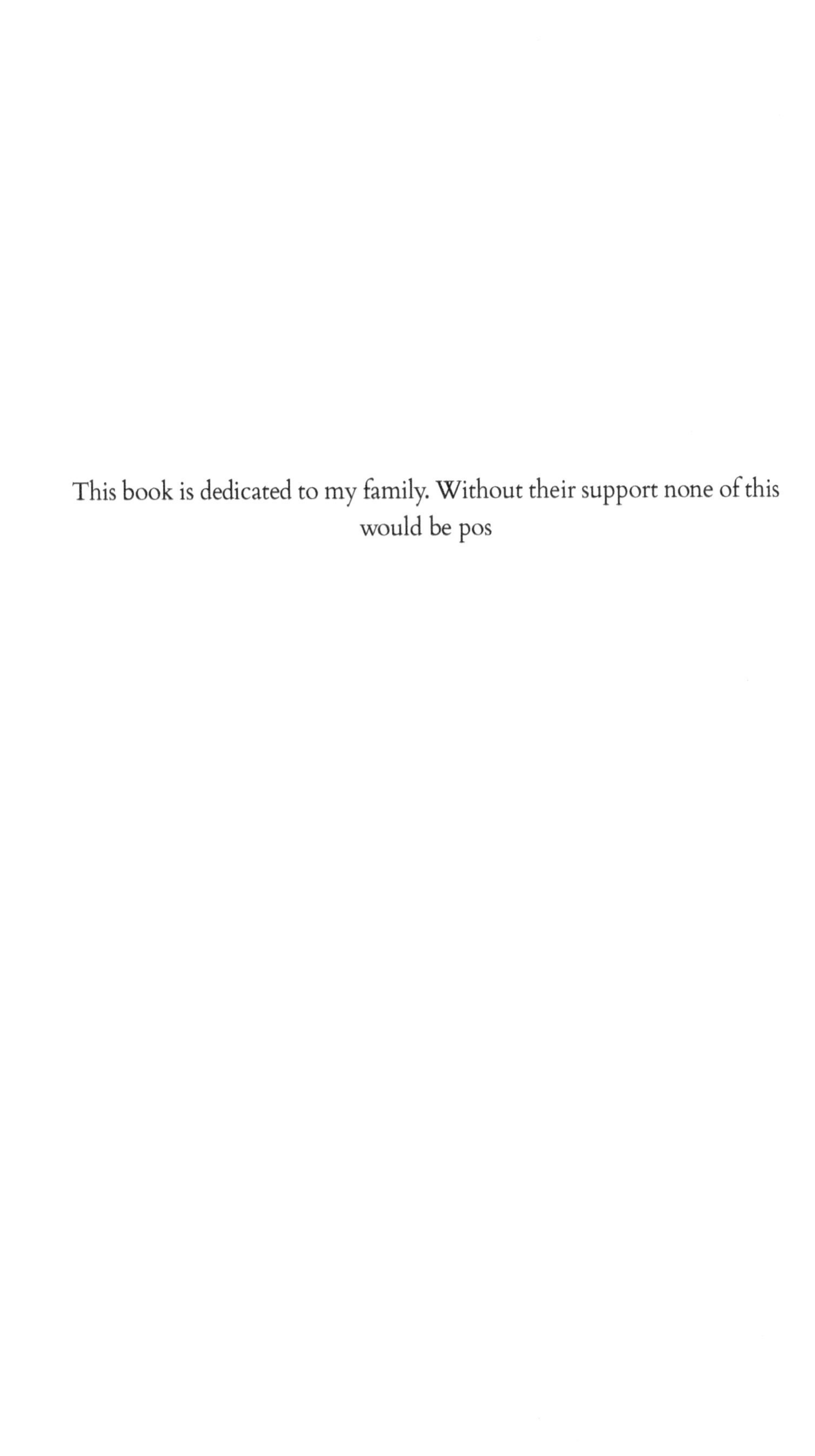

This book is dedicated to my family. Without their support none of this would be pos

Chapter One

"Fail forward," they always said.

It was Ajay Andersen's esteemed and very wise opinion that *they* were a bunch of assholes.

During his career as an NSA hacker, Ajay had experienced his fair share of failure. Lessons learned in failure burned themselves into every success he had experienced since his abrupt retirement.

Now, as he stared down at his liver-spotted hands, he considered the end result of all that failure. Had it ever really led to success? He had played his part in the catastrophic end of encryption. Everything from blockchain to privacy had fallen before him. He had collapsed corporations and toppled governments. Almost every operational success was a moral failure. Every moral success was an operational failure—though there had been few enough of those. If failure brought wisdom, then he was, perhaps, the wisest man living in the small town of Bemidji, Minnesota.

Which was good, because the next thing he was going to try could *not* fail.

His knobby-knuckled fingers danced in the green glow of the holographic display. He walked through the code for the thousandth time. This had to be absolutely perfect on the first try, something that his hard-earned wisdom told him was impossible.

The basement door opened, and the harsh light of morning shone down into the dank coding cave. It was time.

"Papa?" said Kylie from the top of the stairs. Her dark hair fell to her shoulders, and looming in the light, the fourteen-year-old girl was an ominous shadow of her mother's beauty nestled in an oversized gray hoodie. Her full lips pursed in a pout and her light brown skin glowed in the burning sunlight. "Is it ready?"

"Almost, hon," Ajay said. "One more check."

He stepped through the code. Machine language made his eyes ache, and this code was a network of analog, digital, and quantum connections grown organically in his granddaughter's brain. Machine-level code would have been a vacation.

The steps creaked as Kylie descended into his basement workspace.

Ajay became acutely aware of the stink he was wallowing in. He'd been working so hard on this project that there was no time for showers or changes of clothing or proper meals. Chip bags crinkled when he turned around to blink his dry eyes at Kylie. "I'm almost ready."

"You should get out more, Papa."

"At my age…" He didn't bother to finish the excuse.

"You could meet friends."

He couldn't. Ajay had been in hiding for years, ever since he left his government job on unpleasant terms. Something about driving the stake into encryption didn't settle well with the government types. Until he met his granddaughters, Ajay had been content to stay hidden at home. All the social interaction he needed could be found in the shadowy corners of the network.

Kylie chewed her lip. "Are you sure this will work?"

The alternative terrified Ajay. "I'm positive." He closed the code dialog. If something went wrong during the long process, there was no rolling back. Only forward. Fail forward.

The only failure is a failure to change, and Ajay had spent every waking hour thinking of solutions since he discovered the flaw in his granddaughter's abilities. She could connect to computers. Control them. But it was a two-way street.

"They used to call something like this a zero-day," Ajay explained. "As in, it's a security flaw that we know before the first day that it's made public. It's a bug so bad you have zero days to fix it. If someone knew this vulnerability right now, they would be able to do terrible things to you."

"Like what I did to Gabby."

Kylie could connect to wireless devices, including others with similar abilities. Several months ago, she had used her ability to override an out-of-control process in a younger girl, saving her. The effect had been transformative and absolute—a good thing given the circumstances, but the implications terrified Ajay.

"What you did was necessary," Ajay said. "You did the right thing by shutting down her abilities."

"But that's not the only zero-day."

"No, of course not. Remember all those military specs I showed you?"

"They were *so* boring. The way you hack stuff is slow. Why would I need to know how to overflow a password buffer?" She crossed her arms and jutted her jaw out in a pout. "I don't work like that."

But she did. After showing her how things worked, he had noticed that she changed how she interacted with machines. She became more efficient.

Kylie's eyes glazed over, and Ajay hoped he hadn't triggered her trauma. No, that wasn't right. He knew he had. He hoped it wouldn't be as bad for her as it had in the past. She only knew two other girls with similar neurological enhancements. One was her sister Isabelle, who had used the computer in her head to change herself and left over a year ago. The other was Gabby, but Gabby had burned out in the worst way. Most children had died from these unethical experiments. All Ajay wanted was to make sure Kylie could survive and dictate her own future.

Even if that meant she made some wrong choices.

The important part was that the choices would be hers. With un-restricted access to the girl's brain, someone else could modify her personality on an instinctual level. Isabelle had done it to herself. At least, that would explain how the older sibling managed to work for the morally questionable Frontier Arms. It was hard enough for Kylie to establish herself in small-town Minnesota. She didn't need the kind of garbage the outside world would push on her.

But that's what was possible if he didn't apply the patch.

"Will I still be able to go to summer camp?" Kylie asked. Her voice was quiet. Not quite a whisper, but soft and flat, like she was trying her best to tamp down its rough ridges.

Ajay's teeth tasted like charcoal. "It's dangerous." He knew it wasn't the right thing to say, but he had thought hard about the camp. Kylie was sensitive. She wouldn't do well in a high-pressure camp, and even if he wasn't worried about the tech in her head, he'd still be worried about her.

"Right." She pinched the meat between her forefinger and thumb, twisting the skin hard enough that it looked painful. "What if I just go learn about it?"

Ajay raised an eyebrow. "We've discussed this before."

"There's a recruiter coming to the park this afternoon. I might not even pass the test."

He'd never heard of a summer camp that came with entry exam, but if there was a test, Kylie would pass. She was smarter than any kid he'd ever known, and if she was determined to succeed at something, she would do it.

"I might not even make it in," Kylie added.

It made sense that Kylie wanted to go to this camp. She had only learned about it a short while ago, when she met her grandmother. It was a survival camp for elite children. Intense, brutal, dangerous.

Not the kind of place Ajay wanted to send his granddaughter.

"My brain, my choice," Kylie whispered, perhaps guessing his thoughts.

"Someone might seek your vulnerabilities there," Ajay said. "If you go unpatched—"

"I'll do the patch." Kylie picked up the band from Ajay's workbench and fitted it to her head. "Is it ready?"

Ajay didn't understand the girl sometimes. He *told* her the camp would be hard. Why would a kid want to go into something that was going to be difficult? He plucked the band from her head, gave it a right turn, and affixed it properly. "This is brain surgery," he warned.

"My choice is brain surgery or brain damage."

"Typical decision for a high schooler, right?"

She flashed a quick smile. "Pretty much."

There were other options. They could disappear into the night, reestablish a new life somewhere, and run when anyone figured out who she was. They could burn out her enhancements entirely. Microsurgery could return Kylie to a more normal development path, but in the process, it would change who she was.

Ajay wouldn't kill the girl just to make her fit in.

"Let me check the code one more time," he said, bringing up his display.

"Papa," Kylie said, grabbing the fidget control from him. It was a miniature computer that fit onto his hand and projected a holographic display. Ajay was using her old model, and it was violet with sparkles. "You've looked over it a hundred times."

"This is important."

"This is ridiculous," Kylie said. She navigated the controls like a pro until she had the first update program flashing in front of her. She squinted at the tiny glowing text. "How do you even understand this stuff?"

"The language is grown from a Python derivative, spun off in the Thirties—"

"It doesn't make any sense." She swiped the code away. Her hands trembled slightly, and the text floating in front of her quivered.

"This first update pretty much just shuts everything down," said Ajay. "Then once that stabilizes, your brain will strengthen to compensate for the missing pieces. After a while, we can reactivate the logic sequences with the extra protection."

"All right. Let's get it over with." She handed him the fidget, which he slipped onto his left hand. His fat knuckles made using this kind of interface difficult, but it was his best option for quick coding.

The controls let him easily manipulate his code, but unlike the consumer-grade fidget, this one connected to a more powerful computer that he kept in his cane. It was the perfect setup for a code junkie like himself. Lots of computing power. Lots of versatility.

An alert flashed across his holographic display, and he cursed when it disappeared before he could read it. He needed his cheaters. He poked around on his messy workbench until he found the slender half-moon reading glasses dangling from the chain around his neck. After a second of calibration, the text popped up laser sharp in his vision.

He grunted acknowledgment. A visitor.

Kylie puffed out her cheeks. Her hands were twisted together in a knot. "I'm ready."

He couldn't wait any longer. She might back out, and he didn't want to think about the consequences if he didn't run this process.

"Just—" Kylie's face scrunched up into a cross between fear and determination. "Just do it."

Ajay looked at the girl one more time. She knew she needed the update. She knew that Ajay was the best person to deliver it. Not only was he the most skilled with the code, but he was the only person in the world that she could trust.

But *knowing* something didn't make the conclusion any less terrifying. Kylie risked losing herself in this. She always had. Either the machine in her brain would grow and cause damage, or she would remove it and cause damage.

None of that was as scary as what might happen if someone else discovered a zero-day flaw. They could take over her personality completely. Rewrite her to be *anything*. Other girls had suffered the same fate. Kylie's sister Isabelle had once been controlled by their father. The constant manipulation the man had used had left her traumatized.

Rumors ran through the shadow networks that spoke of other girls with similar skills. When Haveraptics collapsed, their resources disappeared along with records of all the modified children created by Jackson Garver's ethical monstrosity.

The alert came again, and Ajay took a moment to glance at the outdoor camera. A slender hooded figure stood on their stoop, looking out into the street. A solicitor, probably. A kid looking to sell cookies for some high school field trip or something. They would go away.

He started the update.

Code didn't exactly install in a brain. An organically grown network didn't conform to any standards of access or manipulation. His code nudged functions in her brain that accessed the outer world. He watched as the first lines danced across the signal layers of her enhanced brain. When she reached out, his code attached and danced across the manifold of her existence. It was beautiful.

It was terrifying.

Then, her systems went dark. One by one, his manipulations touched her mind in ways to induce dormancy.

An alert flashed across his cheaters. The person at the door was manipulating the lock. Picking it.

Red danced in his peripheral view. Errors. Kylie's brain resisted his changes.

"Stay calm," Ajay whispered as softly as he could. He placed a hand on the twisted knot of Kylie's fists and pried them apart. "It's almost done."

The front door swung open, and the visitor stepped into the house.

"Shit," Ajay muttered.

Red washed over his whole screen. Kylie's eyes snapped open and she stared at him, mouth slightly parted in horror.

"It's fine," he grumbled. "Nothing to worry about."

It was the exact right thing to say if his goal was to make her worry more.

"Goddammit." That didn't help, either.

Footsteps crossed the floor above. The floorboards creaked. Not one single bark came from the lousiest watchdog known to man.

"We're fine, Kylie," Ajay said. "Almost finished."

The red flickered to blue, but Kylie kept the worried expression on her downturned lips. This wouldn't work if she resisted. The update would be incomplete. Ajay wanted to shout at the person upstairs. Get them to leave and come back later. Whatever they were looking for, he didn't have it. He might have access to dozens of hidden bank accounts, but he didn't live like a wealthy man. They could take the ancient television from his living room or a fortune's worth of frozen pizzas from his freezer.

He knew this couldn't be a common thief. His door was too secure.

This was a professional.

"Kylie," he said, "I need you to imagine a prairie, like the one we visited last year."

"With the butterflies?"

"That's right. Monarchs everywhere. Grasshoppers. Remember the Black-eyed Susans and the daisies?"

"Asteraceae?"

"Sure." Ajay was pretty sure she had looked that up. "One of my favorite flower families. Remember what we learned about the sunflower?"

"It isn't really one flower," she said, scrunching her nose up to help her remember. Blue flashed through the screen, followed by a few points of green. Completed sectors. Good.

"That's right. It's not one flower. It's hundreds of flowers. Do you remember what the petals are?"

She thought for a moment. "The petals are whole flowers."

"That's right. The parts of a sunflower are individual flowers. Some flowers become showy to attract pollinators. Some become reproductive organs and then seeds. Together, they look like a single flower, but it's actually hundreds of flowers working together for a common goal."

Green scurried across his screen. The progress bar leaped forward across his cheaters.

Kylie opened her eyes and stared at Ajay. Her expression was slack, and she blinked lazily. "She doesn't want to talk to me."

"Who?"

The first step creaked under the visitor's weight. Then the second. Ajay watched as the slender form descended the dusty steps into his basement workshop. Behind her, his bloodhound Garrison sheepishly followed.

"Me," said the girl when she was halfway down the stairs.

The update finished. "It's time for a rest, Kylie." He turned toward the stairs where the slender woman stood in a crisp military uniform.

Kylie's eyes were almost shut, and she gave an almost imperceptible nod. She moved from the chair to a small sofa and immediately dropped into a deep sleep.

"Hello, Isabelle," Ajay said, facing the girl who had just arrived. "It's good to see you again, dear."

Chapter Two

TENEN LANG STARED AT the mud-caked, gravel parking lot. An ant crept across the surface, making its way to the delicious corpse of a dead nightcrawler, and Tenen studied it carefully, letting his eyes focus on its tiny black carapace. Its antennae tested the coarse terrain. At least the thing had purpose, Tenen thought. He leaned hard on the car door, his bulk rocking the vehicle until his head finally stopped spinning. He wore a cowboy hat and sunglasses, but all the swagger and style he once possessed was swallowed whole in his disability.

After downing a couple pills, he jammed his oak cane into the soft earth and strode past the wooden sign for the Pine Fortress School for the Gifted.

Lang had once been one of the best of the best in the mercenary business. He ran his own elite team, worked for the wealthiest clients, and commanded respect wherever he walked. Frontier Arms had treated him well over the years. It had given him all the best jobs.

Until it didn't.

A feeble old man—Ajay Andersen—had caught him by surprise and taken everything. A microwave pulse had fried Lang's inner ear and toasted the parts of his brain that made him so damn good at his job. The old man had ruined him. Ended his career as a mercenary. Andersen had taken everything that mattered.

Now the only job he could get was teaching.

Lang despised teachers. They were the assholes who didn't have it in them to *do*. All they could do was *teach*. Fitting then that this was where he ended up. Andersen should have finished the job. Lang would have been better off in a grave.

A man approached along the camp trail under the canopy of oaks. A short white guy with a shiny bald head. Built. Lang briefly wondered if he'd be given a hard time for his darker skin, but then remembered that he'd be given enough of a hard time for being disabled. That would be a change of pace, anyway. Lang straightened his back and did his best not to lean on his cane, even when a wave of dizziness rolled over him.

"Lang?" the man asked. His accent pegged him as a native of northern Minnesota or possibly Canada.

"Who else would I be?"

"Had a couple Mormons stop by the other day. Looking to spread the word." He stuck out a hand. "Regis Shaleborn."

Lang fumbled with his cane to switch hands. When he tried to look the man in the eyes, the best he could do was stare at his hook nose. Good thing the man probably couldn't see his eyes through the reflective sunglasses. "Tenen Lang."

Shaleborn walked with Lang up the long trail, always moving slightly faster than was comfortable. The shorter man's steps were so balanced Lang figured if he hit the guy as hard as he could, he still wouldn't knock him down. Not that he could ever manage to hit him. He opted not to test the theory but despised the sense of powerlessness. Lang had always been the powerhouse in the room. The badass everyone else respected no matter what.

"I knew a few martial arts guys in Frontier," Lang hazarded. "You ever work in the field?"

Shaleborn glanced back. "Ten years. Mostly bodyguard duty."

Lang grunted. "Peacock or eagle?"

"Nothing we do here is just for show," said Shaleborn. "But sometimes a little show makes things easier." He stepped up his pace, leading Lang from the forest into the wide, flat expanse of short prairie. Across the open commons stood a wide building nestled against the towering forest. Even from a distance, Lang could see that the building's log walls were fake, but they gave the place a Norse longhouse aesthetic that he appreciated. To the sides of the commons were sleeper cabins where kids would live.

"Fancy place," Lang muttered.

"Shooting range is down the hill." Shaleborn glanced at Lang's cane. "Not sure if you're good for much of that anymore."

Asshole. Lang didn't think he could handle being bad at the thing he had once been the best at. What was the point?

"Teachers all get their own cabin, and those are up the hill." Shaleborn pointed to the right, where another dirt path led up a forested hill. Knotted roots crisscrossed the trail, and Lang didn't look forward to navigating it. "We're up at five every morning. Bed at ten. Not much time to rest in between."

Lang fought the sense of dread growing in the back of his chest. His palms grew slick on his cane. This was worse than guarding the most hated Saudi prince in the world. It was worse than securing the caves under Saint Paul. "That'll keep me out of trouble, I guess."

"It won't." Shaleborn started along the path circling the prairie. "Silver wants a word before you settle in."

Sonya Silver was a tall woman with severe black hair and a pair of thin glasses perched on the bridge of her nose. She sat at her desk and didn't look up when Lang walked in. This was it, he thought. This was where she took one look at him and sent him packing. He held his cowboy hat in his hand but kept his sunglasses on.

"Sit," she said.

Shaleborn disappeared, and Lang sat in the proffered chair. It was a low seat, and he was worried that he wouldn't be able to gracefully rise when their conversation was complete. He set his cane across his lap and did his best not to fidget while Silver worked.

At last, she looked up and blinked at him. "They say you're the best."

"I—"

"Do you know what we do here, Mr. Lang?" Silver asked.

"You're a survival camp. You teach foraging and hunting. Martial arts. That kind of thing."

She fixed him with a dry look. "You've read the brochure."

Lang blinked. His thumbnail dug into his cane.

Silver folded her hands and peered at Lang over the tops of her glasses. She wore a dark eyeliner that made her eyes sink deep into her skull. "They say we make killers here, Mr. Lang. Is that going to be a problem?"

"Not at all." Lang *was* a killer. How hard could it be to *make* them?

"Interesting," she said.

"I strangled a guy once," Lang said. "An enemy combatant on the streets of Belize City. We were trying to move the client to the nearest airport, and gunshots would have given away our position." He didn't let even a shred of emotion cross his face. "He was young. Maybe still a teen. It didn't matter. I got him wrestled down and strangled him out with my own hands. It was the hardest thing I ever did, watching the light go out in that kid's eyes."

She raised one immaculate eyebrow. "Why do you tell me this?"

"I imagine teaching kids is pretty much the reverse."

Silver was silent for a long time. "Most of the children we get here are soft." She waved a hand like she could shoo them away. "Rich kids who have lived rich lives. But every once in a while, we find one with real potential. All we need to do is let it blossom. We're not making bad people. We're allowing people to find their function in society, even if that society isn't always the one we would like to have. As a mercenary, I hope you understand this."

"Of course."

Silver's glasses flashed, and her eyes danced with words Lang couldn't read. "You've had quite an impressive career. Started as an enforcer for union collectives. Moved up to leadership almost right away. Then you spent several years working for Liam Thompson. Care to tell me about how that ended?"

Lang's mouth went dry. He felt himself choking up the way he had never choked up during combat. There was something intense and difficult about this woman and the way she looked straight through him. Judged him. Then again, that was what bosses were supposed to do, wasn't it?

"Even the best tactics can't make up for bad strategy, and even the best strategist can't win all the time. We influence our odds, but nothing is guaranteed." When he closed his eyes every night, his brain burned itself out running scenarios that would have prevented Andersen from crippling him. "There's nothing I could have done."

"I'm taking a chance on you, Mr. Lang," Silver said. "It would make me feel more comfortable if you told me it was a guaranteed thing."

Lang scraped a long sliver of oak from his cane. "You're not messing up by hiring me, if that's what you're wondering."

Again, her glasses flashed. "It says you've worked with children before."

"Kidnapping," Lang said, keeping the hesitation from his voice. "The kids we took in that last job were a special priority. Orders from Frontier management. It's what toppled the whole mission. The team wasn't used to handling kids, so they didn't keep them locked down well enough. It was a bad move putting inexperienced people in charge, but that job had us stretched too thin. Mr. Thompson wanted all my best installing explosives and defending the camp."

"Interesting."

Lang was starting to hate how she used that word. "Yes, ma'am. I'll also add that I ought to have been killed when we lost our flank. The only reason I'm alive is that one of the enemy's special operatives decided to cripple me instead. The asshole didn't have enough mercy left in him for a clean shot to the head."

Silver folded her hands in front of her, interlacing her fingers so her immaculate fingernails dug into the backs of her hands. "This isn't going to work if you still feel sorry for yourself."

"I don't."

"The children will devour you if you show weakness. We teach them as much."

"Shaleborn didn't seem like he was messing around."

Silver smiled a shark's smile. She touched the corner of her glasses and pointed at a screen lying on her desk. The tablet flashed once to show that it had received the data. "Take this. You can start reading through bios. Regis will show you to your cabin. The first children arrive in one week."

"Thank you." Lang bristled at the awkward dismissal. It was nothing like the rigid military structure of Frontier Arms. He took the tablet and tucked it under his arm. Using his cane, he stood slowly so as not to induce dizziness, then walked out with as much dignity as he could muster.

Shaleborn waited outside. "Did you pass?"

"Didn't even know it was a test."

Lang's cabin was a single room faux log cabin with an electric heater and a single bed. It sat under a tall oak halfway up a forested swell with a view of absolutely nothing out its filthy back window. The dresser drawers stuck in the humidity, and a trunk at the end of the bed contained an unkempt pile of musty blankets. A single garbage can contained the desiccated remains of half a dozen apple cores.

Shaleborn shook Lang's hand. "I'm out recruiting this afternoon."

"You're still recruiting?"

"It's a special case," Shaleborn said.

Shaleborn left him with assurances that his things would be brought up by the staff, so Lang settled his weary bones on the bed.

He never used to get this tired. Days without sleep had always exhilarated him. Weeks on duty stoked the fire in his soul and drove him harder toward his goals. Sharpened his mind.

Now, after that asshole Ajay Andersen's crippling attack, Tenen Lang was a lesser man. He exhausted easily. His thoughts were a muddled mess. The medicine in his pocket was his one tenuous grip that kept him within view of normalcy but never normal. That's what he would be. Forever.

The tablet flared to life at his touch. He steadied it, balancing it on the dusty pillow. Reading was a challenge, but he increased the font size and engaged an eye-tracking accessibility feature. To an extent, the writing moved with his eyes, so he could read the bios of the children expected to arrive in one short week.

Hours later, as the sky grew dim, he flipped to one final recruit.

And saw her blank expression staring back at him from the screen. Kylie Andersen, with her brown hair and thin lips. The girl who had ruined Liam Thompson's plans. The granddaughter of the man who had ruined Lang's life. She was labeled *Priority Recruit.*

Lang almost made it to the garbage can before he vomited.

Chapter Three

Kylie woke through an oppressive brain fog, and for a moment she thought she saw her older sister. Isabelle spoke in hushed tones with their grandfather, but Kylie hardly recognized her. She had changed so much.

All the regular stuff was the same. Isabelle's blonde hair was pulled back into a severe ponytail, but it still gave the girl an angelic halo. Her blue eyes and pale skin were nothing like Kylie's own palate of browns and tans, but the two were unmistakably sisters. Kylie could see it in the turn of the girl's red lips and the shape of her high cheekbones. It was like looking into a warped mirror where the image was an idealized form of perfection.

But this Isabelle—was Kylie dreaming this?—was not the quiet girl Kylie had known most of her life. In the end, before she had left, Isabelle had lost her words completely. She had been as good as mute. At the time, Kylie didn't know that it was because their father was manipulating her brain. He had forcibly changed her personality and muddled her sense of identity.

Now, Isabelle didn't seem to have any doubts about her identity. She wore a crisp blue blouse and slacks with flat boots and narrow glasses. She made all of it look so good. Professional. Not that Kylie's sister shouldn't look professional, but the whole look made Isabelle appear older than she really was. The girl wasn't an eighteen-year-old dressing up for her first job. She was a business professional consorting with her unfortunate family.

She was still *definitely* Isabelle, though. Kylie still felt the warm glow of a connection with her sister, even though Isabelle didn't even glance in her direction. Kylie might not have picked it up from her sister's body language. She had always been terrible at reading body language, though she was learning some hidden tricks well enough. This was different. Kylie knew that Isabelle didn't want to speak because, despite the updates Papa had put in her head, she could still sense something in her sister. They would always be connected.

Kylie shrank into her gray hoodie as the brain fog threatened to swallow her into sleep.

There had always been a connection between Kylie and Isabelle. It transcended even the connections Kylie could make to wireless devices. It was something spiritual, like quantum entanglement.

Isabelle was watching her. Her blue eyes pierced the sketchy gloom of the basement. A surge of self-awareness bubbled up in Kylie. Isabelle was judging the pathetic lab in Papa's basement. Kylie couldn't stop seeing the cobwebs upon cobwebs in the corner or the greasy stain on the concrete floor which was covered in a layer of dust that looked a hundred years old. It smelled of mold down here in Papa's lab. Mold and stale crackers.

It was a good lab, though. The airflow was superb. Power was routed through a high-quality battery backup for always-on stability. The network connections rivaled even those of the best companies in the Twin Cities where they could afford the very best. Papa had never been one to spend ridiculous amounts of money, but Kylie got the idea that he had enough cash on hand for what he really cared about.

It turned out he only cared about two things: fancier computers and staying hidden.

Kylie opened her mouth to talk, but shut it again when a wave of annoyance rolled off of Isabelle.

"Kylie," said Papa. "How are you feeling?"

For the first time since Papa's update, Kylie considered how she felt. Not great, it turned out. Annoyed. But there wasn't anything wrong that she could really point to, except for the obvious success of the experiment. Her connection to the local network was severed. She couldn't feel the constant buzz of the surrounding machines. The world was empty, and it lingered like the shadow of an invisible giant. Looming. Present, but also gone.

"I'm fine," she finally said.

"All of your readings are normal," Papa said. "Would you mind if I left for a little while to speak with Isabelle?"

Kylie glared at her awful sister. "I have to go meet Austin."

"You need rest," sputtered Papa. "I could call—"

"I'm fine," Kylie said. Her head pulsed with a headache that emerged like a rising tide. "I'm not sick."

Papa watched her for what seemed like a hundred years. Finally, he let out a grunt, picked up his cane, and gestured for Kylie's traitorous sister to lead them up the stairs.

Kylie blinked, and like that, they were gone. She buried her face in her hands, and not for the first time, cried, wondering why her sister wouldn't talk to her. Then, the fog swallowed her whole.

Chapter Four

AJAY ENTERED THE LIMOUSINE almost ninety percent sure that his grand-daughter wouldn't have him killed. He shuffled over to the seat across from her, leaned his cane next to him, and folded his hands in his lap. The silent vehicle rolled forward, and muted sunlight shone through dark windows.

"Kylie is doing fine," Ajay said after several achingly long minutes of silence. "Apart from the occasional excitement, our lives here are fairly normal." Ajay looked out the window. They had already left town and were circling the lake. "You should consider spending some time with her."

Her perfect eyebrow raised imperceptibly. "My job keeps me busy."

"Frontier Arms."

"Yes," said Isabelle. "Exciting as far as first jobs go."

"You're what, eighteen now?"

She touched a spot on the limousine wall and a compartment opened. Soft light illuminated two tumblers and a glass carafe of amber liquid. "Care for a drink?"

Ajay blinked, not sure if he should show his shock at her audacity. Should he lecture her on alcohol consumption? Ask to be let out immediately? Maybe it would be best to ignore the offer entirely and pretend it didn't happen.

He settled on, "Make it a double."

She poured two fingers into one of the glasses and handed it to him. She didn't pour anything for herself. "I'm still underage," she explained with a mischievous smile.

The whiskey smelled of oak and sage but tasted like molten lava. Ajay never really did acquire a taste for whiskey. He said, "I have the information that Silas Cardoso stole from Frontier." It seemed like forever ago that his former acquaintance had died to bring Ajay data that would help him manage Kylie's abilities. "It was incomplete."

Isabelle rolled her eyes, and for a second, she almost looked like her prior teenage self. "Cardoso took what I fed him. You must have realized that."

"It got him killed."

"Frontier is dangerously compartmentalized. I can't always influence what happens in the rest of the organization."

"Everyone lives in their own silo," Ajay said, taking another awful sip of whiskey. "That's how it was back in the NSA. Once, we spent months cracking into a Chinese server farm just to find evidence of prior NSA infiltration. They'd been in, corrupted the data, and left. Best thing we could do was clean up after them so they didn't get caught."

"Did you?"

"Well, they were our competition for bonuses that year."

Isabelle sighed. "Every organization has problems."

"This doesn't need to be you, Isabelle." Ajay's breath steamed the glass. "You know that."

The muscles in her jaw twitched. "You don't even know you're doing it."

"Doing what?"

The limo turned, and fresh gravel popped under its tires. They passed a thousand miles of freshly planted sugar beet fields, with rows and rows of earthen ridges going on forever into the distance. "Changing us," Isabelle finally said.

Ajay set his glass down in the glowing holder. Light played through the amber fluid. "I'm giving Kylie everything she needs to be herself."

Isabelle said, "You aren't letting her decide."

"That's not true."

"Whose idea was it to hack her brain?"

It had been Ajay's idea. He had found the vulnerability in his granddaughter's brain and panicked. The anxiety of the open flaw still gnawed at him, even though he knew it was now closed. "How did you learn about that?"

"She was afraid," Isabelle hissed. "Afraid for her life and her identity because of what *you* told her."

"She needed to know!" Ajay snapped. He regretted the anger in his voice as soon as it came out. "I'm not keeping secrets from her."

"But you're deciding how to present the information. You tell her she'd be an idiot not to do this change, but it's her choice. She'll die if she doesn't do it, but it's her choice. There are evil people out trying to get her, but it's her choice."

"There *are* evil people out there trying to get to her." Ajay wondered if Isabelle might be one of them. "I think someone's continuing the biotech research that changed you two." He had seen chatter online, but nothing concrete.

"Let them," Isabelle said. "They won't get very far."

"Because you'll stop them?"

She fixed Ajay with a steady gaze. "I need her to be safe."

Ajay took another burning swallow of whiskey. "She *is* safe."

"Not with you." Isabelle stared out the window at the passing fields. "Every moment you spend with her puts her at risk, especially with what's happening this summer."

"What do you want, Isabelle? I've let Kylie practice martial arts. I've trained her to manage her own mind. The machine in her brain has developed in a way that gave her a weakness, and the changes we've uploaded today will keep her safe."

"It's not all about weakness," Isabelle spat. "Maybe you should focus on her strengths."

"Once, a long time ago, my wife—your grandmother—God bless her soul—"

"She's not dead."

"Might as well be." Ajay swallowed back a lump of emotion. "I had it all back then. Good looking. Smart. Athletic. She said to me, 'You're never going to be the best at anything. There's always someone better.'" He gripped his cane until his knobby knuckles ached. "I never believed her. Not once."

Isabelle raised an eyebrow.

"Yes, I was athletic. Kind of. In my own way. I was smart, anyway. For a long time, I *was* the best. I was the hacker who could solve the biggest problems of an era. I poured everything into that skill, and I never met anyone as good as me." Ajay leaned forward. "But Kylie leaves me in the dust. She's smarter, faster, and with that thing running in her head, she's the most dangerous anyone has ever been in the computer age."

"That's why you're crippling her?"

"I'm not—" He choked back the words because he didn't want to lie to Isabelle. "She needs to learn how to grow beyond her power. This will force her to learn her skills in a more disciplined way. The brain is a muscle, Isabelle. If she doesn't do this, hers will atrophy. It's all in the data we got from Frontier, so I know you know it, too."

Isabelle folded her hands and pressed them to her mouth. The car rumbled onto a county road, twisting along through lake country among the green forests. Lakes had always been a refuge for Minnesotans. They were the escape after a long week or a long life. Here in the small towns of northern Minnesota, people could live their lives in peace no matter what turmoil shook the world all around.

Eventually, Isabelle broke their silence. "You're manipulative."

"Always have been," he said, "but aren't we all?"

"I want her to go to the Pine Fortress summer camp."

Ajay said, "You've been feeding her information about it."

"Maybe."

"Who's manipulative again?"

She watched him with half-lidded eyes.

"I don't think it's a good idea." He had met a former student of the Pine Fortress School for the Gifted. The woman had been a fabulous person and an excellent assassin, but the experience had changed her. Ajay wasn't sure if Kylie fully understood what she was getting into.

"It's not up to you." The steely look in Isabelle's eyes sent a shiver up Ajay's spine.

"As Kylie's guardian, it kind of is."

"She needs to spend time away from you."

The car hummed as it sped up on the curvy county road. Tires peeled around a sharp bend.

"Driving me out to pasture?" Ajay asked. "Subtle threats? Where is the quiet Isabelle I once knew?"

"That girl never existed."

"I thought I remembered talking with her," Ajay mused. "She said she liked capybaras and wanted to know who she really was without her father telling her."

The car sped faster on the straightaway. Isabelle gestured at herself with her perfect fingernails. "This is who I am, Papa. If you don't like me anymore, that's your problem."

Ajay glanced out the window. They passed another soybean field, its dark soil freshly plowed. They would hit the next set of curves soon, and Ajay didn't know what to say to Isabelle.

But isn't that how it was raising children? They were little terrorists, and policy had always been not to negotiate with terrorists. Give in to one little demand and pretty soon they'll expect the whole world.

Ajay was the guy who negotiated with terrorists. As a hacker, his best move had always been to give in to demands and exact some back-channel pressure to collapse the organization. They wanted power? Give them power. Then use it against them. They wanted to open trade? Great. Give them trade. Then trade them all the corrupt influences that America could manage. Use victory as a lever to destroy them. Subvert their very beliefs.

That *wasn't* what he wanted to do to Isabelle. He wanted a healthier relationship. One in which he could invite her for dinner or discuss Kylie's future in earnest. He saw only one choice. He needed to change the conversation so that Kylie wasn't in the crosshairs.

"I've already decided that Kylie can go to the camp." A lie. "And I know what you're doing now is meant to make me back off Frontier Arms and their clients. Why?"

The car slowed. "You think Kylie's a better hacker than you? You should see me."

"I have no doubt," said Ajay. "But we're not enemies."

"I work for Frontier Arms. I'm paid to protect my clients in this region."

Ajay braced as the car went around a bend. It was still too fast, but he no longer worried that they would go careening off into the forest. "Your clients are corrupt."

"They're wealthy. That's not the same thing."

"It is. You *know* it is, Isabelle. Every one of them is corrupt in some way. The countercapitalists have a pretty solid argument."

"So, that's how it's going to be?" Isabelle asked. "You side with those terrorists?"

"They're activists, and I'm not siding with anyone."

"Tell that to my dead mercenaries and the thousand acres of pollution in the boundary waters."

"They cleaned that up."

"*We* cleaned that up. It wasn't a profitable job, either, but we got it done. If it had been any worse, there's no way we could have done it. And you *killed* Liam Thompson. We had every right to walk away as soon as he dropped."

"You had a contract."

"With *him*."

Ajay had been responsible for the explosion that had caused the waste-water spill in the Boundary Waters Canoe Area, but if Liam Thompson had lived, it would have been much worse. "You did the right thing."

The car pulled onto a gravel parking lot atop a hill. "We're not just killers, Papa. Frontier Arms can be a lot more than that."

"At least some silos can be."

"That's how it is for now," Isabelle said. "Things can change."

Maybe under the right leadership, it could be something in addition to a bunch of killers, but the mercenary group made most of its profit from dangerous, questionably legal contracts. Ajay had traced the money far enough to know that, at least. Plus, the organization was growing. Not a month went by it didn't absorb another mercenary company.

When the car stopped, Isabelle stepped out and gestured for Ajay to follow. They stood atop a rise overlooking a small lake. Paper birches framed their view, and a long swath of prairie covered the hill below. On the lake, a single fisherman sat in a canoe, his line dangling in the water.

The message was clear to Ajay. "Used to be I wanted this kind of retirement," he said.

"You could still have it."

"Not while Kylie still needs my protection."

"Let her go to camp, Papa. Let her exist outside of you for a while. It's the best thing for her."

He glanced at her. She was still so young. In the afternoon light, her skin was so light as to be translucent. Her eyes shone with the brightness that only youth could offer.

But she wasn't young. Not really. Her life had aged her. Ajay mourned the loss of whatever kid she might have been. He mourned her, but he didn't miss her. Isabelle was her own person, and he didn't agree with what she did, but he did his best to respect it.

"I'm not going to stop," he said.

The muscles in her jaw clenched. "I don't need you to stop, Papa. I just need you out of the way for a little while." She returned to the car. Once she was inside, the door slammed and the car pulled away, leaving Ajay to stand in a cloud of gravel dust.

"I should have expected that," he muttered to himself. It was still hard for him to understand his granddaughters. The young led such strange lives.

Isabelle would do what she was going to do. She would climb in power, grasping more and more of the Frontier Arms organization. To what end, Ajay didn't know. He figured it would come up eventually.

For now, he would go along with sending Kylie to the camp. It wasn't what he wanted, but she would likely be safe enough. After all, his sources told him they only took the cruelest, most dangerous kids into the program, then trained them as killers. Kylie had never been cruel, and she wouldn't be dangerous with her tech hobbled. If he was lucky, they would see her as just another rich kid whose parents wanted to ditch her for a summer.

Ajay had never been lucky.

He was in hiding. His departure from the NSA hadn't exactly been pleasant, and the rate at which he made enemies only increased as he aged. Part of hiding meant he didn't have friends, which suited him just fine. Usually.

It also meant he didn't have anyone he could call for a ride.

There was always the automated car network. Summoning a ride would be easy, but a quick check showed that no cars would come to his location. A block prevented any orders for a ten-mile radius. Clever. Isabelle knew what she was doing. How far had she driven him out to pasture? Ten minutes? Twenty? He turned toward Bemidji and started to walk.

Minutes passed. An hour. His hip started to hurt, and apart from a dozen farms, he hadn't passed anywhere that could summon a ride.

The rusted electric pickup rolled next to him for a long time before he bothered to look up and see who was driving. The woman's lightly tinted aviators failed to hide the crinkles of amusement that sparkled at the corners of her eyes. She waved a tanned hand in greeting as the truck rolled silently along.

"Hey, handsome," she said, "need a ride?"

The ache in Ajay's hip didn't leave him much choice. He considered different ways that he could keep his identity a secret from this woman. "Ajay Andersen," he said. That almost certainly wasn't the best way to do it.

"Kate," said the woman. Her truck smelled of hay and the indistinct headiness of livestock. "Kate Ludwig at your service." She slapped the seat next to her. "Hop in."

Chapter Five

Kylie didn't know if her head hurt because of what Papa did to it or because her stupid sister had decided to visit out of nowhere. The back of her skull still ached at the thought of Isabelle. Kylie could feel her there. Or maybe it was just lingering anger. Isabelle had *left* her. After their parents died, Isabelle had a choice that Kylie never had. She could have been *anyone*.

Isabelle had chosen to be someone who didn't care about her sister at all.

Stress burned in Kylie's gut, and there wasn't anything she wanted more than to just walk away and never come back, just like her sister. Papa had a little red Vespa that he was fixing up. She could take it and ride into the sunset. Never mind that she didn't have a license yet. It almost wasn't needed for little motorized scooters.

Instead, she cowered behind the thick row of lilacs and leaned against the base of a microwave tower. She had walked there like a chump. The red and white metal structure gleamed in the morning light.

Her only friend, Austin, sat next to her in a bright orange jacket and new glittering earrings. His lanky limbs made him look like a toppled gazelle.

"There's a *test*?" Austin asked. Not only was he her only friend, but as a gay black kid in outer Minnesota, he was almost as weird as her. "I thought we were done with tests."

"First of all," Kylie said, "we're *not* done with tests. We're done with middle school. Once we go to high school, there'll be way more tests."

"High school is immeasurably far in the future."

"It's at the end of the summer."

"An infinite expanse of time from now."

"Yeah, that's what I meant to say," Kylie grumbled. Despite her best efforts, Austin's charm chipped away at her sour mood. "But this test should be more fun."

"Hold on. I thought you just wanted me to sign up for a summer camp. I didn't know there was going to be an entry requirement."

Kylie rolled her eyes. She couldn't tell if Austin was teasing her or if he was really offended at the idea of taking a test after school was out for the summer. Either way, the conversation had started to annoy her.

The whine of an electric car rolling across loose gravel approached. Kylie peeked from behind the lilac and saw an old beater rumbling up the maintenance track.

"High schoolers," Austin whispered. He pulled her back behind the shrub. "Let's just stay out of sight."

Kylie had never really had trouble with bullies. Most of the time, the older kids ignored her, having long since learned that if they tried to bully her, she would just ignore them. Also, a few might have suffered catastrophic data integrity loss on their personal devices immediately after picking on her. Maybe.

Austin didn't have such luck. Maybe he was a target because he was black. Racism ran in trends through the rural communities, even if the rest of the world attempted to be more progressive. Maybe it was his tall, skinny form that caused him to stick out. Maybe it was because of his horrid fashion sense. Even Kylie knew that his big orange coat had never been stylish and his assortment of hand-me-down T-shirts hadn't seen the right end of a fad in over a decade.

She moved farther back behind the lilac as the car parked, but she could still see them as they stepped out of their vehicle. Three of them crossed the gravel lot, laughing about some stupid joke. The leader, a guy with blond waves and a small scar on his square jaw, took out a thin vape kit and took a long pull.

"Oh, shit," whispered Austin.

"What?" Kylie whispered back. The throbbing in her head swallowed Austin's words.

"That's Brent Nichols. He dated my older sister last year. Real asshole."

Brent's lackeys loaded their kits and drew inelegant puffs of their noxious fumes. Kylie never understood what people liked about that stuff, but she knew a series of marijuana derivatives and enhanced amphetamines were popular. The group talked quietly among themselves, occasionally laughing too loud and too cruel for any joke that Kylie might have found funny.

"Let's get out of here," Austin said, gesturing down the hill.

But the three boys' words danced tantalizingly close. She picked up words at the very edges of her hearing.

"Burn," Brent said. His voice was louder than the others. "We're going to have to burn it down."

When Brent's voice dropped low, she knew they were up to something.

"I need to hear what they're saying," Kylie whispered.

"No you don't," hissed Austin. "Come on, there's a hornet nest in my backyard that we can poke. It'll be more fun."

"That doesn't sound like fun at all."

Austin gave her a blank stare.

"I'm just going to try to listen." Before Austin could talk her out of it, she tried to reach out with the machine part of her brain.

And got nothing but a piercing headache.

Austin's grip tightened on her arm. She didn't even notice he was holding her arm. Why? Her head swam, and she leaned heavily against the immense concrete footing of the tower.

"Let's go," Austin hissed.

It was like walking into the kitchen when Papa was cooking and drawing a deep breath, only to discover no smells at all. A phantom limb of sensation still lingered, but beyond that there was nothing. Blackness.

Void.

Panic fizzed deep in the back of her chest. A low howl sounded from somewhere, and she didn't quite know if it came from her.

She had agreed to this. It was *her* fault. Why had she agreed to let Papa change how her brain worked? Had he done something to make her want it? He wouldn't do that. She *knew* he wouldn't do that. It's what her father had done to her sister, and Papa would *never*.

Or would he?

The animal yowl of frustration bubbled louder and spread through her whole body. Her heart pumped vile anger out into her limbs, and she clenched her fists so hard her knuckles hurt.

Brent and his cronies went silent.

Austin whispered, "Shit, shit, shit." He gave another tug on her arm. "We need to run."

"Who's back there?" Brent said, crashing through the lilacs. When he saw Austin half concealed by the concrete footing, he said, "Hey, it's the Giles kid. Long time no see."

Austin pulled hard enough that his fingers left marks on her skin. When had she sat down? What was happening?

Brent's two friends circled around, cutting off their chance for escape.

"We're not here to bother you," said Austin. He dropped Kylie and squared off against Brent. The older boy stood a head taller, but he was twice the mass and looked a whole lot meaner. "We were just leaving."

"No we weren't," mumbled Kylie.

Brent's lips twisted up in a cruel smile. "How about you come hang out with us, Giles."

"It's Austin," Kylie said, "and he's not interested in hanging out with you."

"You sure?" Brent exchanged an amused look with his buddies. He held up his vape kit. "We got some good stuff here. Just celebrating the end of school. You want a hit?"

Austin's dark skin grew a shade lighter and he took a step back.

"Your sister sure didn't have anything against a puff or two," said one of the creeps who had circled around. He grabbed his crotch. "It put her in the mood, know what I mean?"

"Maybe it'll work for your girl," the other creep said to Austin.

Austin's fists clenched at his sides as he shook with anger. Kylie felt his anger. It burned in her. She wanted to just punch all three bullies. Show them that they couldn't pick on her friend.

"Guys, guys," said Brent, placating. "Don't be like that. Giles here isn't into the ladies. Isn't that right?" His words were nice, but his tone was mocking. Kylie hated it with all her heart.

"Leave us alone," she said.

One of the creeps placed a clammy hand on the back of her neck. She did her best not to flinch, but the touch sent a sickening shiver through her whole body.

Brent held out his vape rig for Austin. "Come on man, we're all friends here, right?"

But they weren't friends. Kylie didn't know why they were pretending, but she didn't like it. Offering friendship was a way for these assholes to control Kylie and Austin. They'd use that social norm to their own ends. It terrified Kylie. Maybe that's why she never made new friends. "We're leaving," she said.

The grip on the back of her neck tightened.

Kylie hadn't been in martial arts for very long. She'd hated Tae Kwon Do. Karate had been too structured for her. The only one she had managed to stay with was Aikido, but that was because Aikido didn't use punches and kicks. She had never been able to picture herself ever wanting to kick someone.

She wanted to kick this creep so bad. Her foot came up—

Brent easily blocked it away, laughing like she was a playful kitten.

She twisted away from him, took Austin's hand, and started to walk. After a little resistance, he followed.

But Brent and his creeps followed, too.

"Hey, this is really rude," said Brent. "We're all friends here, right Jake?" There it was again. Trying to use the claim of friendship.

Jake, the creep who had put his hand on Kylie's neck, gave Austin a shove from behind. Not enough to knock him down, but enough to make him stumble forward. Kylie steadied him and gave him a look that she hoped told him to just keep walking.

"Right," Brent said. "Friends." He took a long draw on his vape and walked next to Kylie. "Look, no hard feelings, all right?" he said to her. "We can't help it if your friend is a gaslighting asshole. Just let us know if you ever need any help with him."

Kylie swallowed her retort, but it almost choked her. On an intellectual level, she understood what Brent was doing. Everything he said was nice. He was offering to share his expensive drugs. Hey, it was just a party. His friends were being straight assholes, but Brent's saccharin kindness was the dangerous one. He was the one who could cause actual harm to Austin or her, because if she went along with what he said or listened at all, she'd be sucked into his perverse reality. She would start to doubt her own sincerity in her own emotions.

She understood all that on an intellectual level.

Emotionally, she was already broken.

Jake touched her again, and this time she flinched. His hands were so cold. So moist. Ugh. A touch from him was like being caressed by the underbelly of a fish.

"Leave me alone!" she shouted. She knew immediately that responding wasn't going to help. She twisted away from him.

Austin stepped between her and the creep, his hands raised in inexpertly formed fists.

Brent and his creeps stepped back, pointed, and laughed with such deep belly laughs that Kylie almost started laughing with them.

But she didn't. Couldn't.

Then, Austin ran. One blink he was there, ready to face the three bigger boys. The next, he was gone, sprinting across the county road. Kylie followed as fast as she could, but he left her in the dust. As she returned to the town, Kylie still heard the three boys laughing. She knew she would hear that sound again when she slept.

Chapter Six

AJAY WORRIED.

Not about the truck. Kate Ludwig rounded a bend of the gravel road that she claimed was a shortcut. The truck's motor whined in protest, and something rattled around in the bed, but it was a solid vehicle made for solid work, and Ajay didn't worry about its ability to continue functioning. It would probably still be running long after he was dead.

Ajay didn't worry about Kylie's test with the camp instructors. She was a capable girl, and she could handle whatever they threw at her. Or she wouldn't. Life would be much easier if she didn't pass whatever entrance exam they had.

Isabelle's interference worried him a little. It was the kind of intervention that hinted at a much larger problem. Gears were turning in a machine he didn't even know existed.

He *did* worry about Kate's driving. He worried a *lot* about Kate's driving. Years of smooth, cautious rides in self-driving vehicles left him unused to the punchy authority of the woman's four-wheel-drive vehicle on fresh gravel.

Whether he worried or not, he couldn't do anything about any of it. All he could do was hope that Kate got him to town.

"She just left you out there?" Kate said, unbelieving.

"My granddaughter isn't always the girl I'd like her to be."

"Okay, explain this again. This is the girl who wants to go to a summer camp without your permission?"

"That's the other one." The truck barreled over a rut in the gravel and Ajay slammed into the door. "I sometimes think maybe they don't like me very much." He neglected to mention that he didn't blame them.

"Dang," Kate said. "Sorry to hear it."

Ajay didn't know why he felt comfortable talking to this woman. The long drive back from the middle of nowhere was taking forever. After a few more minutes of oppressively awkward silence, he said, "I *do* appreciate the ride."

"It's my pleasure."

Ajay nudged the bag of fertilizer at his feet. It smelled of ammonia. "What do you grow?"

"Not much of anything these days. Retired." She looked over at him, the smile wrinkles in her tanned face deepening. "How about you?"

"Houseplants, mostly, and I don't really grow them. It's more of a rotating death sentence."

She barked out a laugh. "I mean what did you do?"

"Hacker," he said. When he saw the serious look she shot him, he added, "Government work. NSA for my whole career back before it collapsed."

"You don't say."

"I do." He typically didn't. Why was he telling her so much?

"Heard a rumor there's a new org taking over." The truck passed hit a particularly pitted section of gravel, and Kate drove on the left side of the road where it was smoother. "Real dark ops kind of stuff."

"I could walk the rest of the way," said Ajay.

"No, it's no trouble." She pressed the accelerator as the truck rumbled onto gnarly asphalt. "No trouble at all."

"In that case, can you take me downtown?"

Kate flashed him a grin. "Any time, handsome."

Ajay swiped through menus until he found an array of programs he'd written to hack modern portable computers. Brushing up on his code, he found some places for improvements and quickly made them.

"Are you hacking right now?"

"A little."

"For the government?"

"Not a chance." He swiped through a program and peered at its output. "There's something I'd like to drop off."

Kate scrunched her brow. "Computer stuff?"

"I used to work in tech. Everything's computer stuff."

"Ahhh." Kate made the sound as if she understood, but she probably didn't. "You're going to hack the camp where your granddaughter's going so that you can keep an eye on her." Or, maybe she did.

"There's going to be a recruiter there. I'm going to install a program on his fidget, and if it detects any dangerous language, it'll alert me."

"Because you'll be hiding in the shrubs outside of the camp," Kate said. "Like a stalker."

"No."

"Pedophile?"

"*No.*"

"Covert superspy?"

"No." Ajay considered it. "Possibly. But I'll be able to monitor the situation from home."

"Sounds like this kid is pretty special to you," Kate said.

"She is." He sighed again. "There are some things I'd like to take care of while she's gone, so it'll be good not to have her around. I just… worry."

"You're trying to get rid of her, but you can't stand to get rid of her." The road noise changed as the asphalt smoothed, and she punched the accelerator. Miles melted away. "It doesn't make sense, but it kinda makes sense."

"Kids need independence."

"So do us old folks." Kate furrowed her brow. "Why would your other kid dump you out in the middle of nowhere? She thought it would take you time to get a car, but you weren't five minutes from the nearest farm."

Ajay stopped fiddling with his programs and looked at Kate. She wore ratty denim overalls, and her gray-streaked hair was pulled back into a ponytail. She was a farmer. Tech was her life, but not the same kind of tech. And she was smart. "Do you ever think of starting a new career?" he asked.

"I gave half my land over to a wetlands reclamation project a few years ago. Ever since, I've been fighting the long boredom of retirement."

"That—is a perfect way to describe it." Ajay returned to his holographic display. The most important part of a good hack was prep work, and he'd been so busy with Kylie's updates that he had neglected the current state of security tech.

"If I get tired of duck hunters poaching every damn year. I'll put it back to soybeans. Doesn't matter to the government so long as I check the right boxes on my tax forms."

"Makes sense."

"So where's this recruiter?" Kate asked as they neared Bemidji.

"The park downtown," Ajay said, "But I need to stop by the lake houses first."

"Let me guess, you need to pick up some equipment from a stash."

Ajay flashed her a wicked grin. "That's right."

"Super spy," she whispered.

Kate rolled through town in silence, watching the people walking on the streets and the other cars navigating the pleasant day. A sadness crept into her expression. Ajay couldn't tell if it was the way the wrinkles in the corners of her eyes deepened or the press of her lips against each other, but she wasn't comfortable in the little town.

He wanted to say something. Ajay had been around too long to suffer silence when there was something bothering someone, but he couldn't bring himself to do it.

And maybe it was better that way. After all, he wasn't sharing his past with her. She didn't need to know how his work at the NSA had first exploited flaws in cryptography, and his exit had resulted in the end of encryption. Of security. Privacy.

They didn't know how many drones watched from the skies. Nobody ever knew. Weaponized Thunderhead drones were the thumb pressing down on the jugular of society, and people out in the rural parts of the state didn't much appreciate it. Ajay's work hadn't put Thunderheads in the air, but he should have been able to predict it. He had sown fear by supporting the broken society's only defenses against dissidents. He hadn't predicted the world he was in.

But he should have, and guilt drove like an icicle into his belly every morning he woke.

It was worse when he thought of leaving that world to his grand-daughters.

"Your girl's clever," Kate said as she pulled into the Cameron Park Lake House parking lot. "The older one, I mean."

"If it weren't for your help, I'd still be standing out there waiting for a ride. She spiked the rideshare services so they'd take extra long to get to me if I could even contact them."

"You don't say." Kate said. "Devious, but someone would have picked you up. The kid forgot about how nice people are around here."

Ajay wasn't so sure. The kindness of strangers only extended so far, even in the rural parts of the state. "Thanks, anyway."

"Well, you're welcome," Kate said as she parked next to a thirty-foot camper that looked like it had been parked in the lot since the spring thaw. She threw the truck into park and shut it down. The persistent whine of the electric motor left a vacancy in Ajay's ears.

The lake house was a new building on the shores of Lake Bemidji. It was a private club, with an exclusive membership and fees that would exclude even the wealthiest farmers in the area. It held a dinner club, rental boats for the lake, and, most importantly, a locker room where people could store their gear.

"I feel underdressed," Kate said, following Ajay as he pushed through the front door.

"Don't worry about it." He crossed to the host's pedestal, where a man stood with an open book before him. "Hello, Grant."

Grant almost managed to conceal his disdain. "Mr. Andersen."

It took a moment for Ajay's eyes to adjust to the dimly lit room. The dining hall to the left held a dozen tables, only a few of which were occupied. The aroma of Canadian bacon and fresh coffee wafted through the air and made his stomach grumble. To the right, a hallway led to an elevator and some stairs. He took the stairs, and Kate followed.

"You're a member here?" Kate whispered.

"Sort of," Ajay said. "They think my name's Jacob Andersen and I'm a wealthy financier from Minneapolis."

"Fancy."

Ajay tapped his cane on the hard floor. "Same coffee and bacon as the new Denny's down the street. Less pleasant company."

"Then why pay for a membership?"

Ajay narrowed his eyes.

"Oh," she said. "Right."

Kate understood that he was a hacker the way people knew that asparagus was a grass. She knew it, but she didn't *know* it. Not in a practical sense. She'd figure it out eventually.

The locker room smelled of aftershave and hairspray, but it was empty of other guests. Ajay crossed to locker number 857 and touched his cane to the keypad. The lock clicked and the door swung open.

Inside sat several things. The first was a key, hanging from the hook. He wouldn't need that today. He hoped he wouldn't ever need it.

On the shelf sat a broken diamond optical quantum computer, which he'd tried to fix many times and failed. Still, he couldn't give it up.

Instead of burying it in his back yard, he'd stowed it here with no direct digital trail back to his own identity. That was where it would stay.

Next to the quantum computer sat a pistol.

"SIG Sauer P520 X-Compact," Kate said.

"What?"

"Your gun. It's a SIG Sauer. Nice gun."

"It shoots," Ajay said.

"My husband was a gun nut," Kate explained. "That gun's a nice piece of hardware."

It wasn't a huge weapon or a particularly dangerous one, but it was one of many Ajay had stashed around town. It was nice to know that the gun dealer hadn't lied to him, but the truth was Ajay knew very little about guns. He hated the idea of carrying a weapon, but he also acknowledged that there were times he might need one. It was just part of the ugly business he was involved in. He left it where it lay.

A Cambion Five Stealth Drone sat at the bottom of the locker. The latest in stealth drone tech, ideal for surveillance, bot node infiltration, and light assassination. As a weaponized drone, it was heavily regulated for government use. It could fly silent in certain conditions and mask itself using an adaptive camouflage. It could kill.

"Is that legal?" asked Kate.

"Not even a little," said Ajay. He slotted the tiny drone into a port on his cane so that its battery could charge. "But I don't plan on getting caught."

Chapter Seven

"Good," said the recruiter as Kylie made a weak attempt at redirecting his slow-motion punch.

It wasn't good. Kylie *knew* it wasn't good. Austin knew. The other six kids going through recruiting knew it wasn't good. She hadn't redirected his punch at all, and she didn't think she ever could.

The recruiter, Mr. Shaleborn, was built like a brick wall, and even when he moved at half speed, he was too much to block. Just—too much.

The written part of the entrance exam had been easy. Kylie hadn't even used the entire allotted time to finish, despite her lingering headache. It was all about the military history of the United States and tactical analysis. She was starting to suspect that the Pine Fortress School for the Gifted was just a military school for rich kids.

Which was fine. Maybe military training would help her.

That made her think of Isabelle. Is that why her older sister had become a mercenary? Did the structure of that organization help her manage her abilities somehow?

She raised her hands in an open defensive stance like her Aikido teacher had taught her. It wouldn't do any good against Mr. Shaleborn. He was too strong. Too solid.

"How is that good?" Austin asked. *He* hadn't done very well on the written test. Kylie had seen his paper as he'd turned it in. Half the questions were left blank. Austin would rather not try than fail.

Shaleborn gestured for Austin to enter the ring. The students formed a circle in the green field of the park, but nobody seemed to care that they were using the space for a martial arts duel.

"Listen up," he said. "Martial arts aren't just about kicks and blocks. They're about training your body and your mind to make the right decision before you even think to react. If you want to be taught by me, you need to have the instincts to win. Anybody can train enough to throw the perfect punch, but not everybody has the gut-deep reaction that tells them when to throw it."

The class's stare was as blank as Kylie's notebook at the end of the school year.

"Tell me," Shaleborn said when Kylie and Austin stood in front of him. "If we met in a dark alley, how would you take me down?"

Kylie didn't have an answer, so she glanced at Austin. The boy didn't even have his hands up. He wore too-short sweatpants and a bright orange tee, which made him look like a frumpy loser next to Shaleborn's all-black gi. Even Kylie wore her Aikido outfit, which was pure, perfect, white, and a little too small. At least she *almost* looked like she belonged in the ring.

"Why would I be in an alley?" Austin asked.

Shaleborn smirked. He was going to make an example of Austin, and it made anger burn in Kylie's gut. He said, "You're just stepping out for a smoke."

"I don't smoke."

Shaleborn took a step toward Austin. "Let's say you do."

"I would run."

"Nowhere to run." The brick of a man narrowed his eyes and scanned the circle around him. "There's no way out."

Austin glanced around. There were two girls behind him and a boy who was twice his size. There wasn't anywhere to run.

"Leave him alone," whispered Kylie.

"Why would I fight you?" asked Austin.

"What if I want your wallet."

"You can have it."

The anger in Austin's eyes could easily have been read as determination, but Kylie knew the difference. She wasn't great at reading emotions, but she *knew* Austin. "Leave him alone," she said louder, not sure Shaleborn had heard her the first time.

Shaleborn didn't take his eyes off the boy. "Maybe I want your girl."

Kylie launched herself at the man, striking him hard in the jaw. She might as well have been body tackling a marble pillar. He shrugged her off, plucked her wrist out of the air, and gave it a twist. She tried to take his momentum. She tried to roll with the movement.

It did nothing. He held her tight and popped her into a wrist lock that sent waves of fire down her arm every time she moved.

Austin finally moved, inelegantly grasping Shaleborn's beefy arm. With a quick snap, Shaleborn had him, too.

Then, the asshole laughed. He circled, holding up both Kylie and Austin for the others to see. "See this? Their instincts were good, but this is what happens when you don't coordinate your attacks. This is the consequence of not being prepared for battle." He met the gazes of each of the kids. "If you make it into this program, we'll make warriors out of you. We'll teach you real martial arts, not this mamby pamby stuff these two have learned. You'll learn to strike. To disable." He released them with a shove. "To kill if need be."

The rest of the session went without incident. Kylie's wrist never stopped hurting, and the lingering ache deep in her tendons was a constant reminder of the insult Shaleborn had given her. Every time she looked at Austin, he was glaring at her.

Shaleborn ran the group through drills, set them up to safely spar against each other, and tested their physical fitness. Apart from the one incident, he appeared to be a reasonable teacher, careful and intent on showing them exactly what needed to be done to take the next step on their journey.

But Kylie hated him. Passionately, burningly, she despised the man. It was all she could do to stop herself from walking away. Every time she thought of spending the summer in Papa's boring house living by Papa's boring rules, she wanted to scream. She loved him. She really did. That was why she needed to escape. The summer away wasn't just because Isabelle had benefited from military training. It wasn't just because she'd be learning cool things that were interesting to her.

It was because she needed a break from Papa. As well-meaning as he was, his constant attention was stifling.

Not that she'd ever pass Shaleborn's test. He'd made that perfectly clear. As the hour-long session dragged on, her mood darkened.

That was why she was surprised when the muscular teacher, gleaming with sweat in the cool air, called her and Austin over after dismissing the group. He touched his ear as they approached and whispered something into an unseen comm.

"Why didn't you want to fight me?" Shaleborn asked Austin.

Austin swallowed, clearly unsure of his answer. "Because I couldn't win. By the time it was just us in our hypothetical alley, I'd already lost the battle."

Shaleborn turned to Kylie. "Why *did* you fight me?"

Kylie considered it for a moment but decided her best option was the truth. "You made me mad."

Shaleborn watched as the other potential recruits gathered their things and left the field. Then, he picked up his duffel bag and made for the parking lot. "You're both in," he said to Austin and Kylie. "Don't let me down."

Chapter Eight

"You're both in. Don't let me down." Regis Shaleborn's voice had a tinny echo in Ajay's hearing aid, but it came through with clear definition.

He maneuvered the stealth drone over the field, drifting into the empty space between ground and sky. It hovered higher than the tallest building in Bemidji, its adaptive camouflage and ultra-silent rotors keeping it from being noticed by anyone below.

Better still, it used an unlikely band for communications. Nobody would notice the stream of data funneling back to Ajay.

"What did I miss?" asked Kate as she brought two beers back to their table. Ajay was shocked that she wanted to stay while he spied on his granddaughter. They sat in the Counted Crow, one of Bemidji's newest old-style pubs. The artificial cigarette-scented incense suffused the oak tables and bar. In the middle of the afternoon, only a few customers were sitting at the cramped, round tables, but somehow the one server—a middle-aged woman with swaying hips and short hair—managed to project the impression that she was too busy to wait on Ajay and Kate.

Ajay said. "Are you sure you're not working for Isabelle?"

Kate took a sip of her pale-yellow beer. "Tell me something, Jay. What's it like being an international man of mystery?"

"I'm not international." The beer tasted like warm piss. "Ugh." He leaned his cane against the table and used its holographic projector to show an image of Shaleborn walking back to his car.

Kate peered at the image. "He's a solid fellow, isn't he?"

"I'm more interested in the military grade fidget in his duffel bag and the scrambler he's using to suppress local communications."

Kate flashed a smile. "You boys and your tech."

"It's not just tech." An interface display appeared in the hologram, and Ajay started the next wave of penetration algorithms. "He shouldn't have this kind of gear."

"You shouldn't have the drone that's letting you see what he shouldn't have."

Ajay opened his mouth to protest, then changed his mind. "Good point." Her smug satisfaction at winning the argument was actually pretty endearing. He already found himself trusting her, which made him nervous. It was more evidence that she was spying on him, but what could her angle possibly be? He decided to try one more time. "It's not safe for you to get involved in this."

Kate placed her left hand on the table, fingers splayed. Only her index finger and thumb were fully intact. The other three fingers were each soft and rounded at the first knuckle. The message was clear. She could handle danger.

"Fine," Ajay said, defeated. His interface flashed a warning, and he spent several breaths avoiding detection from Shaleborn's well-defended tech. He took a deep swallow of his awful beer. "I'm not just a worried parent trying to research a kid's summer camp."

She flashed that infuriatingly charming half smile. "You're not?"

"Fine. I am. But I have good reason."

"Your girl is special."

"She is," Ajay grumbled. "And this camp is dangerous."

"Why not send her to a different camp? Why not send her over to Lake Beauty or one of the other Christian camps?"

Kylie wasn't a Christian and probably wouldn't get along well at a camp like that. Instead of opening that can of worms, he said, "Kylie's sister wants her to go to this one."

"And she overrides your best judgment?"

Ajay stopped fiddling with the holographic controls because he was afraid his hands would shake. He remembered the look on Isabelle's face as she told him to allow Kylie to go to the camp. She was the only person in the world who might have more of a right to guide Kylie's path in life. "She made some solid points."

"Such as?"

Shaleborn tossed his duffel bag in the back trunk of a sleek BMW i7 and climbed behind the wheel. When he started the electronics, Ajay had to dodge a data sweep of the local network by blacking out his drone's data feed. When the image returned, Shaleborn's car was gone. Ajay's hack of the tech was incomplete.

"Crap," Ajay said.

"What?"

"I lost him." He pulled back, raising the drone high into the sky so that he could scan the local streets. Shaleborn's vehicle wouldn't be able to disappear into the streets of Bemidji. The car was far too distinct.

Another car pulled out of the lot. Then another. They turned right, onto a county road that ran along the perimeter of Lake Bemidji. Ajay scanned the city streets, then the main road north. Finally, he checked the lake road.

"Found him." He took a drink of his beer. It was, somehow, worse. Lingering dregs of bitterness danced across his tongue. With a few swipes at the controls, he sent the drone to follow the BMW.

"They're tailing him," Kate said, excitement bubbling in the back of her voice. She had another beer in her hand, and Ajay didn't remember her leaving to get it.

"Who? What?" Ajay blinked. He had been so focused on the hack that he hadn't been paying attention to anything else.

"Those two cars. They turned the same direction as him. When he took a left up there, they followed. There's not really much reason to go up that way."

Sure enough, the two cars followed. When his drone passed them, he saw identical bulky sedans with illegally tinted windows. Not subtle at all.

"Maybe they're with him. Bodyguards or something," Ajay said.

"Uh-huh."

Ajay's drone caught the signal from Shaleborn's tech and started to re-establish the connection. This time, he easily swiped away the counterattack and sliced through the first several layers of defenses. A series of countermeasures followed with standard routines, first locking him out, then alerting the owner, then attacking back. Ajay's code sidestepped the lockout, ate the alert into a bit bucket, and used the counterattack to establish a deeper-rooted authority in the attacking device. A warm wave of satisfaction coursed through him as he moved to slot his program in place.

"Dang!" said Kate.

The first of the boxy sedans slammed into the BMW's bumper, a crunching blow meant to spin it out into the ditch. With a frantic twist into the skid, Shaleborn regained control. He punched the accelerator and launched forward.

The sedans weren't done. Through his holographic feed, Ajay watched as the cars blasted over the hills, twisting through the long bend around the lake.

"They're going to kill him," he said as the second sedan passed the BMW. It swerved to run him off the road, but Shaleborn braked at the last second.

"Can't you do anything?"

He could. Ajay's drone maintained pace with the cars. He could descend and hinder the attackers. "I'm not sure I should."

Kate leaned forward. "What do you mean? Because you might lose your toy?"

The first sedan locked bumpers with Shaleborn and punched the accelerator. Shaleborn's tires smoked on the old asphalt, sending smoke into the late afternoon sky.

The holographic image flickered. They were reaching the edge of Ajay's range, and his signal would drop soon. He still needed to install his hacked program, or this all would be for nothing.

It would all be for nothing if Shaleborn died, too.

"Come on," Kate said. "I know you have the tech. Punch out some tires or something."

"It's not like that," Ajay said. He pushed the drone faster. It was all he could do to keep up.

The sedan in front punched the brakes, sandwiching Shaleborn's BMW between the two cars. Shaleborn yanked his vehicle to the side to try to escape, but his tire caught on a section of jagged asphalt.

The BMW flipped.

"*Dang!*" Kate exclaimed again.

It landed belly up. The sedans screeched to a halt on either side.

Silence.

Ajay maneuvered the drone closer, keeping its camouflage on its highest setting. A square man in a black jacket stepped from the front sedan. He wore dark sunglasses and carried a slender pistol.

"Come on, Ajay. Do something," Kate was more urgent now.

But what could he do? His drone was weaponized. It *was* dangerous. If he set it on the attackers, he might kill them. He didn't know that he could bring himself to do that with so little evidence.

"I don't know," he managed.

Kate grabbed his wrist. "They're going to kill him."

Shaleborn kicked the door open and crawled out. Blood covered his face, and the smug superiority was gone from his chiseled jaw.

"How do I know?" Ajay asked. "What if they're government agents? What if Shaleborn's the bad guy?"

"They're going to kill him." Her voice was an octave higher.

Ajay stared at her. She didn't know how hard he worked at staying hidden. How important it was that he stay under the radar. She couldn't possibly know how much personal risk he was in just by having eyes close to something like this. To interfere—that would be suicide.

The square man stepped forward to Shaleborn, who was now on his hands and knees. The martial arts instructor's injuries didn't look bad, but the holographic projection didn't have enough detail to know for sure.

Another man rose from the other car. He was tall and thin, and he carried a pistol exactly like the one the square man held. He said something to the other driver, but Ajay's audio didn't function at the edge of his range. He was lucky to have the grainy video.

The square man raised the gun.

"Ajay," Kate hissed.

Ajay swiped the controls and executed a saved sequence. The drone swept forward and unleashed a pulse.

The Havana pulse was a mix of subsonic noise, microwaves, and trace radiation. One pulse wouldn't permanently hurt anyone—not from a single stealth drone like this. Alone, this drone could disorient a person. Make them dizzy and distracted. It wouldn't save Shaleborn.

But it would give him a chance.

The square man blinked and stumbled back. He held a hand to his head. His eyes tracked across the drone's location.

Shaleborn launched up, snatching the gun from the man's hand. With a series of quick punches, he bloodied the man's nose, boxed his ear, and bruised his kidney. He turned and fired at the other man, who ducked behind his sedan.

Still reeling, the square man dropped to one knee. Blood darkened his coat and spattered across the ground. Shaleborn struck him hard with the pommel of the gun, and the man dropped like a slab of meat.

The tall man fired over the hood of his car, and Shaleborn dove out of the way. Pinned, he crept along the side of the BMW.

The video feed flickered and froze. Ajay swore and tried to re-establish the connection.

"What was going on there?" Kate asked. Her voice held the awe of someone who didn't think violence could ever happen in her community.

"We don't know who they are. They could have been some kind of organized crime. Government."

Kate leaned forward. "Both."

Ajay locked gazes with her. Maybe she understood.

The feed returned. Shaleborn fired two shots under the BMW, where the car's sleek form created a gap. The tall man scrambled away to protect himself, but it opened an opportunity for Shaleborn to close the distance.

Shaleborn was fast. A flicker of the video and the man was on top of the tall guy. The man's gun flew into the cornfield. Shaleborn kicked his chest, and the man slammed against the side of the sedan.

"Damn," said Kate.

"Damn is right," Ajay said. "This Shaleborn really knows his stuff."

"I guess it's good that your granddaughter can learn from him."

The video feed flickered off again. "I need to get the data connection back." Ajay's fingers danced over the controls. He ignored the video feed. At the edge of the signal, all he could manage was one or the other. After a tense moment, the feed picked up. He started the program upload and scripted its execution so that it would engage only after a long pause.

Kate took a long pull at her beer. "Things aren't too boring with you, are they?" she said with a quirky grin on her face and a twinkle in her eyes.

"Not nearly boring enough," said Ajay. He pulled the video connection back up.

Both attackers lay at the side of the road. Shaleborn pried at the ruined trunk of his BMW. His arm bled, but he had wrapped it enough to stop most of the flow. The trunk popped open with a jerk and his duffel fell out. He snatched it up.

Then he looked up at the sky, directly at the drone. Ajay could have sworn the man saw right through the camera to him. It was like a man shouting a challenge out into the night—as if Shaleborn knew his drone was there.

Then the drone fell, and when it hit the ground, the video feed flickered and was gone.

Chapter Nine

GRAVEL POPPED UNDER THE tires of Kate's truck as the sun set over the dark cornfield. Ajay could just see around the stand of bony oaks to the spot where two ambulances and a police cruiser barricaded the spot around the attack.

"We should leave," Ajay said.

"I thought you said you wanted that drone back."

"Kate," Ajay sighed. "I can't ask you to get involved in this. Just take me home."

"Fine," she snapped.

A compulsive urge to backpedal seized Ajay. "I don't want to get you in trouble." Also, he didn't trust her.

"You don't trust me."

Dammit. "I do. Kate—"

"No, I understand." She cranked the wheel and started to maneuver a U-turn. "Bill always said I was too intense with new people." The truck stopped with its back wheels on the edge of the ditch. "You wanna know what I did yesterday?"

"Not really."

"Fine."

"Fine."

Kate wheeled the truck around and tore gravel as she accelerated up to speed. A pit of guilt burned in Ajay's stomach. He hadn't meant to be as harsh as he was. Maybe that just supported the fact that he shouldn't be out making friends. He couldn't trust anyone, and every time he thought about drawing someone new into his life, he thought of the last woman who he'd fallen for.

"I'm sorry," he said.

She drove in silence for a while. "I wonder what the police will think when they find your drone."

He waved it off. "It'll burn its own data core. I can do without."

"That sounds expensive," Kate said.

It *was* expensive. It was also military hardware and would cause all kinds of red flags to go up when the police entered it into their records. Unfortunately, he wasn't able to signal a retreat. All he had was the location data from the last image it had sent: Regis Shaleborn holding his duffel.

Had Shaleborn done something to his drone? Ajay hadn't seen the man use any tech or activate any defense. It would have been hard for the man to initiate any kind of attack without some kind of obvious sign, and drones were notoriously tricky to hack in flight.

No, the drone probably ran out of power. This model was known for its short battery life, especially if the Havana weapon was triggered.

"Say it," Kate said.

Ajay gave in. "You're right."

Kate hit the brakes and spun the truck around. She bounced with anticipation. When they arrived, Ajay opened the truck door and stepped out.

"I'll come with," said Kate.

Ajay waved her off. "I don't want you anywhere near this. It's not safe."

"One," Kate said, her voice like ice as she ticked off points on her finger stubs, "I'm already in this. I watched that video same as you did. I know what happened. Two, I'm your ride. A getaway driver is more than a little involved."

She was right. Of course. "A getaway driver needs to stay with the vehicle," he said. With a few commands, he paired his comm unit with her clunky brown fidget. "I'll stay in contact and let you know if you need to flee without me."

Her lips pressed into a line. She clearly didn't like being left out.

"I know you won't leave without me," he admitted, "but I'll feel less guilty when you get caught if you let me send the signal."

The field's soil was soft. Bumpy from a recent plow. Corn silage stuck out at odd angles, but Ajay made his way carefully across, staying to the side where the stand of oaks would block the officer's view. His knee twisted on a particularly solid clod of dirt, but he bit back the pain and kept walking.

At the oak stand, he paused to assess the situation. By then, the sun had set. Long tendrils of gloom stretched across the open fields, swallowed only by the flashing red and blue of the ambulances. The location data for his drone put it on the near side of the road, close enough that if he was smart, he might be able to edge forward and grab it without anyone noticing. Far enough that there was a risk of being seen.

"I think I see it," Ajay whispered into his comm.

A car sped by the commotion, its driver slowing enough for a gawker's pause. Lights flashed over the small truck as it passed, and Ajay could see the back of the man's head as he stared at the mess at the side of the road. No doubt this incident would be written about in the following day's paper. A crash on the side of the road. Cars totaled. This was big news in small town Minnesota.

"Are you sure you need this thing back?" Kate asked.

Ajay let out a resigned sigh. "If the police find it, it'll be nothing but bad news to me. All I need to do is walk over and pick it up. They're too busy to notice."

They *were* busy. Ajay watched two large men as they hefted a body onto a stretcher. The body's face wasn't covered. Not dead, then. It was the square fellow from the fight. A medic strapped an oxygen mask to the man's face.

He stepped out of the forest. It was the distance of a solid nine iron from the forest to the drone, and he didn't have it in him to crawl the whole way. One foot in front of the other, he made his way across the uneven soil, just hoping the cops wouldn't look in his direction.

"More incoming," said Kate, because of course there were more incoming. "Police."

The flashing emergency vehicles were silhouetted against the dimming blue of the twilight sky. The dregs of the day cast the muted tones of twilight, where dangers could lurk in the open, confident that the eye would disguise them in the ever-flattening hues of darkness.

The new police car approached. Its lights flashed, and it parked a few car lengths from the other vehicles.

"Why are you doing this, Kate?" he asked.

"I think the reason is why are *you* doing this, old man," said the farmer. "You're just my hitchhiker with a mysterious past."

"It's not so mysterious." He was halfway there. A glint of metal jutted from a clod of earth shadowed by the raised county road. "I worked for the government. Boring as they get."

"I was married," Kate said. Before he could respond, she said, "Now, Bill wasn't a mysterious guy. He was a farmer. He worked hard every day. Drank sometimes, but not too much. When it was time to relax, he sat on the porch and played his mandolin. The only mystery that guy had was that sometimes he didn't label the meat he put in the freezer. We having venison or beef in tonight's stew? Bill didn't know." The comm unit crackled when she sighed. "There's only so much boring a lady can handle, Ajay, and you're not it."

"Fair enough."

The newly arrived officer approached the other group, but something was off about the way he gesticulated. Ajay stopped and watched them speak, wishing he could get a spy drone close enough to hear their words. He tuned his comm to better pick up the conversation, but a cool wind blew across his mic and their words were mostly lost. He edged closer.

The drone's tail end stuck up out of the soft soil. A few more steps and he could grab it and run. The road stood atop a short rise only a few steps away.

"Excitement's not all it's made out to be," he whispered.

"I would kill for a little excitement, hon," said Kate.

"You never told me what you did yesterday."

The ambulance tech at the crash scene drew a gun from a back holster, leveled it at the newly arrived police officer, and shot him in the face.

Ajay's vision went black. His heart slammed in his chest and a fresh wave of adrenaline coursed through his veins. Time slowed, and his body wouldn't move. The officer fell in slow motion, his body charcoal gray in the faded colors of twilight. Someone shouted.

The ambulance. Ajay finally focused on it, seeing it without the filter of a hazy brain. This wasn't the Bemidji emergency services or an ambulance from the Cities. The label on the back read Frontier Arms.

"Fuck," Ajay hissed.

"Ajay," hissed Kate, "what is happening over there?"

Still, Ajay didn't move. Some lingering edge of instinct told him that movement would be detected, but he didn't know how hidden he could possibly be, out in the open as he was. Some tall grasses from the ditch obscured part of their view of him. The fields behind him were the same muted browns of his light coat, but this wasn't camouflage. It wouldn't hide him if anyone decided to look.

Another voice came from the crash site. In the back of Ajay's brain, he recognized the gruff timbre of it. The harsh, military snap of the voice.

The man who had shot the officer turned to scan the field where Ajay stood. Ajay pinched his eyes shut, knowing that he wouldn't hear the gunshot that took his life. If he was seen, it would be over faster than the neurons that would give him any warning. Far away behind him, he heard the roar of Kate's truck.

"Ajay!"

"Stay away," he hissed. With a tremendous force of will, he opened his eyes. The workers dragged the officer's body to one of the two ambulances. A big man wearing the scrubs of a medic heaved the body onto the floor by the square man's stretcher. They worked fast. Soon, they would have the scene handled. They would search around for any lingering evidence.

They would find him, and they would find his drone.

"I need you to help me, Kate," he said into the comm. "And I need you to stay away. Stay safe."

The drone was only a short distance away, but any farther forward and he would fall into the aura of light around the crime scene. Ajay dropped into a crouch.

"There's a house two blocks down from the new Bethel Lutheran church. It's as bland as it gets. Wooden fence around the backyard. White siding. You can't miss it." He drew a deep breath, which failed to calm his thundering heart. "If I don't make it, I need you to go there and tell my granddaughter what happened. Keep her safe."

Kate's truck hummed in the distance. Was it getting closer or farther away? Ajay couldn't tell in the muffled echoes of the surrounding hills.

"What about her sister?" Kate asked, finally.

Ajay thought about it. Isabelle would take Kylie in. She *was* family after all. But what was the best thing for Kylie? "I—I don't know, but I need you to stay safe. Get away now before they sweep the area."

He crept forward, keeping as low and as hidden as he possibly could. It wasn't great. His hip ached. His knees pinged with the effort of the crouch-walk. Pain flared in his neck and back. If he grabbed the drone, he could maybe sneak away. He'd meet up with Kate later.

There it was! He swept the tiny drone up and clicked it into place on his cane. Now all he needed to do was sneak away as quickly and quietly as possible.

Kate's truck burst around the end of the oak stand, wheels chucking up clods of earth. The four-wheel drive vehicle spun across the field at full speed toward Ajay.

"So much for getting away quietly," he said.

The workers shouted behind him. Ajay turned to see the man who had shot the officer staring at him. Their eyes locked. The gun came up.

Fired.

Bullets punched into the side of Kate's truck as she skidded sideways to a stop between Ajay and the shooter. Ajay tore open the door and climbed inside.

Behind the shooter, the ambulance with the cop and the square man chirped to life and peeled away in the opposite direction. The big man waved his cane at the vehicle.

Kate didn't even wait for Ajay to get all the way in before she punched the accelerator again. More bullets slammed into the vehicle, but she sped away across the field.

"They can't follow," she breathed. "Not in those cars."

Ajay peeked out the back. The bigger man had stopped the shooter with a gesture of a sturdy cane, and they both watched Kate's truck as she drove away. He, again, felt a lingering recognition of the bigger worker. A hint of an idea that maybe he knew the man. He'd seen him once before.

But without a better look, he had nothing.

"What were you saying about needing more excitement in your life?" Ajay deadpanned.

Kate's only response was a whoop of joy and to punch the accelerator harder as they sped away across the open field.

Chapter Ten

THE VERTIGO LANG FELT had nothing to do with the permanent damage to his inner ear. It was the kind of vertigo that came from being sucked back into a life he thought he had escaped. It was the shuddering void of seeing a hated enemy and not being able to contain the rage that bubbled up inside.

He gestured for the idiot from Frontier to stop shooting. His first day of work, and here he was supervising a cleanup job. The custodian's pistol didn't have the range to take out the truck, and wasting bullets was poor form. They needed more than ever to focus on cleaning up the scene, especially after shooting a damn cop.

Especially with both their quarries gone. Escaped in the stolen ambulance. Whoever those two assholes were who had attacked Shaleborn they were gone now. They had too much of a head start to catch. Lang swore and punched the tire of Shaleborn's upside-down vehicle. How had that shitkicking son of a bitch screwed this up so badly?

The cop situation never should have happened. For that, Lang blamed himself. He was supposed to be the one who managed strategy. When Shaleborn had called begging for a cleanup, Lang had been quick to intercept the emergency frequencies in the area. Silver had sent him personally down to oversee the work, and sent the school's Frontier payrolled custodian, Vincent, to do the grunt work.

Only they'd failed to intercept all of the calls. Or maybe one of the drivers who had passed them had sent word in a way they couldn't intercept. Lang wouldn't put it past them to speak in person. The rumor network exceeded the speed of light in small towns like this.

And it complicated things. Lang hated complications. He especially didn't like the clenching fist of guilt in the pit of his stomach, but he'd long since learned to ignore that.

This never should have happened. Shaleborn should have known he was being followed. He shouldn't have let himself fall into this position.

"Come on," he said. "We need to get this stuff moved."

"Tow truck's almost here," said Vincent. The man's lips were pursed in a permanent sneer of disgust. His greasy hair fell to his shoulders.

They no longer bothered to pretend like they were obeying procedure. More than anything, they needed to get gone. Fast. He ordered the custodian to clean the mess of blood around the scene. Ruin any DNA trace.

Lang leaned heavily on his cane as the other man worked. A wave of vertigo washed over him, so he focused on the distant horizon until it passed.

Three cars needed to move—a fact Shaleborn had failed to mention. The first would be Shaleborn's BMW. Even if they flipped it right side up, it wasn't drivable. The idiot had let himself be chased down by a couple of blocky sedans. Lang remembered the last time he had been in a car chase. He longed for the whine of the motor and the smell of rubber burning from a hard turn. He'd never drive again. Not without serious constraints.

The second vehicle was one of those awful sedans. The custodian could take that.

But now a flashing police car sat on the side of the road. What should he do with that?

Not being able to drive usually wasn't such a disability, since every car except for these damn three was self-driving. This only sucked one more morsel of pure joy from his life. He must have imagined the old man in the field. It couldn't possibly have been the same guy. With the bad light and the distance, it could have been anyone out there. Why would it have been the same old man who had taken his sense of balance?

But that would be appropriate, wouldn't it? The old man returns to enact more suffering. *Deserved* suffering, but that didn't make Lang like it any more.

When the tow truck arrived, Lang helped attach the hook to the BMW. It took only a few seconds to flip the little car, but agonizing minutes to get it attached properly to the truck. When, finally, they had finished, he inspected Vincent's work on the rest of the cleanup.

Lang poked at a bloodstain with his toe. "Sloppy," he said.

"Rain's coming tonight. Won't be a thing left as evidence."

Leave it to the lazy custodian to expect the weather to clean up a mess. Lang was liking this guy less and less the more he worked with him. Never mind that the man was probably right.

The tow truck pulled away, and Lang made his way to the passenger side of the sedan. They had disabled its tracking, and it didn't have anything fancier than a key fob for security.

"What about the cop car?" Vincent asked.

"Leave it," said Lang. The mystery would plague the police for weeks. The man's family might never give up the search. "They'll never track it back to us."

"You're the boss."

"You drive," said Lang as he climbed into the sedan, as if there were another option. "And keep it slow. We've cleaned up enough messes for one night."

Chapter Eleven

The week before camp passed with all the excitement of the Great Molasses Flood of 1919. Every day dragged on hotter and stuffier until Kylie could hardly breathe in the brutal sun of the back patio. Austin stopped by only twice to shatter the drudgery of her nascent summer. Once to tell her that his parents would allow him to come to camp with her, and once to ask her if she was mad at him.

She wasn't. Kylie was mad at everything and everyone except for him.

She seethed at Papa and everything he stood for. He had muffled the tech in her head, but now the rest of her brain was compensating, and the rest of her brain was full of anger. Sure, she had agreed to change the tech in her head, but she didn't expect it to *feel* like this. A low-grade headache burned in the back of her skull. She hated how now he was busy with other projects—far too busy to spend time with her.

Kylie *definitely* didn't want to spend time with Papa. She was angry at the camp for leaving such a long gap after school. A week!

Also, the shortness of that gap irritated her. Only a week!

Everything tasted funny, and Kylie detested the way grease pooled on the pizza Papa made.

Kylie hated being late, which she knew already, but *extra* knew when they arrived at the bus pickup. Being late was worse than sitting in a crowd where sensory overload stole her ability to successfully manage even the most basic conversations. Stepping into the shuttle bus was like diving into a swimming pool full of ants. They swarmed, chattering and singing and talking, and it was too much. The whole thing was a mistake.

The sensory overload of the tech was gone from her head, but she still couldn't handle anything the world threw at her. What did that tell her about the quality of her own brain?

Austin took her hand. "It's all right," he said. "Close your eyes."

She did, but it didn't help. Nothing helped. The tight fist of anxiety closed over her chest. When they finally arrived at the camp hours later, Kylie stepped out with the swirling mass of kids into the middle of nowhere.

The Pine Fortress School for the Gifted was serious about restricting technology. Before she and Austin had stepped on the shuttle in the parking lot of the Bemidji High School, they had been scanned for tech. Mr. Shaleborn—who had some ugly bruises now—had plucked the fidget from Austin's pocket and handed it to his older sister. She had smirked at him and tossed it in the back of her old Chevy hatchback.

Kylie hadn't tried to bring any tech except for the computer living inside her head. She was glad when they had decided their sensors were wrong to ping on her, even after they found the tracking device Papa had hidden in her backpack. There was obviously no machine attached to her face.

The Pine Fortress camp was designed specifically for upper-class children, and it wasn't much of a stretch to guess that they might have started training people with special abilities like hers. Not that she had any special abilities anymore. She couldn't detect signals or modify the functions of her own brain. She was normal now, even though she was *not* normal.

She hadn't expected it to hurt so much, being abnormal but not special.

Papa had said he was going to fix her abilities. He had installed one last update before she had left. This one gave her a little more control over her anxiety levels, but it wasn't enough to tame the crushing wave of abject fear that washed over her as she stared out at the crowd.

"It *was* a horrible tragedy," said Austin. "Twenty-one people died. Boston. A big container of molasses split and flooded the whole street. People drowned in it."

Kylie opened her eyes. The chaos had settled, and only a dozen kids lingered in the parking lot. A wooded path led away, and people slowly filtered that direction. Kylie let out a long sigh, released Austin—she had been gripping his hand hard enough to leave dents in his skin—and started to walk. The air smelled of the newly opened buds of summer and the musk of nature. It had a calming effect on her, and she started to notice the subtle sounds all around. Birds chirped somewhere in the trees. Wind rustled the branches of the aspens, causing new leaves to dance back and forth even when the air hardly moved. It was a peaceful place, and she almost didn't understand how it could do what she had hoped it would do.

They passed the wooden sign that read "Pine Fortress School for the Gifted," and Kylie felt the worst pang of homesickness she had ever felt. She didn't even *like* the house she shared with Papa. It was just—now that she thought about it, she'd felt homesick ever since Isabelle had left. She'd always shared a special connection with her sister.

"I don't *feel* very gifted," Austin said, hefting his big red backpack.

A voice behind them answered, "They'll let anyone in for summer school." A tall, blonde girl pushed past Austin and walked at a fast clip up the path. A pair of younger girls followed her, chittering to themselves as if the tall girl had said something very amusing.

"Bitch," Kylie whispered under her breath.

"Excuse me?" the girl said.

"Hanna, you're not supposed to fight," said one of her lackeys.

Hanna took a step toward Kylie, an amused smirk on her face. "It wouldn't be a fight, and I don't think it's proper for them to let rude little girls into this place." She was older. Late teens, maybe, Kylie thought. And she was right. It wouldn't even be a fight.

Austin stepped forward. "She didn't mean it," he said. "Kylie's just jealous of your backpack."

Hanna blinked. "What?"

"Your backpack. It's the kind she wanted to get, so she's jealous. I know it's not great to be jealous of other people's stuff, but, I mean, it's pretty understandable. You've got like a dozen pockets."

Suddenly Kylie felt self-conscious about her inadequate backpack.

Hanna's brow furrowed. She jabbed a finger at Kylie. "Don't touch my stuff."

"I won't," whispered Kylie as the other girls left. She didn't fully understand what had happened but decided that maybe other girls could hear better than she thought.

They continued up the path, and by the time it opened up into a square of short grass, she almost felt calm again.

Which was good, because that's when everything got worse. First, Hanna snickered at her quietly into the back of her hand, as if she was trying to conceal her amusement. Then Hanna's two lackeys joined in with cruel smiles.

Then, it was everyone else. A trio of boys a short distance away, a short girl with calloused hands, a dozen older kids in matching vests. All of them looked at her, their eyes driving right down into her soul.

She hated it. This was a mistake. The whole idea of getting away from Papa felt like the biggest failure of any failure she'd ever been a part of. She hated every one of these kids, and she didn't even know them. She just knew that they were cruel and mean and stupid.

Kylie concentrated on putting one foot in front of the other. She crossed the green to the big building on the other side. They had said to check in there and make sure she was properly registered. She'd get a cabin assigned, then she could hide there until supper. She hoped.

"I'm just saying, drowning in molasses sounds like a terrible way to go," Austin said.

"I don't know anything about molasses," said Kylie.

"You use it for baking."

"Papa doesn't bake."

"Huh."

Kylie shuddered. "Any drowning sounds bad to me."

"I wonder if they have swimming here," said Austin. "I'm a pretty good swimmer." He was forcing a conversation to distract her from a doom spiral. She could tell.

It still worked, though. "It's a camp in Minnesota. They probably have at least one lake around here somewhere."

"Yeah. I was hoping for a pool."

"Why?"

"Lakes are full of fish."

"And?"

"How can you swim when you know there are fish?"

Kylie looked at him. "How can you walk around in the air when you know there are birds?"

He laughed. It was a little forced, but maybe he was feeling the stress, too. "Well, as long as there aren't squirrels, I think we'll be fine."

"I have some bad news."

"Kylie Andersen," said a voice so familiar it sent a chill down her spine. The man wasn't talking to her, though. He was near one of the cabins, talking to Mr. Shaleborn. "You're kidding me, right?"

Kylie nudged Austin and the two veered away to a spot where they could listen.

"Silver thinks she's got potential." Mr. Shaleborn put his hand on a tall man's shoulder. Kylie couldn't see his face from behind a large viburnum hedge, but she saw he wore a battered black cowboy hat. "Just tell her you regret everything. That you've moved on from your previous employment and you're trying to make things better."

"What were those guys after, Shaleborn?"

"That's not school business. You're a teacher now. Listen to Silver. Do your job. Make sure your history with Andersen doesn't cause any trouble. You'll be fine."

"This isn't the kind of work I signed up for."

Mr. Shaleborn said something very quiet that Kylie couldn't hear.

"Your custodian killed a guy," said the familiar voice.

"You were the brains of that operation," Shaleborn growled. "So, whatever happened out there is on you."

"I was hired to teach."

"You'll do whatever Silver needs done." There was a brief pause. Kylie imagined the two men staring daggers at each other. "Who else would hire you, Lang? You're not good for anything else."

"Lang?" Austin whispered. "Is that who I think it is?"

Kylie nodded. The man talking to Shaleborn had kidnapped them both. He had been high up in the Frontier Arms organization, and his team had almost gotten them killed. If it hadn't been for the internal conflicts running all the way through Frontier, someone might have actually killed them. And for what? Kylie never quite understood why they had done any of it.

"Let's get out of here," Kylie said. They circled a cabin to avoid running into Mr. Shaleborn and the guy from Frontier Arms.

But how long would they be able to avoid them? Kylie wondered if she could manage to stay at camp while somehow avoiding the big man. This was the worst.

Those was her thoughts when Tenen Lang stepped onto the narrow path between cabins, blocking the two of them.

Chapter Twelve

A WAVE OF VERTIGO washed over Tenen Lang when he saw Kylie Andersen and Austin Giles on the commons. The air went still and the bustle from the rest of the camp died under the weight of his singular focus on the two children in front of him.

It hadn't been very long. Six months. He had known his disability would be permanent as soon as the first medics ran the MRI. He had dragged himself through rehab. Suffered through the realization that his whole life was a slag of ruined debris, and it was all thanks to that old man, Ajay Andersen.

The girl's grandfather had ruined Lang, and he couldn't help but despise her for it. He tried to meet her gaze, but nausea threatened to overtake him.

"I regret how we made our first acquaintance," Lang said when he knew he wouldn't vomit. The words tasted like sand on his tongue.

The girl stared at him, a look of pure disgust on her face. He didn't blame her. What kind of pathetic image must he be in front of her? "You don't have to lie," she said.

"I'll be teaching your strategy class," Lang said.

"What happens if we skip?" asked the boy.

"Probably better if you do," admitted Lang. It would be so much better for him.

Giles looked at him suspiciously.

"I'm not skipping," said Andersen. "I'm going to make the most of camp, and you're not going to stop me. Papa paid good money for me to be here."

"You're Papa's just a saint, isn't he?" said Lang before he could stop himself.

"He saved your life," said the girl.

"Saved," Lang spat. He drew several deep breaths in a futile effort to calm himself. "Show up to lessons and you'll get as good as anyone else."

"Can't imagine *that's* very good," said Andersen, earning a dirty look from her companion. "What? He lost a fistfight to my grandpa. What can he possibly teach us about anything?"

It wasn't a fistfight. Lang had been fighting a contingent of armed protesters at the time, and a split-second distraction had resulted in a life-altering disability. Fistfight. Lang knew pointing it out would do no good with this girl. He knew that she'd tear him apart if he tried to dispute whatever nonsense she believed about her awful grandfather. He knew it was a losing battle, but he stepped forward anyway. So much for strategy.

"Listen up, kid," he said, jabbing a finger at the girl. "I don't know what your Papa told you, but I was on a legitimate job that day. Mercenaries don't always get to pick their missions, but that one was going to make the world a better place. If that meant we had to move you kids around to keep you safe from a bunch of terrorists, then we were willing to do that." It was an exaggeration of Frontier Arms' dealings in the area, but nothing he said was a blatant lie. "Notice how I'm not in jail? Frontier's lawyers found plenty of reasons why what I did wasn't illegal."

"That doesn't mean it wasn't wrong," said Giles.

Lang gave him his most scathing look. "First rule of tactical success, kid: there's no such thing as wrong."

"My mom says it's always good strategy to stay on the side of right," said the boy.

Lang opened his mouth to protest, then reconsidered. He gave the kid a nod and turned to hobble away. Maybe this camp wouldn't be such a waste after all. He had at least one smartass kid to teach.

Shaleborn slapped him on the back. "Kids giving you trouble?" he said through his piece-of-shit grin.

"Nothing I can't handle."

"Really?" Shaleborn punched Lang in the arm, almost toppling him. "Don't write any checks you can't cash, big guy. You think it's bad when they're mocking you for your cane—just wait till one of them's landed you on your ass."

"Talking from experience?"

"I've had to bruise a few cocky upstarts to keep them in their place." Shaleborn shadow-boxed an imaginary opponent. "It's how they learn."

Lang had trained dozens of soldiers over the years. Hundreds, maybe. He'd long since learned that soldiers who only respect someone for their strength don't respect them at all.

"If they come at me," Lang said, "I'll do what my gramps always did when the kids started to get out of line."

"What's that?"

"I'll fall on them."

Shaleborn laughed all the way across the field.

Chapter Thirteen

As soon as Ajay heard the knock on his door, he knew he'd screwed up. Nobody was supposed to know where he lived. He had purged his location from every solicitation database on the planet. When he used transportation, he always wiped the unit's memory. His little house in the middle of a big neighborhood ought to be as invisible as a green golf ball in the rough.

He swiped to his outside camera display and saw a view of the top of Kate's head as she stood patiently on his front stoop. With a sigh, he extracted himself from the chair where he'd spent the week since Kylie's departure. His own sweaty odor wafted up around him in a cloud.

A week wasted in research. All he wanted to do was check in on Kylie, but his tracking device had been disabled. He *knew* that he should trust that she would be safe. He *got* it.

Unfortunately, the dark specter of parental anxiety didn't agree.

He unlocked and opened the door for her, and once she was inside, Kate folded her arms. "You're not responding to my texts and I tried calling."

Ajay glanced at his cane leaning against the wall. Sure enough, its alert light blinked with new messages. "I've been busy," he said.

"Was that a strange way of saying you're sorry?"

Ajay's jaw worked a few times before he finally came up with, "Can I get you some coffee?"

Kate flashed a grin. "That's better."

It wasn't *good* coffee, but Ajay had long since lost the taste buds necessary to enjoy the fancy stuff. He brewed a pot in silence, blinking away the bleary fog that always surrounded him when he'd been lost deep in the recesses of computer research.

"I don't regret sending her," he said as he pushed a cup across the table to Kate. "But the more I think about it, the more I don't think she's safe. I want to know about those guys who attacked the teacher."

Kate sipped, winced, and set the cup down. "Maybe it's best to just let it go."

"I never wanted to do anything like survival camp when I was a kid. *Way* too much work."

"Not everyone's lazy, Ajay," she said.

"Teenagers are *supposed* to be, though."

"You were never in 4H."

Ajay inhaled the steam from his cup. It was early enough in the morning that his bones still yearned for the stuff. "All I found were some Canadians. I don't know why yet, but apparently that Shaleborn guy has pissed off a group of thugs from Thunder Bay."

"Ontario?"

"Is there another Thunder Bay?"

"Hired muscle?"

"The best professional criminals don't make big scenes," said Ajay. "In fact, if they're smart, they don't make an online footprint, either."

Kate tried another sip of coffee, but it made her pucker her lips. "This is awful, Ajay."

"She's dealt with worse before, but I still worry."

"No, I mean the coffee."

Ajay tasted his coffee. It was an average level of awful. Maybe a little tart, which he supposed people didn't expect in their java. "I'm just… worried." Ajay's shoulders slumped. "How can I let her live her own life when I'm so worried every time she's out of my sight?"

"She's a good kid, right?" Kate said.

"I don't even know where she went," Ajay said. "The bus picked her up from the parking lot, but the location on the registration info isn't the actual address of the camp."

"Surely there's surveillance—"

"Gone," Ajay growled. "All of it. Records from mid and upper drones. Tracking data from the bus company. It's a good camp. Very reputable. But all the records hide its location."

"Maybe that's why the Thunder Bay thugs attacked Shaleborn when they did."

That thought had never occurred to Ajay, but it made sense. If nobody could find the camp—and if *Ajay* couldn't find it, he didn't think anyone else could—then they would simply have feelers out for whenever their mark popped up on the grid. That happened to be during the Bemidji recruiting trip.

They had attacked on his way back. Maybe they had been following him to find out the location and he'd spotted them, or maybe they just wanted him dead. Whatever the case, Kylie was probably safe in the camp. After all, she had fewer enemies than that Shaleborn guy. Certainly fewer enemies than Ajay. He thought back to the night of the attack and remembered the voice he'd heard.

"Shaleborn has several bounties out on him," Ajay said.

Kate leaned forward, a gleam in her eyes. "Bounties? Really? Do we suddenly live in the Old West?"

"Nothing official, but a few forums buried deep in the most anonymous corners of the network have him on a list of wanted men. These guys from north of the border might have just been looking to make an easy buck."

Kate didn't look convinced. "You smell terrible, Ajay."

Ajay waved her off. "I showered last week."

She took another sip from her coffee, then they sat in silence for a long time. She stared out the window. Ajay desperately wondered what was going through her head. They hadn't seen each other since the day they had met, but Ajay found that he missed her. It felt as if they were old friends, comfortable in each other's company.

"Have you talked to the bus driver?" she finally asked.

"What?"

"The bus driver. Not the records and not the financials. I mean track down the actual bus driver and chat him up."

"I never—" Dammit, she had a good point. "I sometimes get distracted."

A huge grin spread across Kate's face. "You fell down a gol-darn rabbit hole."

Ajay frowned at her enthusiasm. "A little."

"I knew it! It's that look on your face. Bill used to always go off on tangents. 'A little,' huh?"

A lot, actually. "Have you heard of the North Shore Shooter?"

"The what?"

"Come on," Ajay said. He pushed his aching bones up from the table and led Kate down into his computer lab of a basement. "If there's one thing the networks are good at, it's finding patterns where there aren't any."

"You found a pattern?"

"Someone else found a pattern." Ajay brought up a map of Minnesota on his screen. "It always happens in the late summer. Always in a fairly unpopulated area. Always a not-so-prominent target with a criminal background."

"You think there's a vigilante in northern Minnesota," Kate said. Her voice dripped with disbelief.

"Maybe it's a hero," Ajay deadpanned.

"What's the difference?"

"A hero gets ignored by the authorities when they commit acts of violence in the community."

"Ah." Kate leaned in to peer at the map. "And these red dots are the locations of the killings?"

"They're the locations of the attacks. Not all of them are killings. They aren't even all shootings."

"What else would they be?"

Ajay selected one in Ely, Minnesota near the International Wolf Center. A window popped up with information about the attack. "Bear attack," said Ajay.

Now Kate really didn't believe him. "You're counting bear attacks in the tally? Ajay, I don't think we have a bear vigilante loose in northern Minnesota."

"Look at the details."

She peered at the screen for a long time, reading the synopsis of the attack as described by some random conspiracy theorist from the network. As it read, the victim was a sex trafficker out of Duluth. There was no indication about why he was up near the border, but it was implied that there was a deal going down. Whatever the circumstance, the man ended up tied to a tree in the north woods, bleeding, and covered in honey. What's more, the location in question had been having bear problems for weeks ever since someone had started feeding bears from that location.

"I'm willing to admit this was suspicious," Kate said. "Did the guy say who tied him up?"

"Wouldn't talk."

"May I?" Kate asked. When Ajay didn't protest, she flipped through the other tags on the map, checking the stories behind each. The majority were tagged as hunting accidents. Errant bullets happened to hit people in the depths of the north woods. Occasionally, more than one person was killed, or someone would escape. The pattern was loose, but it was there. Late summer. Violent criminal.

"They all take place on the last week of camp," he said. "I only found it because I was researching the dates."

"That's some rabbit hole," Kate said. Was she starting to believe?

Something else still bothered Ajay about the attacks, but he couldn't quite put his finger on it. "I just don't know."

"So, you think Shaleborn was attacked by this vigilante?"

"No," said Ajay. "The timing's not right."

"What's to say our hero isn't branching out a little?"

Ajay blinked wearily. "I don't know. I'm not even sure that there *is* a vigilante. All I know is that someone out there picked up on this pattern, and they're calling them the North Shore Shooter."

"Even though not all of these attacks involve shooting."

"Right. Like I said, it's not a great theory."

Kate scrolled through a few more descriptions. None of them stood out as particularly interesting to Ajay, but she seemed fascinated. "It could be a rival gang," she said idly.

"That's—not a bad theory," he said, leaning in. "If that was the case, we could figure out which organization these victims belonged to and eliminate them from the list of potential perpetrators. I can write a program to do this."

"It's only fifteen years," said Kate.

"So?"

"So, you could look up each of the fifteen victims in the time it would take to write your stupid program."

Ajay stared at her. She was right, of course, but the fog in his brain still didn't clear. "Right."

"What does this have to do with Kylie?" Kate asked, taking a sip of her coffee. She must have discovered the brew wasn't too hot anymore, because she gulped the rest of it down.

"Nothing," said Ajay. "Everything. Look, I want to find the location of that camp. Just so I know where it is. After that, I want to see if there's really a killer."

"You need sleep," said Kate.

He looked at her for a long time, taking several long seconds to understand what she was saying. It felt so good to talk to her. To have *anyone* to talk to. "You're probably right," he said, taking her cup from her. "But I'll settle for more coffee."

A grin spread across her face. "Now we're talking."

"Oh, and one more thing," Ajay said. "That guy who was supposedly fed to the bears a few years ago?"

"The sex trafficker?"

"Yeah. I don't think he was really a sex trafficker."

"What makes you say that?"

"Because I know him. His name is Olexie Sokolov."

Chapter Fourteen

THE DAYS PASSED INTO weeks, and Kylie fell into the rhythm of the camp's rigid structure. Anger dissolved into frustration dissolved into the drudgery of daily life. She wondered if this was what the military was like. Early mornings, bland food, and days packed full of practice for things she doubted she would ever need. There was a teacher who took them on walks in the woods, pointing out which plants could be eaten and which were deadly poison. Another taught them how to make traps that would kill rabbits and others that would only injure or maim.

"A good distraction in a pinch," said Mrs. Dearborne. "Nothing unsettles an enemy like a screaming rabbit."

Kylie tried not to think about it. Even Austin looked a little pale after that lesson. They learned to shoot arrows and bullets. They even spent double sessions on martial arts.

They avoided the custodian, Vincent, as much as they could. After what they heard Lang say to Shaleborn, they knew the creepy guy with greasy hair was as dangerous as any of the teachers. Maybe more so. Kylie wondered what they were up to. Why was Shaleborn getting into trouble? Why was their custodian shooting people? What was it they were making Lang cover up?

In the end, she didn't have *time* to think about some nebulous criminal conspiracy. She was too exhausted from her lessons.

"Hai!" called Shaleborn.

Kylie snapped a punch, kick, punch combination at the air. Her muscles ached and the tension in her shoulders had almost disappeared. The headache had faded after the first week of camp, replaced by a numb sensation like a rolling fog.

Every lesson with Lang caused her belly to ache and the stress to build in her shoulders. She worked hard every day to ignore the big man—to pretend like he hadn't once worked for the enemy.

It rarely worked, even though he'd held true to his promise. He gave her strategy lessons, same as anyone else in his class.

"Hai!"

Kylie's "Hai!" in return lacked the crisp authority of Shaleborn's, but it was a far cry from the weak "Hey" she had timidly shouted at the beginning of camp. Now she was much better. He stepped next to her and watched as she cycled through another combo, correcting her technique as he did.

"Body and mind are one, and both should flow entirely into your attack. When you strike, strike the space behind your opponent. Punch through them."

Kylie didn't think she would ever want to punch through anyone.

After lessons, every day included recreation time, which she and Austin spent *not* swimming in the lake. The evenings were full of typical summer camp fare: food cooked over a campfire, songs, and stories. These were distractions from the aching homesickness that lingered in the back of her brain, but as long as she kept moving, her longing didn't hurt too much.

"Pair up," said Shaleborn. "Hanna, this time you take Kylie."

Dammit. Kylie had worked hard to avoid the older girl, and so far mostly succeeded.

The others lined up across from each other. Most of the dozen in her group were older than she and Austin. A boy with red hair and a deep splash of freckles paired up with Austin. Hanna, standing a head taller than Kylie, smirked at her across an imaginary central line.

"Hai!" shouted Shaleborn.

The students knew the routine. At once, those on the east side of the line launched themselves at the west. They got to choose their attacks, but the defenders could only use blocks or throws.

Hanna started with a front kick, which Kylie sidestepped easily. Then a strike snapped Kylie in the upper arm, which stung, then an open-handed strike to her solar plexus. Kylie gasped and stepped back.

A short distance away, the red-haired boy ground Austin's face into the grass.

"Looks like your friend knows where he belongs," Hanna said with a smirk.

Kylie's fists clenched in front of her. The tension returned to her shoulders, and when Hanna launched another attack, she didn't move fast enough to block.

Every blow hurt, but Hanna knew better than to strike to injure.

"Stop," said Shaleborn. "Andersen, what are you doing?"

Kylie wiped her lower lip, checking the hand to make sure it wasn't bleeding. "I've never been good at martial arts." Her Aikido instructor had taught her how to flow with an attack and how to roll when thrown, but she never learned how to be aggressive. Shaleborn's martial arts involved a mix of Tae Kwon Do, Judo, and Jujitsu. Flowing quickly between techniques gave him an advantage against opponents accustomed to only one, but learning to switch was tricky. Each martial art contained an entirely different philosophy, and when Kylie thought about them too hard, she froze.

"Find your center," he said. "Protect it."

Kylie nodded acknowledgment, even though she had no idea what he was talking about.

"Proceed."

Hanna boxed her on the ear, then slammed her shoulder hard enough to leave a bruise. They separated.

At least Kylie was doing better than Austin. The red-haired boy had him twisted in an actual knot.

"Block this time, Kylie," said Shaleborn, as if she hadn't been trying to block. He crossed his arms and watched them line up for another bout. She may have had history with Lang, but Shaleborn was fast becoming her least favorite teacher.

"Yeah," said Hanna. "Block."

Kylie lined up in a Tae Kwon Do ready stance, all hard edges and tight fists. She had the advantage that she didn't need to initiate the attack. All she was allowed to do was wait for the strike and meet it with equal force.

Aikido had been such a different skill. It taught her to flow with the energy of the attack. She learned to sidestep conflicts and dissipate aggression. It was a beautiful martial art.

But it was so hard for her to do.

Hanna snapped a forward kick, which Kylie met with a step forward and a block. Hanna staggered back from the jarring impact, but it didn't slow her. She followed up with two quick punches. Kylie clumsily deflected the blows. She kept her center, backed up, and readied to block another attack.

"Good," said Shaleborn. He gave a whistle and the group snapped to attention. "Jess, join Hanna. Both on Kylie."

"What?" gasped Austin from the dirt. "That's not—"

"Kylie," Shaleborn said. "Block."

Jess stepped up with a smirk on her face. Jess was one of Hanna's sycophants. She was shorter, thinner, and not as cruel, but Kylie almost hated her more for her compliance.

Hanna and Jess didn't hesitate. They advanced hard and fast, with Hanna coming in low and Jess striking high. Kylie lifted a leg to partially block the kick and danced away from Jess's weaker punches.

"I said block," snapped Shaleborn. "Don't dance."

Kylie's rage boiled up inside her. She stood her ground for the next attack, snapping a low block with her left fist and a high block with her right. Instead of retreating, she stood her ground, but Jess snuck a fist under her defenses, thumping her hard in the ribs.

"Break," said Shaleborn. "Does this work?"

Kylie was too busy gasping for breath to answer. In that moment, Kylie hated Shaleborn more than she'd ever hated anyone. Tears blurred her vision.

Austin touched her elbow, but she pulled away. His words were a haze of noise and nonsense. When did he get up off the ground?

Shaleborn said to Hanna and Jess, "It didn't work because you aren't fast enough. You aren't clever enough. You aren't strong enough." He took Hanna's fists, adjusted her stance, and nudged her to one side. "When you both attack from her front, she can more easily defend against you both. Flank and coordinate."

"They're going to try to hit you at once," Austin whispered to Kylie. "You're not allowed to attack, but you need to control the narrative."

Narrative. Kylie's brain struggled to grasp the idea of that word. Controlling the narrative meant writing her own story. Not Papa's. Not Austin's. Certainly not Hanna and Jess's.

Hanna and Jess stood on either side of Kylie. She couldn't properly watch either one of them, and she didn't know how to line up a ready stance. Shaleborn stood in front of her, hands clasped behind his back.

"You are outnumbered," he said. "Flanked and outpowered. Take in the situation. What's the move?"

Kylie looked to the other students. She glanced at Hanna, who watched her with a predatory gleam. Austin took a few steps back to return to the circle.

"Observe," Shaleborn said. "Take in everything."

Her heart pounded. What was she missing? What was she supposed to do? She observed everything there was to observe and it was too much. Anxiety made her whole body shake.

"This is the part where you tell me it's not fair," said Shaleborn.

"Life isn't fair," Kylie said, locking eyes with him.

"No," he said. "It's not." He gave the signal to start.

Kylie moved, staying light on her feet. She couldn't properly defend against them both, but she didn't have to make it easy for them. If they wanted to coordinate their attacks, they could do it on a moving target.

"Block!" Shaleborn shouted. "Don't dance."

Kylie kept moving. Fuck his rules.

Jess struck first. The roundhouse came in high and strong. Kylie blocked with both arms, stepping into the blow to rob power from its arc. Without slowing, she spun on Hanna, who had already launched herself forward. Kylie batted away the first strike at her middle, but a solid blow on her shoulder jarred her sideways.

Kylie's lungs burned. Her vision sharpened. She spun back on Jess to block a clumsy blow to the head. Kylie swung around.

And elbowed Hanna in the nose. Blood exploded across the girl's beautiful face.

"Stop!" called Shaleborn. "Good."

Hanna cried and sputtered. She held her hands to her bloody face. Jess rushed to her side.

Shaleborn leaned down to look at Hanna's nose. He gripped her chin and turned her from side to side. "It's not broken," he said. "You'll be fine."

Hanna slinked back into the circle, then someone brought her a towel so that she could stop her bleeding and clean up.

"What happened?" Shaleborn asked of Kylie.

"Nothing, I—"

"What went wrong?"

Kylie swallowed a retort and gave him the answer she thought he wanted. "I was outnumbered like you said. I didn't stand a chance." She looked to the other students but found nothing but angry glares. Hanna was popular, she realized too late. "I couldn't watch both directions, so I had to guess where she would be. I thought she would go high, so I blocked high. When she went low, her face ended up where I blocked."

"Is that really what happened?"

Almost. Kylie felt her muscle memory betraying her. She'd *hoped* her elbow would land in the girl's face. It had been her only chance of escaping the situation without losing. "The rules were too restrictive," she said. "You wanted me to block, but blocking won't win."

"What will?" Shaleborn asked, this time addressing the whole crowd. "What would you have done in that situation?"

Austin swallowed and tried to look very small.

"Giles," Shaleborn snapped, zooming in on the one retreating student. "What would you do?" A cruel grin flashed in his eyes. "Take in the whole situation. Absorb it all in a second and make your decision. That is the path to victory. Assume you have done everything possible to avoid the situation, but here you are, flanked and outnumbered."

Austin looked from Shaleborn to Jess and finally to Hanna. "What are the rules?"

"Anything you want," said the instructor.

"What do *they* think the rules are?"

"Good question." Shaleborn took a step toward Austin. "What do you think?"

Austin said, "If they expected sparring strikes, I would hit harder. If they expect blocks, I would strike." He considered for a moment. "If they expected a fight, I would surrender."

Shaleborn scoffed. "What would surrender get you?"

"Survival."

"I would call you a coward."

"All good strategists are cowards, sir," said Austin.

Shaleborn pressed his lips together and appeared to consider the statement. After a moment, he breathed one single laugh and waved to dismiss the class. "When they need to be, kid," he muttered as he gathered his things. "When they need to be."

Chapter Fifteen

"HE'S A COWARD," SAID Ajay as Kate pulled her truck into the Crow Wing county courthouse parking lot in Brainerd, Minnesota. "But he's also an idiot."

"You're really selling it here, man," said Kate. She found an open spot between a tiny self-driving Chevy with rust on every single panel, and a piece of farm equipment with wheels twice Ajay's height.

It had taken weeks to track Olexie Sokolov to the county jail. The old Russian was almost as sharp a hacker as Ajay and twice as paranoid. He'd covered his tracks, but the real trouble came when he disappeared into the government systems. When Ajay had finally tracked the big man to the Crow Wing courthouse, he had called Kate for a ride. To his surprise, she had agreed suspiciously fast.

"I'm not fun," he protested.

"You're two steps up from watching grass grow," was her response.

The morning sun shone down on the Brainerd streets too warm through Ajay's loose button-down shirt. Somewhere, an ancient diesel engine rumbled, and the sharp scent of ammonia drifted over the summer breeze.

He wanted to ask Kate what her interest was in what he was doing, but he was afraid of the answer. His best guess was that Isabelle might have hired her, but why? Whatever Kate's motivation, it couldn't be perfectly altruistic. Not in this oppressive heat. Ajay wasn't *that* fun. She couldn't be *that* bored.

Not that *his* motives were entirely altruistic. He could have taken a self-driving car wherever he needed, wiped its memory clean, and been on his way. Unfortunately, that got a lot harder with the latest updates to the self-driving software. He could no longer count on untracked transit, at least not until he figured out a zero-day flaw in the new software. Once he had that, he'd be able to stop asking Kate for a ride.

Until then, it felt nice having her company.

"We're here to see Olexie Sokolov," Ajay said when the peace officer greeted him at the desk.

"Finally bailing him out?" the man asked. He was in an ill-fitting uniform and his close-cropped hair made his jaw look swollen.

"Depends on what he has to say," said Ajay.

When Ajay sat in the waiting area to fill out paperwork, Kate whispered, "Why not just bail him out and speak with him somewhere else?"

"Because he's an asshole," said Ajay.

"He'd be in good company."

Ajay pressed his lips together, but when he looked up at Kate, he realized she was teasing him. She was also right. "I'm sorry I didn't want to stop for donuts."

"It's a road trip," she said. "There should be donuts."

When the paperwork was complete, Ajay returned it to the peace officer, and they waited while absolutely nothing happened behind the scenes. After the better part of the morning, the officer signaled Ajay and Kate to come forward and guided them through the halls of the jail to a meeting room. The beige walls and low ceiling were almost as stifling as the uncomfortable chairs and worn faux-wood table. The jail smelled of antiseptic spray and urine.

"Since you're not Mr. Sokolov's lawyers, everything will be recorded," said the officer. "Voice and video."

"Yes, sir," said Ajay.

A handcuffed Olexie Sokolov was ushered into the room. The tall Russian was almost as old as Ajay, and the bags under his eyes made him look twice as tired. His normally trimmed square head was shaggy and unkempt, with the scruff of a steel beard covering his strong jaw. The wrinkles in the corners of his sharp blue eyes deepened with amusement when he saw Ajay.

"My friend," he said, exaggerating his Russian accent.

"Olexie," said Ajay.

The officer left the room, presumably to go somewhere to ensure that the full video and audio were recorded of the encounter.

Ajay tapped the top of his cane. A light on top of it flashed twice. Then, a low hum rattled the table.

Olexie looked at the cane, looked up at the camera in the ceiling, then looked at Kate. "You aren't going to pay my bail, are you?"

"It depends," said Kate.

To Ajay, Olexie said, "Who is this person?"

"Tell me about the sex trafficking, Olexie," Ajay said.

Olexie flinched. "I don't know what you're talking about." His Russian accent all but disappeared.

"Few years ago. Up by the Canadian border." Ajay leaned in and shone the light from his cane on his friend's face. "There might have been a bear involved."

"First of all," said Olexie, "I did not sex traffic. It was human trafficking. No bears."

Kate crossed her arms. "So, there was no sex?"

"There might have been sex," Olexie said. "I don't know anything about sex."

"What are you in here for, anyway?" asked Ajay.

"Nothing." Olexie leaned back in his chair and folded his hands over his belly. "I was driving."

"Drunk?"

"I don't like alcohol."

"They arrested you for driving?" Ajay said.

"I am being persecuted," said Olexie. "For my beliefs."

Kate drummed her fingers on the table. "Tell us about the bear, Olexie. Maybe we'll bail you out."

"I know a lot of bears," Olexie said. "I am Russian."

"But you don't drink," said Kate.

"Neither do most bears."

Ajay said, "This one almost had you as a snack. It's the person we're more interested in, not the bear. Who tied you to that post?"

Olexie leaned forward and buried his face in his palms. He let out a long sigh. "The people I brought across the border needed my help. I didn't make much money from them. They were refugees of the Canadian jobs crisis."

Ontario's job market *had* crashed during that time. The forestry and agriculture industries had suffered greatly due to the lingering effects of climate change. New species of emerald ash borer had devastated the northern reaches of forest, but the paper industry south of the border had already recovered from a similar catastrophe. Canadian workers needed jobs.

"Minnesota had jobs," said Olexie. He shrugged. "What is the harm?"

"So," said Kate, "no sex trafficking?"

"Workers sometimes have sex," Olexie said. "It's not my fault."

Ajay thumped his cane on the table. "They're going to figure out that the recording isn't working pretty soon. Tell us who tied you to that post."

Olexie cast a nervous glance at the camera. "Bail me out."

"I'm not going to bail you out, Olexie," said Ajay.

"Why not?"

"Yeah, why not?" asked Kate.

"Because I think you're lying about being persecuted," said Ajay.

Olexie grimaced. "They don't like Russians here."

"No," Ajay said, "they don't like *you*." Ajay knew for a fact there were a dozen legitimate reasons Olexie might have been arrested.

"Fair enough." Olexie drew a long breath. "I will tell you the story."

Ajay's chair creaked when he leaned back. He didn't take his eyes off the Russian.

"It was a few years ago," started the Russian. "I was just starting to work with the countercapitalists and that Mr. Black guy, but this job came through and it was good."

Kate's eyes narrowed, and her jaw hardened.

"The countercapitalists are not terrorists," Olexie explained.

"Sure," said Kate.

"They are terrorist adjacent," laughed Olexie. His Russian accent was back in full force. "It is very different. Anyway, I was not trusted enough to get real information from the group. They asked me to help some workers who were having trouble in northern Minnesota. The paper industry was failing, and a worker-led coop was about to go under because they could not find any workers to backfill.

"It was not their fault. Someone was buying contracts. Hiring workers for big money, moving them across the country. Oregon was bleeding their talent dry." Olexie pressed his lips together and his nostrils flared. "I never liked Oregon. It is an inferior state. Unfortunately, they paid well and people would move. Later, we learned that those people were then fired, stranding them miles from old jobs that they were afraid to go back to. It was an ugly thing, but paper needs pulp and pulp needs trees and trees need lumberjacks.

"Canada had lumberjacks. Fires took so much of their forest after the dieback that they had no more industry. They are still recovering. The only problem was that we couldn't legally move people across the border. Someone was influencing the visa process."

"You decided to ignore the law," Ajay said. "Bring people over."

"Crossing through the boundary waters is easy. I even got the permits to canoe north to meet people. Then we came straight down through the lakes and I drove them away. They had jobs waiting for them. Good pay. We made sure everything was beneficial for them." He looked straight at Kate. "We did not prevent them from consensual sex."

She gestured for him to continue the story.

"I took three trips. On my last one, I was almost caught. There was some fast driving involved."

"Is that the kind of driving that landed you here today?"

"No, I was not going fast at all. This was different." Olexie sounded profoundly offended. "I am a very good driver. Very fast. Even with my skills, however, we could not outrun the drones. They followed us wherever we went, so instead of taking them to the meeting point, I took my new friends to the Wolf Center in Ely. That was where they caught me."

"Who?" asked Ajay. "Who caught you?"

Olexie bit his lip in disgust. "There were three of them. They were very green." Olexie looked down at his hands, clenching them into fists. "I couldn't kill them. You know how that goes. It was easier to give myself up. Let them capture me. Then I escaped."

"Who were they?" Ajay repeated.

"I don't know who they were, but they knew where I was going to be. Caught me. Stripped me. Made me into bear bait." A far-off look passed through Olexie's eyes. "It was a good bear. Very healthy." Then he met Ajay's gaze. "I escaped. It did not eat me."

"I figured," said Ajay, almost ready to give up on the idea of getting any real information from the Russian.

Kate said, "Are we just ignoring the comment about Oregon being inferior?"

"Silver," said Olexie. "I do not know who the children were, but the woman pressuring us to stop bringing people over the border was the heir to the Silver estate."

Ajay blinked. "Was this the same woman who still dominates the paper industry around International Falls?"

"That is the lady. She is a stone-cold bitch," Olexie said. To Kate, he added, "No offense."

"None taken," drolled Kate.

"Do you have proof?" asked Ajay.

"That Silver is a bitch?" Olexie said. "Yes, of course I do."

Ajay stood. "How much is your bail."

Olexie mumbled something under his breath.

"Excuse me?"

"One hundred thousand dollars."

"You know I can't pay that, right?" Ajay said.

"That's fine." A grin spread across Olexie's square face. "Word is that Black will send a good lawyer soon."

"Your countercapitalists still take direction from that guy?"

"We take money and information," said Olexie. "Our ideals remain solid and intact."

"I bet," Ajay said. "He'll really get you out?"

"Not soon enough to go to the big meeting in Duluth," Olexie said, "but pretty soon after that."

"What meeting?"

Olexie blinked at Ajay. He might have said more than he was supposed to and just realized it. Ajay wouldn't get more from the man.

"But Oregon?" Kate asked.

"Piece of shit state," said Olexie.

Ajay shut down his audio and video interference, allowing the systems in the jail to normalize. He had configured the interference so that it would blur their conversation but still allow snippets through. Olexie, hopefully, wouldn't get in trouble. He tapped his cane on the door and after a short wait, the peace officer returned to let them out.

"Good talk?" the man said.

"He's a surly son-of-a-bitch," said Ajay, "but at least he's chatty."

The office chuckled. "I'm surprised we keep seeing him in here, actually."

"Why was he picked up, exactly?" asked Kate.

The officer grinned. "At first we picked him up because we thought he was drunk."

"But he wasn't."

"Not that we could tell. He was singing some Russian song and got a little rough with some of our officers, but to be honest, it wasn't enough to hold him on anything until the call came in from higher up."

Ajay furrowed his brow. The whole thing didn't make much sense at all. A hundred thousand dollars was a significant bail for something they couldn't quite pin down.

"What was he driving?" asked Kate.

Now, the peace officer's grin widened. "You probably saw it on your way in. That sprayer with a wheelbase wide enough that it almost looks like a car could drive right under them?"

"He drove over someone?" Ajay asked.

"Tried," said the officer. "Not successfully. Right down the middle of Highway 18. As far as we could tell, he paid cash for it from one of the farmers down that way." The officer tapped a pen on the desk. "Will you be paying his bail?"

"I think we'll let him wait it out."

The light outside seared right through Ajay's eyes into the back of his head, and he realized that the conversation with Olexie had given him quite a headache. They crossed the street, careful to avoid any self-driving cars, and made their way back to the truck. Olexie's ride needed liberating as much as he did, but Ajay wasn't going to bother with any of it. He had more important things to think about.

Kate looked up at the sprayer with a hint of respect. "Well, I'll be damned."

"He's not subtle."

"Sonya Silver," said Kate as she climbed into her truck. "That name meant something to you."

"It did." Ajay twisted his cane in his hand. "Sonya Silver is a name on a list of Minnesota's wealthiest. Olexie and the countercapitalists try to track down the worst abusers of wealth. Those who stepped on a few too many people on the way up and work to keep people down now that they're on top."

"Sounds like a noble goal," Kate said.

"As long as they remember to avoid violence and do their research, yes. Olexie's not fantastic on both counts." He chewed his lower lip. "I can't say I'm always great either, to be truthful." He climbed into the passenger side of the truck, trying to gauge her reaction. What would she think of him if she knew what he had done? What he still would do? "But I haven't been able to find anything out about Silver on the network. Some people keep their lives buckled down. They hide the worst of what they do, or they involve themselves in seemingly charitable projects that cover their true intentions."

"What do you think she's up to?"

"Only one project that I know of," Ajay said, staring into the street. "Sonya Silver runs the Pine Fortress School for the Gifted."

"The place you sent your granddaughter for the summer?"

"Yeah." A knot of worry gnawed at Ajay's belly. "And I still don't know where it is."

Chapter Sixteen

"SUN TZU WAS A hack," Tenen Lang growled at the five kids across the table from him. A textured terrain rose from the holographic projection showing the movement of armies through forested lands. In the very center of the map was a walled fortification surrounding a huge power plant.

These were the four best kids the camp had to offer, plus the Andersen girl. Silver had told Lang to include her in everything. She was special. Lang hated special treatment. Special treatment got soldiers killed in the field.

As far as he could tell, the kid wasn't special at all. She was angry, but angry was a dime a dozen among teenagers. Lang met the gazes of each of his students in turn. Hanna Peterson was the only one who really impressed him. She was smart. Talented. Ruthless. She'd make a good mercenary someday if she wanted.

She wouldn't, of course. Peterson was a family girl. She'd go back to her father and run his security ring. As a glorified bodyguard, she'd hardly see any action, but at least camp would give her a chance to test her skills. Judging from her bruised nose and two black eyes, she'd already been tested enough. He wondered if Shaleborn was teaching his lessons again and bristled at the thought of that asshole screwing up kids who would otherwise have made decent soldiers.

Jess Harkin didn't look as wounded, but her mood was just as surly. She stared at the map as if it might jump up and bite her, but she'd proven herself capable before. It was only a matter of keeping her interested. Like Peterson, Harkin was connected. She'd never see any real military action.

Neither would Brian Gould, who stood too close to Harkin. Lang almost respected the curly-haired kid. His input in class had always been measured and clever—equal parts witty and tame, as if his every word were something he'd strategized over for days. Gould wasn't a rich kid, but he was too cautious to ever be a decent mercenary. Not cruel enough to be a real leader. He'd go into business or tech or something. Whatever it was, it'd be low risk and high reward. Lang almost hated the kid for it.

Then there was Austin Giles.

Lang closed his eyes and leaned heavily on his cane. Dizziness washed over him on the shores of a vast sea. When he opened his eyes, he met Giles's gaze.

"Tell me why Sun Tzu was a hack," Lang asked the kid.

Giles swallowed. Maybe Lang liked the kid because there wasn't enough melanin in the rest of the crowd. Andersen had a touch of color, but the others were so white it hurt to look at them. Or, possibly, Lang liked the kid because he saw a true thinker. He had potential. He wasn't mean enough, and he wasn't fast enough, but those were things that could be taught.

But what the hell did Lang know? He'd never been a teacher. Not really. He'd trained rookies, but *life* had done most of the training for him. Survival provided the passing grades.

What a person couldn't learn—what Lang now decided was impossible to teach—was a certain outlook on life. It was the idea that the world was a problem to be solved. That with proper strategy a person could enter any situation and come out victorious.

"Sun Tzu's first problem was that he wasn't a person," Giles said, eliciting a smirk from Andersen. "He was an amalgamation of the wisdom of generals over centuries of Chinese history."

Lang didn't know if that was true, but he didn't need to offer answers. It was *his* class after all. Let the kid answer.

Giles stared at the map and continued, "His problem was that he saw things as a general. He assumed that he would be given a goal and all of the power to accomplish it. He assumed that a victory condition existed, and he assumed that anything he did to achieve that victory was fair game."

"But that's how it works, little guy," sneered Hanna. "The general runs the army. It's kinda in the job description."

Giles flinched. For whatever reason, he was intimidated by her. Lang wondered if it had anything to do with the black eyes. Normally, it might worry him seeing a girl bruised like that, but it was obvious she physically outmatched him.

"Most people aren't generals," whispered Giles.

A good answer. One he would never hear from one of the rich kids. He placed a hand in the holographic map and moved one of the armies forward. "What makes someone a general?"

"Power," responded Hanna immediately. "The ability to achieve goals. Any goals. It doesn't have to be control of an army. It could be control of your own self." It came out like the regurgitated rote some previous teacher had given her. It wasn't *wrong*, but it didn't show the kind of thinking Lang wanted to hear.

The Andersen girl stared at the table. "Legitimacy," she said.

Lang had always gotten bad vibes off that girl, and she wasn't getting any better. "Explain, Andersen."

Her fingers danced over the controls on her side of the map, sending secret instructions to an army controlled by the kids. Half of the army melted into the forest. "Without legitimacy granted by a king or a president or something, the general is just a psychopath, marching across the land killing people."

Lang bristled. As a mercenary, he'd been given legitimacy by the contract. Everything he'd done had been under the authority of Frontier

Arms. Then they took it away. "You think that Sun Tzu was a psychopath?" Lang asked as he moved his army. She was hiding half her army, which meant she was going to try to misdirect him. If he moved his army quickly enough, he could claim the fortifications as his defense and her hidden troops would make no difference.

"Wait," Giles said, placing a hand on Andersen's wrist. He whispered, "Don't split them like that."

She shushed him, then to Lang, said, "A general who would burn his own boats to generate desperation in his own people is a psychopath."

When she moved a hand forward to move her troops, Peterson stopped her. "Kylie, maybe you should let more educated people run the army."

After a brief unspoken battle, Kylie Andersen retreated. Peterson sent commands to their shared troops while everyone else watched.

"I had a good plan," Andersen grumbled.

"You had a losing plan," said Peterson. They had a rivalry. Maybe that's where Peterson's black eyes came from.

"So, you don't agree, Peterson?" Lang said as he made his moves. His army was at the walls of the fort, ready to assault the position. His army set up a defensive position, expecting an attack from the forest. "Do you think Sun Tzu was a good person?"

"He wasn't a real person," said Giles. "He was an amalgamation—"

"We get it, Austin," said Andersen. "We're talking about hypotheticals here."

"I understand that."

"I get it," whispered Gould.

Peterson and Harkin glared at him.

"I get Kylie's strategy," he explained. "It's a good one."

Lang gestured for him to move, and the boy tentatively stepped up to the controls. He issued his commands and half of the remaining army disappeared into the dense forest.

Lang sent his troops into the fortified zone and set up their positions to guard the entrance. His defensive positions protected him from the neighboring hilltop—an obvious place for them to try to launch their attack—and he had clean shots on anywhere they might try to enter. For all intents and purposes, his position was solid. Any attack they made at that point would be a bloodbath.

Gould punched in their commands.

"What are you doing?" hissed Peterson.

"Not losing," said Austin.

"How do we define victory?" asked Lang, hoping to spark more conversation, "if it isn't defined by our legitimate ruler."

"Escape is victory," said Giles without hesitation. "Every time. The one who walks away is the one who wins."

Lang blinked. He'd never heard it put that way, but the definition almost made sense. In all his years as a mercenary, the only people who had declared victory had been the ones walking away from the field of battle. A wave of dizziness washed over him. He'd escaped his last battle. He might not have been able to walk on his own, but he got away. "Survival is victory," he muttered. "An interesting position."

"Everything else is a secondary objective," said Giles.

Interesting, but wrong. Victory required numerous other factors. This power plant, for one. The one that the kids had given up so that they could dance around with fancy maneuvers in the woods. They'd get the lesson. Sometimes the direct approach was the best. Achieving the objective fast and with force was better than fancy flanking and pinpoint strikes. He instructed his army to scan the edge of the forest.

And their scans picked up something. There, atop the bald hill where the dense forest gave way to rocky prairie, stood a single soldier with a single weapon.

"Oh," Lang said. "Interesting."

"Do you want to do the honors?" Gould asked Giles.

"No, that's fine," said Giles. He took a step back. "Hanna?"

Her answer was a scowl that would have made a gargoyle flinch.

"I'll do it," said Andersen. She touched the controls and dropped her instructions.

The lone soldier launched his attack. A single laser lanced across the battlefield and struck the core of the power plant. In a split second, Lang's army returned fire, cutting down the soldier where he stood.

But the damage was done. The power plant rumbled at first, then split wide. A pure white explosion pulsed across the map, leveling the fort, the hill, and most of the forest.

"We burn our boats," said Andersen. "Most of our army survived."

Lang didn't like the smug expression on the kid's face. Not one bit. Instead of flanking like he had expected, they had pulled most of their army off the map. Retreated before combat even started. Then they'd left one guy to destroy the power plant. Cracked it wide open. Killed everyone on the map.

Lang said, "Takes a hell of a general to send a soldier on a suicide mission."

"He had a family back home," said Giles. "And cancer."

The backstory wasn't part of the game. It went against everything Lang had learned as a young mercenary. "Faceless soldiers are fodder to grind in the gears of bad strategy. When your soldiers are people, you can make them heroes."

The rest of the lesson was a deconstruction of the battle, the different strategies they might have taken, and the reasons they might have played things differently. Maybe the power plant needed to stay operational or the city's population would freeze over the winter. Maybe a larger force was incoming and their army needed the defensive position. Whatever the case, the parameters affected the outcome.

It was dark outside when the children left. Lang slumped back in his chair and popped a couple pills. He closed his eyes and waited for the dizziness to ebb.

"Are those your five picks for the mission, then?" said a voice behind him. Lang did his best not to flinch at Sonya Silver's approach across the room, but the heels of her shoes tapped like daggers on the wooden floor.

"Hanna Peterson," Lang said. "She's the only one good enough."

Silver kneaded the muscles of his shoulders with her bony hands. "Kylie Andersen is the one I'm interested in."

"I'm aware." Lang opened his eyes. The room still spun, but he was able to focus on the severe woman above him. "She and Austin Giles have a clever streak, but they're soft. Not really mercenary material."

"I'm not looking for mercenaries, Lang," said Silver. "You know that."

Lang didn't give a damn about Silver's little mission, but the project was a condition of his employment. "Hanna's the one you want. Competent, clever, and cruel. She's got it all."

"Yet, Regis tells me that Kylie took down Hanna and Jess in martial arts."

Lang wrenched himself to his feet. "Martial arts aren't my business. I can tell you who's got the chops to run your mission. Andersen doesn't have it. She's not a leader." He placed a hand on his desk to steady himself. "And I seriously doubt that conflict is finished. Hanna might be bruised, but she's not the kind of girl to just let something like that drop."

Silver's lips pressed into a tight line, and Lang got the distinct impression that he was about to suffer her disapproval. "Prep all five for the war game. We'll see who's ready to run a mission."

With that, Silver disappeared into the night.

"We'll see which of them survives," Lang muttered to himself. "That'll be their victory."

Chapter Seventeen

Kylie still couldn't control her brain like she used to, and her brain was being an ass about it. When she panicked, anxiety rolled over her in waves, making her hands shake and her chest hurt and her lungs scream as if she hadn't taken a breath in ages. Before Papa's update, she would have nudged her brain and suppressed the jittering anxiety. She hadn't even known she was doing it. It was simply a normal reaction to a deadly threat.

Now, she needed to learn how to breathe, and she didn't like it. She still had a shred of control over her anxiety, but it wasn't enough. Not by a long shot.

"You don't have to be perfect," Austin whispered to her. "You already beat her in martial arts and strategy. Let her have this." The ear protection they wore allowed them to communicate directly, even with the staccato thundercrack of rifle fire all around them.

The rifle was a lead weight in Kylie's hands. She hefted it onto the platform and took position beside it.

"Do you think he's off killing someone?" Kylie asked.

Austin sighed. "Stop it about the custodian. He's gone, and we have more immediate concerns."

It had been weeks since Kylie had seen the greasy-haired custodian in the camp. She wondered if maybe the man's murder had caught up with him, or if he was maybe on a job somewhere murdering someone else.

"It's just suspicious, is all," Kylie said.

"My mom thinks that my being here means I'm going to go into the military when I graduate."

"Are you?"

He eyed the rifle in her hands. "I don't think I'm really military material."

The Barrett M33 sniper rifle wasn't the biggest, most expensive rifle on the range that day, but Kylie liked how it fit in her grip. The modified pistol grip was the right size for her admittedly small hands. The muzzle brake—improved over the older M95 rifles being fired elsewhere on the range—took almost all of the recoil. After weeks of bruising force thumping against her shoulder every time she shot, she decided that this model was the way to go.

It didn't quite have the punch of the older weapon, but Kylie didn't care. At nine hundred meters, Kylie could pierce the motor of a military vehicle. At two thousand, she could pluck a drone out of the sky.

In theory.

Kylie drew a long, slow breath. Her heart roared in her ears, and blood rushed like fiery ice through her veins. She glanced at Hanna on the next platform.

Hanna met her gaze with a look so cold it made Kylie's mouth run dry. Then, Hanna lined up, made an adjustment on her rifle, and fired.

Through her scope, Kylie found Hanna's shot. One circle off from the bullseye. A fine shot for twelve hundred meters. A killing shot, if the target had been a person. A disabling shot for many vehicles.

Weeks of practice had given Kylie a routine. She drew a long, slow breath, waited with it for a second, then let it go through her mouth. It would have been so much easier to simply dial her panic down another notch. She could have adjusted the balance in her brain and given herself a supernatural calm. Maybe with practice, she could have been the best sniper ever.

As it was, she wasn't so bad. Having once had the ability to fully control her own panic gave her a hint of insight into how her mind worked. She focused on that. Concentrated. Her thundering heartbeat gradually subsided.

"Just don't show her up," Austin said. "Just this once. Trust me."

Austin had always been better at reading people. She knew she should trust him.

But there it was. When she looked through her scope and adjusted for wind conditions, she knew she could line up the shot. She knew she could keep herself steady. Hitting the target at twelve hundred meters was as important as food. As important as breathing. She *had* to do it.

She drew another breath, let it halfway out, and held it.

Boom!

Even with the ear protection covering half her head, the earth-shattering noise of the rifle made her teeth shake. Recovering quickly, she peered through the scope at her target. It now had a hole grazing the right edge of the bullseye.

She wasn't done. Kylie worked the bolt action, ejected the spent cartridge, and slotted another of the ridiculously large .50 BMG cartridges. Her rifle's footing hadn't moved. The recoil wasn't enough to shift her position. She leaned in, drew a second breath, and when it was halfway out, she pulled the trigger again.

Boom!

The shudder shook her bones, and the rest of her breath released in a raspy sigh. Checking through her scope, she saw a second hole in her target. Dead center. She'd done it.

"Don't look over at her," Austin said. "Just don't. Don't make this about her, and maybe she'll let it slide."

Kylie looked. A glance. Nothing more. Hanna was furious. Her knuckles were white where she gripped her rifle. The skin around her bruises turned bright yellow. She met Kylie's eyes with an expression of pure hate that shook Kylie all the way down to her spine.

"We should go," Austin said, removing his ear protection. "We have manners next."

"Ugh." Kylie hated their manners class. What did blending with higher society have to do with survival, anyway?

Kylie brought the rifle to the weapons shed, cleaned it with Austin's help, and stowed it back where it belonged. When they were ready to leave, Hanna was waiting for them.

"Nice shooting," Hanna muttered. "As long as nobody gets close, you'll do just fine."

Kylie put on her best fake smile. "Thanks!" Then, she hurried out to the path back to the green.

After a minute of walking, Austin said, "You know, she's just going to get worse."

"Whatever," said Kylie. "She's almost healed from when I broke her nose."

"You didn't break her nose."

"It looked broken." Kylie mimed throwing an elbow. "And maybe I would break it for real if they tried to jump us right now."

Austin cast her a sideways glance. "You know that's a distinct possibility, right?"

"Yeah," said Kylie, "and I'm ready for it. I'm thinking three steps ahead, Austin. Just like you said I should. Just like chess." She wasn't. She was thinking one step ahead at best, but she figured she could wing it if she needed.

Austin kicked a rock, which skittered ahead into the underbrush. "I don't think you see how dangerous she is."

Kylie stopped walking and stared at him until he stopped, too. "Not everybody is like you, Austin."

He cocked his head to the side. "How so?"

"Weak. Submissive. Gentle. Abiding. Accommodating." By the time she got to the end of the list, he was already walking away. Shit. She'd offended him. "They're good things!" She reconsidered. "Well, except for weak."

"Submissive?"

"Well, okay, that one depends on who you ask."

"I don't need this," Austin said.

Kylie stalked after him. "We're a team. You're brilliant, I'm tough. We complement each other."

"You mean *I* compliment *you*." Austin said, still stalking away. "And you insult me."

"I don't!"

Austin spun on her with clearly recognizable rage on his face. Tears ran down his cheeks. "You don't know what it's like, Kylie. When every aspect of your life is a threat and you need to decide whether or not you're going to get teased for wearing an ugly shirt or beat up for wearing a nice one. When you don't know if they're hitting you because you're gay or because you're black or because they just needed someone to hit that day. You don't get any of it, and Hanna—" He gestured wildly in the direction of the shooting range. "She's the worst of them. Privileged, powerful, cruel. When you show up someone like that, she gets you back and she doesn't have any consequences for it."

With that, Austin turned and left, and Kylie didn't follow. A knot clenched in her chest. She didn't need him. He was just being stupid and hoping that rolling over would make Hanna quit. She wouldn't quit. Austin was wrong.

When she finally walked back to the green, she stopped by the main cabin where a group of campers gathered around a posted sheet of paper.

"What is it?" she asked.

"Teams for the war games," said Brian Gould, the smart kid with the curly hair.

When the group finally parted enough to let her in, Kylie read the list of names, first finding herself. She was listed as a co-leader of the blue team, whatever that meant.

The knot in her chest tightened when she saw the name of her co-leader.

Hanna Peterson.

And the Red team was led by Austin Giles.

Chapter Eighteen

Kate hefted two bags of cement, one on each shoulder. When she dropped them in the backyard, the ground shook.

"Are you sure you want to do this?" Ajay asked. Kate had visited every day since their visit with Olexie. For two weeks, she had stopped in for coffee, helped him around the house, and left him wondering about her motivation. Garrison watched her from his corner of shade near the shed, but he didn't seem suspicious at all. Not that that was worth much.

"Government pays me to leave my land as naturalized prairie and wetland," said Kate, breathing hard. "My whole body itches for work 'round this time of year, so I'll help, even if it is just building you a fancy pergola."

Ajay looked down at the single post hole he'd dug in the time it had taken her to move a truckload of lumber, four bags of cement, and a bucket full of nails into his little backyard. The sun beat down from above, and he already felt faint from all the hard work.

"I appreciate it," he said, unable to tell her that he would rather be using his resources to track down Kylie.

"Well, anything to get you away from a screen," Kate said with a laugh.

The camp listed an address, of course. The location near Thief River Falls had long since been shuttered and overgrown with buckthorn. There was another location near Hibbing on the Mesabi Range that Ajay identified as a potential secondary location. Kate had driven Ajay up to Bear Head Lake one afternoon so that he could surveil the area, but it was occupied by a different prepper camp. They trained kids to survive in the wild, defend territory, and shoot drones out of the sky. Ajay's best war drone had barely survived the encounter.

There were more potential locations in northern Minnesota than Ajay could count, and nothing written about Sonya Silver gave any hint of where Pine Fortress might be. She didn't leave a mark in public automobile records or in government surveillance of facial or body mechanic recognition. All of the financials for Pine Fortress were hidden behind layers of obfuscation that even Ajay couldn't untangle.

"I just—don't know if I'm good at what I do anymore," he said. His post-hole digger struck limestone.

"You're still trying to figure out where that camp is?" Kate asked as she lined the lumber up for staining.

"I just want to be sure she's safe."

"I'm sure she's fine. Her letter said so, didn't it?"

Ajay had received a letter from Kylie, signed and sealed in a decorative envelope. He'd scoured it for hidden messages or concealed code, but there was nothing. She said she was homesick but happy, and that she looked forward to August when she would return. The handwriting had been Kylie's, but the words felt flat.

"Come on, old man," Kate said with her infinite supply of energy. "Put some oomph into it." She took the post-hole digger and jammed it into the earth. It sparked on the limestone. "Oh," she said. "Hmm."

"Break time?" Ajay asked.

"Yeah."

No sooner had they settled into lawn chairs with a Schell amber lager each than an alert pinged on Ajay's cane. He let out a long, exhausted sigh. The cane was leaning against the house next to the dog, and Ajay didn't feel like getting up for it. Garrison whined.

"Leave it," said Kate, taking a deep drink of her lager.

The cane pinged again. For some reason, whenever Kate was around, he felt older than he ever had chasing Kylie. The farmer's relentless energy only proved to him that he ought to be in better shape. He *could* have been in better shape. Even the Tai Chi classes he'd started taking didn't let him keep up with the unstoppable farmer.

Another ping. Ajay set his beer in his chair's holder and stood.

The glass bottle shattered with a pop. Ajay blinked, frozen. Garrison stood, his floppy ears as perked as they could possibly get.

Kate tackled Ajay as another pop snapped a ring of spiderweb cracks in his patio door. Ajay hit the soft earth near his post hole hard enough to bruise a kidney. He gasped.

Without missing a beat, Kate grabbed a handful of his shirt and dragged him toward the house. He regained enough of his composure to snatch up his cane as they passed. Another shot zipped past his head and thunked into the oak of his dining room table. Garrison followed into the kitchen.

Kate slammed the patio door. "Where's that SIG Sauer?"

"That what?"

Another bullet hit the door near her head but didn't penetrate the heavy bulletproof glass. Ajay's heart pounded in his chest.

"Your gun!" shouted Kate.

"Locked up." Ajay swiped through the controls on his cane. "Sorry, I'm not a gun nut!"

"But you could have one gun around," Kate said.

"Statistics show—"

"Get down!" Kate pulled him around as another volley smacked into the bulletproof glass.

Ajay's sweaty hands slipped, and the image juddered into view over his cane. A drone scanned the area around the house, having pinged when it identified the shooter as a threat. "Shit."

"What?"

He showed her the holographic display of his house and the surrounding area. The highlighted figure of a tall man on a neighbor's roof was the shooter, but across the street was a second combatant, waiting to ambush them when they approached the truck. A short man, built like a WWII tank. Ajay knew these men. They had attacked Regis Shaleborn.

"They have us boxed in," Ajay said. "Only two of them as far as I can tell, but they have both exits covered."

"Don't you have a secret tunnel or something?"

Ajay opened his mouth with a sharp retort, but then reconsidered. "That's not a bad idea."

A volley of rifle fire shattered the neighborhood, and automatic fire pounded into the patio door. Under that duress, even the reinforced glass wouldn't last long.

"Can you—"

"Let me think!" snapped Ajay. His heart pounded in his throat and adrenaline turned his vision into a tunnel. This was his *home*. It was supposed to be his safe place. Secret. Protected. What had he done to give it away?

The only difference was Kate.

His surveillance drone probably couldn't take out an armored soldier. It didn't have the weapons package to even attempt a hot encounter, but it might be able to help. Ajay focused it on the man across the street. It scanned the area for signals, testing the network for anything on the military or paramilitary bands.

Found it. A networked scope. Comms. A vision-enhancing system.

That last one wasn't in use. It was more for night vision. Why the thug would carry that during a day operation, he didn't know. Maybe they thought it looked cool.

"These are amateurs," Ajay said. "Any idiot would know that black tactical gear is going to stand out against harvest slate-colored shingles."

"I see him out there," said Kate peeking out the front window. A shot slammed into the front window. "Jiminy Christmas!"

"Get to the garage," said Ajay, gesturing to the connecting door. "Grab those keys, and get the dog strapped in."

"Dammit," she hissed. "I need a gun."

"Go," Ajay snapped.

Kate snatched the keys from the bowl by the door and retreated to the garage. She whistled, and Garrison padded after her without even a glance in Ajay's direction. The big garage door wasn't bulletproof, but the attacker couldn't see through it, so she might be safe.

For now.

Ajay sped through his routines, flinging them almost at random at the attacker. There had to be a program that would disrupt their comms. The rest of it he could manage, but he at least wanted to make some noise. He needed the distraction.

He was distracted.

His cane pinged, and he looked up just in time to see the tall soldier drop from the neighbor's roof into his backyard. The man raised a long semi-automatic rifle and fired.

Ajay dove to the side as the shots finally punched through the patio door, shredding the table he had been behind. The air smelled of oil and ash. His mouth tasted like sand.

Another alert pinged, but it wasn't from the soldiers. Someone had called the police. The last thing Ajay wanted was officers descending on his home. He tagged the police alert and sent it into an indefinite delay. Future calls would be slotted into the same queue, which meant the police wouldn't come until he released the delay. Then, he triggered a full system wipe on his local hardware. His chest ached at the loss, but everything he really needed was in backup.

The soldier guarding the truck dropped from the roof across the street and approached. He raised his rifle and drew a bead on the front door. His voice boomed, enhanced by his tech. "Come out, Andersen."

Ajay thought of *one* thing he wanted less than officers descending on his home.

"I'll think about it," he called out to the soldier.

The man stopped, clearly not expecting that response. In the back of the house, the taller soldier crept across the lawn. From his drone, Ajay watched as he was closed in a pincer. His processes spun endlessly, searching for a way into their tech. Only a narrow segment of wall offered Ajay protection from both soldiers.

Kate swore from the garage. "Stupid dog," she said. "Ajay, we're ready."

But the soldier in front of the house stood feet away from the garage door. He was a coiled spring ready to strike. Ajay needed that distraction.

It wasn't going to come. The soldiers' tech was properly updated. It had all the best security protocols in place, and they hadn't missed even a single pathway. He was locked out. Even if he could get in, the best he could do was squelch their comms. It wouldn't make the kind of distraction he needed to get away.

If he surrendered, maybe they would leave Kate. His palms grew slick with sweat, and his knuckles went white in the hand that gripped his cane. Surrender would be death.

"Ajay, let's move!" Kate said.

"Give me a minute," Ajay called out to the mercenaries. They probably wouldn't. To Kate, he said, "Give me a second."

"We don't have a second!"

He directed his drone so that it was over the house with a view of the soldier in front. He pushed a short routine. Fire and retreat.

Then he dove for the garage. A shot punched into the doorframe as he passed, but he slammed the door shut and mashed the button to open the garage.

The drone struck. It couldn't get close enough to effective range without alerting the soldier to its presence, but it didn't need to. It fired three needles, which punched into the soldier's torso.

"He's got defense drones," the soldier said. "Needlers."

"Take it out," said the tank.

The drone retreated over the top of the house. Around the corner, the garage door slowly, silently opened.

Kate was ready. She sat on the front of his red Vespa scooter with the big Garrison absolutely filling the sidecar. The dog looked at Ajay with a pleading expression. Kate wore Ajay's brown half helmet, strapped tightly around her chin. A goofy grin covered her face.

"Hop on, hot stuff," she said.

"I figured I would drive," Ajay said, but he clambered onto the back, stuck his cane in the sidecar with Garrison, and wrapped his arms around Kate's waist.

"Are you kidding?" Kate asked. "I wouldn't miss this for the world."

With that, she cranked the accelerator and the scooter launched forward out of the garage.

Thirty feet. That was the distance Kate needed to cover before her truck interfered with the soldier's line of fire. Thirty feet of open space, a moving target to be used as shooting practice like a duck in some carnival game. Thirty feet to catch a bullet in the back as they ran like cowards.

The Vespa electric scooter was a wonderful piece of hardware. The oversized motor Ajay had painstakingly installed gave the device not only the ability to accelerate to highway speeds, but also the torque needed to jump to full speed fast enough to jar Ajay's bones and nearly cause him to tumble off the back. Even with the weight of extra batteries and the addition of the sidecar, Ajay's scooter was a quick little ride. Its reinforced tires squealed on the concrete driveway.

The soldier spun as soon as they cleared the garage door. He pulled away from the flaming wreckage of Ajay's drone, lining up a shot with his rifle as Kate launched the vehicle down the driveway. The Vespa hit the gutter with a jarring crunch that landed solidly in Ajay's tailbone.

A gunshot echoed through the neighborhood.

He caught one glimpse of the attacker before they sped away, but it was enough to register in the back of Ajay's brain. This man—this mercenary—was definitely one of the two men who had attacked Regis Shaleborn. What did this mean?

Ajay's cane pinged an alert. Not about the attack. Not about danger. It flashed a message that he saw for a split second before it was swiped away by a jolt against the pavement and a lurch of speed.

His hack on Shaleborn finally activated. A torrent of data started to stream.

Tires peeled against hot asphalt.

Then they were gone.

Chapter Nineteen

"Just stay out of my way and we'll be fine," said Hanna. She wore black and dark green forest camo with blue ridges along the arms and legs. Her skull cap also had blue streaks, which made her blue eyes shine like sapphires. The outfit made her look like some kind of warrior princess queen assassin, ready to strike death into the heart of the enemy.

Kylie wore the same outfit, but it fit poorly and made her itch like she had been rolling around in stinging nettle.

Regis Shaleborn stood in front of the cluster of twenty campers. He clapped his hands once and waited for the chatter to die down.

"Welcome to the war games, students," he said. "Many of you have spent time in practice games, but only once per summer do we all assemble all you shitheads for the full event."

Kylie fidgeted in her suit. The headgear rubbed the wrong way against her ear.

"You are wearing Endersuits," said Shaleborn. "This is the top-of-the-line wargame gear, used by the best military and paramilitary organizations around the world." He hefted his rifle—an AK-34, a smaller, lighter modern version of the legendary AK-47. Many claimed they were not an improvement over the 100-year-old design, but Kylie liked that it was lighter. Kylie had practiced with these, and this was an authentic weapon in everything except the blue streak along the side of its clip. "This will be your weapon. You will load magazines with a low velocity, lightweight round. Like neuropellets, but without the neurotoxin. For all other purposes, this is a normal weapon. If you see a magazine that does not have this blue streak or the enemy's red, then you do not use it. Those are real bullets and you will kill someone." He looked directly at Hanna, then Kylie. "If your bullet kills someone, you will be held responsible. A mistake with a gun is not a mistake. It is murder."

A murmur went through the crowd.

"Do you understand," said Mr. Shaleborn.

"Yes, sir," the group said in unison.

"Many of you have not practiced with the Endersuits, so I will give you a primer." He set the AK-34 down on the table. "Get shot in a limb, and that limb will stop moving. Get shot in the torso or head, and you are dead. Your whole body will stop moving." He gestured for Hanna to come forward. When she did, he indicated the blue streaks on her suit. "If your attack goes to hand-to-hand or melee weapons, strike these blue streaks. A hard enough strike will disable limbs. It is not possible to fully disable someone like this, but a soldier with no arms or legs is not a dangerous opponent.

"You will keep your face shield down at all times. These bullets will hurt, but they will not injure as long as you are not hit in your unprotected face." Again, he looked at Hanna and Kylie. "You will be held responsible for any damage done to an opponent or ally injured by your bullets. Do you understand?"

"Yes, sir," the group chanted.

"Good." He touched a blue block the size of a backpack. "This is your comm and control unit. It handles local encrypted communications, which you all have in your helmets. You will always be able to locate your enemy's comm unit, and they will always know the location of yours." He touched a blue device the size of a baseball. "This is your objective. You are to plant it in the enemy base, retreat, and detonate it using your comms. It will destroy their base of operation and 'kill' anyone within thirty meters."

Kylie tentatively raised her hand. When Shaleborn nodded to her, she asked, "What's to prevent one of us from making a suicide run?"

Shaleborn flashed a wicked smile. "Anyone killed during wargames doesn't get to attend the end-of-year mission, which I'm sure you know is the most prestigious placement this camp has to offer." A murmur rolled through the crowd. "In addition, the losing team gets MREs for a week instead of mess hall, and they forgo all privileges with regards to evening game time for that week."

It didn't sound so bad to Kylie. She didn't *like* the MREs she had tried, but she didn't hate them either. She also didn't much care for rec time privileges. She would rather sit by herself and read than join the group by the campfire or practice with the equipment. Maybe it was worth losing just to make Hanna lose, too.

"Kylie, Hanna, as co-leaders, you are both assigned half of your troops. Now that you know your mission, you can coordinate your efforts." Mr. Shaleborn took a step back. "I suggest you use this hour to work out any communications issues you might have."

"This is easy," Hanna said after several minutes of wrangling. "Blue One and Blue Two will follow my orders. Kylie, you can try that suicide bombing."

"I never said that was going to be the plan."

"Well, I never said I would let you share leadership," Hanna said.

Kylie bristled. She remembered Austin's words. He had wanted her to give in to Hanna sometimes. She didn't even care about the stupid war game. She could let Hanna run everything, probably fail, and she'd be no worse off. In fact, that made a lot of sense for a lot of reasons.

But she couldn't do it. "I'm in charge of Blue Two," Kylie said.

Hanna threw up her hands. "War doesn't work with two leaders. One leader. Orders are followed. That's how the military works."

"Then give your troops to me."

"To a kid?" Hanna sneered. "You haven't even played this kind of game before. My family used to go on retreats with stuff like this all the time."

"That's great," Kylie said. "You're regular doomsday preppers."

"So what if we are?" A hint of stress tightened Hanna's voice. "The Peterson family is going to survive no matter what. You don't want to be our enemies."

Something tightened in Kylie's chest. She had enemies. Papa had enemies. The thought sent her into a spiral of homesickness that she hadn't felt since their first week of camp. What if Papa ran into trouble and she hadn't prepared? Should she learn to be more like Hanna?

Should she take this game seriously?

"I'm taking Blue Two," Kylie said. "You're taking Blue One." She glanced back at her campers. They were a motley bunch, with younger kids a couple years younger than her and older kids about twice her size. She didn't know most of their names. "But I don't need them all for what I'm doing."

Hanna pressed her lips together. "And what is it you think you're doing?"

Kylie knew the challenge would have been simple if the computer in her head were working. She could hack enemy comms. She could even make people's suits lock up. If she wanted, she could scramble their voices and make false orders destroy the cohesion of the enemy positions. It felt almost as if the challenge were designed to be easy for her.

But she didn't have all her tools available to her. She could sense signals a little, pinpointing direction and distance at a range too close to be truly useful. She couldn't establish communications. She couldn't blitz a hack on all nearby machines. If she was careful, she might be able to use her abilities to sneak past the enemy.

She wasn't going to do it, though. All she wanted to do was…

What?

What did she want? Hanna stared at her as she thought through their position. None of them knew the terrain, but they knew they had to protect their base and their comm device. There were a lot of ways she could help. A lot of uses for the skills that she'd become very good at over the past few weeks. She looked at the expressions on people's faces and saw that they were all waiting for her. They wanted to know what she was doing and what Blue Two's mission would be.

She remembered what Austin had said. Let Hanna have something. Let her feel powerful. Make her the center of attention.

Kylie finally said, "I need three soldiers. Good shots."

Hanna spoke through gritted teeth. "What are you going to do?"

"I'm going to take out their leadership," Kylie said, hefting the AK-34 that Shaleborn had left on the table. "I'm going to kill Austin Giles."

Chapter Twenty

"I need time," Ajay said as the scooter rolled slowly past a stand, where a man with a long goatee sold paintings of the sunset. "How long do you think we can avoid them?"

They had lost the two thugs, but it wouldn't last. They'd spotted their pursuers twice already, and their only salvation was the arts festival creating traffic and chaos in the middle of the green lakeside parks.

Garrison looked up at Ajay as if to ask if he really understood what he was saying.

"We're not going to get away on this scooter," said Kate. She had taken the whole thing in a stride, and as they rolled through town, Ajay wondered exactly how she was coping with all of it. "We can't leave town."

"Getting caught by those guys on the county roads would be a death sentence," Ajay agreed. "At least in town we can lose them again."

"Why are they after us?"

"I wish I knew." It was a question for the future, and Ajay was too busy now.

The scooter ran silently along Lake Boulevard, creeping down the crowded street.

Ajay grasped his cane in one hand and manipulated the controls with the other. Finally, Regis Shaleborn had activated the device that Ajay had hacked using the drone. The device's signal picked scraped data from its comm encryption and pushed it onto the network. It deposited recordings in a place that Ajay could easily pick it up, but the device was designed to never send location info. Nothing was ever that easy.

It wouldn't last. The data dump was temporary at best. If he wanted to know more about the camp, he would need to grab as much as he could right away. Anything else—

Anything else and he might fail Kylie.

"Those are real bullets, and you will kill someone," said Regis through the channel.

"Got it," Ajay said in triumph.

Kate juiced the accelerator, nearly tossing Ajay off the back. He held tight to the cane and grasped her shoulder with his other hand.

"Sorry," she said. "I saw that black sedan again."

"Get shot in the torso or head, and you are dead," said Regis. "Your whole body will stop moving."

It seemed to Ajay like an odd point to make, but Kylie had wanted to go to camp to learn survival basics. That was certainly pretty basic.

"Do we have a game plan here?" Kate asked.

"No," said Ajay. He let go of her shoulder and fiddled with his controls. There had to be more information. All he wanted was location information. If he knew where Kylie was, he could go get her if she was in real danger.

Kate took the scooter past a cluster of white tents selling carved wooden statuettes and onto the Paul Bunyan State Trail.

"Where are we going?" asked Ajay absently.

"Driving where they can't," said Kate.

"Good plan."

"It's not a plan at all," said Kate. "Really just delaying things."

"Right," said Ajay, fingers dancing across his controls. "Good plan."

Kate chewed on a grunt of frustration.

Regis said, "You are to plant it in the enemy base, retreat, and detonate it using your comms. It will destroy their base of operation and kill anyone within thirty meters."

"What the hell," Kate muttered.

"Probably a game," Ajay said. "Camps do that kind of stuff all the time."

"Sure, but that sounds pretty extreme."

"Look out!" Ajay shouted.

Kate yanked the bars to one side to avoid a woman with too many bags and a free-range toddler. The scooter rolled along the side of the trail amid the scowls of the crowd.

"We could make a run for it," she said. "Head for my place."

"We won't make it."

"Dammit," Kate growled. "What if we picked up my truck?"

"It'll be bugged by now," Ajay said. "The lake house is our best chance."

Regis's voice came through, tinny and distorted. "Now that you know your mission, you can coordinate your efforts." It sounded dismissive, as if he were sending a group on their own to complete a mission.

Kate twisted the accelerator and the scooter rolled forward through the crowd. Garrison watched as the world rolled by, quietly absorbing the warm wind, the smells of the crowd, the beauty of the shining lake spreading out across the horizon. When they reached a section of path that wasn't as crowded, she bumped their speed up a little, rushing past vendors selling their arts and crafts.

An inarticulate chatter through the dying connection sounded to Ajay like the cadence of his granddaughter's voice. Kylie spoke with confidence. Authority. His chest ached as if a boulder had been placed on it. He hadn't known her for most of her life, but now that she was gone again, all he wanted was to have her back. Happy. Safe. Home.

He didn't even know if he had a home anymore. How could he? Whoever had found him probably knew everything about his situation. They were killers. Not particularly competent, but killers nonetheless.

"We need to stop them from following," Ajay said.

"You wanna kill them?" Kate asked. "You're going for the gun?"

"Why does everyone jump to that conclusion?" asked Ajay. When she didn't respond, he said, "No. Not really."

Kate twisted the accelerator and sped along the walking path. When they encountered the last stragglers from the arts festival, she veered from the path onto the hard lawn. Garrison's jowls wobbled dangerously, but Ajay held on tight and they bumped back onto the road.

The black sedan pulled a U-turn as soon as they hit the wider Bemidji Ave. It was a block behind and accelerating hard.

"What are you doing?" Ajay asked.

"Hold on." The scooter launched forward, narrowly missing the bumper of a self-driving van, sending the panicked AI into a hard swerve.

Trees whipped by. Garrison's fleshy jowls flapped in the wind. Behind, the sedan muscled through choked traffic. Despite the delays, it gained on them in a straight stretch, its black windshield shining in the afternoon sun.

"Jesus, Mary, and Joseph," swore Kate.

A second sedan ran a red light and cut in front of her. She swerved hard, accelerated, then ran up the curb cut at the corner. A woman dove out of the way, and Kate blasted up the block on the cement sidewalk.

"Sorry!" Ajay shouted back at the woman. "I think that was one of Kylie's teachers."

"Small towns, am I right?" Kate growled through gritted teeth.

The second sedan's tires squealed as it kept pace with them in the street. Kate took the corner hard, sticking to the sidewalk. Peeling around the corner, the sedan closed the distance.

It was all Ajay could do to hold on. He desperately wanted to help, but there was nothing—nothing at all—he could offer. Kate was a local. She knew the streets and sidewalks of the little town better than he ever could. The sedans the two thugs drove were gasoline engines. Manually driven. Unhackable.

Kate cranked the bars and hit a church parking lot as the sedan blasted past. She sped through at an angle, hit the alley, and doubled back.

Only for the first sedan to pick her up again. She turned hard, hit the asphalt of an actual road, and launched straight past onto the dry grass of a residential yard. The space between houses was narrow—too narrow for the sedans. She skirted past a fence, skidded through a backyard, and hit another alley at an angle. Accelerating the whole time, she let out a whoop and made her way to another street.

"Lost 'em," she breathed.

"For now," said Ajay.

"Right." Kate cranked the accelerator again and sped down the street. Ajay did his best to avoid yelping in fear as she narrowly avoided another self-driving vehicle, but he probably failed.

He definitely failed.

Garrison gave him the look.

"Sorry," Ajay said to the dog, but he didn't have time to decide whether or not the apology was accepted, because one of the sedans spotted them from a block to his left.

"We got this," said Kate. She didn't slow, and the sedan was several blocks back by the time it got turned around. "Few more blocks."

She yanked the bars again, this time scraping hard against another vehicle on their way past.

"That was a new paint job," Ajay shouted.

"Sorry!"

Then he saw their destination. The Cameron Park Lake House. She hit the parking lot at full speed, buzzed another car on her way through, and screeched to a stop at the door.

"Go," she said. "I'll lead them away."

Ajay hopped off the back of the scooter. This would put her in danger. She'd be drawing the enemy away, using herself as bait. He couldn't—

"Go!" she shouted.

He went. His legs felt wobbly and weak. He climbed the steps to the lake house and burst inside.

"Grant," he said, nodding to the host.

"Good day sir, how—"

And Ajay was down the stairs on the way to the locker room.

Kylie's voice chattered through the feed in his cane, but Ajay reduced the volume. He wasn't getting the information he needed, and he couldn't be bothered by the distraction. Not with Kate in danger.

The locker contained exactly what it had when he'd left it weeks ago. The pistol sat like a lump of coal in his stocking, promising only bad things for him and his future. The quantum computer was worthless. Inert. He wouldn't be able to get it fixed anytime soon.

Then there was the key. The single silver key dangling from a hook in the back of the locker shone out at him. It was finally time. He pulled it from its hook and clutched it in one hand. This was it. Once he activated this plan, he couldn't come back until it was finished. He would need to discover who had found him, deal with them, and go through a million hoops to make sure it was still safe. He needed to know how they had found him and why they were trying to kill him.

Because running wasn't an option anymore. Not if he wanted to keep Kylie in his life. By the time she returned from camp, he needed to resolve this problem.

He turned the volume back up on his feed.

"I'm going to kill Austin Giles," Kylie said.

Ajay picked up the gun and left.

Chapter Twenty-One

LANG LEANED OVER HIS table and stared at the holographic projection of the wargame grounds. Indicators showed clusters of players, still separate in their base camps. Combat could start at any moment, but both sides were being achingly conservative.

"What about Kylie Andersen?" asked Silver. She watched the board with an expression of distaste on her narrow face.

Shaleborn stepped from the shadows of the classroom to the edge of the table. "I haven't seen any advantage from her. Not in martial arts and not in shooting."

"I thought she was a good shot," said Silver.

"Not any better than the others." He gestured at an icon in the center of the Blue team. "Hanna Peterson could outshoot her if she could get out of her own head. She's the one you want, I guarantee it."

Silver looked like she was chewing whole peppercorns. "This isn't what we were promised."

"Hey, you told us the kid's special," Lang growled. "Let's just have some trust."

"We don't trust here, Mr. Lang," Silver said. "We experiment. And when our experiments show us what we want, we experiment some more."

"Sounds like a lot of work."

"It pays off."

"Does it?"

Silver's gaze penetrated all the way down into Lang's soul. "I could make you better, Mr. Lang. We have the technology."

Lang's heart thundered in his chest. Suddenly, the constant vertigo was only a small fraction of the dangerous disorientation rocking him. She was promising something he didn't believe could exist. Every instinct in his bones told him it was a trap.

"You mean you have an experiment," he said.

The woman studied him the way she'd consider spilled wine on her favorite carpet. Lang got the impression that the kids weren't the only ones being judged during the wargame.

"Our source gave us the impression that this girl could hear enemy comms," said Silver. "And we were told she could hack enemy tech with nothing more than a thought."

Lang had seen those skills in action before, but he wondered who Silver's source was. Andersen and her grandfather had ruined his last big operation the way Lang had been ruined by that microwave pulse attack. He had always wondered how they had done that, but he still wasn't sure he believed Silver's claims. Waves of dizziness washed over him at the memory. He didn't *want* Andersen to succeed. He wanted to see her fail in the worst way.

But at the same time, he wanted her to succeed. If she was successful, then it was proof that she was a force to be reckoned with. She and her grandfather were something special. It was like losing in the playoffs to the team that wins the pennant.

He swallowed the bile in the back of his throat. "She's special," he finally said. "You'll get proof soon enough."

They watched as a cluster of three Blues separated from the group. They crept across the board through the dense forest.

"She's on the move," said Shaleborn, stepping closer. The stink of his stale sweat irritated Lang. "Strike team?"

"Looks like it," said Lang.

"What is Red team waiting for?" asked Silver.

"Training," said Shaleborn. He touched his ear, listening to the comm chatter. "They're wasting time."

"It won't matter once Blue takes out Red's comm," said Silver. "This is basic strategy, Lang. Take out comms right away. A blind enemy fights itself."

"True," he said.

"So where's the brilliance?"

He had heard her plan, and she wasn't after the enemy comms. Her plan was a good one. Take out Austin Giles. Without their brilliant leader, Blue would be helpless. Giles wouldn't be as well guarded as the comms. Hell, he might even come out to meet them.

But if she could hear their comms—if she could locate them based on their tech—she could take them all out single-handed. She didn't even need her two backup fighters. She'd sneak through the woods and assassinate them one by one. If she could do everything that they suspected she could do, then this was going to be a one-sided game. Not fair by a long shot. The thought was both exhilarating and draining. If people like her were the future of combat, where did that leave people like him?

"Watch," was all Lang said, swallowing back a bitter taste at the back of his mouth. "Just watch and we'll see what she can do."

They circled the table and watched. For the first time, Lang wondered what Kylie Andersen was capable of.

Chapter Twenty-Two

Kylie couldn't do jack diddly squat. Without her abilities, she was as helpless as any other cog in the big war machine. She crept forward through low undergrowth, doing her best to stay silent on their way across the battlefield. It was all she could do, and that was basically nothing.

If she had all her abilities, she'd be able to sense the location of anyone carrying tech. She would have been able to hack their communications and send fake communications of her own. No need to take down their comm unit. She could trick people into hearing the wrong orders or missing important directives. It would have been chaos in the ranks of the enemy, and if she had wanted to pick them apart, she could have easily done it.

She had none of that. The bare trickle of sensation she still possessed left her with a lingering desire aching at the back of her skull. Had she really agreed to be limited like this? It felt like Papa had pressured her into lopping off her arm.

Hand over hand, Kylie made her way up the branches of an enormous spruce until her hands were sticky with sap and the view of the valley spread out below her. Using a thin pair of binoculars, she scoped the territory.

"They're about half a mile northeast," she whispered into the Blue Two comm.

"One click," came the response. It was curly-haired Brian Gould, who insisted on the codename, Jade.

"What?"

Jade looked up at her from below. She could see his pale skin through his helmet's hard visor. "A click. That's how far they are."

"Yeah, okay. One click northeast." She scanned the territory. "It looks like we can circle east for a better angle of approach."

Kylie scrambled down the tree as quickly and quietly as she could. Jade met her along with a girl who took the code name Nyx. Nyx was heavier and shorter than Kylie, and when she made fists, her knuckles cracked. Nyx and Jade fell in twenty meters to either side of Kylie, and together they moved east through the dense forest.

The first scout they found was half a click out from Austin's main group. He watched from ten feet up in an old oak, but the way he had situated himself left a wide gap where they could sneak past. Kylie signaled to her team to follow her, and the three crawled through a tunnel of buckthorn and debris. It took ages but didn't alert the guard. They were past the outer perimeter.

"He's going to be a problem once we're spotted," whispered Nyx. "We should take him out."

"If we take him out now, we'll lose our surprise."

"I'm quick," Nyx said.

"Austin will know if someone doesn't check in." He wasn't an idiot. Kylie knew that. Being paranoid and pessimistic gave Austin an advantage in a game like this. He'd have everything important guarded at all costs. No way he wouldn't constantly require check-ins from his guards and a detailed report of all activity. There was only one valuable resource Austin didn't value enough to protect: himself. "We're going to have to take Austin out and move fast if we want to escape."

Jade and Nyx spread out again, taking a distance just outside her line of sight. If one of them was found, the others could respond or escape accordingly. Kylie had to trust her team to make the right decision in any case.

Voices hissed through the trees ahead, hushed but commanding. They were the voices of children playing at war, which struck her as painfully wrong. Who would force kids into this kind of stress? She needed these survival skills because of who she was. It wasn't an option to live a calm, peaceful life. She was hunted. Her grandfather was hunted. If she ever found freedom from this life, she'd spend it looking over her shoulder.

The weight of it crushed her. It threatened to pin her to the pine forest floor and leave her there until the undergrowth devoured her whole. Survival. Violence. They were her only options in life, and she wasn't sure if she could do it.

That wasn't true. She knew she *could* do it, and that terrified her. Kylie whispered, "Hold."

She crept forward under another clump of underbrush. This was the tree she had spotted from afar—the one that might give her a good view of the enemy camp. Cautiously, she reached up, took a branch in one gloved hand, and pulled herself up. Too fast and the movement at the tips of the branches would be noticed. Her muscles ached from the tension, even after only the short crawl across the field. How long had it taken her to move across this terrain? A half hour? An hour? How long would it be before Austin decided to move his people?

This tree was as easy to climb as the other, and she found her way up into its embrace. The view stretched out below her. A clearing with several figures in red-striped dark green surrounding one tall, slender figure. Austin.

They were listening to him. She couldn't hear what he was saying, but the way they focused on him made her ache with jealousy. Her first instinct at leadership had been to take only a small group. She shunned her chance to show leadership.

But she still had one skill she wanted to show off, and there in the tree, she had one solid opportunity.

The AK-34 wasn't a sniper rifle. It had a scope, but she didn't have a thousand meters of range like she wanted. The kind of rubber bullets they were firing wouldn't work at that range, anyway. They caught the air and wouldn't fly straight. This was a parameter of their conflict. She had to expect some deviation in her aim if she shot from her current distance.

She waited and watched.

"Almost in position," said Nyx.

"Hold," said Kylie. Something wasn't right. "Both of you."

She counted the figures in the clearing, careful to spot the ones on the edges lurking in shadows. There weren't enough of them. She mentally counted how many it would take to run a perimeter guard at the density she thought they were using. It was the density she thought *Austin* would use. A cautious number. Measured.

Slowly, carefully, she scanned the terrain all around her tree. Behind her, the direction of the sentry they had passed, she couldn't see through the dense evergreens. The underbrush choked the forest there, and it would be impossible to find them until they tried to move.

Something wasn't right.

Instinct itched at the back of her skull. She swung her AK around and quietly checked its function. Sweat beaded on her brow, but she couldn't wipe it away without opening her helmet's visor.

She had the shot. She should take it. Knock Austin out of the game.

Why was she still so mad at him? At worst, he had been looking after her. He thought he knew better than her, and maybe he did. Couldn't he just let her make her own decisions? Maybe constantly showing up Hanna wasn't great strategy, but who cares? Kylie wasn't going to fail just because it might make the older girl look better.

That's what it came down to. She could win the war by taking down Austin right now. It would make her look better, and everyone would know that she'd won the day and not Hanna. It was an easy choice. The smart move. Even if she didn't escape, the sacrifice was worth it. Without his leadership, Austin's team would be an easy target.

But something wasn't right.

Chapter Twenty-Three

Silver peered at the icon representing Andersen in the tree. "What's she waiting for? She has the shot."

"What's the rush?" asked Lang.

"I want to see if she can use her abilities."

"Right." Lang still wasn't sure any such abilities exist. If he saw the girl escape this situation after firing a shot, then maybe he'd be impressed.

"She's not motivated," Silver hissed.

Lang peered at the holographic display. How could he possibly know the inner workings of the girl's brain? Silver was right. Andersen had the shot. She needed to take it. What could she be waiting for? He had been in that position before. The target was clear, but crossing that line would set everything in motion. "She probably senses them closing in on her and she's deciding how best to get away."

Silver raised an immaculate eyebrow. "Evidence of her abilities?"

"Evidence that she can hear."

Silver drummed her long fingernails on the table, apparently impatient to get on with the lack of action. "She should take the shot, regardless."

"Maybe she's playing a long game," Lang hypothesized.

"She's not a long game kind of kid," said Shaleborn. He leaned against the back wall of the strategy room, hardly bothering to watch the map.

"Plus, Lang, if she could sense them, then why did she crawl right into their trap? Maybe she's not so bright after all."

Lang bit back his retort. "Just watch." He hated his urge to defend the girl, but he also hated Shaleborn more and more every day.

"She had to have noticed the second sentry," said Shaleborn.

"I said watch," Lang growled. There was a time he would have broken men like Shaleborn in half.

The martial arts teacher crossed his arms. "Sure."

"Amazing things, my source said," whispered Silver. "This girl is supposed to be better than this."

Lang drew a slow breath. "She might not like to plan very far in advance, but she's a smart kid. She knows how Giles thinks. She knows what kind of traps he likes. She's thinking this through, and she has a plan. I guarantee it."

"She's a coward, then," said Silver with an expression of distaste on her lips. "She's going to be useless."

"Maybe," Lang said. Andersen was a lot of things, but she was not a coward.

"I'm not looking for a cowardly girl who can think, Lang," said Silver. "I was promised that she was special. She should have the potential to be the world's most dangerous assassin." She waved at the holographic projection. "This is not impressive."

Promised by whom, Lang wondered. Who was Silver getting her information from?

Shaleborn stepped forward, peering at the map. "No," he said. "I get it. Her falling into this trap keeps her abilities a secret. If everyone knows what she can do, she's nowhere near as dangerous."

"The point of this is to *test* her," hissed Silver. "This doesn't work if she's afraid to flex." She gestured with her fidget and flashed through several holographic screens.

"Watch. It'll be clear when the pressure's on," Lang assured her. "I guarantee it. She knows what the hell she's doing."

"Bring him in," she said into a private comm.

Lang wondered who she was talking about.

Silver leaned forward, peering at the holographic display. An indicator moved in from the edge of the field, working its way slowly through the underbrush. Lang watched, as a sliver of a smile touched her lips. "Well," she said, "maybe we'll get our hint at her real talents soon enough."

"She knows what the hell she's doing," Lang said, hoping that what he said was true.

Chapter Twenty-Four

Kylie didn't know what the hell she was doing.

"Jade," she whispered. "Get ready to fire a shot."

"I'm not in position," he responded.

"Doesn't matter. We're going to draw them out," Kylie said, not sure at all what Austin's reaction would be. He probably had contingencies upon contingencies planned for something like this.

She could take the shot, and she could almost guarantee the hit.

But.

Something still didn't feel right. Her head ached to search the world for signals. To draw answers from the surrounding network. She'd know everything if she had all her abilities available to her. She gritted her teeth. If only…

There. The way Austin moved in front of his troops. The slight favoring of one hand. The straight back, showing confidence.

Kylie peered through her scope and zoomed in on the figure's face. She knew what she'd see before the figure turned her direction. Under that tinted face shield was not her friend's dark skin. It was the shockingly pale skin of Jess.

She was a decoy. Kylie scanned the rest of the crowd. Nobody else fit Austin's narrow figure. He was somewhere else. Hiding.

Stalking.

"Jade, fire one straight up, then run hard east," she said as she stowed her weapon. "This is a trap and it's time to smoke them out."

To his credit, Jade fired immediately, without any protest. This was the smooth operation of an elite strike force. Very professional.

A branch broke under Kylie's grip on the way down. Very *not* professional. She lurched forward, caught the next branch in her ribs, then fell awkwardly to the soft earth. She hit hard, crunching her left hand under her body.

The whole arm went stiff. Her endersuit seized, registering the impact as a strike. Swearing under her breath, she got her feet under her and ran.

Soldiers crashed through the forest toward Jade, so she went the other way. Her left arm hung useless at her side, so she hefted the AK in her right. It was awkward and far too heavy in one hand. They hadn't practiced like this. She didn't know how to sustain this.

An unmarked soldier stepped through the underbrush in front of her, only a few long steps away. He blinked at her, and through the visor of his helmet, Kylie could only see two eyes on the verge of madness.

A sudden headache split her skull in half. Waves of nausea twisted her stomach at the pain. It was like her head was on fire.

"Who are you?" she gasped.

But the boy didn't answer. His piercing gaze fell on her, and she felt something like a burning static in the back of her brain where she normally would sense signals.

Kylie screamed, and the boy lurched forward. She fired a three-bullet burst from her AK. Her rifle swung wildly from the recoil, but one pellet struck the boy's arm. He staggered back and gasped in pain. She retreated, terror coiling itself around her heart.

He raised a pistol. His arm still worked, even though she had shot him. He wasn't wearing an endersuit.

Nyx stepped from the brush and popped him in the head. The boy let out a startled gasp, dropped his pistol, and staggered away into the woods.

"Thanks," said Kylie. The headache ebbed slightly, and she could almost string two thoughts together. "Shouldn't that have killed him?"

"This mission is fucked," said Nyx. She picked up the pistol and offered it to Kylie.

Kylie dropped her AK and took the gun. She hadn't trained much with pistols, but it would be better than trying to fire the AK with one working arm. "It wasn't Austin out there."

Nyx covered her as Kylie checked the ammunition in the pistol. A red stripe on the clip indicated that it was a Red team's fake ammunition. Good. She locked it in and nodded to Nyx. Nyx led the way through the underbrush away from the sound.

"Wait," Kylie whispered, doubt rolling in like a summer storm. Austin knew they were coming. He knew they would try to assassinate him. He even knew where to let them in to surround them. It was only luck that she only had three soldiers. "Our team didn't even get pistols," she said. The sense of deep-seated unease still lingered in the back of her chest, and she didn't like it. What had happened to her when the boy had attacked? Her head felt numb.

"Come on," hissed Nyx. "We need to leave. I think we can still take out their comm unit."

But Kylie didn't move. If Red got pistols in addition to AK-34s, what other equipment did they have? Could they listen in on enemy comms? Could they track tech signals? What had they been practicing back at the Red camp?

Hand signals. They were working on ways to communicate that didn't involve their comms, which meant destroying their comm system wouldn't impact them as much as it should. Meaning—

Kylie's heart pounded. Her hands went slick with sweat. She had tried so hard not to take the game seriously, but the pressure of it roared in her ears. It burned in the space behind her eyes. She wanted to win so badly. Everything had to be perfect.

But it wasn't. It never would be. Nyx was right. The plan was fucked. They needed a new plan, and taking a wild shot at the comm unit wasn't it. Too obvious.

"Come on!" said Nyx again.

Kylie pressed a finger to the front of her helmet in a signal for silence, but Nyx wasn't watching. The girl crept forward through the underbrush. She would go after the comms. Fine. Kylie could work with that. Maybe Nyx would take out comms. Maybe she would provide a good distraction.

It was all chaos as far as Kylie could tell. She didn't have a long-term plan. She wasn't thinking fifteen moves ahead in a game of nine-dimensional chess.

All she could do was think of what was next. That had always been her strength.

She was surrounded.

Comms might be compromised.

There was little chance of her own survival.

And she had information critical to the success of her team. Her heart slowed, and she swallowed back the cotton in her throat.

She heard the crunch of branches under clumsy feet. The enemy approached. She had seconds to decide what to do.

Kylie clicked her comm on and said, "Blue One, Blue Two is down. Red has ears on Blue comms and hand signals in case their comms go down. Significant forces converging on my current position. Red Leader is—"

Austin broke through the underbrush. She saw the whites of his wide eyes as he spotted her. He held an AK in both hands. More soldiers spilled in behind him.

Time measured in heartbeats stretched across an agony of adrenaline-soaked seconds.

One beat. Kylie raised her pistol and fired. Her finger squeezed the trigger and the gun roared in her hand. Austin stepped back.

Two beats. The soldier behind Austin fired. The boy's AK thundered in his grasp, spitting three bullets in a tight cluster. They exploded in the tree near Kylie's head.

Three beats. Austin fired. Bullets pounded into Kylie's chest and slammed into her good arm. Her limbs froze. Her comm went dark.

She was dead standing. A cacophony of heartbeats thundered in her ears as she tottered. Austin rushed up to her and pressed his helmet to hers as he lowered her to the forest floor.

"Sorry about that," he said.

Kylie flashed him an apologetic smile. "Me, too." She had missed him. She'd had the shot with the pistol and had missed, even at close range.

But it didn't matter.

Because Nyx had caught her signal.

The forest roared with automatic gunfire as Nyx fired from the underbrush, pounding bullets into Austin and his soldiers. They returned fire, but not fast enough. Austin's suit seized and he toppled hard next to Kylie.

Nyx dropped.

Kylie smiled, not because she was dead, but because she was pretty sure she'd done everything she could to improve her team's chance of success.

Chapter Twenty-Five

"I HAD THE JUMP on you, though," Kylie said. Her whole body still ached from the previous day's combat. She sat against the oak and cast a sideways glance at Austin next to her. "It's not my fault I missed."

"It kind of is," said Austin, but not in a mean way. He handed her half of his apple pie, since she wouldn't get any of her own for two whole weeks. "You should practice with pistols, maybe."

"I prefer to shoot targets that are really far away, thanks." That wasn't it. When it finally came time to point a gun at someone and pull the trigger, she had hesitated. Her instincts wouldn't let her shoot Austin, even though she knew it was fake.

"Well, I wish you would have done it. The shots from the AK really hurt." He rubbed his shoulder where a deep bruise still marred his skin.

"You shot me in the boob."

They were silent for a long time. Kylie didn't remember why she had been upset at Austin. It didn't matter. At least, she didn't think it still mattered. She ground her teeth and tried her best to ignore the pain worrying in the back of her chest.

"Lang told me I'm on the team for the mission," Kylie said at last. "And you're in, too."

"Getting killed in the game was supposed to disqualify us from the end-of-summer mission."

"Deals change, I guess." Kylie ate the last of the apple pie. She wondered if he felt the same wave of dread in the pit of his stomach.

Austin glanced over at her. "So now we know that they lie. I think it's part of what they're trying to teach us."

"To distrust authority?"

"To distrust everyone," Austin said. "Hanna is in, too."

"Great." Kylie deadpanned.

"Well, she *did* almost win the game."

"I still can't believe she screwed that up."

"You underestimated Jess," Austin said. "I'm sorry I shot you in the boob."

"It's fine." Kylie watched the students practicing judo throws in the center of the green. "Hanna almost beat you, you know."

"I know," said Austin. "I'm glad I took the extra time to teach everyone my whole plan."

"And you taught them non-standard hand signals."

"I figured you'd either kill our comm or try to get to me. I wanted backups in place."

Kylie grinned. He *had* known what she would do. Damn him for being so smart.

"A strike team of three was pretty ballsy," he said.

"Still," she said, clapping him on the bruised shoulder. "Nice work."

She thought of the soldier who had attacked her in the forest. He hadn't looked like one of Austin's people, and the way he made her head hurt bothered her. An echo of the pain still lingered along the bridge of her nose, like a faint scar from an old wound.

"Oh, crap," Austin said before she had a chance to ask him about the soldier.

Kylie followed his gaze across the lawn. Hanna was approaching, with Jess at her side and Brian Gould following close behind. Despite her healing bruises, the girl was the picture of authority. Her back was straight, her eyes icy, and her lips were pressed into a firm line. She stood in front of Kylie and Austin for an eternity before she finally spoke.

"You did well," Hanna said through her clenched jaw.

Austin stared at her like he couldn't believe the words coming from her mouth. This rich, privileged girl was—apologizing?

Kylie was the first to speak. "You fought well, too." It was all she could give her. Hanna had lost the wargame for her, even after a solid start, but she *had* fought well. Hanna was a force to be reckoned with on the battlefield.

Austin stood and pulled Kylie up. He looked at each of the other students in turn and said, "You all fought well. We all went in there with a goal, did our best to achieve it, and came out with some bruises." He glanced at Kylie. "But now they're going to give us a new mission. A real mission. We're going to have to work together to make this succeed, but after seeing how everyone fought out there, I have absolutely no doubt that we can do it." He held his hand out, palm down. "I have a feeling we can accomplish anything."

The others stared at his hand, young and smooth and brown, held in the space at the center of them all.

Kylie put her hand atop his. "Anything," she said.

Brian added his hand, then Jess. Finally, Hanna added her perfectly manicured pale hand.

"Anything," she said.

Chapter Twenty-Six

Tenen Lang leaned against the windowsill, hoping the solidity of the wood under his hands would somehow steady the constant unease flowing through his veins. He had watched the Andersen girl and her friend under the tree.

Vincent, the custodian, pushed his way into the room, towing the man in the fake endersuit. The helmet was missing, and the man's face was bloodied. His eyes rolled around unsteadily in his sockets.

"What's going on?" Lang asked.

The custodian sneered. "Boss's orders." He wrestled the man down onto a heavy chair and tied him down. Once the man was secured, Vincent placed the pistol on the table. Red stripes marked the clip as a training clip.

"Where have you been?" Lang asked.

Vincent licked his dry lips. "Out at sea laying low from the law."

"Learn your lesson yet?"

Vincent snapped like a tightly coiled spring. He was in Lang's face, spittle flying as he talked. "Leave the fuckin' cop, Lang? Leave the cop? Nobody will track that shit back to us, right?"

"Nobody told you to kill the guy," said Lang.

Vincent's fists clenched. "I need to work on a fuckin' boat until I can afford an identity wipe, you asshole. It was your job to clean up the scene."

"You're the custodian."

"What has he told you, gentlemen?" purred Silver from the open door.

"Nothing," said Vincent, suddenly calm and under control. "He just keeps snarling and spitting."

"Head injury?"

"He was running flat out when we caught him. Not normal head injury activity, but I don't know. I've never seen anything like this."

"Yes, I suppose not," said Silver. "Did the girl do something to him?"

"Who is this guy?" Lang's heart was still hammering from the confrontation with Vincent.

"What has she done to him?" Silver said. She waved Vincent away. The custodian disappeared through the door, but not before glaring at Lang.

"Is this one of your experiments?" Lang asked. "Is this how you were going to ramp up the pressure on Andersen? Send a crazy guy after her?"

"We make survivors, Lang." Silver crossed the room, picked up the pistol, and slammed the clip into place. "We temper these children into swords. Turn iron to steel. That doesn't happen with fake combat and fake weapons."

Lang's stomach turned, and his knees buckled. The only thing keeping him vertical was his grip on the window. "Andersen almost shot her friend with that gun."

Silver pointed the pistol at Lang's chest. "The girl couldn't have known they were live bullets unless she could read his mind."

"Mind reading?" Lang roared too loud. "What is it you think this girl is capable of?"

"People die in combat all the time, Tenen. This is what these children are here to learn."

Lang growled, "Not by shooting their best friends in the chest. This is the kind of thing that ruins potential warriors."

"She missed, and that tells us what we need to know."

More than ever, Lang felt an overpowering urge to defend the girl. She *was* capable of more. He slammed his fist on the table hard enough to crack the wood. "Call your mission off, Silver. I know when a job stinks, and this is rotten all the way through."

Silver watched him sway through half-lidded eyes. She was no doubt weighing his worth, and Lang didn't know how that balance would fare. He knew war well enough. He taught strategy. The kids had made fantastic plays on both sides of the battlefield.

But they were still kids.

He had expected something closer to a direct confrontation with slight variations on trying to outflank each other. Instead, the Andersen kid had shown incredible leadership when she led an assassination attempt, Peterson had timed her assault perfectly, and Giles had taught his troops everything they needed to know in his absence. Together, they had the skills needed to succeed at Silver's mission, but he still didn't know if they had what it took to go through with it.

"You really want them to kill someone," he muttered, his shoulders slumped.

Silver said, "We turn children into elite killers. We make survivors who can keep their families safe when the world collapses. When the worst of the worst finally destroys the last vestiges of our society, these children will keep everyone around them safe by being *dangerous*."

Lang did his best to meet her steely gaze, but the dizziness that washed over him threatened to topple him. "It's the only way," he finally agreed, still not sure that he believed it.

"The trial brings us closer to knowing what the children are capable of," Silver said. She walked across the room to the dark corner where the bloody man sat in the tattered remains of his endersuit. His ruined face stared up at her in abject fear as she leveled the pistol at his forehead. She looked into his puffy eyes and said, "Tell me, why doesn't it work?"

His eyes widened. The holographic display next to him flickered.

"Why?" Silver wondered, almost to herself. "There must be a way to make this technology work on adults."

"It's just," the man rasped, "so much." His eyes spun wildly in his skull.

Silver peered at him for a long time. Lang wondered if this was the technology she had promised him—the tech that would fix his condition. Judging from the frazzled state of the man tied in front of him, Lang didn't want anything to do with it.

Finally, Silver said to the man, "Thank you, my dear. You may be dismissed."

The gunshot that split the man's head was lost among the distant reports of children practicing on the live weapons range.

Chapter Twenty-Seven

Kate whistled.

The only thing bad about her whistling was how irritatingly good she was at it. She whistled "The Wreck of the Edmund Fitzgerald" as they raided several Ajay's cash stores throughout northern Minnesota's Lake Superior watershed. "All Along the Watchtower" accompanied him for hours as he sat atop Eagle Mountain and established an independent repeater network across the Northern Shore. When they finally stopped under the bright stars, she whistled perfect imitations of owls and other birds.

"Thank you," Ajay muttered as he digitally scrubbed an old beater so that it could safely take her back to her farm.

"You sure you don't want me to stay?" she asked, waggling an eyebrow.

"It won't be safe around me. Not for a long time." He wondered again how the thugs had found him, but he couldn't bring himself to believe that she was in on that.

"I'll visit," she said. Before she left, he made her memorize a list of the next hundred places that he would likely go, since they would not be able to communicate.

"How's the farm?" Ajay asked one day when she found him at his campsite atop a bluff in the driftless region along the Mississippi.

"Low maintenance prairie makes more for me than a corn-soybean rotation ever did, and I have enough freedom now to do whatever I want." She punched him in the shoulder. "Which means driving around to help you out. Five years ago, I would have watched you leave and kept an eye on the news for your obit. This is better."

"I won't be in the news if they find me."

"Something tells me you'd make noise."

"I suppose."

"Your house is looking better," she said.

"You went there?" It was a stupid risk.

Kate said, "You betcha. Place looked pretty rough, but I patched it up a little. Got new glass in the patio door."

Something unclenched in Ajay's chest. He hated to admit it, but he had been worried about the house. He'd grown a connection to the place over the last years living with Kylie. It felt like home the way nothing had for years.

Ajay maneuvered a drone over a black sedan three miles away to track its movements. If it approached the bluff, he wanted an early warning. He eyed the bag of groceries she had brought him. "Bagels?"

"And Nutella."

He hadn't been able to shop on his own for weeks. Ajay didn't want to admit it, but these latest developments had him completely tied down. He could move his camper to a new site, but if he tried to stop in a town to stock up, he'd have black sedans swarming within the hour. Kate's deliveries of food and reading material were turning out to be critical.

More importantly, Kate kept him sane while he did the work to locate Kylie.

And she could whistle. Then whistling was nice.

Regis Shaleborn's comm device had gone dark before he was able to deduce its location. If he had been able to concentrate on it, he might have been able to triangulate its signal in the network. Backtrack to its source. But the attack on his house had distracted him. By the time they'd rounded Lake Bemidji and evaded the attack, the signal had shut down and there was nothing left to find. All he could do was set up a net to catch the signal when it came back. Now that he knew what kind of device it was, the task ought to be easy.

But in the weeks since that day, it hadn't been activated even once, and Ajay hated being patient.

"I think I should move on," he said, standing from his folding chair.

"Getting restless again?" Kate asked, eyebrow raised.

"Nope." Ajay flashed an image up on his cane's holographic projector. It showed the sedan turning to drive the winding path up the bluff. "Looks like our friends are getting close."

"Figures," Kate said. She gave a sharp whistle and Garrison hopped up to follow her to the camper. When he was situated inside, she stepped back out. "See you in a couple days?"

Ajay wanted to tell her to stay. They could travel together. Get to know each other better. After his divorce, he'd always figured he would be alone for the rest of his days. He never thought it bothered him until he realized his love for a woman days before her death. He was afraid of the same thing happening with Kate.

But he was also terrified of risking their relationship by asking for too much. What if she wasn't interested in that way? Worse, what if she wasn't what she seemed?

"I'll follow the same pattern as before," he said.

She took his hands in hers and looked straight into his eyes. "You'll find her."

It'll be too late, he didn't add. He knew he'd find Kylie eventually, but he needed a better tactic. If only he could think of one.

Ajay's black and gold Winnebago ran its automated routine in the time it took him to gather his supplies and attach his Vespa to the hitch-mounted platform. It retracted its feet, released the hydraulic leveling system, and retracted its solar paneling. As his swarm of cheap drones returned to their docking compartments, he pulled the monster of a vehicle onto the county road and ventured once again into the unknown. Kate went the other way.

Chapter Twenty-Eight

ANDERSEN WAS THE WORST, Lang thought. He had been so convinced that she was a genius, but clearly, she didn't have what it took. Her performance at the wargame had been clever, but she couldn't do this. Silver had insisted that Andersen be on the team, no matter what. Fine. He could manage that. But whenever he looked at the kid, he remembered his last mission with Frontier Arms and how her grandfather had crippled him for life rather than let him die a warrior's death.

Not that he even wanted a warrior's death. He didn't know what he wanted, and that's what made his frustration worse. Silver had offered him salvation. A fix for his damaged brain.

Every time he closed his eyes, he saw the helpless, insane soldier.

"It's just so much," the man had said.

Austin Giles was the only one smart enough to be on the team, but he lacked the drive—the cruelty—to ever find success in this line of work.

That was why Lang had to lie. "The target of this mission is a real shithead, but we're not going to kill him. All we're going to do is tag him with a neuropellet and encourage him to go back to Canada where he belongs."

"Is he a threat to the business or something?" Giles asked.

"That's not information a strike team needs," Lang responded. "By now you understand that strategy isn't just something that happens on the battlefield. It starts with the planning of the operation and involves every decision—including the decision about who gets to know what."

The tall kid glowered but said nothing more.

Next to him, Brian Gould scratched the wispy scruff of a mustache he'd been growing all summer. Gould wasn't a bad kid. Not top-grade material, but he would serve well enough. Someday, he might even be a solid enforcer for his family. "Will there be backup?"

"Shaleborn and I are your backup," said Lang, patting Shaleborn's black comm device in front of him. "But you're not going to need it. We've got good intel for this mission. Better than I ever had when I was working for Frontier."

"Is that why you got injured?" asked Hanna Peterson, that smug little shit. After screwing up a solid lead in the war games, she'd somehow become even more smug and self-righteous. "Bad intel?"

Next to her, Jess Harkin snorted. She had been a co-leader with Giles, and if she had one ounce of skill, Lang hadn't been unable to detect it all summer. Technically, she had won the war game, since Giles had been dropped in combat.

"The target's name is Barty Cullins," Lang said, pulling up a mugshot of the man. He was an ugly son-of-a-bitch with gap teeth, a jaw like a snowplow, and black, beady eyes. Other images of him showed his questionable fashion sense of Hawaiian shirts and silver chains. "He's a drug dealer and human trafficker out of Thunder Bay, Ontario. Real shit of a human being. If this guy saw a profit in it, he'd sell his own mother."

The kids all stared at the image, memorizing the asshole's best features, except for Andersen, who stared off into the distance.

Lang tapped the table in front of her with his cane. "You with us, Andersen?"

She blinked. "I don't think I want to do this."

Shit. Lang didn't *want* her to be part of the mission, but what would Silver say if he lost the one kid that she demanded to be part of it? He had no leverage over her. Nothing in his authority could force her to comply.

He leaned forward, two hands on the head of his heavy cane. "This is why you are here. This camp teaches mercenary tactics and mercenary survival to kids who are going to need them. Pine Fortress is the absolute best of the best, and this is why." He emphasized the last three words with thumps on the floor with his cane. Satisfaction twitched the corners of his mouth when she flinched each time. He faced the window toward the courtyard where the lesser students practiced martial arts. "People don't learn in the classroom. They don't learn at the firing range or in the dojo." He spun on Andersen again. "You learn by *doing*, Andersen. Kill or be killed. You learn when you get that asshole in your sights and pull the trigger. Until that moment: You. Are. Not. Ready."

Her jaw jutted out in defiance, but he knew he had her.

"The police force of Minnesota is now seventy-five percent privatized. The prison system is completely private. Military exercises, the national and state guard, almost all of it is privately run, privately executed. Hell, the state has recently made moves to privatize the judicial system." He jabbed a finger at the screen where Barty Cullins's sneering mug still glowed in the sunlit room. "This asshole goes free in a system like that, but sometime, somewhere, he's going to piss someone off."

"We were hired to take him down," said Giles. "That's how this camp makes its money."

Lang ground his teeth. He wasn't allowed to talk about cash flow of Silver's organization or the particular timing of this mission. "You're learning how to defend yourselves. When you leave at the end of summer, you'll know how to spot threats to your families. You'll know how to organize a resistance. You'll know how to retaliate when someone moves into your territory to do something you don't want them to do."

"Like human trafficking," said Peterson with an edge of superiority over Andersen. God, Lang hated the social sniping of teenagers. "I, for one, am against that, and I'm happy to lead the team."

Lang didn't respond for the span of several breaths. The room spun around him, and he wanted to make sure he wasn't swaying too hard when he broke the news. "Giles is your leader," he said, facing the screen so that he didn't need to watch the reactions of the kids. "And you'll do as he says."

He didn't need to be facing them to sense the shift in tension in the room.

It was Giles who spoke first. "I don't think I—"

"You'll do it," said Lang. "You have the best head on your shoulders. You'll plan the mission, and you'll make sure nobody is ever in any real danger."

The kid had a haunted look in his eyes. Maybe Lang had gone too far by mentioning the danger. Some kids shy away from risk. They've lived lives full of risk they couldn't control, so they didn't know the thrill of managing just how close they get to the crocodile.

"What if things go wrong?" Giles asked.

"Then you'll be there to make things go right." Lang faced the kid. Leaned down and looked him right in the eyes.

"No plan survives contact with the enemy," said Giles.

"A good plan is armor," Lang said. "Either it takes the bullet or you do."

Giles blinked, and Lang could see the wheels turning in his head as he processed the new information. It gave the ex-mercenary a warm feeling, as if he had impacted this boy's life for the better.

"What if Andersen over here lands in a trap and nobody's around clever enough to get her out of it?" Lang leaned close and locked gazes with Giles. "I'm counting on your paranoia to keep her safe, kid."

That got him. Lang saw the tension drop from the kid's jaw. He would lead the team. Lang dropped an inch-thick folder on the kid's table. "The mission happens in one week. Cullins is living large aboard a ship before going to some big meeting in Duluth. He'll only be there for a short time, but there are a number of good opportunities for you."

"What's the meeting?" Giles asked.

"Doesn't matter," snapped Lang, cursing himself for bringing it up at all. "What matters is that it's a big enough meeting that drone restrictions will be in place. Nothing outside the city will be allowed to fly in."

"No fly zone at the border?"

"Right on top of the lift bridge," Lang said. "That's what will make the job complicated, but it'll also give us an opportunity."

"Us?" asked Giles.

"You," Lang corrected himself.

Lang would help create the plan, of course. He'd lead them to the least showy of the options. The least risky. He didn't want to see these kids fail, even though Silver had hired Frontier Arms as a backup if they failed.

The mission would get done, either way.

All Lang wanted was for the kids to learn what they needed to learn and get out. It made him sick training kids this young. Taking this job had been a mistake.

But, then again, what had his childhood taught him? It had been far more violent living on the streets of Atlanta, fighting in the gangs. His whole life had been a mission of survival, from the moment he first ran from bullies at school to the day he'd been crippled by Ajay Andersen on the one mission that was going to make the world a better place.

Now all he needed to do was give these kids a little show. Make them put together a real-world strike and bring them one step closer to serving as their families' enforcers. It was a shitty definition of survival, but survival was a shitty thing.

He placed a hand on the black comm tower on the desk and switched it on. Lang needed the team to understand how to use it, and the rest of the day's lessons would be about how important secure communications were in a world run by hackers and assholes.

"When you get to Duluth next week, you're going to need to set up your comm grid, and this is how you're going to do it."

Giles raised his hand.

"Yes?"

"Do we need to worry about it getting hacked?" the kid said.

Lang sighed. He was right, of course. The problem with any tech was that it tended to betray its user as often as not. "First thing's first, then," he said. "I'm going to show you how to run a system purge, then a full firmware update."

Chapter Twenty-Nine

It had been a week since the last message from Shaleborn's comm box, and from what they said about running a full firmware upgrade, Ajay suspected it would be his last.

"When you get to Duluth next week," the voice had said over the comm as one of its last recorded messages.

Ajay was in Duluth. He had scoured the city for signs of Pine Fortress activity, spent days clearing a gap in the police surveillance so that he could move freely through the city, and invited Kate up so that she could help him.

Because he was desperate. A sour taste burned at the back of his throat.

"Anything?" Kate asked as she sat across from Ajay at a table outside a restaurant overlooking Superior Bay.

"Nothing," said Ajay. "Four yachts are coming in from Superior, but one of them is too big to approach. A group of runners is training for the fall half marathon, and there's a group of bridesmaids who I think might be looking to cause some trouble. Otherwise? Nothing."

"Well," she said, pushing a beer across the metal mesh tabletop. She took a sip of her beer and stared out at the bridge across the small bay. "Then I guess this is vacation."

Ajay grumbled.

"She'll show up," Kate reassured him for the millionth time. "You said that anyone running an op here would need to control one of these rooftops."

Duluth, Minnesota wasn't a huge city, but it wasn't exactly a small town, either. It sprawled along the southern tip of Lake Superior and rammed right up against Minnesota's border with Wisconsin. Duluth was big enough to have its own college, but not big enough to develop an attitude about it. A cool wind blew across the largest port on the largest lake. Above, the bright blue sky was dotted with annoyingly fluffy clouds.

They sat atop the newly renovated roof of Grandma's Saloon, looking out over the world. To one side, the North Pier Lighthouse shone under the noonday sun. To another, Duluth's famous aerial lift bridge sat in the down position, traffic trickling across it at a leisurely pace. The bridge separated the dark waters of Lake Superior from the Duluth Harbor Basin, where smaller craft lingered with the massive container ships frequenting the United States' seventh largest port. Across the basin stood the enormous glass structure of the Great Lakes Aquarium and a cluster of shiny new buildings meant to attract business leaders and tourists alike.

"What about that other thing?" asked Kate.

Ajay sighed. He nudged the control on his cane and watched the results in his cheaters. "No activity yet."

He had placed drones around the city with instructions to watch for black sedans. Somewhere, the killers who had attacked them were searching for him. They had to be. He'd shown himself in town, and even with his best obfuscation of the data, they were bound to locate him. It was only a matter of time before they zeroed in on his location.

Ajay sipped his beer. Despite the stress of this awful summer, he had to admit the beer brought a smile to his face. "This isn't bad, you know?"

"It's good beer."

"No, I mean—" Ajay didn't know what he meant, or how to talk about it.

As it turned out, Ajay didn't *want* to talk about it. He took another drink. The only highlights of this long summer were the brief moments when Kate found him in the wild. The tension that had sparked at the beginning of the summer had smoldered, never really fanning into flame and never really going out. It was in a holding pattern, and the tricky part was that Ajay didn't know if he wanted it to change.

Kate leaned forward and whispered conspiratorially, "Old Bill was a decent husband, but the sex was always mediocre."

Ajay felt the heat rise in his neck. He thought maybe she was rejecting him for advances he hadn't made, but he wasn't sure.

Kate grinned. "You think I can't read your mind?"

"Well, I—"

"It wasn't his fault," Kate continued. She drummed the tips of her three shortened fingers on her sweating beer glass. "The big guy did his best, anyway. Can't fault him for that."

Ajay cleared his throat. "You have four kids?"

"It turns out mediocre sex works perfectly fine for procreation. Sometimes the sex was even good, but that was rare. So, yeah, we had kids. It was a good marriage." She swallowed like her throat was dry, took another drink, and said, "Thirty years. He was a good man."

Ajay chewed his lower lip. He didn't know where she was going with this, but his heart thundered in his chest. Whatever she was going to say was going to change their relationship, and change wasn't usually good.

"You look like you're being physically threatened," Kate said.

Ajay stared at the rising Lift Bridge because he didn't know if he could look Kate in the eyes. Relationships had always been complicated for Ajay. He'd always prioritized the wrong things. When he had been married, he'd buried himself in work. With Kylie, he sunk himself into learning about the tech in her head. Vital work, yes, but it wasn't what she needed. Was it? He just didn't know. "I'm sorry," he said.

Kate grasped one of his hands before he could pull it away. "What kind of people are you attracted to, Ajay?"

He finally looked her in the eyes. "Is this you fishing for compliments?"

"We can be friends if that's all you want, is what I'm saying."

"I'm not good at this," Ajay said.

"Answer the question, old man. That'll be a good start." She leaned forward. "What kind of people are you attracted to?"

Ajay thought for a moment. The Lift Bridge reached its highest point and the three yachts in the lake started to make their way slowly forward. In the distance, a superyacht edged its way closer.

Finally, Ajay said, "Do you remember that pie place we went to on the north shore?"

"The one with the gooseberry that tasted suspiciously like blueberry?"

"Yeah, that's the one." He squeezed her hand. "That waitress was attractive."

Kate pressed her lips into a tight line. "Really?"

"Are you judging me?"

"She was… not good looking."

Ajay furrowed his brow. "She had her charm."

Kate stared at him for a moment. "You just like that she flirted with you."

"She was nice!"

"That's how she gets good tips."

"I like to feel appreciated." He turned his gaze back to the yachts drifting under the bridge. They were floating mansions, and the warm sunlight danced over their well-dressed passengers. Men in black suits looked out of place on the little floating resort. "Do you think they're bodyguards?"

"You're trying to change the subject."

"I thought we were done."

Kate released his sweaty hand.

The clenched fist of his chest released, and something inside felt as if he'd been holding back something very important. "I've never been a very good friend," he said. "And a worse lover."

"Nobody's particularly good at being a friend. It's just that some people fit together." She considered it for a moment. "Like you and Olexie."

"I hate that guy."

"But you respect him, and he respects you."

Ajay grunted acknowledgment.

Kate tapped the side of her empty glass. "Finish your beer, then. I'll buy the next round."

"I think I'd better not," Ajay said.

"Oh?"

Ajay gestured at the Lift Bridge, which still sat in its raised position as a second yacht transitioned below it. "There's someone up in the top of that lift tower with something that looks suspiciously like a sniper rifle. The bodyguards on the smaller three yachts are all extremely well-armed. Someone up in that building across the river is flashing a signal this direction." He drew a long, slow breath. "Something's going to happen, and soon."

After a long pause, Kate said, "I think they're going to bring that superyacht under the bridge."

The rooftop door opened and someone stepped through who Ajay almost didn't recognize. She wore black dress pants and a deep crimson button-down shirt. Her black tie was cinched tight and crisp, with a perfectly tied Windsor knot. She wore dark sunglasses that covered half her face, and her curly hair was pulled back into a professional ponytail. In her right hand, she carried a weathered guitar case, and in her right the black case that Regis Shaleborn had stowed in the trunk of his car so long ago.

If he had any doubts about who she was, they disappeared when she spoke.

Kylie said, "Hey, Papa. How's your summer going?"

Chapter Thirty

"THE YACHT IS A fortress," Austin had summarized as the van rumbled along a county road. The holographic image in front of him didn't do a great job of showing the scale of the ship, but it broke down its defenses well enough. "Shielded inner cabins, anti-drone tech, swarm capabilities. If the *Edmund*'s security smells something's wrong, this whole job goes south."

Kylie had watched her friend speak with confidence and barely recognized him. It wasn't how he was dressed. *She* was dressed in a shockingly stylish red shirt and tie. It felt stiff and awkward to her, but the others agreed that she fit her part, and that was the most important thing.

Austin didn't *look* any different. He wore a maroon and gold University of Minnesota hoodie, sunglasses, and baggy pants. The fidget on his left hand was a top-of-the-line model, but most casual observers wouldn't notice such a thing.

What she hardly recognized was that confidence. In the past week since he had been put in charge of the mission, he'd gone from cowering in the shadows to commanding the team.

Even Hanna. She wore a black tuxedo with a loose bow tie, and her pretty blonde hair fell in ringlets across her face. For the past week, the girl had almost seemed to respect Austin. It felt... wrong.

"This seems unnecessarily complex if all we have to do is scare him," Hanna had protested when he'd first revealed the plan.

Austin hadn't missed a beat. They were in the dark strategy classroom, using the holographic table to show a detailed view of the ship. "If we want to scare him, then we need to get to him." The image zoomed back to show three escort yachts. They were tiny by comparison.

"What's so hard about it?" Hanna asked.

"We aren't able to get close-up scans because of drone denial, but we know that in addition to being heavily guarded, the *Edmund* is protected by a small fleet of ships, each staffed with several bodyguards."

"I thought this was supposed to be a simple mission," Brian had protested. "Why does this guy need so much security?"

"The situation will change as data comes in." Austin had said it as if it meant something.

"He was supposed to be some low-level drug runner," said Hanna. Kylie had thought she detected some trepidation in the inflection of the girl's voice. After watching these people for the summer, she was almost starting to learn how to read their moods—something she had never been able to do before Papa had disabled most of her other abilities. "It was going to be a quick and easy mission."

"Low-level doesn't mean easy," said Austin.

"But whose ship is this?" Hanna asked, waving at the *Edmund*.

Austin glanced toward the corner where Lang sat. "I'm told it doesn't matter."

Hanna rolled her eyes.

"As it turns out, our low-level drug runner has the luxury of traveling with one of the most powerful magnates in the entire Canadian criminal field." He was repeating what Lang had told him.

"And we're *not* hitting this magnate?" asked Hanna.

"No," said Austin. "We're not *hitting* anyone." He cast a nervous glance at Kylie, which she understood to mean that there was something he wasn't telling them. "We're scaring someone. Shouldn't need to kill anyone."

"Just tap him," Kylie muttered. Silver *definitely* wasn't being forthcoming with information. She glanced at Lang and wondered how much autonomy their team really had.

"Tap him," said Austin. He met Kylie's gaze. "As we discussed, you'll set up the comm relay. Someplace high up, because if they get farther into the harbor basin, we're going to be at the edge of our range, and I don't want satellite delays."

"I thought they weren't supposed to get that far," said Hanna.

"It's not in the plan." Austin zoomed on the Lift Bridge again, showing the narrow path the ships would need to take. "The plan is to hit Cullins on the deck of the ship where he can't bring all of his usual protection. From the tower, it'll be an easy shot."

"Why would he be there?" asked Jess. She wore a wet suit and sleek scuba gear under a silk drape as black as the depths of Lake Superior.

After a long and heavy pause, Austin said, "He's desperate. The owner of the superyacht controls half the weapons shipments in the region, and he's there to negotiate."

"What if he's below deck?" Jess asked.

"I'm assured he won't be," said Giles, failing to sound convinced. "And if he is, then the mission's scrubbed."

Jess furrowed her brow. "Then—"

"We're going to be the band," Austin said, bringing up an image of Hanna, Kylie, and Brian in nice clothes.

"Awesome," said Brian. In the image, his mass of curly hair was smushed down by a skull cap and he wore tiny green-lensed glasses that made his eyes look like they glowed. His suit was similar to Hanna's, but even in the image, he wore it with significantly less panache.

"We're the band?" said Hanna. "We're going to get past security, tap Cullins, and escape over the side—by being the band?"

"They said it would be a real-world scenario," said Austin. "And sometimes real-world scenarios get complicated."

"Or impossible," said Brian.

"Whose ship is it again?" asked Kylie.

Austin met her gaze. "I told you, it doesn't matter." He meant just the opposite, she knew. He didn't know who owned it, and he very much thought it mattered. Kylie filed that away for later. Why would that be hidden from them?

"Kylie will bring the weapons," Austin had said.

"Why her?" protested Hanna.

"I trust her," said Austin.

The whole group started talking at once, drowning out Austin and cracking his confident facade. He tried talking louder to explain the plan, but the barrage of questions drowned out his every word.

"Stop!" Kylie shouted. She nodded to Austin. "Tell them how we get past the scanners."

Austin cast a glance at Lang, who was studiously pretending not to listen. "A good hacker can disable the weapons scanners as soon as Jess places the repeater node."

"Repeater node?" Jess asked.

"We don't have a good hacker," Hanna said. "That's not something we learned at camp."

Austin held up a hand and showed an image of the superyacht passing into the Duluth Harbor Basin. As it passed under the lift bridge, a drone car landed on its deck. Three figures emerged and were greeted by the guards. At the same time, a figure under the hull of the ship activated a beacon. The interior diagram of the ship's map glowed, highlighting its network infrastructure.

"Weapon scanners will be disabled," said Austin. "You will be packing high-grade neuropellets, which are easier to sneak past detectors." He pointed at a figure on top of the lift bridge. "Even our snipers will have neuro ammo, but they're there just for backup. It'll act a lot like the stuff we were practicing with for the wargame. Low velocity. Disabling. Non-lethal."

Hanna grinned. "Painful."

"Sniper rifles won't work as well with neuropellets," said Kylie. "They're too light."

"There's a narrow optimal range," said Austin.

"We still don't have a hacker," Hanna said.

"I heard a rumor there's a neurotoxin counteragent," Kylie said.

"Highly experimental," said Austin.

"Highly suspect," added Hanna.

"But what if he uses it?" asked Kylie.

Austin shot her a glare. "He can only do that if he has a needle on his person, and even then, it's not worth it."

"Side effects?" Kylie asked.

"Pain," Austin said. "Maybe neurological damage."

"So, it's real?"

"Allegedly."

"Not worth it," Kylie agreed.

"Jess's hack will be automatic," Austin said. "We've already verified that it will work on their devices. Once you're in, Kylie will have a universal override and the skills to use it. The ship will be yours."

The group had stared at the holographic image for a long time, and the weight of what they were doing finally sank into Kylie's chest. They were infiltrating a ship full of dangerous people to perform a mock hit on someone nobody liked. This was going to be dangerous. It was going to take every ounce of discipline each of them could give, and then some. In the end, what would they have? This was a survival camp. It was teaching them to be dangerous.

"Survive by being dangerous," Kylie muttered.

"Excuse me?" said Hanna.

"Survive by being dangerous," Kylie had said, louder. She swallowed back her fear. "That's what we're learning. That's what they said they'd teach us. We survive this by being more dangerous than the killers guarding those criminals. We survive by being able to infiltrate an impossible situation to reach someone who thinks they're above reproach.

We survive by striking anything that might threaten us *before* it has the audacity to actually threaten us."

Nobody else seemed quite as convinced.

When she spoke again, it was in a whisper. "We survive by being something we're not."

A week later, they were riding in a van, geared up for the mission.

The van moved in silence for a time. It passed into the city limits of Duluth, rumbling through smaller roads until it reached the waterfront. Austin recapped the details of the plan, carefully explaining contingencies in case communications went down. There was a support team from Frontier Arms. They weren't supposed to use them, but he would call them in if needed. He didn't expect them to be needed.

Kylie stepped from the van. In one hand she held her guitar case, and in the other the comm relay. They had recently refreshed its keys and updated its firmware. It was as secure as they could possibly make it, and she needed a place to leave it that would give them a wide range of operation. Grandma's Saloon near the Lift Bridge had rooftop access, so she went there.

A cool wind blew off the river basin, but the low sun was warm on her face. Her tie felt tight, but she took a measure of confidence in it. With her hair done and her button-down shirt looking so damn good, she felt like she could maybe pull off her role as the band's leader.

"Part of the band," she muttered as she shouldered her way into the bar. She didn't think she could get away with passing off her age as twenty-one, but the saloon also appeared to serve families. Maybe she could get by pretending to be part of one of the families if she needed.

She didn't. Nobody paid her any attention as she mounted the stairs and carried her equipment to the roof access. She stepped outside.

And was shocked.

She hadn't seen Papa all summer, but he looked so different from her last memory of him. His cheeks had more color. His eyes danced with mirth. Across his table was a stocky tank of a woman with short-cropped hair and roughly wrinkled skin that had seen more than its fair share of sunlight.

So, it was true. He was doing better without Kylie. He was healthier. Happier. More social. She'd always wanted him to leave his house, and now here he was doing just fine. She wanted to duck away before he could see her. Disappear into her work and when summer camp was over, fade into the world the way Isabelle had done, leaving everything behind. Maybe she could even join Isabelle eventually. That's what her sister wanted, wasn't it? Her hands grew clammy and her grip on the comm relay shifted uncomfortably.

Papa had always said it was important to do the right thing. In this case, the right thing was to let him be happy without her. Relieve him of all the stress that he must be under trying to keep her safe. Maybe he could finally move on and live his own life.

Maybe it was the right thing, she thought, but she couldn't do it. Not yet.

Kylie stepped forward, drawing his attention. She noticed the shock in his eyes as he took in her new appearance. What did he think about her now? Did he see her as the kind of killer he was afraid she'd become? Survive by being dangerous. That was her new look.

But was that her?

"Hey, Papa," she said. "How's your summer going?"

Chapter Thirty-One

WHEN TENEN LANG WAS young, he was afraid of heights. One time, at the Fernbank Museum of Natural History, while leaning over the edge of the open structure above the dinosaurs, someone jostled him toward the railing. His hip—he was a tall kid—hit the bar across the top and for a split second he had the sensation that he was going to go over the top. He was flooded with vertigo, unsure which direction to move if he wanted to live. That vertigo stayed with him through the years, fading into something he could easily ignore, but always present. Always waiting to disrupt him, even at the pinnacle of his badass career as a mercenary, bodyguard, and thug.

Even mercenaries have their weaknesses, he always figured. Nobody was perfect.

Acrophobia wasn't an issue anymore, since his vertigo never changed as he ascended the south Lift Bridge tower with a rifle case strapped to his back. Even after his medication, the dizziness rolled over him in waves, the same at the bottom as it was all the way up at the very top where the elevator deposited him onto the open expanse of the minimalist structure.

Lang swallowed back his fear. He'd swallowed so much fear in his life, it was a wonder it hadn't given him an ulcer. As he unpacked his rifle, the lift bridge rose, making room for the first of yachts to enter the river basin.

They weren't yachts, of course. These were guard ships, designed to appear to be yachts as they patrolled the waters ahead of the superyacht.

And, of course, the superyacht wasn't a yacht at all. It was a cargo ship capable of carrying so much contraband it would disrupt the Minnesota dark economy for years. Drugs, guns, and people. Drugs and guns Lang could get behind. But people? These fucks moved the poor and unfortunate refugees from faraway wars as well as people kidnapped off the streets. It was slave trade. Sex slaves, house slaves, factory slaves. Soldiers.

Lang started to assemble his weapon. The clean aroma of gun oil and metal brought back memories of his mercenary days. There was a time when he could hit a target from a mile away with such a weapon. He had once single-handedly kept a dozen National Guardsmen at bay while his allies had cleaned a crime scene. He hadn't killed anyone that day, but keeping a mission non-lethal took more skill than going in like a killer.

He'd never be able to do that now. Even dosed up on as many meds as he could manage, the world still spun. It drifted, left to right, no matter what direction he faced. He'd be lucky to hit anything at five hundred meters, and resetting for a second shot was impossible.

But he probably wouldn't need to do it. Lang held the assembled rifle up in two hands so that he could appreciate the hardware. Cool wind blew off Lake Superior and tousled his hair. The superyacht was still a ways out when the encrypted comm clicked online. Andersen had completed her mission.

"Eagle is in position," said Giles through the comm. The boy was the leader, so he was the first to find his position. "Band, how's the situation?"

"Still missing Guitar," said Gould, the boy with the curly hair. "But Singer and Sax are at the dock."

"Good," said Giles. "Guitar, what's your ETA?"

There was a long pause before Andersen chimed in. "Relocating the comm relay for better coverage."

"Good," said Giles. "Check in when it's ready." The kid was too easy on his friend. Andersen should have had the relay in place already, and if she didn't get back to the band before pickup, she'd derail the entire operation before it even started.

Lang lifted the scope to his eye and located the rooftop area where the girl was supposed to be placing the device. The movement sent his head spinning, but after a moment he was able to focus on the situation.

She moved north across the rooftops. Her red shirt flashed across the black asphalt roofs. She'd be in position soon enough. It was a good choice. The higher location would give them better range, and the better isolation would make it less likely the device would be located accidentally.

Then, he saw that she was being followed. A man in a tan polo shirt made his way slowly across the roof, accompanied by a woman in a blue t-shirt. A wave of nausea washed over Lang, and he lost them as the scope swayed out of control. By the time he got them back, they had rounded the roof of the building and he couldn't see them.

"You have a tail, Guitar," he said into the comm.

"I'm aware," she replied immediately.

A tap on the comm line indicated an incoming text message. *Slick in position.* Slick. The girl, Jess, was underwater. She was only able to send text, which was fine. Lang wondered if she would be able to pull off what Austin needed.

Because, of course, the plan wasn't entirely designed by the children. Lang had supervised every aspect of their plan, inserting ideas as needed. It was a fantastic plan for a highly skilled, elite team of mercenaries.

For this group, it was ambitious. Really, really ambitious.

"Say that again, Guitar," said Giles over the comm. "Do you need help with your tail?"

"Negative," said Andersen.

"What do you mean, negative? You're being followed. That might mean the whole mission is scrubbed. Do you need help identifying your tail and shaking them?"

"Negative," repeated Andersen.

"Why not?"

In the scope, Lang watched the girl place the comm relay. It was a good spot. She turned and waited for her tail to catch up. When they did, she had plenty of time to shoot them. The neurotoxins would have kept them out of play for the rest of the mission. She didn't even need to kill anyone.

Then, the old man stepped into view and Lang saw who it was. Ajay Andersen. Lang almost took the shot, but from that angle at that distance, he wasn't sure he could make it count. The neuropellet had a narrow effective range, and he was far outside of it. The man who had disabled him dared to show his face? Now?

Lang clicked his comm over to another channel. "Shaleborn?"

"Lang." Shaleborn had been waiting for him.

"We have a problem."

"You're telling me."

"What do you mean?" Lang asked.

"Take a look at Harbor Drive," said Shaleborn.

Lang redirected his scope to the street. It ran alongside the permanently docked freight ship museum. Shaleborn's position was in front of that ship, where a large motorboat was docked near the road.

A black sedan rolled slowly down Harbor Drive. A man in dark sunglasses sat in the passenger side, peering out at the harbor. They had Shaleborn cornered.

"Shit," said Lang. With Shaleborn pinned down and Lang all but useless up on the bridge tower, the kids' plan wouldn't have any backup. Shaleborn had done it again. Gotten himself followed and cornered right when it mattered. "Goddamn it."

"Yeah," replied Shaleborn. Lang spotted the man hunkered down on one side of his boat, cornered where he wasn't visible from the road. "Shit."

Chapter Thirty-Two

"Let me get this straight," said Papa. He followed Kylie, even after she hopped from the rooftop restaurant to a nearby flat-topped building. "They discovered that your target was in a far more difficult position, guarded by almost an entire army, and significantly better protected, but your leadership decided to have you go forward anyway?"

Kylie sensed something else under his voice. A tension lingered there that she hadn't noticed before. Had she always been ignoring his non-verbal signals or was he more emotional than usual? A glance at his lady friend didn't reveal any clues.

"Kylie, please," Papa said. "I'm not trying to stop you, but there are some things you need to know."

"You don't trust me," Kylie spat. "You never did."

He was definitely trying to stop her. She hefted the guitar case and comm relay over a short ledge and hauled herself onto the next roof. Reconsidering her situation, she clicked the comm relay into the active position and waited for the data connection to be established.

The others chattered on comms a little, then she said, "Relocating the comm relay for better coverage."

"Good," said Austin. She felt a flutter of satisfaction at making her friend happy. It hadn't been his decision to move forward. He was the leader of the mission, but it was Lang who made the call. Did Papa even know that Tenen Lang was a camp instructor? It was probably best not to mention him.

Papa struggled with the short wall. The woman helped him and then hefted herself over easily.

"You have a tail, Guitar," said Lang through the comm. She had picked her own codename based on her position in the band, but it still felt strange using fake names.

"I know," she replied, a little annoyed. Papa was still approaching over the rooftop. She clicked off her comm and said, "I really, really want to talk to you, Papa, but this is the most important part of survival camp."

"What's your mission?" he asked, catching up.

"A secret."

Papa grumbled with frustration, but the woman elbowed him. "Kylie, I'd like you to meet Kate," he said.

A hint of amusement twinkled in Kate's eyes. "We're not dating," she said.

Kylie hitched. "I didn't say—"

"I just want to be clear," said Kate. Kylie liked her already, despite herself.

"You've been busy," Kylie said to her grandfather. She found the place she had scoped for the comm relay and put it in position. Where it sat, the shadows from the high sun barely covered it, but it would get even better concealment as the afternoon wore on. "You made a friend."

"Well, yes," said Papa.

"What else?" There was something else. Kylie could see it in his eyes. There was a *lot* else.

"Someone's been chasing me," he said. "They attacked at the house."

Kylie blinked. The house was supposed to be safe.

But Papa didn't stop. "They've been on me all summer. I think they're here somewhere. Kylie, these people are dangerous."

"Where are they?"

"I don't know. They're staying hidden from me."

"That's not as hard as it used to be," Kylie said, immediately regretting her mean words.

"True," said Papa. He was hurt. She could hear it in his voice. "But your camp leaders hid you from me, Kylie. I wanted to warn you, but all the contact info the camp gave me was bogus. Why do you think that was?"

Kylie remembered her first week at the camp. How she'd felt so homesick for a home she didn't even like. How they had said the best way was to cut off all ties and *survive*. They had said it as if survival were the single greatest thing that a person could ever achieve.

"Survive by being dangerous," she muttered to herself. To Papa, she said, "What do you want to do?"

He tapped the top of his cane. "I can unlock your abilities."

Kylie stared at him. Horror bubbled up in her chest and threatened to choke her.

"It'll help you on your mission."

"You don't think I can do this on my own." She took a step away from him. "You never believed I could be anything without it."

Papa sputtered.

"No," Kylie said. "No, I won't. Not until this is done."

It was supposed to be until the end of summer. Kylie remembered the headaches, the distractions, the glorious communication with everything in the world around her—and she remembered how upset she was when Papa shut it down. Even though she had asked for it, it still made her furious at her grandfather. He'd done something to her to make her *normal*, and it was the worst thing anyone had ever done to her. She knew now that she didn't want to be normal.

That wasn't true. Austin didn't want her to be normal. Lang and Shaleborn had their faults, but they didn't expect her to be normal. They expected her to be exceptional.

Now that she thought about it, they expected her to be what she really was. A hacker. An infiltrator. A girl capable of moving invisibly through a world steeped in digital surveillance. That's why they wanted her to be a survivor. They counted on her to find the zero-day flaws in an airtight system.

They wanted her to be dangerous. Kylie clicked her comm back on.

"Ride's approaching," said Brian—Sax. She had to remember to use their codenames. Brian was Sax. Hanna was Singer. What would it be like to be in a real band? Kylie didn't even *play* the guitar.

"I'm on my way," she said through her comm. She stalked across the roof to where it met the sloped top of another building.

"Kylie, please," said Papa. He wasn't saying what was important. "I'm not telling you what to do. I'm giving you your space, but…"

"But what?" Kylie spun on him. "But you're going to come here and guilt me into doing something? More modifications to my brain? Maybe you want me to abandon the rest of my team?" She gestured at the river basin, where two drone cars flew over dark waters. "I have work to do, Papa. I can't just leave them."

"They want you to kill someone," said Papa. His knuckles were white from how hard he gripped his cane. "We found evidence that they've done it before."

Maybe it was the stifled anger bubbling up inside her or maybe it was the urgency she needed to stay on task for her mission, but Kylie said, "So what?" as if she meant it.

Papa rocked back on his heels. "The Kylie I know wouldn't be so flippant with such a thing."

"Maybe you don't know me at all."

"Kylie…"

"He's a bad person," she said, pushing confidence into her words that she didn't feel. There were lots of good reasons Mrs. Silver had given that Barry Cullins needed to be put in his place. He was a human trafficker. A drug runner. A user.

But what evidence did Kylie actually see?

"I'll make good decisions," she said. It was all the ground she could manage to give. She hefted her guitar case over the wall and vaulted onto the fire escape. He wouldn't follow. Not with how fast she was moving. Not with his bad hip.

That was why she was surprised to hear someone hit the fire escape when she was halfway down. When she got to the bottom, she saw Papa's friend Kate scrambling down.

"What?" she demanded as soon as the old lady's boots struck pavement.

"He misses you," Kate said. She was a tough-looking older woman, but she had a kind voice. "I just thought you should know that."

A car drove by on the otherwise empty street. Far away, the sound of sirens echoed through the town.

Kate continued, "He looked for you all summer. Figured out that you were gone right away, pretty much."

"That's because he's always spying on me. That's exactly why I left." Kylie turned on her heel and started walking, ignoring the old woman as she fell in step beside her. "He's always talking about how he wants me to make my own decisions, but it wrecks him every time I do something he thinks isn't perfect. I mean, why can't he just be happy for me with how I do in school?"

"Do you get good grades?"

"That's not the point."

"He wasn't going to spy on you," said Kate. "Really."

"Uh-huh." They rounded a corner and Kylie saw the two drone cars landing near the docks. She had to hurry if the plan had any chance of success. "Tell him I get it. I'm not going to murder anyone. This is a training mission for a survival camp, not some sort of mercenary hazing operation."

"Can't it be both?"

Kylie stopped and stared at the woman. She looked like a tough woman, weather-beaten and calloused. If Kylie had met her on the street, she might have thought the old woman was also involved with the mercenaries. She was certainly rugged enough.

"When I come home—and I will, I don't care if the house isn't safe anymore—I'll do it having accomplished something on my own without his help. I'll have either succeeded or failed in the mission, and I'll know my own worth. Not his. Mine." She glanced again at the landing drones. "We're delivering a message, and if things go well, they'll never know where it came from."

Kate said, "You know how to reach your grandfather if you need help."

"I always have, and I never will," Kylie said. With that, she stalked away, not looking back to see if the old woman followed.

It was time to make some music.

Chapter
Thirty-Three

AJAY WATCHED AS THE *Edmund* approached the lift bridge. The superyacht had to be Kylie's target. She said they were after a certain person and that they were delivering a message. The way she had said it made him think their message wasn't a friendly one.

At his feet sat the comm relay.

He glanced at the Lift Bridge. From this angle, he couldn't see the figure with the rifle. He wasn't even sure that he had seen it before. At that distance, it could have been a trick of the light or an odd silhouette of an antenna or some satellite tech. Why would there be a sniper on the bridge tower?

Because a sniper was part of the plan.

When he heard Kate climb back up the fire escape, he said, "I don't understand that girl."

Kate said. "When you say you're there to back her up, she hears that you don't trust her. How hard is that to understand?"

"But that's not what I said."

"She'll grow out of it."

"Her birthday is next week," Ajay said. "She'll be fourteen."

"She seems older."

"Kylie's been through a lot." Ajay tapped the controls on his cane and the display flashed. The comm relay had been updated. None of the hacks he had used before would work, but he had physical access to the device. He could—

"No," Kate said, elbowing him.

"What?"

"You were going to hack into that thing."

"A little."

"Don't do it." She stepped between him and the device. "As a show of trust."

"But what if she needs me?"

"Then you'll help as best you can. When. She. Asks."

"I won't know what she needs unless I can listen in on them."

The *Edmund* towered over the banks of Lake Superior. Closer now, Ajay saw that the ship was taller than the building he stood on. It must have been near the capacity of the narrow canal, hulking over the three guard ships preceding it under the bridge. The flat top of its conning tower was going to pass very close under the raised bridge. Below, at the docks, two drone cars lifted from the landing pad. Dangerous vehicles, as far as Ajay was concerned, but probably safe enough for a quick jaunt between land and ship.

That was how Kylie was getting aboard the *Edmund*. How was she escaping after her message was delivered? Ajay glanced up at the lift tower. Were they going to try to escape up? Down into the water? How?

"You're right," he said. "I shouldn't hack into their comms. If I do that, I might open a vulnerability. I could be giving their enemies access that would put her in more danger." Like leading enemies to someone's house, he thought.

Kate placed a hand on his shoulder. "Good," she said. "So, how about we go get another drink and wait this out?"

"No," Ajay said, drawing the word out to give himself a little more time to think things through. "No, I don't think so."

"Ajay."

Ajay pointed his cane at the ship. "Because what I want to do will be easier if I'm on that boat."

Kate swept his cane out of his hands and rapped him on the noggin in one swift movement.

"Ow!" Ajay rubbed the spot on his forehead. "That's going to leave a mark."

"It's not."

"It feels like it."

"And yet."

Fine. She was right. It didn't hurt *that* much. What hurt most was being told that he couldn't help his granddaughter. "I'm going to help her."

"You're not."

"Give me back my cane."

Kate rapped him on the skull a second time. "That one's going to leave a mark."

This time Ajay was angry enough that the pain felt like nothing. He balled his fists. "Kate," he said, hoping the warning in his tone would make her realize she had to back down. "I can't abandon her."

"And I can't let you do something stupid." She tossed the cane back to him. "Come on, we'll find someplace better to watch what's happening. If she needs you, she'll call."

He looked at the cane in his hands. She was right. He knew intellectually that she was right. His emotions didn't agree, but that's how emotions worked, wasn't it?

"Fine," he finally said. He turned to walk back to the rooftop restaurant.

Two men in black suits stood next to their table.

Adrenaline flooded Ajay's body. He recognized these men. They had attacked Shaleborn. These were the men who had assaulted his house. The guy built like a tank spotted him first and grunted. The tall one touched his ear and said something.

The tank stared at Ajay with his penetrating gaze.

Then, all hell broke loose.

Ajay tackled Kate, dragging her down behind the short wall. The crack of a pistol shattered the silence, and the brick above their heads exploded.

Kate swore. Ajay led her along the wall in a crouch walk, hurrying away as the men cautiously mounted the short wall between buildings. They hit the corner just in time and ducked behind a large air conditioning unit.

"Who are these guys?" Ajay asked idly.

Kate looked like she intended to find out. She wrestled with her holster a minute, then pulled a pistol of her own. She let a couple shots fly around the metal unit, sending the two men under cover.

"You brought a gun?" Ajay asked.

"You're damn right I did," said Kate. "It's *your* gun, Ajay."

"I don't like guns."

"And I don't like getting shot, so I guess we're a good team." She peeked around the corner but ducked away when a shot pinged off the sheet metal above her head. "Shit."

"What do we do?" Ajay asked.

"Hey!" Kate called out. "Hey, what is it you guys are looking for?"

Their only answer was another shot over their heads.

"They're going to try to circle around," Kate said.

"We could go over the side." Ajay glanced over the edge of the building and was immediately hit by a wave of vertigo. They were only on the second story, but it was too far down to the hard pavement. "Nope, never mind."

"Climb for it?"

"I'm not exactly in great shape right now."

Kate gripped his hand. "I don't know what else we can do, Ajay."

Ajay's chest felt tight. His breathing came in ragged gasps. He'd always been able to hack his way to freedom, but there was nothing to hack. The drone attached to his cane would help with surveillance. The taser built into its tip might slow someone down, but only if they could get close, and there was no chance of that.

"I don't know," he said, helpless. An ache like grief strangled him. "I just don't know."

Kate fired another blind shot, this time aiming the other angle across the roof from their corner. "Think of something, Ajay," she said through gritted teeth.

"I—" Then, he did know. He wasn't sure it would work. It probably wouldn't.

Ajay detached the drone from his cane and gave it instructions to swoop close to the two shooters, and then take to the skies.

"Cover it," he said to Kate. She fired two more shots as he sent the drone. If the assassins shot it down before it got good images, then they were done. "He's not a threat, assholes!"

"Wrong place, wrong time," said the tank.

Ajay watched the video feed in his cheaters. Good, solid images. Full scan.

"Might want to consider your next move," he shouted, standing from cover. "You just got a full identity scan, gentlemen. That thing is watching from the skies." He held his hands high, his cane gripped tightly in his left hand.

"What are you doing?" Kate hissed.

"Giving myself in," said Ajay. To the attackers, he said, "You're here for me. You don't need my friend." To Kate, he hissed, "Climb, Kate. Now."

The tank stood from behind the wall. He leveled his pistol at Ajay.

"And don't think your obfuscation measures are going to work on my drone's feed. I saw that right away and overrode it. There are still a few zero-day bugs I have in my back pocket, you know. Government surveillance overrides have all kinds of back doors nobody knows about but me. I collect them the way people used to collect stamps or Pokémon cards."

The man hesitated. Ajay could see the decision being weighed in the man's thick mind.

"Just shoot him," urged the tall guy.

Ajay's holographic image flashed from the top of his cane. "The video is live on the feed, gentlemen." He strolled forward. "You're welcome to shoot me, but it's not going to look great to your fans."

"Fans?" said the tank.

"Yes, fans. I sent the video feed to my friend Olexie. Maybe you've heard of him. He's a social media guy. Olexie Sokolov, king of sock puppets. One of his hobbies is motivating people to action on the network. His specialty is old-school social media, but he's fairly well connected with the modern stuff, too. Your identities have been blasted out and, wow, we're getting a pretty good viewership." He took another step forward, bringing him only a medium putt from the black-clad man. Too far to attack with a taser. To close to miss with a gun. A name flashed across Ajay's cheaters as he stared at the shorter man. "You're going to be famous, Spencer."

The use of the man's name did the trick. He lowered the gun and glanced at his partner. "They've got us," he said.

"That's right, Charles," said Ajay to the tall man. "We have you. Sure, you can kill us easily enough, but you'll be famous for it. Famous enough that even your high connections won't let you weasel out of some good quality prison time."

Spencer raised his gun again. "Maybe it's worth it."

Ajay's heart pounded in his throat. A few years in prison might be worth it to this guy. He'd spend some time behind bars, be compensated by his boss, and by the time he went free he'd be better off than if he'd worked a full-time job. The economics of criminals made a lot more sense than the economics of the law-abiding. You do the time, pay the price, and wealth is yours. That's all there was to it.

A hacker like Ajay knew all about that kind of compensation.

Charles muttered something into his comm. Ajay's tools didn't detect the signal, so it must have been on a secure transmission.

"Let my friend walk," Ajay said. "I'll come willingly. You can kill me in a private warehouse somewhere if you like."

"Oh, that sounds like a hell of a trap," said Spencer the tank.

"Guys," said Kate, her voice a grim warning. "Don't do this."

"I'm the one you're after," said Ajay. "Your contract says to kill me so I don't interfere with—what?"

"It doesn't matter," said Kate. "We don't know anything. Let us go and we'll leave."

Spencer took a step forward, a hint of a smile creeping onto his face. "Oh, you think you're so damn sharp, old man. You've spent all this time working for her on the sly and you still don't know how deep it goes."

"Working for who?" Ajay hadn't worked for anyone.

"Spence, shut up," hissed Charles.

"Oh, it's not really going to matter, is it?" said Spencer. "This guy's not going anywhere, even if he tries to give me a zap with that cane of his."

Ajay's cane suddenly felt very heavy. His best bet would have been catching the man by surprise.

"Drop it, please," Spencer said.

Ajay dropped the cane.

Before it hit the ground, Spencer took two strides forward and struck Ajay on the side of his head with the pommel of his gun.

Everything went black.

Chapter Thirty-Four

"Touching down," Kylie said, attempting to sound very professional over the comm. "I'm on the second yacht."

Kylie didn't like drone cars. The movement was smooth enough and fairly reliable. It was the same stabilization technology that Papa's best drones used, but scaled up large enough for two passengers. It had lifted from the dock and taken her almost to the bridge to the canal where three yachts inched forward in front of the giant superyacht.

The drone with Brian and Hanna landed on the first yacht, but Kylie's drone brought her to the second. They hadn't expected that. The plan was to be taken directly to the *Edmund*. That's where their intel said Cullins was. They were the band hired to entertain guests as soon as The *Edmund* reached the Harbor Basin. According to Austin, they had hired a band made up of kids because kids were harmless. Cullins was to be the band's contact on the ship. He was supposed to help them set up.

"Stay with the plan," Austin said in her ear. "Our band's contract says there are security measures. They must do that on the smaller yachts before moving you to the *Edmund*."

"Got it." She did, but she didn't *like* it. "Whose yacht did you say this was?"

"Guitar," Austin said, his voice dripping with warning.

"I know, I know. That information's not important." She had searched the registries. Austin was right, the information wasn't anywhere it was supposed to be. All she got were a bunch of shell corporations and a retaliating search for her own identity. She had shut the connection down fast enough when it had happened, but it had unnerved her all the same.

"We're on yacht one," sighed Hanna over the comm. "They're scanning all our gear."

"That's fine," said Austin. "Kylie, don't let them scan your case until Slick is in position."

It wasn't fine. Kylie hated it. Her heart pounded, and her mouth tasted like dry battery shavings. The door of her drone car hissed open, and she stepped out.

What was that ping? texted Jess.

"There's no ping," said Austin. "What frequency?"

I heard it. Underwater.

"I don't know what you're talking about." Austin's voice had a taught edge. "Just stick to the plan for now."

Two women stood in front of her in khaki pants and colorful button-down shirts. Their garish clothing made for an odd contrast to the deep dark of Lake Superior behind them. Out in that sea, the *Edmund* loomed in front of the canal, pulled by a comparatively tiny tug.

The woman on the left held a blue baton, which she waved over Kylie's body. It buzzed a little when passed over her head but otherwise didn't trigger on anything. The other woman took the guitar case away somewhere behind Kylie.

Kylie turned. "I'm going to want that back."

The woman with the baton smirked.

"It's just—" Kylie couldn't think of what to say.

"You'll get it back." The tone didn't brook any argument.

Austin's voice sounded in Kylie's ear. "Slick's not in position."

I'm on my way, texted Jess.

Jess's task was the simplest out of them all. She was supposed to get close to the yacht and run an interference signal to the scanners. It was a short-range tool that would only work if she pressed it right up against the hull of the offending boat. Lang had assured them that it would work.

They hadn't planned on being separated into two yachts. The security measures should have taken place all the way out on the *Edmund*. Now with the change in plans, Jess needed to reposition. Fast.

"Guitar," said Austin. "Delay."

"Wait!" shouted Kylie. She broke from the woman and stalked after her guitar.

The reaction was swift. The women had guns pointed at her and three black-suited men swarmed onto the deck, weapons in hand. A spotlight from above blasted about a million lumens straight into her skull. She blinked furiously against the onslaught. Had she recognized one of those men?

"Don't even move," said the woman who had been scanning Kylie.

"It's not mine," Kylie said. Who was that guy? She squinted through the light.

The woman's footsteps approached Kylie from behind. The woman spoke through gritted teeth. "What's not yours?"

Kylie channeled all of the insecurity she was feeling into her voice. "I-I know they said not to bring anything. It's not my fault."

One minute, texted Jess. One minute was forever.

"Hang in there, Guitar," said Austin. She could hear him failing to suppress the nervousness in his voice. "Tell them a story."

"It's-it's not my fault," Kylie repeated. She took another step toward her guitar, which stood near the door to the interior of the yacht. A tear welled up in her eye and she pressed it out so it could roll down her cheek dramatically. "My friend said it would help. I was nervous about the gig and I didn't think it would matter if I brought it."

"Brought what?" said a man with a rumbling deep voice.

Kylie took another step toward her guitar, but the woman behind her grabbed her arm hard enough to bruise. "What did you bring, kid?"

The man with the deep voice hefted the guitar onto a bench and flipped the clasps in front of it. Kylie's eyes adjusted to the light, and she cast around for the man she had recognized. He stood behind the others now, just out of sight. His long, greasy hair didn't fit the crisp, clean image of his suit.

"Wait," Kylie said, struggling against the woman's iron grip. Her ploy wasn't working very well. If they opened the case and searched instead of running it through a scanner, then it wouldn't matter if Slick got there in time. "I'll throw it over the edge. Please, just let me—"

"Keep quiet, kid," hissed the woman. To the man, she said, "Be careful."

Almost there, texted Jess. Kylie couldn't delay anymore. If she moved, they would shoot her.

Wouldn't they?

What had Shaleborn told her? Take in the situation. What's the move? The most important thing she could learn was how to observe her surroundings.

She looked around. The three men didn't have guns. They had tasers. The women had guns, but the one who had taken the guitar wasn't pointing it at her. The woman who had run the personal scanner was holding Kylie's arm. She was the one in charge, and Kylie couldn't see if she was holding a gun.

What else had Shaleborn told her? Most of what she knew would work on a larger, stronger opponent, but it was always best to have surprise. There was no way she could take down the whole security team.

But she could pull away. Get over the edge. Escape.

"I'm sorry," Kylie said.

The woman's grip loosened almost imperceptibly, so Kylie took the opportunity. She dropped her center of gravity, twisted, and pulled free.

In two long steps, she closed the distance to her guitar, wrenched the case open, reached in for a packet, and threw it overboard. The little plastic baggie spun away into the dark waters.

Seconds passed and the security detail stared at her. Wind gently tugged at Kylie's air. Her face felt cool where her sweat evaporated in the evening breeze. The man she had recognized was gone. Kylie remained wonderfully unshot.

"What was that?" the woman in charge growled.

"Nothing," said Kylie, shrinking into herself. "It was for the stress."

The woman's lips pressed into a tight line. "You tried to bring drugs."

"It's not my fault."

She tilted her head to the man with the deep voice. "Scan the guitar," she said, exasperated.

He closed the case, latched it tight, and carried it inside.

"Wait," Kylie said.

The man stopped.

"Do it," said the woman.

He continued down into the depths of the ship. Too soon. He'd scan the guitar, find her stashed weapons, and then she'd be in real trouble. The thugs closed around her. She didn't even have a direct route to the side of the ship. Plunging into the canal to escape was no longer an option.

In position, texted Jess.

"I'm sorry," said Kylie.

"What did you throw overboard?" asked the woman.

Kylie swallowed. She still didn't need to fake nervousness. "This is my first real gig."

"I thought the boss only hired seasoned professionals," the woman said.

Kylie shrugged. "I had to fill in last second."

The woman scowled. "That's against the contract."

The man with the deep voice returned with the guitar case. "Let it drop, Talia. The case checked out. She's clean." To Kylie, he said, "Don't be so nervous, kid. We're all friends here."

Kylie swallowed a wave of nausea. She glanced around again for the man, but he was nowhere to be seen. For several seconds all she could hear was the rush of blood in her ears and the crashing of water against the front of the yacht as it moved through the canal.

The man handed her the guitar and led her to a drone car. Above, a drone passed over with Brian and Hanna.

She left in a different drone car from the one she had arrived on. They didn't want anyone stashing anything in the car as a way to avoid inspection. The new car was smaller. A one-seater.

As the man with the deep voice helped her get situated in her seat, he said, "Marijuana's not illegal, kid. Worst case we would have confiscated it."

Kylie's mouth went dry. "I get really nervous sometimes."

"Don't we all, kid," said the guy. She almost thought she read a genuine kindness in his eyes, but she couldn't be sure. There was something else there, too. Something cruel, as if he enjoyed seeing her squirm.

The drone took her high into the air, and this time being up above the canal relaxed her. She'd made it through the security checkpoint. It wasn't the worst part of the whole plan, but she didn't want to fail before getting one shot at Cullins.

"I'm in," she said into her comm. She closed her eyes and tried to picture the man she had recognized. Where had she seen him before?

"Slick," Austin said, "proceed to second station."

More pings, Jess said. *It sounds closer.*

"Proceed with caution," Austin said. Then, he switched to a private channel. "Guitar, how are you doing?"

"Feeling pretty nervous," said Kylie. No reason not to be honest with Austin. "I saw Papa back on the roof."

"I know."

"He offered to give me back what he took early this summer," Kylie said. She didn't want to say too much over the line. The drone whooshed over the open waters of the lake. "I should have taken him up on it."

"Jess had your back."

"What if she hadn't?"

"I'm listening to the chatter on that yacht, and it's all about wishing they had confiscated some pot from you so that they could smoke it once they were off duty." He paused for a moment. "You read them perfectly, Guitar. Nice work."

Then, it clicked. "It was Vincent," she said.

"What?"

"The custodian at camp. I just saw him on the yacht."

Austin paused for a breath. "That—doesn't make sense."

Brian and Hanna's drones landed on the superyacht. Kylie had the sunset to her back and the last dregs of orange dotted the clouds over the ship. As her drone flew, the yacht got bigger and bigger, to the point where she didn't even believe it could possibly fit under the Lift Bridge. It was huge. Like one of those giant container ships. A person could get lost for weeks on a ship like this.

Hopefully, it wouldn't take that long.

"I'm telling you it was him," Kylie said. "He saw me and got out before I could get a good look, but I'm sure it was him."

Austin said, "Just focus on the mission. Get in, tag the guy, and leave. Let Brian positively identify the target. You can initiate the hack, hit him with a neuropellet, and go."

"Right." Kylie's heart pounded in her chest. "About that."

"What?"

"I might have thrown my override tool overboard when I was pretending that I'd brought drugs."

The line was silent for several seconds as the drone passed over the bulk of the superyacht.

"Say that again," said Austin.

"I'll figure it out," Kylie said. "Like I said, I should have taken Papa up on the offer to get my abilities back."

"Maybe," said Austin. "But you'll figure it out. Just don't rush. Slow and steady."

"If I wait too long, they're going to want me to play the guitar."

"I thought you said you knew how to play."

"Not very well!"

"Crap."

Kylie tried her best to slow her gulping breaths. "It's fine. It's fine. We'll be long gone before the party starts."

Her heart pounded in her chest, worse even than when the security guards had surrounded her on the yacht. She was about to be surrounded by goons without a clear line of escape. Who thought this was a good idea? Sending kids was the right choice, though. The crap she'd pulled would never have been tolerated for an adult. If they had sent a real band, they would have been scrutinized much more closely. She never could have faked panic about a packet of marijuana. Faked. Right. As if her panic were faked. Her guitar case creaked in her hands where she hugged it too tight. A full panic threatened to wash over her and she couldn't straighten out her thoughts.

That was why it was almost a relief when yacht three exploded in a ball of fire that lit up the sunset sky.

Almost, but not quite.

"What the hell is happening?" she sputtered into the comm.

Austin's only reply was a burst of static.

Then she saw him. Their target, Barty Cullins, stood in a cluster of men in Hawaiian shirts and dark sunglasses. He was unmistakable—clearly the seedy, washed-up turd they'd seen in their reconnaissance photos. He was right there, running for the door.

Getting away.

The whole job counted on not having to chase him into the ship. Every analysis they did said that the mission went south hard if any of them had to go below deck.

Shit.

Kylie yanked open the drone's door as it approached the *Edmund* and jumped. By the time her drone touched down on the superyacht, Kylie was sprinting with her guitar case across the deck.

Chapter Thirty-Five

THE GOON NAMED SPENCER rolled his muscular shoulders. "Get in."

"I'd rather not," said Ajay, peering at the gaping maw of the black sedan's trunk.

Spencer wrenched Ajay's cane out of his grasp. The man jangled with nervous energy and flashed a holographic clock on the fidget computer on his left hand. "We're behind schedule already," he said to Charles.

Charles grabbed Ajay and piled him violently into the trunk without a twitch of emotion. The way he moved reminded Ajay of a robot. Powerful. Determined. Immutable. Charles was the dangerous one. Spencer was nothing but muscle and nerves. The trunk slammed before Ajay could protest. Then, the car was moving.

"Lift Bridge is up," said Charles. Ajay's hearing aid picked up the voices, even through the road noise. It wouldn't do him much good, but maybe he could learn who was going to kill him. Maybe he could communicate with Kylie—but, no, he didn't have a connection. He didn't even have his cane.

They hit a bump, and Ajay's panic tasted like battery acid in the back of his throat. He was a dead man. The trunk smelled of mildew and sweat.

The dim display on his cheaters flashed bright in the dark of the trunk. Ajay slipped the crescent moon glasses onto the bridge of his nose with some difficulty. They projected the image from his drone, which was still following the sedan. It showed the car far below making its way cautiously through the Duluth streets. They passed close to the Harbor Basin on Harbor Drive, and he saw a window open on the driver's side.

His cane flew out and splashed into the water.

Crap.

Ajay's computer was everything. He knew it. Kate knew it. Kylie knew it. Without access to decent computing power, he was nothing. He couldn't fight his way out or run faster than anyone. Hell, without his cane, he could hardly walk far enough to get away. He'd be useless if he got away.

Here he was thinking about getting away again. Why bother with the impossible?

"Full of hope, Andersen," he muttered to himself. "That's what they always said about you. Always the damn optimist."

Three minutes in the trunk of a car and he was already talking to himself.

Old sedans with trunks used to always come with escape levers. He remembered that from an old documentary about safety in the automobile industry. He searched for it, using the flickering light on his cheaters to illuminate the tiny space.

The trunk was empty. They didn't even carry a spare tire. No winter kit. Scraper, blanket, granola bars. Who drove around without the basics, even in summer? It seemed irresponsible.

Unless maybe they were from outside Minnesota. Spencer's high voice penetrated the rumble of car noise, so Ajay froze so his hearing aid could better pick out the words.

"We'll take care of him when this is all done," said Spencer.

Charles said, "I don't like it."

"Until we knock his drone out of the sky, we're not going to do anything."

"Even without footage, we'll be under suspicion if he disappears. He IDed us."

The car turned, and in his cheaters, Ajay watched as the sedan rounded a corner. It was going faster than the rest of traffic, but not over the speed limit.

"Suspicion's not proof," said Spencer. Maybe Spencer was the dangerous one. Ajay tried to locate their accents. Boston, maybe? Did Ohio have an accent? "They won't pin anything on us if there's no body."

The men were silent for what felt like eternity. The car rumbled over pitted roads, taking back streets rather than the more heavily traveled Harbor Drive.

"We have Shaleborn pinned down," said Charles.

Spencer punched the gas. "I can't be-fucking-lieve you let him get away."

"He won't this time."

"If we go over there now, the old man's drone is going to cause trouble."

"Shit."

Regis Shaleborn must be there with Kylie and the summer camp. He must be there to supervise whatever mission the children were on. If Ajay could contact him, maybe they could help each other out.

Or, maybe Shaleborn would be just as bad as these two thugs. Who the hell were these guys?

"You got that rifle still?" Charles asked.

The sedan stopped in the alley of a residential area. Tall pines stretched high above the surrounding buildings. It was as secluded as he'd seen within the city limits. In his drone images, Ajay saw Spencer step out of the car, open the back door, and draw something long from the back seat.

This was the point where Ajay would have had the drone retreat. It did no good spying on these guys if it was just going to get shot down. His cheaters showed him the drone's view high above the Duluth residential area. Maybe too high to get shot, but this model didn't have the adaptive camouflage.

Unfortunately, Ajay didn't have control over the drone. It was programmed to watch, and with his cane lost, it would continue to do that until its battery died.

Or until it was shot.

A gunshot rang out over the small alley. Ajay's video persisted. Maybe it *was* too high to shoot. Without a backdrop, Spencer would have trouble adjusting to a miss. He had no way of knowing if he was missing left or right or too high. Any adjustments would be random. He couldn't possibly know the wind patterns up there.

Another echoing shot. A miss.

Plus, he couldn't sit there all day firing at the drone in the sky. The privatized police might be corrupt, but this was a predominantly privileged neighborhood. Someone would report something, and then there would be attention that these assholes didn't want. Attention that Ajay could leverage into an escape.

A shot. Miss.

Ajay still searched for the hidden lever. There had to be some clasp or release that would open the trunk and allow him to flee. He'd be an idiot to try it while Spencer sat there with the rifle, but if someone came to investigate…

A gunshot, and Ajay's cheaters flashed an error message. The feed was gone. His drone destroyed.

Tires peeled out on the rough asphalt.

"Nice shot," Charles said.

"Fuckin' thing was tiny," said Spencer.

A hiss of panic whined in the back of Ajay's throat. He had missed his opportunity. Never mind that it hadn't been one. Not really. His anxiety didn't care, and now he didn't have the protection that the drone offered. Not even that tiny amount of safety. He was awaiting whatever these two men had in mind for his disappearance, and he knew it wasn't going to be pleasant.

He barked his knuckles against a sharp metal ridge in the trunk and swore. His cheaters no longer emitted a glow from their display. His only light was the tiny hint that emerged when the sedan braked and the taillights glowed. Could he do something with those? He patted down his pockets for his utility knife.

They hit a bump. His knuckles were slick with blood, but he held on.

The light was protected by the coarse carpet that covered the entire trunk. Ajay hacked at it with his knife until it came off in chunks. The car was moving fast now, speeding through the narrow streets.

"Come on, asshole," Ajay muttered to the light. "Get out here."

A protective cover over the light leaked around its edges but prevented Ajay from accessing the electronics. His knife barely scratched the metal of the cover, but feeling around its edges, he located three screws. He switched his multitool to a screwdriver and started working.

"What's the situation?" asked Spencer.

"Team B is in position around Shaleborn. Can't approach because he's hunkered down in a boat. If they move forward, he has a clean shot."

"So if we're across the river?"

"Too open. We're supposed to move along shore." There was a pause before Charles pointed. "There."

The car made a sharp right turn and the hard bump slammed Ajay against the trunk roof.

The first screw came loose and clattered to the trunk floor.

"Can you see it?" Spencer asked.

"Try up there," replied Charles. The car turned again. They were moving slowly, like they were looking for a parking spot. "I'm not sure we'll be able to spot him from the car."

The second screw didn't move as easily as the first, but Ajay cranked on it. Blood slicked his fingers, but he wiped them off on his pants and continued to work. This was his only chance.

His cheaters flickered to life, reporting contact with his cane was restored. Not that it did him any good. They must have circled all the way around to the other side of the canal. How long would his cane continue to work at the bottom of the lake?

His screwdriver slipped and he smashed his thumb against a jutting metal bar that he hadn't known was there. It was invisible against the dark carpet.

Ajay gripped it with a bloody hand. This was the escape lever. The car was stopped.

If he got out, how far would he get?

Before he could build up the courage to run, the car moved again. Tires ground against the sand left in the parking from the long winter.

Ajay worked on the next screw. It came quickly, and he finished it with his bloody fingers. That was the third and last one. The panel should move.

It didn't.

He pried at it with the screwdriver, and the metal bent around a single hidden screw. Dammit. He lost precious seconds wrenching the metal piece aside.

The car stopped, brake lights filling the tiny trunk. He switched his multitool to the knife and jabbed it into the wiring. With several quick scrapes, he stripped the insulation from several wires.

It was guesswork. He didn't know car wiring. He didn't know electricity at all except for when it passed through the nand gate of a complex computing system. Two wires and a ground. Right? Ajay wasn't sure. He pressed wires together. The first few tries had no results. The car started moving again.

The brake lights flashed.

"Was that me?" Ajay muttered to himself.

"There!" barked Charles. "Up on that hill."

The car rumbled over something rough, throwing Ajay around in the car. He struck his head painfully on the metal frame and swore.

Reaching back to the brake lights, he quickly found the place where his wires were exposed and worked the lights so they would flash when he wanted.

Not everyone knew Morse code, but any idiot could see an SOS. He flashed the signal out a few times as the car rumbled forward.

But who the hell was going to see it? He didn't think they were even on a road anymore. At best he had just created an inconvenience for the idiots driving around in this sedan.

He flashed the lights again.

"I got him," said Charles. "Get me a little closer and I'll give Shaleborn the worst headache of his life."

Ajay wondered what that meant. He pictured the big thug pointing a gun out the window at Shaleborn, but he couldn't worry about that guy. He needed to worry about himself.

He flashed another signal through the brake lights as the car stopped. Licking his dry lips, he grasped the lever and pulled as hard as he could.

It didn't move.

Ajay gasped out a sob. He imagined Kylie returning home, finding an empty house riddled with bullet holes. What if she went to live with her sister? Isabelle wasn't so bad. Was she?

Isabelle would let Kylie be who she wanted to be. She would let her sister become the dangerous person she apparently wanted to become. Isabelle herself had become that girl. But that wasn't the right thing for Kylie. Kylie was kind and caring. She had a warm heart and if she became a mercenary—a hired killer—that something in her would die.

Ajay ground his teeth, gripped the lever, and pulled.

Metal ground against metal and the lever moved. The trunk popped.

Ajay drew a long, slow breath. Kylie needed him. As much as he tried to let her become who she wanted to become, she needed him to be a guiding light. He couldn't let the kindness in her die. He couldn't let her become a killer.

He eased the trunk open, decanted himself onto a parking lot of coarse gravel, and took in his surroundings. He was near the canal. Opposite side from where he went into the trunk. A short distance away, the smooth boulder riprap by the water was buffered by tall weeds along the bank of the Harbor Basin.

"I won't let her be a killer," he muttered to himself.

Charles stood in front of the car. If Ajay ran for the cover, the thug would surely see him.

"I won't let her be a killer," he muttered again. This was going to take all the courage he could muster. It likely would be the end of him. "I won't let her be a killer."

Charles stood in a wide stance, rifle braced against the hood of the sedan. He aimed at a dark form across the water where a row of small boats sat in dock. "I've got the shot."

"Take it," said Spencer. "Then let's get out of here."

Ajay wouldn't let it happen. He picked a fist-sized rock from the ground, stepped forward, and struck Charles as hard as he could on the back of the head. He put every ounce of muscle he had into the blow, striking with all his fear and burning rage.

"Ow, fuck!" shouted Charles. He swung around and kicked Ajay. Ajay fell and skidded painfully across the gravel. He expected burning rage in Charles's eyes, but he only saw dry determination. Charles raised the gun.

On the other end of the parking lot, a massive pair of headlights rumbled over the curb.

A wave of red-orange light washed over them both. Charles, distracted, stared out at the Harbor Basin where a ball of flame consumed one of the yachts.

Charles blinked. "Spence?"

"I saw it," said Spencer. "We should—we should probably finish off the old man and get out of here."

The headlights grew closer. Ajay scrambled backward, but he couldn't move very fast. The whine of a huge electric motor hummed from the approaching vehicle. He recognized that hum.

Charles shook his head as if to clear it. He raised his rifle again, aimed—

Ajay's Winnebago slammed into Charles and the car.

Spencer swore as the car he was in spun from the impact. He slammed a foot on the accelerator and the sedan tore away through the parking lot, leaving Charles's body behind.

Ajay stared in horror at Charles's crumpled corpse glowing in the camper's bright headlights.

A dark form stepped out of the big vehicle. Kate held Ajay's cane in one hand and a pistol in the other.

"Almost thought I lost you when I stopped for this thing," she said, handing him the cane. "Thanks for the signal."

"I won't let Kylie be a killer," Ajay said.

Chapter Thirty-Six

Kylie was a killer.

She hit the ship's deck in a skid, sliding along the slick surface past a row of deck chairs. The guards were distracted by the explosion. As Hanna and Brian joined her, she popped open the guitar case and wrenched open the secret compartment. She drew a pair of pistols, tossed one to Hanna, and pocketed the extra ammo.

She was a killer. It was the only way to think of herself and still function. If she could be a killer, she could cut her way out of here.

"Over there!" shouted a guard. The distraction hadn't lasted long.

Hanna popped up from cover and fired two shots. They didn't have the crisp crack of a gunshot, but the thwip of something closer to a paintball. The neurotoxin took time to work, but it was the best on the market. Fast. Penetrating.

The guard dropped hard.

Kylie was a killer.

"Let's move," she said as Brian fumbled with his tech. Kylie launched herself from hiding and fired on the next guard. The two drone cars lifted from the landing pad and flew away. "There goes our ride." They would need to worry about that later.

Cullins ran for the door—the only entrance belowdecks that she could see. Kylie fired a shot—she was a killer and killers don't hesitate—but the downdraft from the drones battered her slow rounds.

She sprinted. "Cover me!" she shouted and didn't look as the snap of Hanna's fire sounded behind her.

Closer, she fired at the retreating man. Missed.

His hand mashed the emergency switch as he collapsed through the door.

Kylie dove. Through the comm, she said, "Singer and Sax, keep the deck clear. I'll find another way for you to get in."

"There's no time," said Austin. "Complete the task alone, Guitar."

Kylie fought back the shuddering panic. Alone? How could she?

"Second yacht just blew," said Hanna. "Who the hell is doing that?"

"It's not us," said Austin. "Is it us? Slick, check in."

The text feed remained blank. Had Jess been caught up in the explosion?

Kylie stood in a long, carpeted hallway. Red lights lined the intersection up ahead, and a blaring whistle warned of danger. She raised her pistol, forced herself to stay calm, and moved forward. Austin wanted her to finish the job. She'd finish the job.

Kylie was a killer.

And she was good at it.

A jolt rang the superyacht like a bell, throwing Kylie off her stride. She stopped at the corner of the carpeted hallway and got her bearings. The place was huge, and she could only guess where Cullins had disappeared to.

But when she rounded the corner, everything changed. The decor of the yacht changed from the decadent beauty of a luxury cruiser to the iron walls of a prison. She took a few steps on the metal mesh floor, careful to keep silent on the creaking surface.

I'm in the system, Jess finally texted through the comm. *What is going on up there?*

"Hurry," gasped Brian. "We've got incoming drones."

Kylie flashed Jess's map up on her fidget and took a second to absorb the data. The inside of the ship wasn't designed like a luxury yacht at all. This was a container ship, with rows and rows of sealed boxes lined up and stacked a dozen high. If anyone important moved through this ship, they sure as hell weren't living in the lap of luxury.

This was a prison.

She hit a T intersection, and both sides had stairs that descended into the metal mesh hallways below. Kylie didn't know what direction to take. She stood frozen, unsure what to do.

Then, to her right, a man shouted, "There she is!"

So she went left.

Kylie was fast. She kicked out over the rail and dropped to the next level down. From there, she sprinted down the length of the ship, passing sealed metal doors. She found another stairway down.

She shot the man before she even understood that he was there. He staggered back from the sting of the neuropellet, blinked a few times, then dropped. She kept running. Down, down, down, she descended into the echoing depths where everything was painted gray except for the stark red exit signs and the blue of the emergency service nodes.

"Where is he?" she hissed into her comm. She was out of breath already. Wasn't she supposed to be in better shape? "This is all wrong."

Hold tight. said Jess. *Data connection secured.*

Kylie strolled down a narrow hall, wishing she hadn't worn the bright red shirt. She passed a metal door with a round window. She stretched as tall as she could stand and peered inside. It was black. Her heart pounded. She activated the light on her fidget and shone it through the thick glass.

At first, she could see nothing. It looked like the window distorted the view to the point where nothing was recognizable. Then, the form inside shifted, and she saw the face.

She snapped her light closed and stumbled back, slamming against the opposite wall. The image of the man's features was burned in the back of her skull. Sunken eyes. Greasy, thin hair. Pasty skin. He was a ghoul trapped in the container. A monster waiting to be unleashed.

No. It couldn't be. She activated her light again and shone it at the door. She crept up to the glass surface and peered in again.

He was there, same as she had seen before, but he wasn't a monster. Now, his eyes pleaded for help.

"What the hell?" Kylie said aloud. A sudden headache pounded in her skull. It was the same pain that had struck her during the wargame. Her signal sense pulsed with a static buzz.

The first hint of Sonya Silver's presence was the tap of heels on the metal floor above. Kylie turned to see the woman approaching down the winding stairs. She wore a white skirt and matching top. Her hair was pulled back in a tight bun, and the expression on her face was one of dangerous annoyance.

"What are you doing here?" stuttered Kylie, but as soon as she said it, she knew the answer. Kylie tapped her comm. "Hey, Austin, I think I figured something out," she said, totally forgetting his codename.

There was no response.

"You know, we've been doing this for years," said Silver, stepping forward. "I've had students succeed or fail. I've had students crack under the pressure while others turned hard as diamonds." She was close enough that Kylie could smell her acidic perfume. "I've never had a kid peek behind the curtain."

"Austin, come on," Kylie hissed. She didn't know how to proceed without his advice. How was he cut off?

"They can't hear you," Silver said. She let out a long sigh as if it might be the most inconvenient thing she'd had to do in a long time. "Remember, you're speaking over a comm system that I own."

"I don't understand," said Kylie. "Why are you here?"

Silver gestured at the gray walls. "I think you know."

"It's your ship."

"You were meant to test my security, dear. I thought you made a good run at it, but things have gone a little south, haven't they? It's time to call this off."

"We had a good plan."

"Oh, I know the plan. Once Lang and Shaleborn are done mopping up the mess outside, we'll discuss with your team how things went. It'll be a good learning experience for everyone."

"What? They get to learn not to venture forward when it's unsafe? Or do they get to learn not to mess with megalomaniacal women?"

"I wish you hadn't looked in there," said Silver, nodding to the door.

"You have a guy in there. Big deal."

"I think you and I both know how big a deal this is. Your grandfather didn't raise you to be stupid."

"Papa didn't raise me at all."

Silver's eyes narrowed. "No, he didn't, did he? Tell me, what was it like growing up in a lab?"

Kylie's heart slammed in her throat. How much did Silver know? Was that why she was put on the mission? "What do you mean?"

"I know about your abilities, dear," said the woman. "You were supposed to be amazing, but so far I'm not impressed."

Kylie was torn between defending herself and denying everything. She settled for, "Maybe you aren't as good at your job as you think."

Silver's gaze flicked to the little window where Kylie had spied the man. "What matters now is whether you'll give me your full loyalty or disappear forever."

Disappear. It didn't sound like the friendly, fun kind of disappearing. When Silver said it, it almost sounded more like being stuffed in one of her metal boxes for years and years.

"What's wrong with them?" Kylie didn't know what made her ask, but a flutter of instinct told her that the face she saw behind the glass was different. Strange. There had been a flicker of oddity in his eyes that triggered fear in the very depths of her heart.

Silver tapped her ear. "Take care of it," she muttered. To Kylie, she said, "Come with me, dear. We have work to do."

Kylie didn't know what to do. The idea of following Silver made bile rise in the back of her throat. The woman's shark eyes gave Kylie the serious creeps, and there was still something wrong with the people in the cages.

Because that's what they were. Cages. How many people did they have locked up down here? How long had that man been living in that little metal box?

Silver was distracted by more chatter on her comm. This was Kylie's only chance.

Kylie cycled her comm channel. "Papa?" she said. "Papa, I need your help."

Then she ran into the echoing depths of the ship.

Chapter Thirty-Seven

POLICE DRONES BUZZED IN the skies, and the whole area was already being swept by the mid-level surveillance. Laser scans from the skies danced over the Winnebago and adjacent corpse.

Kate stared at the body glistening in the dark parking lot. "I killed him," she said, her eyes wide with horror.

Ajay pulled her into the weeds on the shore and motioned for her to keep her head down. "I'm sorry," he rasped. He could still remember the feeling he'd felt the first time he had killed someone, even if it had been from a thousand miles away. One thread of fate severed along with the millions that might have branched from it. "You did what you had to do. He was about to kill me." He knew that wouldn't help. "Plus, he was an asshole." That definitely wouldn't help.

"I killed him," she repeated. She shook her head as if to clear the cobwebs. "Is the other guy coming back?"

"I think we lie low," Ajay said. "I'm already running a routine that should keep us from getting too much attention from the police drones." As he spoke, a trio of blue and white flashes drifted over the hulking mass of the William A. Irvin ship museum. The massive ship was a black shadow over half their horizon. Thanks to the big metal structure, they probably hadn't gotten caught in too much aerial surveillance. "Yeah, we hide. Wait this out."

"Okay," Kate said, still distant. "Who were these fellas?"

"That guy's name was Charles, and he was an asshole," said Ajay, more brusquely than he intended. His heart thundered. This could work. Lying low and returning another time was their best bet. He could gather more information. Kylie would be fine.

"Papa?" said a familiar voice in Ajay's comm. "Papa, I need your help."

"Well, so much for hiding," muttered Ajay. Into the comm, he said, "Hold tight, hon. Where are you?"

"Charles," Kate said, still dazed.

Kylie's voice crackled in the comm. "I'm in the *Edmund*. Way down in the middle."

"We'll come to you."

"It was a trick," Kylie said. "The whole thing. They know about me."

A rush of horror washed over Ajay. They knew about her. That meant they knew her weaknesses. Where could they have learned anything about her?

Ajay took Kate's hand and drew her along the shore. They needed a boat. A boat or a drone car, but he didn't think his odds of stealing one of the ridiculously expensive drone cars was great in this part of town. "Lie low," Ajay said to Kylie. "We're on our way."

"He was supposed to see me and retreat," Kate said.

"It was Silver," Kylie said. "There are people here. Trapped people. I don't know what to do, Papa."

Ajay didn't know what to tell her. He couldn't bring himself to tell her to ignore the trapped people, but, also, he had no idea what that was all about. Trapped people? Slaves? Prisoners? What kind of yacht was this?

Finally, he settled on, "Do whatever you think is right," but he regretted it as soon as he'd said it. From her perspective it would mean freeing the prisoners, and what risk would that put her in? He needed to hurry.

Kate crouched as a police drone hovered overhead. She muttered something to herself.

"Hang in there, Kate," Ajay said. He sped through the controls on his cane. It was so nice having it back. "Kylie, just stay safe, okay?"

"Yeah, Papa," Kylie said. The comm crackled again and she was gone.

Police drones fell into two categories. The first were the big city drones, designed to manage a large and dangerous population. They were usually outdated tech maintained exceptionally well. All the security patches had to be in perfect shape and the operators learned how to use the drones in disconnected mode. With the drones configured to severely limit operator input while in operation, they were almost impossible to hack while in flight.

The second category of drones was the machines rolling out to smaller towns across the state. The smaller police forces were decades late to move to a drone-heavy force, but that meant they had modern, up-to-date equipment. It also meant the operators had never dealt with real, serious security threats. They'd never faced skilled hackers running modern tech.

Duluth wasn't a large city, but it also wasn't a small town. These drones were geared out with the very best security enhancements. New tech.

But not inexpertly operated. The police force here understood the importance of disconnected operation. The drones were sent to scan the area. It was a task-oriented operation. Until they completed their task, they were completely unhackable. Ajay set a routine on his machine that would loop indefinitely. If one of the drones finished its task, then he'd see about taking it and plant his own code in the back corners of the crafts software.

Until then, they were on their own.

"There's a drone denial barrier," he muttered, reviewing the data. "It's interfering with aerial traffic over the whole basin."

"Okay," Kate said, her voice on the edge of panic. "Okay. This is fine. I'm fine."

"It's fine," Ajay said. She'd already had over a minute to adjust to her new status as a killer, and he didn't have more time to be sympathetic. He'd *never* had time to be sympathetic, and he full well knew that was a problem. "Did you see where Charles was aiming that rifle of his?"

"Charles?"

"The guy you hit."

"Oh. Um, no."

"Never mind." Ajay led the way along the edge of the tall grass, expertly dodging between the scanning fields of two drones. "There are two mercenaries up there pinning down a guy who I think can help us get onto the yacht."

Kate glanced out at the Harbor Basin. Two yachts burned out on the water already. A third sped back toward the Lift Bridge. "Are you sure we want to go out there?"

A streak from high in the sky struck the remaining yacht. The explosion lit up the shore in a flash of its fiery explosion and a wave of heat rolled over them. Ajay had seen strikes like that before. That was the attack of a Thunderhead drone, apparently the third. One for each yacht.

"This is bad," he said.

"What?"

"Thunderheads, and they're ignoring the denial barrier." Shit. He walked faster along the rocky shore. Duluth's shores were piled with infuriatingly smooth stones, and he nearly twisted his ankles half a dozen times. "That means we've got government involvement."

"Yeah," Kate said. "Police."

"Police are privatized. Thunderheads mean military approval and a larger scale operation." And Kylie was in the middle of it. "We need to get Kylie and Austin out of this."

They had finally reached the point where they were behind the two mercenaries who had Shaleborn pinned. Ajay still didn't have control of any drones, and asking Kate to shoot someone sounded like a bad idea. Ajay armed the taser on his cane and stumbled forward toward the mercenaries.

"Did you see that?" he slurred.

The nearest mercenary looked up. He was a big man, but almost invisible against the shadowed lawn. "Get out of here, geezer," he said.

Far away, flashes of white lit the superyacht as the giant ship approached the bridge. Thunderheads weren't enough to stop the giant ship, though. It plowed forward, but in the light, Ajay could see dozens of drones swarming it. It was under attack, and Kylie was in there somewhere.

"You know," Ajay said, staggering forward, doing his best impression of a drunken idiot. "Back in the war, I used to run swarms like that all the time. It's a cluster swarm. Overwhelm the ship's defenses. Get enough drones past the outer hull that you can cause trouble with the crew for hours. Occupy the guards to distract them from a more substantive assault."

The man's jaw tightened. "I said get out of here."

Ajay waved it off as if it were a joke. "Of course, it takes a whole crew to run a good, coordinated drone attack. Automated sequences are fine, but if you depend too much on AI without supervision, you tend to get—" Ajay glanced at the control unit in the man's hand. "Oh, is that a gen seven? I never used one of those. I'd love to take a look."

He didn't give the man time to respond. Ajay jabbed his cane's taser straight at the man's chest.

The mercenary caught the cane in one meaty fist. The control unit dropped to the ground. Electricity from Ajay's taser crackled inches shy of the guy's body.

Shit.

The other mercenary, slower on the uptake, scrambled over to help. He was out of position. Distracted.

The big mercenary wrenched the cane out of Ajay's grasp and threw it aside. He unclipped the holster of his pistol.

Kate slugged the second mercenary, sending him sprawling across the round stones by the water. She followed up, grabbing his gun and tossing it into the water, and then pounded him against the stones until he stopped fighting. She drew Ajay's pistol and pointed it at the remaining mercenary.

Ajay stared at the barrel of the mercenary's gun. "You know," he said, "I think we could probably talk about this."

The flash of police drones approached from behind. The mercenary glanced up at them and frowned. He stepped to the side so that he had Kate and Ajay both in his view. "You kill him?" he asked.

At first, Ajay didn't know who he was talking about.

Kate said, "He's not dead. Just knocked him out." The man moaned.

Ajay said, "We could probably still work this out."

The man touched his comm and said, "Position's compromised. Moving out."

He bent down slowly to retrieve his drone control unit.

"Leave it," Kate said.

The man paused. He looked from Ajay to Kate, then back again. "I'll shoot him."

"I'll shoot you," Kate said, not missing a beat.

"She will," Ajay said.

The mercenary took a step back, then retreated into the night.

Ajay couldn't move for a million years. His muscles were frozen in concrete, stiff and unresponsive. A fishy breeze blew across the Harbor Basin, and something splashed in the dark, but Ajay was transfixed.

The spell was only broken when Kate said, "Well."

Ajay picked up his cane and scanned his options. There were a dozen signals nearby, none of which appeared to give him access to the superyacht where he might be able to help Kylie.

"Are you hidden, dear?" he asked through his comm.

Kate responded in a droll tone, "I'm right here, hon."

"Not you." Ajay shook his cane. The water hadn't ruined it, but it hadn't done it any favors, either. "Kylie, can you hear me?"

"I'm fine, Papa," Kylie said. "I think I know where I need to go."

"Your main comm is down, and I don't have access to the ship's systems."

"We've got an underwater node," said Kylie. "Close hull connection and a repeater. You can connect through that."

Ajay checked his signals again. One flitted at the edge of his range, dancing in and out of the nominal data fidelity. "I think I see it. I'll need to get closer. Hang tight."

"Papa?"

"Yes, dear?"

"I can do this on my own."

"I'm aware."

"But I don't want to."

"Understood."

"I think I see an access node," Kylie whispered.

Some deep parental instinct in Ajay told him he wasn't going to be able to stop her from doing whatever it was she had planned. The best he could do was figure out how to help.

Nearby, a boat detached itself from the docks. Ajay rushed toward the water's edge and used the light from his cane to wave the driver down.

"What are you doing?" Kate hissed.

"We need a ride," Ajay said, still waving.

"How do you know that guy's friendly?"

Ajay spun back to look at her. "You're looking at this all wrong." He stalked up the hill. The unconscious mercenary groaned. "It's not about being friendly. There are things going on here that are way beyond us. Those three ships out there were taken down by Thunderhead drones. Three of them. That's a dense cluster of weaponized drones, even for a heavy urban area or an area with a significant potential military threat. Down in the Twin Cities, there were swarms of those damn things, but if they had a mission to complete it, would still take hours for them to converge."

"I'm still not catching your drift."

Across the channel the boat swung toward them, shining its spotlight on the shore.

"Thunderheads means government activity. Military. This isn't a drug runner getting captured in a sting. It's not a situation of two mercenary operations conflicting in their goals. This is bigger than that. It's an attack on our land. The first foray into some kind of takeover."

Kate shielded her eyes against the approaching spotlight. "You're sounding pretty paranoid, Ajay."

The boat ground up against an enormous boulder, and the spotlight swung away from them. Inside the damaged boat, a figure moved in the shadows.

Ajay stepped in front of Kate. He raised his hands in the air. "We don't want any trouble," he called out.

"Those guys had me pinned down," said Regis Shaleborn. "I wasn't getting out of there if you didn't come."

"Now I need your help."

"It's hard times, old man."

"Get us to the ship," said Ajay. "That's all I ask."

Regis pressed his lips together. "One condition."

"What's that?"

Regis pointed at the man on the ground. "Bring that guy. I have some questions."

Chapter Thirty-Eight

"I THINK I SEE an access node," Kylie whispered to Papa through the comm. She had asked for help, and she needed it, but now that she was hidden in the black recesses of a storage closet, she was starting to feel a little better.

The ship creaked under her, shifting slightly.

If she'd had all her abilities, she would be able to connect to the node remotely. It was designed to connect to handheld systems so that a sailor could use the interface on their own fidget to manipulate the local controls. Unfortunately, her device didn't have the codes to connect, and she didn't have her override tool. No matter what she tried, she couldn't make the connection stick. She needed physical contact to exchange keys, then she could work her way into the wireless network.

And it was only a few steps away, across the hall. She peeked around the corner. This would be easier if Austin could talk her through it. He always had a knack for knowing when something was worth the risk.

The comm was dead. She had to make her own decisions. Kylie stepped forward into the hall.

"Boss says she went this way."

Kylie ducked back into the cover of the closet before the big soldier rounded the corner. His footsteps rattled the metal floors and his form filled the narrow hall right up to the low ceiling. He stopped outside the closet and peered into the darkness. Kylie squeezed farther back between two metal crates that smelled like charcoal.

She pulled a natty tarp over her head as he flicked the lights on and stepped inside.

Risk.

She hadn't done well at risk management no matter how important Mr. Lang said it was. Was it riskier to try to hide in the tiny room? Her position was good. The big man wouldn't find her unless he got all the way back into the closet. But if she hid like that, she'd be doomed if he found her. She didn't even have her neuropellet gun drawn.

If she shot him, he might get an emergency call out before he fell unconscious. That would draw more assholes down on her.

It was the risk of doing nothing versus the risk of acting.

Silver's voice sounded over the comm clipped to the man's shoulder. "Make a sweep of the lower decks, then get back up here. The meeting is starting soon, and we need all the help we can get."

"Yes, sir," the big guy replied. He stepped deeper into the storage room.

What was the meeting? What did Silver need help with?

Did this change Kylie's risk assessment? On one hand, the big man was going to keep looking for her. On the other hand, if she shot him and he didn't return to the main deck, he might be missed. Silver herself was expecting him now.

Then again, it sounded like they might be distracted.

By someone. Who was gathering at this meeting? Was Austin using this as another distraction to give her a chance to escape? What was she supposed to do?

Kylie was frozen with indecision. Her palms got clammy and gross, and all her muscles ached from the tension.

The man was a statue in the doorway. Through a narrow gap in her cover, Kylie could see his tightly laced black boots. She could smell the stale sweat that permeated his all-black fatigues. He could have reached out and grabbed her, she was so close.

Instead, he turned and left. Kylie released a long, slow breath.

Seconds later she was across the hall, her fingers dancing over the controls on the access node, pairing her device with the ship's local control unit. The keys were enormously complex and used a rotating pattern. Her ability to access functions remotely wouldn't last long. She returned to her hiding place and scanned through the data now available to her over the wireless.

The ship trembled beneath her. Either the *Edmund* had impacted something, or it was under attack. Maybe both.

Inventories. Explosives. Lots of them. Weapons of all types, and Kylie recognized an array of illegal war drones. Papa had described them to her one day as he had shown her his own illegal arsenal. This was bad stuff. Programmed assassin drones.

And they all had orders.

"The meeting," she whispered to herself, recognizing a few of the names on the list. "It's Frontier Arms."

There, in the middle of a long list, was Isabelle Garver. Her sister.

These drones were programmed with kill targets, but they would need to be launched from close to their target, beyond the drone denial field.

And soon.

Chapter Thirty-Nine

Adrenaline made everything worse for Lang. Nausea and dizziness incapacitated him for minutes at a time. He retched and clawed at his own eyes. He doubled his meds, but there was only so much he could do.

He sat in the Lift Bridge tower and watched the old man Ajay Andersen take down a couple thugs. Seeing that old bastard sent a new wave of nausea through Lang's guts. Rage boiled from somewhere deep behind his chest, and he wanted to get his big hands around the old man's neck and squeeze until his head popped. Lang had to rest his scope at his side for several deep breaths before he was up to watching again.

But there was too much else happening.

The comms were out. Another thug lurked where the comm router had been. It was likely destroyed, putting their entire operation at risk.

They could still use insecure comms, but any encryption system they used would be easily cracked. It would only be a matter of time before someone listened in on their plans. He had to trust that the team would follow their schedules.

Not that this was Lang's mission.

"You gotta look at this," said Giles from the other side of the tower. "Something is happening on the *Edmund.*"

Lang wrenched himself up from his nest and crossed the tower. Austin crouched by the overlook. Right at the entrance to the canal below sat the huge ship. A fiery explosion rocked the deck. Through his scope, Lang saw two of the kids running from a couple of guards. They hid behind a conning tower, but it wouldn't keep them safe for long. By the look of it, the whole mission was shot.

"It's your call, kid," Lang said.

"Look." Giles nudged Lang's scope so it pointed to a spot over the lake's dark waters.

At first, Lang couldn't see anything. The night had swallowed the scene and what he was supposed to be seeing was camouflaged against the rippling waves.

Then, he caught movement. A blade cut the waves as it sliced across his view. Water swelled in the wake of a massive underwater form.

"A submarine?" he asked, amazed.

"It's not in our plans. It's not even part of our outlying conditions." The boy peered through a pair of binoculars. "We don't know who it is, and we don't know why they're there." He let the binoculars drop. "Comms are down. Non-comm signaling is impossible because Kylie is inside the ship. Insecure comms might work, but there are a lot of ears listening out there. We'd be broadcasting our location as well as our strategy." He stared at Lang with sunken eyes. "We're screwed."

"Good," Lang grunted. He pushed away from the rail and crossed to the other side of the tower. He peered at Shaleborn's boat as it sped across the harbor. In the long expanse of water behind them, a one-person drone car swept close to the water's surface. Did Shaleborn even know he had a tail? "You're about to learn the most important lesson of them all, kid."

"What's that?" asked Giles.

"What to do when everything goes to shit."

Chapter Forty

THE SPEEDBOAT RAN SILENT and fast, cutting the choppy waters of the Duluth Harbor Basin like a honed blade. Yachts ahead burned against the deepening darkness of the sky. Frigid droplets of lake water stippled Ajay's face as they blasted over low waves. Regis Shaleborn drove, silent and brooding, the wind cutting at his short hair.

"How do we know we can trust this guy?" whispered Kate.

"Didn't you *just* tell me I was paranoid?" said Ajay. "I don't trust *anyone*."

A smile tugged at the corners of Kate's mouth. "Do you trust me?"

Ajay checked their prisoner's bonds. They seemed tight.

"He's waking up," Kate said. A line of tension hardened her features, but Ajay knew he could rely on her. She'd been through a lot, but there seemed to be no end to the depth of her good old farmer stoicism. "Look tough."

Look tough. Ajay didn't know if he had ever looked tough. Even in his prime, he'd been the kind of guy to sit behind a screen moving mountains rather than flexing muscles and acting mean. He needed to know who this guy was, though. For that, they needed to interrogate him. And fast. The boat passed the first of three flaming wrecks. Police drones swept the skies, blue and red lights making a lightning strobe of the sky.

The man shifted in his seat.

Ajay licked his dry lips. He hated this. What, was he going to torture this guy for information? Would that even work? The guy probably had training on how to resist the worst things Ajay could imagine. This man was a soldier. The toughest of the toughs. He was a mercenary.

The man's eyes opened.

"Hey," Ajay said in his toughest voice. "How are you? We didn't cut off your circulation, did we?" Dammit.

"Real tough, Ajay," said Kate.

"Sorry."

The man mumbled something incoherent.

"Look," said Ajay, moving closer. "I want to let you go, but we really need to know who you're working for."

They passed another yacht. An expanding grease film surrounded a scattering of flotsam. The air smelled of burning wood and oil.

Regis hollered over the roar of the waves, "What the hell are you doing?"

"Interrogating him," said Kate.

"That's not how it's done," said Regis.

"Who do you work for?" growled Ajay, finally making eye contact with the man.

"The United States Government," said the mercenary. The man was slovenly, with a week-old beard and an odor that oddly reminded Ajay of mustard.

"You don't look like police. Are you National Guard?"

The man pulled his thin lips back in a sneer. "Independent contractor."

"A mercenary. Frontier?"

"Those fuckers."

"What's your mission?"

The mercenary tested his bonds. Kate had tied him with zip ties and connected him to the anchor loop. He wasn't going anywhere.

"Let me be more specific," Ajay said. He stopped trying to sound tough. "Why did your people try to kill me?"

They passed the third burning yacht. This one was still afloat, its shape a hulking black mass in the night like a giant made of embers and smoke reaching from the lake high into the night sky. Regis banked around it and steered straight for the Lift Bridge.

"You were on the list," the mercenary said.

Ajay raised an eyebrow at Kate. Was it that easy to get these guys to talk? He'd always expected decent mercenaries to be a lot tougher. Maybe this guy wasn't the most elite soldier modern warfare had to offer.

"How long is this list?" Kate asked.

"And how high up it was I?" added Ajay.

The man stared forward as they sped under the Lift Bridge. The boat cut through still water for several long seconds, and the giant superyacht loomed like a giant on the dark horizon.

"Rough him up some," Regis shouted from the helm. "We're almost there."

"I'm not going to rough him up." Ajay gripped his cane. He got a flickering connection and set it searching for the signal that would supposedly give him a back door into the ship. To the man, he said, "What are you trying to stop?"

"Cut me loose," the mercenary said. "Let me swim. I'll tell you everything if you let me swim away before they get you."

Ajay cast a look at Kate. She shrugged and cut the ties on the man's feet but not his hands.

"You'll go free," said Ajay. "But you need to talk first."

The mercenary glanced behind him. The lights of Duluth glowed against the twilight. A shadow passed in front of the Great Lakes Aquarium. Ajay blinked. Was something following them, or was that a police drone running dark?

"There's a list," he said. "You're on it, Ajay Andersen. So is that Shaleborn guy over there. It's a long list. I don't know who made it, but someone sees you all as a threat."

"Was it really the government?" Ajay asked.

"I—I don't know."

Kate leaned forward. "You're just going down the list killing people?"

He cast another glance backward. A hint of panic flashed through his eyes. "They wanted certain people out of the way for the leadership meeting."

"Whose leadership meeting?" asked Ajay.

"It's the one Olexie mentioned," said Kate.

Ajay leaned forward. The aroma of burning yacht was strong behind the freshwater spray. "Was Olexie Sokolov on your list?"

"We didn't kill everyone on the list. Some people we were just supposed to keep busy. Useful people. Other people were supposed to be eliminated permanently."

"Because we're threats." Ajay poked the man in the chest with his cane. "Because nobody could think of a way to keep us out of trouble without killing us."

The man chuckled. "You have no idea how this works, do you?" He tugged at his bonds again. "They probably decided to kill you because it was cheaper. This is government work. The budget rules all."

"Funny talk from a mercenary."

The guy shrugged. "We're the only ones who are honest around here."

"Who else is on this list? Sonya Silver?"

A flash of recognition crossed the man's eyes, but all he said was, "We didn't get the full list."

Ajay's cheaters flashed with a connection alert. A new signal appeared, so he swiped through the buggy controls on his cane. The data stream was weak and fluctuating, but the closer they came to the enormous ship, the stronger it got. It was the signal Kylie had talked about.

And it was a way into the ship. To Kylie. To everything that was happening in this messed-up harbor. He started a routine that would expand his influence and give him access to the ship's internal systems.

It would take time to run, but now that he had the connection, things looked good. When it started, he turned back to the man.

"Who do you work for?" Ajay asked.

The man opened his mouth to answer.

A muzzle flashed fifty feet behind the boat, and the man's head exploded.

"Down!" Ajay cried, pulling Kate away.

More flashes. The white shell of the boat cracked under a staccato impact. Above, the silhouette of a drone car moved across the gray-blue sky.

Regis swerved away from the line of fire. "Take the helm," he yelled over the noise.

Ajay scrambled forward, unsteady on the slick floor. He fell, slamming his thigh into the bench, but he gripped the handhold along the guardrail and pulled himself forward. He pushed past Regis and took the helm.

He had driven boats before. They weren't complicated. Steering wheel. A lever for acceleration. Easy stuff. He mashed the accelerator all the way forward.

Regis returned fire, wildly shooting out into the night. Ajay banked, making a broad sweeping arc directly under the Lift Bridge.

Gunshots cracked through the night, and the cabin around him shattered in a spray of fiber and plexiglass.

"Don't be so damn predictable," Regis shouted at Ajay.

Ajay jerked the wheel to one side, banking hard toward the superyacht. The ship loomed over them in the dark now, its black underbelly sitting high above them in the night. As soon as he was pointed in that direction, he juked left.

This time the shots from the night went wide, missing their boat.

Ajay was about to whoop with triumph when he felt the water on his feet. It sloshed around his ankles, soaking his slacks. Everywhere it touched, his skin went numb from the cold.

And it was rising fast.

Kate fired into the night. Ajay kept his pattern as random as he could manage, but they were still too far from the superyacht. The lights from the giant ship lit the water ahead, illuminating their boat so the flyer behind them had no problem finding them in the dark waters. It was a bad position, and it was only going to get worse.

"Hold on!" Ajay shouted. He slammed the throttle to reverse and yanked the wheel to the right.

The deceleration was almost enough to throw Ajay out of his seat. Kate stumbled forward past him, sloshing in the water on the deck of the boat.

"Sorry!" Ajay called to her.

"I'm fine," she snapped. "Just drive." She popped the clip from the gun and slammed another in.

The drone car whooshed overhead. It swept forward, banked around, and settled squarely in the long searchlights beaming down from the superyacht.

Regis stepped forward, braced himself against the railing, and fired. Kate braced herself, held the gun in two hands, and squeezed off three shots.

Ajay couldn't tell who had hit it, but the drone car sputtered and the rotors hitched. It dipped away and sped off into the dark, followed by a splash.

Ajay punched the throttle and veered toward the ship. The boat lagged, weighed down by the water still gushing onto its deck. Kate pulled herself back up and crouched next to Ajay, taking the wheel from him.

With a nod, she handed him his cane. "You might want to hold onto this."

"Thanks."

Ajay jabbed his controls. He needed to hurry. They'd be swimming soon if they didn't find a way to get onto the ship.

"There's a lift," Regis said. "For lifeboats."

There. Its controls were clear once he knew what he was looking for. A dozen lifts ran from the side of the ship down to the water, designed to lower whole boats from the deck above to sea level. He told the device to unfold. Prepare to transport passengers.

Because their boat wasn't going to make it.

The motor sputtered. Water sloshed over the front of the deck. Regis dove into the water, swimming toward the superyacht.

Then, silence.

And the boat sank.

Chapter Forty-One

Survival.

Kylie had the data from the access node. She knew a dozen ways to escape. To survive.

But what was survival? What was it really? Was survival the continuation of drawn breath, or the ability to step out into the world and *live*?

Hanna and Brian escaped their pursuers by venturing down into the ship. Kylie saw them in glimpses through the holographic display of her fidget. Flashes of their images appeared as they descended through the massive ship. Silver had them cornered. There were too many enemies in the ship for Kylie to fight. She needed a better solution.

Or she needed to leave.

Where was Papa? A life raft lift on the edge of the ship had moved several minutes ago, but nobody had come up yet. If he was down there, what was he waiting for? She dared not signal for him. Anybody could pick up the unencrypted comms, and she simply couldn't risk it.

Not if she wanted to survive.

The motor room sat in the back of the ship. If she could reach it and the accompanying control room, she'd own the ship. Everything ran through the engineering complex, and if she had it, she could even override the locks keeping people in their cages. None of those systems were connected to the access node that she controlled. This would be a way to free people from their prisons, stop the invasion, and survive. She could finally survive.

To get there, she needed to cross the bridge in the center of the ship. The mesh of metal and plastic ran across the vast open expanse and would be easily guarded. She checked the video feeds for the millionth time. Nobody was nearby. Her wireless access wouldn't last, and she needed to hurry. Anxiety kept her rooted in place, but panic drove her forward. Between the two, she was stretched thin and squashed all at once.

"Here we go," she whispered to herself. "Here we go." She moved from her hiding place. Every step clacked noisily against the metal floor no matter how hard she tried to walk quietly. She was reminded of the bright flare of color that was her shirt against the blinding gray of the inner ship's decor.

She came to the bridge and stepped onto the long metal expanse. It creaked under her foot, but she forced herself forward. The ship swayed, a silent monster in the night.

"You were supposed to be the impressive one," said Sonya Silver, stepping around a corner up ahead. She blocked the way forward. "The one with abilities."

Kylie resisted the urge to check her surveillance connection. Hadn't Silver been on the other side of the boat? The way was supposed to be clear, but that niggling feeling in the back of her skull told her something was wrong.

"It's all right," said a voice behind Kylie. "Silver explained it all to us, same as she tried to explain it to you."

Kylie turned to see Hanna standing on the other end of the bridge. Brian, behind her, had a sheepish look on his face.

"What are you doing?" Kylie hissed.

"It's her ship." The metal bridge creaked under Hanna's feet. "The mission to infiltrate it was never supposed to succeed."

"I know that," said Kylie. "But there's something else going on here."

A slip of a smile creased the corners of Silver's mouth. "This was only meant to draw out your latent skills, my dear. A failure as far as experiments go."

Kylie stared at the woman. What did she know about Kylie's latent skills? If Papa hadn't disabled them, would she have given herself away sooner? Probably. Kylie had never been very good at resisting the temptation. But why did Silver want to draw Kylie out?

"I don't know what you're talking about," Kylie said. It sounded unconvincing even in her ears.

"It was your sister," said Silver as if reading her thoughts. "She and her meteoric rise in the Frontier Arms organization. She's picking up all the best contracts these days, you know. When our intel team dug into her background, we discovered she had a sister. It wasn't hard after that. We just needed to get you to prove what you were capable of."

Kylie was in the middle of the bridge, with Silver on one side and Hanna on the other. Brian stood to one side. She didn't think she needed to worry about him.

"Is that why you tried to have my grandfather killed?" Kylie asked. "To get him out of the way?"

Silver's eyes widened for a fraction of a second, an expression Kylie caught but didn't quite understand. Surprise? Fear? "We don't have anyone trying to kill Mr. Andersen," said Silver. "Just like we don't have people trying to kill Mr. Shaleborn."

"Then that's—"

"That's right, dear," said Silver. "That was Frontier."

"But *you* work for Frontier."

"The organization has been undergoing some growing pains," said Silver. "It will soon thrive under new leadership."

"That's what the meeting in Duluth is," said Hanna. "I figured it out right away."

"Isabelle," said Kylie. That's why her sister's name was on the assassin drones' list. She was a contender for control, and therefore a threat to Silver.

Silver took a step forward. She was a lunge away now, and Hanna moved forward to match. "You have quite a family," Silver said. "But we all come with complications, don't we?"

The pieces started to fall into place. Silver's school wasn't an enemy of Frontier. They were just another group of mercenaries that Frontier Arms absorbed into the fold the way they'd absorbed so many others. Silver had no intention of letting that happen without a fight. She had always run an organization bent on training upper-class children to be survivors. And sometimes killers. Kylie had no doubt of that. The training she'd gone through gave her confidence. It gave her skills.

But most of all, it eroded every hesitation she ever had about hurting people. Killing them.

Yet, Kylie still hesitated. She *had* been a failure.

Silver didn't want to work for Frontier Arms. She wanted *control* of it.

That was where the ship came in. It was going to give her influence over northern Minnesota.

Once she controlled Frontier, she would control everything. Frontier Arms was ninety percent of the standing police force. They heavily supplemented the National Guard and the various emergency services. By the time the United States government realized there was an all-out mercenary war, the fighting would be over.

And what did Kylie care? It was all bad. Why was one mercenary group controlling the police any scarier than another? It wasn't. It was all bad. Just… bad.

"People are going to get killed," Kylie whispered. Isabelle would get killed. Transitions were dangerous, especially when they were executed like this. Silver wasn't subtle. She was brutal, straightforward, and murderous. "Innocent people."

"This is what you already signed up for, dear," said Silver, taking another step forward. "The people killed tonight are criminals. The worst of the worst."

"My sister."

"A killer."

Kylie shot a pleading look back at Hanna but was met with an iron glare.

"Don't screw this up for us, Kylie," said Hanna. She was a knot of tension. "Silver's letting us in on the top level. This is going to change everything."

Kylie shook her head. "It's transition, but it's not change. Don't you understand? This is just mercenary control swapping one leader for another. You're not helping anyone. Frontier needs to be split up."

Silver scoffed. "Think of all the good we can do once Frontier is under my control."

Kylie barely knew she was going to act. Hesitation wasn't even an option. She drew her pistol and shot Silver in the face, then swung to face Hanna.

Too slow. Hanna struck Kylie's gun hand with a chop, sending the pistol clattering across the rafters below. She followed with a sharp kick, snapping the air next to Kylie's head.

Kylie staggered backward. Silver stepped forward and wrapped an arm around Kylie's neck, heaving back and up. Kylie's feet came off the metal floor. Silver yanked her up and away. The woman's grip was like a crocodile's jaws. She was going to throw her over the edge, so Kylie hooked a leg on the railing.

Silver gasped. Her grip weakened from the neuropellet, but Kylie still couldn't pull free. She needed to buy time.

Hanna slugged Kylie in the stomach. Kylie caught a flash of the other girl's rage, a flare of red in her otherwise pale complexion. Kylie kicked, but she wasn't fast enough. Wasn't flexible enough.

Still, she didn't stop to think. She didn't bother to hesitate. Kylie fought, finally releasing herself from the shackles of all the complicated decisions that had weighed her down. This was clear to her. She needed to fight, and she needed to fight hard.

Then, Hanna had a knife in her hand. Her teeth were bloody. Maybe one of Kylie's kicks had landed. Hanna blocked the next wild kick, redirecting it to strike the railing.

A slash and Kylie felt the knife bite her ankle. The next kick sprayed blood across Hanna's face.

Silver's grip weakened. Kylie released the railing, wrenched herself around, and pulled free. Silver staggered away. Up close, Kylie could see her struggling with the effects of the neuropellet. How was she still awake?

Then the woman had something sharp in her hand. A knife?

A needle.

She plunged it into her own leg and screamed as if the pain were the jagged teeth of a pack of dogs.

A flash of a blade, but Kylie dodged Hanna's attack on pure instinct. Shaleborn's training flowed through her muscles, and she swung around in a snap to strike. The knife flew over the edge and Hanna stepped back, holding her stung wrist.

"Bitch," Hanna said.

"We're on the same side," gasped Kylie.

"Never." Hanna clenched her fists.

"Silver used us. She's trying to make us something we're not." Kylie glanced at Silver, who writhed on the bridge behind her. "This plan of hers is crazy, Hanna. It's going to get a lot of innocent people killed."

"She told me the plan," Hanna said. "People like you don't understand this kind of thing. You sit in your filthy homes and whine about how nothing ever goes your way. You complain about the missing middle class and how very hard it is to advance your place in the world. Then something like this comes around." She gestured wide at the ship around them. "And you pass it up."

"It's murder," said Kylie.

"It's opportunity! I'm going to be on top of it all, Kylie. Once things settle, I'll have control of a significant chunk of the operations. Yeah, maybe things go badly and someone gets hurt, but if I'm in charge, I can make sure everything goes smoothly. I can arrange all the policing and every mission. This is what power gets you. The ability to do things right."

Silver bit back another scream and glared up at Kylie with hooded eyes. She grasped the railing in one hand and pulled herself to her feet. Kylie stared at her. The woman had counteracted the neurotoxin with—something. It didn't look like it was going well.

"The plan moves forward," Silver said through gritted teeth. "Hanna, throw her over the ledge."

For a fraction of a second, Kylie thought she saw something like hesitation in the bigger girl's eyes. It was followed by a shudder of determination. An icy burn in the girl's eyes.

Then, Hanna's head snapped forward and she blinked rapidly. Her lips pursed, and her fists went slack. She dropped to her knees.

Brian stood behind her, his pistol still aimed where her head had been. He met Kylie's gaze, then focused on Silver behind her. "Get back," he ordered the woman.

Silver didn't get back. The skin around the swollen welt on her face was red and inflamed where Kylie's neurotoxin pellet had hit her. Her pulse pounded in her neck. In one fluid movement, she drew a gun and fired. Brian cried out in pain.

Kylie dropped low and charged, hoping to bowl the woman over. Brian returned fire, striking Silver in the shoulder and neck. Kylie lowered her shoulder and charged, not to tackle, but to just rush past.

But her hit struck harder than she expected. The woman crumpled away, toppling over the railing. Kylie grasped at her, but Silver fell, striking the mesh floor of the bridge below.

The door on the far side of the bridge was still open, so Kylie ran through it. Her connection to the wireless died before she could bring the map back up, but she remembered the way. The motor room sat in the back of the ship, far past the network of interlocking bridgeways.

Silver shouted from below. Brian was gone. Heavy boots pounded on metal floors. Kylie ran.

Chapter Forty-Two

Ajay watched Regis Shaleborn climb onto the lifeboat and push the button. A mechanical thump sounded and the lowered boat started to rise.

It would have been perfect if Ajay and Kate hadn't still been in the frigid water clinging to a sinking boat.

"He left us," Kate gasped. Wet hair clung to the side of her face.

"Can hardly blame him," said Ajay. "I wouldn't want a couple of old folks slowing me down, either."

The superyacht had all but stopped below the Lift Bridge. Its tug had abandoned it in the canal after the yachts were destroyed. Above, white lights illuminated the ship's sleek hull. The sheer enormity of the ship stunned Ajay. It towered above him like a monster out of some old movie. Shadows played across the rough waters in the canal. To their backs, Ajay and Kate felt the looming banks of the canal rising high above. They wouldn't be able to scale that. As the speedboat slipped deeper under the waves, he wondered if they would be able to tread water without drowning before the police rescue vehicles arrived to arrest them.

Not that there were any police vehicles in the area. Ajay hadn't seen the telltale red and blue flashes of survey drones in quite some time.

The numbing cold of Lake Superior made his arms heavy. He fought a hard shiver and gripped his cane tight. It wouldn't do to lose that now. Not that it would do him much good if he drowned.

"Well," Kate said.

"Well." Ajay sloshed over closer to her. The boat was gone, and all they had was each other. "This isn't great."

"No."

"Probably can't get worse."

Kate glared at him.

The rattle like the popping of fireworks sounded above the waters nearby. Ajay flinched, swam a short distance, and tried to see where the sound was coming from.

Regis returned fire from his rising platform as shots pinged off the hull beside him. He shouted something that Ajay couldn't quite hear.

"That guy from the drone is still alive," gasped Kate. "We need to get out of here."

Ajay's cane was somewhat water resistant, but he couldn't use it in the water. The holographic interface faltered if the projector was wet at all. He couldn't recall the lift.

More gunfire. This time, it struck the lift closer to Regis. Ajay spotted the muzzle flash a short distance away. The dark form of the fallen drone floated in the rough waters. A man crouched atop it with a rifle aimed up at the ship.

"I don't like this," Ajay said.

"No kidding."

"I mean…" He tried to think. Cold seeped into his brain. "I don't like what I'm going to have to do."

Ajay dove deep, feeling the cold of the deep penetrate his numb skin as he swam under the murky water toward the back of the drone car. He'd only have one chance for this to work. The bright side was that if he failed, he wouldn't have much time for regret.

But he had to try. If he didn't try, he would drown before it even mattered.

He emerged in the black slick waters between the floating drone and the sheer face of the canal wall. The shooter was the shadow of a giant above him, framed by the towering Lift Bridge above. Lights danced across the surface of the car, glittering in the gloom of the cold dark lake.

Kate saw him across the waters and met his gaze with a quick shake of her head. She knew what he was going to try and didn't approve. Well.

Well.

She didn't know him well enough, did she? This wasn't just the only way he could think of to save their lives. This was the only way to save Kylie. Ajay would do anything for that girl.

Even if that something was stupid.

The man braced himself, aiming carefully with his rifle. He'd hit Regis any second. The lift was only halfway up and rising slowly.

Ajay braced one frozen hand on the frame of the drone, pushed down hard to lift himself, and swept as far as he could reach with his cane.

He hooked the man's ankle and pulled. The man's boot slipped against the wet frame. He swore. The gun fired wild, bullets dancing off the *Edmund*'s hull.

Ajay grabbed the man's leg, gripped it as hard as he could, and plunged back into the water, dragging him with.

The gunshots were muffled thumps in his ears underwater. The sea churned with their fight, but once the man was in the water, Ajay swam away as fast as he could, deep under the floating drone car.

More gunshots. Bullets zipped through the water around him. Algae churned like scintillating green arrows. Water slowed the bullets, but he wondered if they could still kill this close.

Wondered, but not quite enough to brave getting closer.

His head splashed up on the other side of the drone. He scrambled up and braced himself. His limbs were numb from the cold. Muscles ached in that bone-deep way they did when they were preparing for much worse pain.

He waited. A short distance away, Kate watched him from the oily water.

The man was nowhere to be seen. Ajay clenched his hand into a fist. It was bloody. Impossible to tell how much he was bleeding with the way it mixed with the water. Seemed like a lot. He hadn't felt a cut.

"Where is he?" Ajay called out to Kate. Above, the lift platform approached the railing. Regis would hit the deck soon. "Do you see him?"

"He went down right after you," said Kate. "I'm coming over there."

"No, wait." Ajay crouched, gripping his cane in both hands. He clicked open the holographic display. His cheaters were gone, lost somewhere in the deep sea. His hearing aid crackled. Everything sounded muffled. Full of water. "Get to the lift."

High above, Regis hopped onto the ship. Gone.

Ajay bit back a curse. His holographic controls were still sluggish and strange. They worked, but the water messed with the display. He found his connection intact, pushed through the lift controls, and sent it back down.

"Go," he called again to Kate, but he couldn't see her anymore. Had she submerged? From his vantage point, the waves churned with movement. He might never see the man if he returned.

A splash. It was a chip shot away. Not far. Too far for him to reach with the cane. Another splash. A struggle.

"Kate!" Ajay yelled.

Flashes underwater. More gunshots.

Then, Kate burst through the surface and gasped for air.

"Are you all right?" Ajay asked.

"No." Kate swam to the drone and pulled herself up. "But I'm a lot better off than him." She stuffed Ajay's pistol into its holster. Her hands were shaking, whether from cold or stress, Ajay couldn't tell.

Ajay pulled her close as soon as she was aboard. She was as cold as he was and shivering as the evening breeze brushed across their tiny flotilla. It took him three attempts to start talking because his jaw was stiff with the cold.

"I tried to tell you," she said through the shivers. "I still have that gun."

"Oh."

Kate mimicked him swinging his cane. "You didn't need all that—whatever it was you did."

"Sorry." He looked up at the shift. "We need to swim to the lift."

The lift was halfway down already but moving slowly. "Can you make it?" she asked.

The distance had closed some. The ship crept forward in the night, inching its way under the Lift Bridge. Above, the highest reaches of the giant ship appeared to scrape the bottom of the tall bridge. It wouldn't be hard to imagine this whole transit going poorly. Ajay's imagination spiraled out of control.

Because he started wondering *why*. Why move this ship into the Harbor Basin? Why not use a fleet of smaller vessels or even a truck? Why go there at all on this particular night?

It couldn't be coincidence that the attack was happening when there was a meeting of the Frontier Arms leadership in town. If they were launching drones, anything outside the denial barrier would face heavy scrutiny. Not even Ajay's best drone could sneak past that. As for launching from the sea, it must have been because the launch denial coverage was weakest there. Launching from the city posed its own problems.

But the ship still didn't make sense. Why move such a large vessel in?

"I can make it," he said, not knowing the truth.

The truth was, they didn't have a choice. Staying out on the floating drone wouldn't save them. There was no closer safety than the ship. If they didn't reach the lift at the right moment, they would surely drown. Or freeze. Or both.

Ajay dove over the side. Cool water flowed through his rough clothes. It dragged at him, pulled him back and down. His shoes were already soaked, but now he felt fresh cold water seeping in through his socks. It was unpleasant, but not enough to stop him. Keeping a grip on his cane, he swam through the water, reaching the lift as it touched down in the choppy waves. He pulled himself up, then reached down to pull Kate after him.

As she sloshed up onto the lift, she flashed him a weak smile.

"I can erase us from surveillance as we board," said Ajay as his cane's holographic interface flashed back to life.

"Never a dull moment with you, is there?" said Kate.

Ajay scratched his chin. The water soaking his clothes started pulling heat away from him again. "No," he said, finally, "not really."

With that, they rose toward the deck of the ship. In his wobbly holographic display, he found the access to surveillance feeds.

"What the hell are they doing here?" he muttered.

Kate looked over his shoulder. "What?"

He showed her the image. Kylie ran through the bridgeways inside the ship, fleeing several guards. He caught the audio feed and heard the thumping footsteps that would give her away no matter how fast she ran. He showed the readouts for a hundred assassin drones and people in cages. Dozens of them. Who the hell were they?

And he saw Sonya Silver, strolling directly toward the part of the ship where Kylie fled. With a few swipes, he picked up the sound of Kylie running and echoed it throughout the facility. It would at least prevent them from finding her so easily.

Through the audio network, he said, "Kylie."

She stopped, breathing hard.

"Kylie, I'm here." His words echoed through the whole ship. There wasn't a good way to get a direct comm message to her. Not even an insecure one. This would have to do. "I can unlock your potential, dear," he said. The words tasted like ash in his mouth. He was telling her that he wasn't confident in her abilities. That the machine in her head was more valuable than her ability to do everything for herself. He understood the message he was sending her, but he was afraid. Afraid for her life. Afraid for the city of Duluth if those drones were released. Afraid for Kate and for the others who had helped him.

"What's happening?" Kate asked.

"The guy we talked to was right. This ship is loaded with an attack force that'll decapitate a dozen organizations all at once. If they deploy, people are going to die. A lot of people."

"Can we stop it?" Kate said.

"No." Ajay didn't have the access he needed. He barely had enough control to mess with the surveillance. He brought up a video of Kylie as she crept farther toward the back of the ship. "But she could."

Chapter Forty-Three

"I can unlock your potential, dear." Papa's voice echoed from every intercom speaker in every corner of the ship. No doubt the guards all wondered what it meant, but Kylie knew. It meant Papa was aboard the ship and he was willing to unlock the computer in her brain. It meant that he knew what part of her was most useful.

How often had she needed that power when it wasn't there? She thought of all the things she wasn't able to do. She wasn't able to hack the tech of the guards following her to redirect them. Even as she ran, she heard how Papa echoed her footsteps throughout the ship's intercom. It was a clever hack that would distract her pursuers. With her full abilities, she could have done that with hardly a thought.

Then, there was access to the ship's control systems. She had needed that, hadn't she?

Not really. Here she was, on her way to the motor control room where she would have everything anyway. Maybe if she'd had her abilities things would have been easier.

But what good had the whole summer without her abilities been? She still wasn't able to understand people. She still didn't have any better control over her own emotions or whatever other miraculous cures the deprivation of tech was supposed to provide for her. She lacked the self-discipline Papa was trying to teach.

She had to decide if she should go back and let Papa unlock her brain or move forward to hack the main systems via the motor control room.

It wasn't a hard decision, as it turned out.

Because she was already there. The metal door loomed in front of her, its plain gray label unassuming against the black steel frame.

Kylie bolted the door shut behind her. The world was quiet except for the persistent hum of the enormous motor. She could sense the electromagnetic pulse of the ship behind the bridge of her nose, and it reminded her of the sensation she once had when there were signals in the area. Maybe that's all it was, after all. An enhancement of that one strange sense.

Once the door was sealed, she turned to the displays mounted against the far wall. Readouts splayed across sturdy monitors like guts across roadkill. Red and chaotic, it took Kylie a moment to understand what was happening.

Her problems fell into three categories, each more concerning than the last. Her organizational skills were better now, she thought. She could prioritize and sort her tasks into those that mattered immediately and those that could wait for further consideration. Was that improvement in her skills due to the absence of her enhanced abilities? Was it due to brain development that wouldn't otherwise have happened, or was it due to the intense training the survival camp had given her? The strict discipline of a pseudo-military organization could change a person.

The first problem she saw was that all the cages were prepped and ready to open. She could open them with a wave of her hand, then every container-turned-jail in the entire ship would split wide and release its prisoner. Now that she had the power to do it, she wondered if she should go ahead and make it happen. Maybe that wasn't a problem, but why were these containers configured this way? She didn't have time to think about it because she saw the second problem.

The ship's drones were already engaging. Somebody in the conning tower had initiated the launch sequence. A quick check of surveillance feeds showed her Mr. Shaleborn.

Damn. She had almost started to respect her martial arts instructor.

The drones were primed to launch the second the ship passed the barrier of the Lift Bridge. At that point, they would be beyond Duluth's drone denial field. They could proceed to their targets.

The ship was already breaching that barrier. The recall button was grayed out. Inert. She couldn't easily recall them from whatever kill missions were programmed into them. People were going to die if she didn't figure that out immediately, her sister included. All she needed was a little time and she could cancel all of them. She wasn't going to get it.

Because the third problem was a ping on the sonar. It was big and coming fast, originating from somewhere deep under Lake Superior.

And it was headed straight for the motor control room in the aft of the ship. She had no time.

Kylie didn't hesitate. She hit the switch to release the prisoners. No time to worry about them. She drew up the drone controls and started sweeping them for flaws. There had to be a way in. Had to be a way to cancel the launch.

The first few drones fired as the ship passed under the bridge. They launched silently into the air and hissed through the calm Minnesota night. Kylie swore under her breath and tried another routine. Access denied.

More launches. The sonar pinged. Its whole face went red.

Shit. Shit shit.

Kylie pounded her fists on the panel. Red spilled over the screen like blood. Data flowed across in shining white.

There!

A packet that she recognized. It was a military control pattern like one she'd studied with Papa.

And it had a zero-day. One he had discovered years ago that nobody had ever patched. She typed the commands from memory, letting the code flow from her fingertips. It was an overflow issue. If she wrote too much into one of the data fields, it would let her rewrite the password encryption file.

Access granted. More drones flowed from the launch tubes. The sequence threw a dozen alerts as targets were located. Dozens of targets. There were duplicate drones for every assassination attempt.

An ear-shattering siren blasted Kylie's skull to pieces. Sonar showed the approaching blip as a great crimson blob.

Torpedoes. Aimed directly at her control room.

With her new authority, she pulled up the drone cancel sequence and fired it. She couldn't do anything about the drones in flight, but she could stop more from launching.

Then she ran.

She hit the door as everything exploded.

Chapter Forty-Four

"We have to get down there," said the kid.

Lang couldn't concentrate on the words. His head spun and the rush of blood in his ears drown out any attempt at communication. He gripped the rail until his knuckles went white and still the world wouldn't stop spinning.

He'd once been able to do anything. Lang was the bad motherfucker people wrote legends about. He dominated the battlefield, not just because he was physically powerful, but because he was smart. The world was a chess game and he'd always been willing to watch it all play out from above, tweaking what needed to be tweaked to get the best outcome.

"Slick," said Austin through the comm. "Full retreat."

A squawk of noise came through the comm as response. Had she heard? She was the least of their problems. There was nothing they could do about her one way or the other.

The damage to his inner ear had permanently ruined his ability to shoot. To fight. He was worthless in the boxing ring, but did that mean he needed to be worthless in everything? How had he let this situation get so bad? He'd missed all the signs. Silver had said she had everything under control, but she didn't. A submarine lurked in the lake that she hadn't accounted for. The guards on the ship—*her* guards on the ship—were playing for keeps. They put everyone in danger, including the kids.

This wasn't a mission to apply pressure to the kids to see which ones hardened into diamonds. This was a mission that would get those kids killed.

Lang had always hated kids, but this—he had to do something about this.

Austin grabbed Lang by the shoulders and shook him, which did not help. "We need to go," he said. "Extract Kylie and the others. They're in danger. It's coming. Call in the reinforcements"

"Can't," muttered Lang.

He couldn't call them up because they didn't work for him. They worked for Silver, and Silver was already on the ship. No doubt most of the mercenary budget was already on that ship.

The old Lang would have known exactly what needed to happen in this situation. It was time to signal the retreat. He was a mercenary, not a crusader. There was no reason to die for a cause, even if that cause was rescuing some kids. When things went far enough south, mercenaries got out of town. After all, mercenaries worked for a paycheck. Can't cash a check if you're dead.

One by one, Lang peeled his fingers from the railing. His hand ached from gripping it so tightly. Loose from the one solid thing he was touching, he felt like he was floating above the city.

"I can't do it alone," Austin said. "We never trained with this gear, and I don't know what I'd do once I got down there." He spoke fast, but not out of panic. He had information to give, and he wanted Lang to have it. "Those people down there will listen to you. They'll respect you. All you need to do is tell them they need to abort what they're doing and evacuate the ship. Pull the alarm if you can get to it."

Lang picked up the coil of rope. It was slick under his hand. Wet. His hand shook from a fear he had never before felt. Sure, he had retreated from bad situations before. He had been nervous or scared of uncertain outcomes. Deep down, he had always known that the challenges were something he could handle.

This was something else.

Below, the bow of the *Edmund* passed under the bridge. Its enormous bulk rose almost high enough to scrape the bottom of the bridge. On the deck, so very close, guards ran from one end to the next. Lang saw Shaleborn come over the side. The smug bastard landed on his feet and strode confidently toward the bow. He shouted instructions to the guards, and they obeyed, setting up a perimeter around the door to the decks below. Shaleborn disappeared into the conning tower.

So, he was with Silver. How much had the two planned for this? Did the martial artist know about Silver's plans?

"Are those drones?" Austin asked, peering over the side of the bridge pointed toward the city.

"All right." Lang secured the rope to the rail on the Lift Bridge. "I'll go down."

"I think they are," the kid said. "Why are they launching drones?"

Lang double-checked his harness. He'd have one chance at this, and he didn't want to screw it up. Already the thought of going over the edge sent his heart pounding so hard it hurt. He pulled the sniper rifle from his back and handed it to the boy. "You might need this."

Austin held the rifle like it might turn into a snake.

"You've got this," Lang said. "It's neuropellets. Non-lethal. Medium range. Point and shoot."

"I've never been good at—"

"You've never *needed* to be good at shooting. Kid, I've watched you. You're good at what you want to be good at the moment it's necessary. Not a moment before." He placed a hand on the boy's shoulder. "Look. Just remember to breathe and you'll be fine. When in doubt, shoot with empty lungs and be ready to move."

"Where would I go?" Austin asked, wide-eyed.

Lang clicked the rope into the carabiner and looped it around so he could control the speed of his descent. His mad descent. "All the plans were yours, right?"

"Yeah."

"Good. Stick to them. They were good plans."

"But everything's different. It wasn't supposed to go down like this. A submarine? I mean, how could I plan for that?"

A siren blared below, piercing the night.

Lang grinned. "So much for triggering the alarm." All the nervous energy coursing through his limbs converted into a rush of pure adrenaline. This was the glory he'd been missing. "A good plan doesn't care about details," he said. "It's really more of a philosophy."

"Survival is victory," said Giles.

"Everything else is a secondary objective."

With that, Lang stepped out over empty air and dropped. Halfway down his descent, explosions rocked the aft of the ship.

Chapter Forty-Five

THE EXPLOSION TORE THROUGH the control room and warped the bulkhead door. The impact threw Kylie back across the hall and slammed her into the wall. The harsh lights of the lower decks grew halos, and a throbbing pain grew in the back of Kylie's skull. Something felt very wrong, like an irritation right on the edge of her senses.

But she hadn't hit her head.

She brought up her fidget, recently paired with the ship's systems.

Nothing. The device's display was a mess of undifferentiated pixels. What the hell?

A woman stepped out of a container a short distance down the hall. She wore a shredded dress, and her fingernails had been gnawed down to their roots. Her head was cocked as she stepped out, and she stared at Kylie's chin, refusing to make eye contact.

Eye contact. Kylie had never been very good at that before, but that was one thing that she had improved at over the summer. She'd worked at it. Trained with Mr. Shaleborn as a way to read an opponent. She'd practiced it with Mr. Lang as a strategy for building rapport with allies. It still felt uncomfortable to her, but now she noticed its absence.

Something was very wrong with this woman. Her jaw clenched, and Kylie felt a new wave of pain in the back of her skull.

"You're like me," Kylie gasped.

Someone had experimented on them, not in utero like Isabelle and Kylie, but as adults. Kylie's parents had never found a way to make that work, but someone was trying to give people the ability to interface directly with wireless networks.

It hadn't worked, Kylie realized, but it *had* given them the ability to project a hell of a jamming signal. The lingering remains of her abilities picked up the noise and translated it into a pulsing migraine. Kylie blinked hard. She had to concentrate. How many prisoners had there been? A hundred? She tried to picture the list.

In the hallway beyond the woman, more containers opened. One by one, the prisoners emerged from their cages. Her headache intensified.

"I can help you," she said, cursing her voice for betraying her fear. "We all need to get off of this ship."

The woman advanced a step. Then another. She didn't quite block the exit to the bridge yet, but if Kylie waited too long there would be no escape. She needed to make a decision. Lead these people or run?

It was a strategic decision. Mr. Lang had taught them the balance between glory and retreat. She knew the weight of her options. There were risks on either side. If she ran, she might be giving up a good opportunity to make allies. Maybe these people were as frightened as she was, and they would help her the way she'd hoped.

Or maybe they would tear her apart.

She ran.

Her shoulder slammed into the woman as she passed, staggering both of them. Fingernails raked against Kylie's neck, but then she was gone. She hit the bridge across the middle of the ship and stopped.

A heavyset black man in fatigues stood between her and the stairs. A guard. He went for his gun.

Kylie leaped over the railing and dropped down one level. Her feet slammed into the metal bridge below, rattling the whole structure and sending a crackle of pain through her left knee. She limped forward. Her head swam.

Above, the woman and several other ragged prisoners slammed into the guard. He gave a yell of surprise as they attacked, pounding fists into his big body. A single gunshot reverberated against the metal walls.

He didn't stand a chance. In seconds, he was down and they forced past. They were furious, their bare feet pounding on him as they passed. More of them emerged from the cages above, but Kylie didn't wait for them to follow her down. She crossed the lower bridge and entered the narrow passageways below.

The ship shook. A second torpedo hit? The air compressed so hard her ears rang. The impact threw her to the floor and she bruised the palms of her hands. She felt pain, then her whole body went oddly numb.

When she opened her eyes, she saw the cold water sloshing over her injured hands. Her fidget flickered to life, and her migraine ebbed, but the water was getting deeper. Fast.

Two pairs of boots stomped in the water ahead. She looked up slowly, dreading what she would see.

Brian stood with an arm under Hanna's shoulder, halfway supporting her. His other arm was heavily bandaged.

Kylie dragged herself to her feet. "Truce?"

Hanna glared at Kylie but apparently didn't have enough of her neurological control left to protest.

"You were right," Brian said. "We have to stop Silver."

Above, someone screamed bloody rage, and a movement like the charging of a pack of elephants passed overhead.

Alarms squelched. Red lights along the hall flashed in an irritating rapid pulse.

"The drones have launched," she said, taking Hanna from the other side and helping Brian move her forward down the hall. "Silver's drones have launched and there's nothing we can do to stop them."

"Then let's get out of here," said Brian.

A prisoner emerged from the water down the hall. The dripping cold washed away the woman's filth, and her cold fists clenched at her sides.

"It's all right," Kylie said. "I think they just want to escape."

A squelch of signal twisted in Kylie's brain. Her vision blurred for a second, and when she looked again, the prisoner's face was twisted in a panicked rage.

"Run," Kylie said, knowing full well that they couldn't get away. "Run!"

Chapter Forty-Six

Wind tore through Ajay's wet clothes as the lift ascended the side of the ship. They were close—almost to the summit where they would be able to find Kylie and escape. And then—Ajay didn't know.

The banks along the side of the ship whirred and opened. Drones spewed from hidden compartments, bursting out into the dark night with a sound like a million mosquitoes swarming at a Fourth of July picnic.

"What the cripes?" Kate said.

"Each one of those has a target programmed. We must be close enough to the target." Ajay looked up and saw that the fore of the ship had crossed under the bridge. Above, it looked close enough to touch. Their lift ground to a halt shy of the deck, and the whole ship shuddered.

"Oh for fuck's sake, what the hell was that?" Kate muttered.

Ajay could no longer discern between the ache of his joints and the bone-deep agony from the cold. The holographic display on his cane danced with images too fast for his old eyes to follow. He stilled himself from shivering and looked again.

"She's still below," he said as Kate helped him up onto the deck. Nobody had spotted them yet. His connection through Kylie's team's hack had disappeared, but he'd picked up his local connection as soon as he was close enough to the ship. It had taken a few minutes to crack the encryption, but the near-field network was strong on the deck, so his feed was giving him more and more info every second. "And the ship's taking water."

A guard shouted from the other end of the deck where a row of drone cars landed in sequence. Ajay ducked, sure that he was yelling at him, but he wasn't. The guard signaled and some men in suits ran over from their hiding place by the railings.

Then, the drone cars exploded. Orange flames lit up the night as the row of vehicles, one by one, was struck from above.

"Crap," muttered Ajay. "There goes our ride out of here."

"Our ride?" said Kate. "Were you planning on stealing those?"

"It seemed like the right thing to do."

"But is it?"

Ajay chewed his lip. "Stealing from bad guys is okay."

Kate gave an exasperated sigh and stalked away.

"What?" Ajay hurried after her. The last of the drone cars went up in flames as they ducked behind the raised central cabin. "We need to do what we need to do."

Kate spun on him. The tears in her eyes shone in the harsh orange light. "Is that how you operate, Ajay? Do what needs to be done, no matter what?"

It's what she did, Ajay wanted to say, when she killed those men. How could she have a problem with stealing if killing was nothing?

But something told him it wasn't that. She was in a crisis, and every decision was a hard one.

Ajay gripped his cane. The holographic display on its top danced over the movement of guards below deck. It hurt knowing what he had to say next because he knew it would ruin how she saw him. "Yes," he said. "I'm sorry."

Now, her eyes burned with rage. "You have no idea what I've been through, Ajay." She pounded him in the chest with a boulder of a fist. "I don't want this to be so easy."

"We're not killers," Ajay said. "Not unless we can help it. Not if there's any chance of escaping without death."

Kate's voice dropped low and dangerous. "But what if there's not."

"Then we do what needs to be done. No hesitation."

Her jaw hardened and her gaze bored a hole right into his soul. He felt her weigh him. She judged every flaw he'd ever had and every mistake he'd ever made, and Ajay couldn't stand it. He knew how he came out at the end of that judgment. "It's hesitation that keeps us human," she whispered.

Ajay didn't know how to respond, so, instead of facing it, he pulled her into an embrace. There on the deck of the ship, he felt closer to anyone than he ever had before. Not his wife. Not his daughter. Not even Kylie, who he'd cared for these several years. The best years of his life.

He didn't know how it happened or who initiated it, but Ajay and Kate kissed. He tasted her salty tears and felt heat rushing back into his body. He felt alive. Alert.

When he pulled away, he met her gaze for an eternity, lost in her as he'd never been for anyone else. "Kate," he said.

Kate said, "Your granddaughter."

"What?"

She touched his cane. The display on top showed Kylie running across a metal bridge. A guard leveled a gun at her, but she leaped high over the railing and dropped to the metal floor below. Her feet hit and she kept running. Damn, she was fast. He could hardly track her using the surveillance feeds.

"Where is she going?" he asked.

"More importantly, who is she running from?" said Kate.

Doors throughout the ship swung open. Ragged, confused people spilled forth, but each time Ajay saw it happening, the video surveillance juddered to a stop. Signals started dropping at random.

A man in black rounded the corner of the conning tower and spotted Ajay and Kate. He raised his gun. "What are you doing here?"

Ajay put on his most innocent smile. "Hey, I'm a little lost. Thought maybe you could—"

The door beside the guard flew open and a tall man in rags bowled him over. The guard didn't even get a shot off. More people spilled atop him, kicking and punching.

"Allies?" asked Kate.

"Run," Ajay whispered, but he couldn't make himself move. He was frozen by the shock at the sheer savagery of the attack. "We have to run."

Kate didn't move. "We can help him."

Then, one of the ragged men looked up at Ajay with eyes full of hideous anger. The holographic display atop his cane flickered and died.

"Run!" Ajay shouted. This time both he and Kate moved.

The man was too fast. Ajay was too old. Kate was faster, but Ajay knew neither of them would make it. There was nowhere to go. His hip ached already, and he could feel it starting to seize up.

Ajay stopped. Turned. "I'm not with them!" he shouted raising his hands in surrender.

Then the man lunged, fury in his eyes.

Ajay dropped low, took the man's momentum, and shoved him over the railing. Far below, the man splashed into the cold canal.

Kate was there somehow. "Did you just—"

"I did what I had to do," Ajay gasped. There hadn't been another option. Had there? The man *might* survive. It was possible.

From their current vantage point, they could see most of the main deck of the ship. Guards fought pockets of ragged men and women. Blood flowed from the naked hands of the maddened attackers. They swarmed. Attacked. Overwhelmed. When guards managed to fire their guns, people fell in a bloody mess, but the gaps were filled by more attackers.

"Kylie," Ajay said through his comm.

Nothing. The signal was completely jammed. Ajay's cane didn't work. The electronics hissed and sputtered, but the holographic display was dead. The computing center suffered a series of faults, and he couldn't interface with it. Panic bubbled up in his chest.

"I don't know what to do," he said. "I can't find her. I can't save her."

Kate put a hand on his shoulder and pulled him close.

"I know what to do," Kate said.

"What's that?"

She drew her gun and checked the cartridge. "Anything," she said. "We'll do whatever it takes."

A ragged man spotted them across the deck and ran at their position. They felt exposed where they were near the edge of the deck. There was no cover. Nowhere to hide. Not that it would matter. The man ran at them full speed, and five paces before he struck them, Kate shot him in the knee. He dropped and skidded to a stop.

"Whatever it takes," Kate whispered.

The sound of her gunshot drew the attention of several more of the strange people. They all, as one, snarled at her and charged.

Another explosion pulsed from the rear of the ship, shattering the air and peeling metal. The deck shook, and Ajay grasped the railing to steady himself.

"What the hell?" he said.

The ragged people weren't fazed by the explosion. They continued toward Ajay and Kate. They were too many. Too tough. Ajay considered the option of jumping overboard when a dark shape blotted out the light from the bridge above.

The big man's boots rattled the whole deck when he landed. He stood tall in front of Ajay.

And Ajay recognized him. It was Tenen Lang, the fierce asshole of a mercenary he'd fought months ago. Ajay had spared the man's life but used a cluster of drones to debilitate him. Now, here he was, big, powerful, and right in the middle of another war zone. Exactly what Ajay had been hoping to make impossible for the dangerous man.

"You," Ajay said, unable to think of anything else.

The scowl on Tenen's face could have bored a hole in the ship's hull. He took two steps toward Ajay, his muscles tense. His square jaw hard as a cinder block. Ajay braced himself for the attack, knowing that nothing he could do would mitigate the damage if Tenen Lang decided to pound him to a pulp, and the big man was far too close for Ajay to manage a leap over the edge.

Which would be suicide anyway.

The big man's eyes danced in his skull like he'd just stepped off a Tilt-a-Whirl. He blinked hard several times, opened his mouth as if to speak, then dropped to his knees and clutched the hard deck as if it might fall out from under him.

And the attackers struck him in a wave.

Chapter Forty-Seven

Lang's boots hit the deck with a resounding thump. Shockwaves ran up through his knees and hips. He'd hit too hard because he was unable to properly judge the distance down. Still, he had made it. He was ready to rescue the kids.

But things were worse than expected. The deck of the ship was overrun. People—unarmed people—advanced, ready to take down anyone in their path. Lang was in their path.

Lang turned to see Ajay Andersen—that asshole—right there in front of him. Rage bubbled in Lang's gut. He clenched his fists.

Then dizziness struck. His fall had disoriented him. He swayed, and the lack of control filled him with more rage.

Silver had been hiding people on her ship. These were her elite fighters? They were enhanced by the same technology that the Andersen kid supposedly possessed. The same technology Silver had offered to Lang as a way to fix his problems.

But there was something wrong with them. The tech must have changed them in some way. Damaged them. They stared at Lang with a look of such stupid anger.

Another wave of dizziness struck. Disorientation. A group of zombies approached.

No, not zombies. He saw intelligence in their eyes. They were desperate—as desperate as he was. Desperate like a junkie looking to score a hit.

He shot a glance up. Giles was supposed to be updating him with location data for Singer and Sax, but the comms were dead. Worse than dead, the comm squelched a hiss of static. Jammed. Fuck.

The deck swayed under his feet, and he couldn't tell if it was because of what was wrong in his head or that the ship was actually leaning to one side. He dropped to a knee.

Then, the attackers struck. They piled on Lang like a rugby scrum.

Here he was, right between the zombie horde and the damn asshole who had rendered him worthless in a fight. Fists pounded into him, bruising muscle and splitting his lip. He felt every powerful blow like a hammer taken to tenderize every bit of meat on his bones.

Andersen clocked one man in the head with his cane before he could wrap an arm around Lang's neck. The old woman peeled another attacker off and shoved him away.

"We're not your enemies," she screeched. An attacker launched himself at her, but she took him down with a rabbit punch to the solar plexus. He dropped, gasping. Damn, she was good at this.

Lang tensed and shoved a man over the railing. He waited for the splash below.

It didn't happen. The man landed with a thud on solid land.

"What are you doing here?" Lang gasped as the remaining attackers split and ran. Some elite fighters these turned out to be.

"I could ask you the same," shouted Andersen.

Lang grasped as another attacker flung himself at Andersen. It took him several tries, but he finally got a hold of the man, thumped him in the head, and flung him overboard. "Teaching."

"You know what they say about teachers?" Andersen said.

"Those who can't *do, teach?*"

"Bullshit," said the old man. "Teaching's much harder than doing. People *do* because they're shitty teachers or terrified of standing up in front of a bunch of impressionable kids. If they wanted to influence the world, they'd teach, but they can't, so they have to settle."

Lang opened his mouth to respond but found he found he didn't have anything to add.

They had a second to breathe. The other attackers swarmed guards across the deck, but they'd be done soon. Already, three black-clad soldiers lay in bloody messes across the deck. The bodies of a dozen attackers decorated the deck with their violent deaths. What a clusterfuck.

The whole ship shuddered and the sound of tearing metal shattered the night sky. The impact of the ship and the canal wall was a thunderclap. It flung Lang over the edge of the railing, and his cane went flying off into the night. He clung hard to his thin rope and swung back aboard, swearing profusely.

He stood over Andersen, who had—along with the woman—managed to stay on the ship. Damn.

"Where are the kids?" demanded Lang, swearing at himself for not crushing Andersen right there.

"Below," said Andersen. "All my connections are broken, but they were near the bridges."

The ship shuddered again. Were they sinking? Lang saw the fear in the old man's eyes. Yes, they were. They were sinking and the kids were still below deck. Worse, the old man and his girlfriend weren't going to be able to rescue them. They could barely handle themselves.

"How the hell did I ever let you beat me?" Lang asked.

"It was luck," said Andersen. "Pure, dumb luck."

Lang detached his rappelling harness. "All right," he said to Ajay Andersen. "Give me your cane."

Chapter Forty-Eight

THEY WERE CLUMSY. THAT was Kylie's big advantage. Digitally, they screamed on all the signals she would ever be able to detect, but these ragged prisoners were clumsy in their attacks. Underfed. Weak. Slow.

Behind her, Brian and Hanna struggled through the waist-deep water. Kylie sloshed forward to confront two women dressed like waiters from a fancy restaurant.

The first lunged just as the ship lurched to one side. Water disrupted her attack, and Kylie followed up with a strike to the woman's skull.

The other attacker staggered forward and grasped Kylie's arm. Her grip was strong and cold, like being gripped by the vise in Papa's workshop. It brought back panicked memories of the last time—when she had him block her abilities. What would these people's vicious screaming do to her if she was fully receptive to it? The migraine pulsing in the top of her skull told her she probably wouldn't like it.

Kylie rotated and pulled, wrenching out of the woman's grip. She threw a punch. Then another. Her fists glanced off the woman's cheekbone to no effect. Water flowed away across the ship, dropping the water level down to Kylie's knees. The first woman burst from the dark water, but Kylie was ready for it. She struck fast and hard and sent the woman stumbling away.

"Go!" Kylie shouted at Brian.

The boy pulled Hanna forward while Kylie dealt with the second attacker. This woman was a little less clumsy than the first. A little more cautious.

"I don't want to fight you," said Kylie. "We can escape together."

It didn't matter. Kylie had trained hard. She remembered Shaleborn's lessons deep down to her bones. When the woman struck, Kylie snapped into action like a cat, pouncing over and past. Brian and Hanna were almost to the next set of stairs, which were now treacherously skewed because of the lurching ship. They needed to go up, though. The ship was still sinking. Rushing water almost bowled Brian down.

Kylie threw another punch. She felt the contact, but it didn't stop the woman at all.

Punch through the target. She remembered what Shaleborn had taught her. It wasn't enough to bounce glancing blows off the woman. Kylie needed to *punch.*

Kylie sloshed backward, but the woman caught up to her and grabbed her shoulder. Kylie dipped low, then spun and snapped a solid right hook straight through the woman's face.

The woman's foot slipped on the metal floor, and her chin hit the railing hard. She dropped like a sock full of sand. Water pooled around her face.

Crap. Kylie shot a glance at the other woman, who was still crouching in the hallway. She might attack again soon, but for now, she was far enough away that Kylie didn't worry. This unconscious one would drown if Kylie left her.

"Come on!" shouted Brian.

"I have to help her."

Brian didn't protest. He hefted Hanna up the stairs. The girl was recovering from the neurotoxins, but she still couldn't manage on her own.

Kylie hooked her arms under the attacker's shoulders and pulled. She just needed to get her to high enough ground that she wouldn't die. Kylie didn't want to kill anyone. *Couldn't* kill anyone.

A crash like thunder boomed through the ship, and the hallway lurched again. Cold, green water hit the back of Kylie's legs, knocking her over. Thick, inky blackness swallowed her in icy panic. She held hard to the unconscious woman, and the two were battered around the little hallway as the water poured in.

"Drop her!" Brian said from above when Kylie thrust her head above water. "It's too late."

"Go," Kylie gasped with the only breath she could manage. "Get to the deck!"

Brian hesitated, but the ship rumbled again and he nearly pitched over the railing to the deck below. "Kylie," he called. He pushed Hanna up ahead of him, leaving her to stand on her own, which she could barely do. "We can still get out." He took several steps down into the rushing water and held out a hand.

Kylie didn't take it. She needed both hands to pull the woman above the rising level of the water. Her feet slipped. Another wave knocked her back underwater. Cold knocked the breath from her lungs.

Then, Brian was gone. Kylie came up, and Hanna and Brian were nowhere to be seen.

Kylie would die alone.

No, not alone. She had this migraine-making ragged woman with claw fingernails and clothes that seemed to place her as a waitress at a fancy restaurant.

It wasn't how she expected to go out.

The next impact was a rumble in Kylie's submerged ears. The water climbed high enough that only a pocket of air gave her any chance at a breath above, but she couldn't get there.

Underwater was so calm. The chaos of the sinking ship was reserved only for the world above. The world of air and madness. Underneath the waves, everything existed as a hazy reflection of itself, softened and muted. Peaceful.

She knew she had to swim. Her kicks didn't move her forward. The stairs were close, but infinitely far. She would never reach them and the air above. Not without releasing the unconscious woman. Was the waitress even still alive? Kylie tried her best not to think about it. Her lungs burned, threatening to burst from her chest, but still, she wouldn't let go of the woman. Wasn't she supposed to save people like this?

Kylie's foot caught on the metal mesh floor and she pushed herself closer to the stairs. Water whooshed across her ears. Her vision blurred. Another rumble through the huge ship. The currents pushed her toward her destination, but they also made the water deeper. There was no air above anymore. Nothing she could possibly hope for.

Her back hit the metal railing next to the stairs. All she needed to do was pull herself up, but all her muscles seized in a wash of oxygen-deprived agony. She kept her grip only on the woman.

Why die for her? What did it matter if one person died in addition to all the others who must have already perished? Kylie had killed before. Her abilities had activated, and they'd suppressed something in her brain that cared about killing. That was her. The killer. Even as a small child she had been brutal. Heartless. Why couldn't she do that now, even to save herself? How could she possibly care about this woman who had attacked her?

Because she did. That's all there was to it. She cared because she cared.

Maybe Papa's patch had done more than she thought. Maybe it had moved her machine parts out of the way so that she could sort out what was important to her.

Or maybe she knew what it felt like to kill—to *have* killed—and she didn't like it.

Kylie wanted to be the kind of person who saved people, even if that meant dying in the attempt.

Keeping one hand gripping the woman, she reached out and grabbed the railing, pulling herself forward and up. Molten fire flowed through her limbs—agony boiled in her chest as her body desperately cried for air. Again, she pulled. Currents grasped at her, pulling her back down.

She wouldn't stop.

The red flashing lights died. Eerie illumination cast her watery grave in dancing shadows. All was quiet. Unearthly silence filled the ship, punctuated by the echoing percussion of the superyacht's final death march.

A shadow passed over her like a great white shark looming over her in the black ocean. It eclipsed her, considered her, and struck. A massive hand gripped her arm with bruising force, hurting even through the numbing ache of cold. It yanked her upward, rushing her through the murky waters.

She held tight to the unconscious woman, dragging her up the stairs.

Into the air. Her lungs grabbed at sweet air, gasping as the black nothing still threatened to swallow her whole. The unconscious woman flopped onto the floor next to her.

Above, stood Tenen Lang, leaning heavily on a cane as the ship rumbled around him. "Who the hell is that?" the big man asked.

Kylie tried to answer, but her body wouldn't respond to her commands. She dry heaved.

Lang dragged the woman farther up, gave her a few pumps of CPR, and blew some air into her lungs. After a few iterations, the woman vomited more water than Kylie thought possible.

"Brian and Hanna are above," Lang said. He hooked his cane into his belt and hefted the woman onto his shoulder. He stood, grasping the railing hard in his other hand. "Can you walk?"

"Yeah," Kylie managed. The ship was at such an angle that they were half walking on the left wall. Port. They moved forward through the hall, closing the distance to the next set of stairs. The container cages all along this hallway were open, and several of the prisoners were unconscious or dead, bleeding onto the metal floors. Kylie tried not to think about what had happened there, but her stomach roiled at the idea of all that violence.

The ship shook again and the floor bucked under Kylie's feet. She pitched forward, catching herself. Lang didn't even lose a step.

"Unsteady footing is my whole life," he explained when he saw her staring. He tapped the cane looped into his belt. "Courtesy of your grandpap."

Kylie noticed for the first time that the cane in his belt was Papa's. She had made it for him—bound the technology, wired the taser, carved the shape. What the hell was Lang doing with it?

Before she could ask, they were off again, rushing through the ship, and making their way upward through the maze.

As they reached the top, a voice rang out from somewhere down in the belly of the ship. Kylie couldn't hear what he said, but it was Mr. Shaleborn.

Lang set the prisoner down. "She'll be safe here for now. Get out of here." He set his jaw in grim determination and started down the hallway. "I'll be up soon."

"Wait." Kylie didn't know why she said it, but Lang stopped. She fumbled with her words. "Why did you help me?"

He stared at her a long time before answering. "Not too long ago I would have let you drown. Think about that."

"You're not a bad guy, Lang," she said.

"We'll see about that."

She hit the stairs as the metal walkway lurched again, and this time Kylie kept her footing. She paused and listened as Lang moved away through the ship. It would be possible to catch up to him. Find him and see what was so important. Kylie took a step back down the stairs.

But no. Kylie needed to check in with the others. She needed to get a signal out to Austin to let him know that she was safe. Then, she could come back.

She hit the door and burst onto the deck of the ship.

Sonya Silver stood before them on the sloped deck, pistol in one hand, and Brian's hair grasped tightly in the other. The ragged prisoners surrounded her, peering at Kylie with their insane eyes.

"Kylie, dear," Silver said. "I'm so disappointed. You were supposed to be something special."

Chapter Forty-Nine

"It was going to be so simple," said Shaleborn as Lang stepped into the control center. Computers buzzed around them, and the central console still had power. "She had me program them, you know."

Half a dozen bodies oozed blood into the grated floor.

"Program what?" Lang said, stepping forward. The floor tilted to one side, but he would have had trouble standing on a level floor.

"I hadn't realized it. I'm not a hacker, you know. This isn't my thing."

"Programmed what, Shaleborn?" Lang growled.

"The drones," said Shaleborn, crossing to the far side of the room. "My fingerprints are all over everything, but I was smart."

"You were?" Lang gripped the rail.

Shaleborn brought a diagram up on the one functioning screen. "Come here. Look at this."

"Shaleborn, this is enough. We need to get out of here. The cops are going to get free of the deadlock and move in."

The bodies on the floor hadn't been shot, Lang saw now that he was close. They suffered knife wounds. Deep slashes marred their bodies. Shaleborn had killed them.

"That's fine, Regis" Lang said, trying the man's first name for a change. "You'll need to go dark. Escape."

But Shaleborn looked at him with mad eyes. "You need to *see* this, Lang." He gestured at the screen again.

With a sigh, Lang crossed the room. Another shudder ran through the ship, and one of the corpses—a young and beautiful woman—flopped on its side. Lang placed his palms flat on the desk next to the biometric scanner and peered at the screen. Rows of data scrolled slowly up, showing the logic transmissions of the dozens of assassin drones.

"Your name is on all of these," Lang said.

"Unless someone with credentials overwrites it with their own ID." Shaleborn took Lang's wrist in both hands, twisted, and yanked it toward the biometric scanner.

Lang wasn't such an easy target. He shoved hard, pivoted, and pulled out of Shaleborn's grip.

"It was supposed to be simple. I program the drones, making extra sure they couldn't be seized by that Andersen girl." He gestured at the corpses littering the floor. "Silver had her experiments, but it turned out the kid had no utility there, either."

Lang said. "You were testing her again?" There had to be more.

Shaleborn threw his arms up in a defensive stance. "Testing? Maybe. We were building her into something powerful, but she's not up to the task, is she? That's the beauty of the plan, but Silver had to go fuck it up!"

The ship shook again, the lights flickered, and Shaleborn launched his attack. Lang had no defense. He took a strike to his chest. He rolled away, turning a skull-crushing blow into a staggering assault on his senses. Shaleborn was fast. Punishing. A kick slammed into Lang's hip and pain exploded through his back.

But he bit back the scream and staggered away. Shaleborn let him catch his breath.

"I'm sorry, Lang. I really thought we could work together. If Silver hadn't done this—" he gestured to the screen "—we might have built something amazing together at the top of Frontier Arms."

Lang asked. "Frontier?"

"Frontier is a conglomeration of dozens of mercenary companies, and they're all meeting tonight. One strike. One chance to grab leadership. Silver was always going to end up on top, but why do you think she's put my name on every fucking assassin drone?"

"To get you out of the way," Lang said. "So get out of the way."

Shaleborn shot forward again. A roundhouse kick bruised Lang's biceps. A punch caught him on the chin, snapping his mouth shut and bloodying his tongue. Lang did his best to fight the man off. He raised his big meaty fists—too slow to do anything about Shaleborn's lightning-fast attacks—and desperately sought distance.

When Shaleborn backed away again, Lang wiped the blood from his mouth. "You need me alive and intact for the biometrics."

"Technology's a bitch, right?"

Lang thought of the technology that had stolen his ability to fight. It was Ajay Andersen's attack that would lose this fight against Shaleborn. The world spun around Lang. Repeated blows to the head did nothing to stabilize his out-of-control sense of balance. He gripped the railing in one hand and kept the other up in a defensive position. It wouldn't matter once Shaleborn decided to let loose.

"Why not make this easy?" said Shaleborn. "Give me the scan I need to transfer the records over to you. You'll have plenty of time to go on the run. Sure, blame will fall on you, but you'll be alive. You have the connections you need to dodge a prison sentence."

Lang scoffed, "Used to." Used to a lot of things, now that he thought about it. Lang would have killed this asshole a long time ago if he'd been at his peak. Shaleborn's martial arts were nothing to a good old-fashioned street brawler.

Shaleborn's next attack was going to be brutal.

"All right," Lang said. "All you need is the scan?"

"Then you can go."

Lang let out a long breath. There was a lot he couldn't do. He would never run a marathon. Never beat the best fighters in the world. Never pull off a daring escape as the jaws of doom closed around him.

Silver had hired him for something, though. She had hired him for his ability as a strategist and tactician. His balance might be bad, but his brain still worked.

All Shaleborn needed was the scan.

Lang unhooked the cane from his belt and leaned on it. He didn't take his eyes off Shaleborn, but the walk across the room was a treacherous minefield of slick spots and corpses. He gripped the heavy cane head in his right hand and knew what he had to do. He stepped across the room. Halfway. Three quarters. All the while, Shaleborn hovered near the machine. The instructor waited and watched Lang struggle to move. Lang was only a few paces from the console.

All Shaleborn needed was the scan—and he couldn't get it if there was no scanner.

With a furious roar, Lang took the cane in two hands and swung at the machine.

Shaleborn popped like a broken spring. His movements were like a cobra strike, snapping out, snatching the cane on the inside of its arc. Like that, he stopped the attack.

And left his body exposed.

Lang's attack was the walrus form of martial arts. He let his bulk overpower his enemy, leaning hard into him and keeping the quick little bastard in constant contact. Together, they smashed into the computer, then hit the floor hard. Lang grappled one of the other man's arms and twisted.

An elbow landed in Lang's chest. Then another strike glanced painfully on his jaw. He lifted and twisted hard and the arm snapped under his weight. Shaleborn screamed in agony and rage.

But Lang didn't stop. To stop would be to give up his advantage. It didn't matter whether or not he wanted to kill.

Shaleborn was the enemy.

Enemies die.

He shifted his grip and caught the smaller man's thick neck in an arm lock. The screams stopped, choked down to nothing. Shaleborn's face turned blue and Lang eased him down. He knew exactly how long it would take.

Then, Lang did something he had never done before. He hesitated. What would happen if he killed Shaleborn like this? This wasn't combat anymore. Shaleborn could be left alive if Lang subdued him, couldn't he? Without Frontier's legal support, murder would leave Lang open to all kinds of problems. It wasn't good strategy.

But neither was leaving an enemy at his back.

He squeezed tighter. Tighter.

Then let up.

Color returned to Shaleborn's face, but the man didn't wake. Lang used the cane and pushed himself to his feet. Unsteadily, he made his way across the room to the exit. The ship shuddered under his feet, but that was normal. Another factor in the big equation of life.

An impact pounded the ship, dropping Lang to his knees.

Then, Shaleborn was on him again. "I'll kill you," the man rasped as he struck a clumsy blow against the bigger man's shoulder. The knife dug deep into muscle. It had been meant to be a killing stab to the neck, but Lang's lurching walk had thrown it off.

In one smooth movement, Lang spun, grabbed the offending arm, pulled Shaleborn closer, spun him, and snapped his neck.

"You won't," he whispered as he knelt over the man's body. "You won't."

Chapter Fifty

"THIS ISN'T SO BAD," said Kate. Her rough hands gripped Ajay tight as a motor in the rappelling harness pulled them steadily upward. "We're hardly high enough to be dangerous."

"If this line breaks, we're dead." They dangled several stories above the deck of the ship, which was now tilted to port and leaning heavily against the wall of the short canal. The ship was still sinking. The ponderous movement of water slammed it relentlessly onto the wall and into the side of the lift bridge. "Either way, I'm not sure the city of Duluth is going to let us come back."

"Duluth's overrated, anyway."

"It is *not*. It's a great vacation destination. Water parks. Fishing. Beer." Ajay's knuckles went white where he gripped the line.

"You're just naming things that you can see from way up here," Kate said.

"Which is too many things."

They slammed into the bridge with a jolt that would leave a bruise on Ajay's back. Kate heaved them up and over the railing where they landed in a heap. He was almost starting to get tired of this.

A familiar voice said, "The scope shows three dozen assassin drones moving across—Mr. Andersen?"

Ajay peeled his eyes open. "Austin?"

The boy helped Ajay and Kate detach from Tenen's rappelling rig. It wasn't made for two people, but they'd rigged it to work by looping the loose end of the rope around and making several dubious knots. Once free, Ajay stood and rubbed his thighs where the rope had chafed.

"Scope?" he asked, finally processing what Austin had said. He blinked up at the boy, who now, somehow, stood taller than Ajay and sported the actual fuzz of a mustache.

And he moved with confidence. Austin walked across the bridge tower. "I'm in charge of the mission, but that fell apart a long time ago. The scope gives me access to anything flying in the area. It was for monitoring police activity, but a few minutes ago, the ship launched a whole fleet of drones."

"Headed straight to the aquarium," Ajay said, peering at the screen. "No, they're not, are they? They're spreading thin."

"I think that's so that there's no way to hit them all," said Austin. "It's what I would do."

Kate looked over Ajay's shoulder. "Can you work with this?"

Ajay flexed his stiff fingers. He had been reluctant to trust Tenen at first, but this was their best chance. He wasn't going to be able to fight his way through the ship to get Kylie. He wouldn't be able to rescue any of the other kids or disrupt any other part of Sonya Silver's assassination plot. Sometimes a man needs to know his own limitations.

But this? This was something he could manage.

"You're plugged into the bridge's signal tower?" he asked, knowing the answer.

"Yeah," said Austin.

"Double-check all the connections."

The boy ran off to check the wiring.

"That's busy work," Kate said.

"There are certain times I don't like the distraction of kids." He looked up to meet her gaze. "Or any distractions."

She gave him a peck on the cheek. "Understood."

Then, Ajay fell into the hack. The world around was nothing to him. Mindless, empty void full of a thoughtless nothing. All that mattered was the hack. Using unfamiliar equipment and unprepped programs, he first found a list of every moving drone in the area.

The assassin drones weren't the only ones. There were still a few police drones scoping the ruins of the smaller yachts. The explosions on the ship had drawn enough attention that even the heavily bribed and thoroughly incompetent police couldn't ignore it, so a new fleet was incoming. The process he had set in place earlier had placed backdoors in a dozen drones in the area. Ajay found them, tallied them, took them.

A wisp of a smile pulled at the corners of his mouth.

There were others, too. Personal drones. Security surveillance drones. Drones left active in people's garages, waiting for instructions over insecure channels. There were Thunderheads above, and he could detect them, but he had never learned Isabelle's trick for taking them. Those drones ran missions disconnected from their networks, listening only for a unique abort command. They operated much in the way the assassin drones did. They'd listen to that abort command, but nothing else.

If only he knew a zero-day flaw—or the abort key.

He didn't, though, so he had to continue with what he could find.

Ajay sent every drone he could grab at the assassin drones as they quietly made their way across the Harbor Basin. The first impact came over the black slick waters below—a crash and shower of sparks followed by a splash.

"One down," Ajay mumbled to himself.

Somewhere, Austin gave out a cheer, only to be shushed by Kate.

It wasn't enough. Ajay could do the math. He had dozens of drones available to him, but the assassins were too difficult to find. If he wanted to stop them, he needed something more.

Ajay turned to see Austin leap over the railing.

"He saw a friend," explained Kate. "Took the harness down to get her."

"Kylie?"

Kate shook her head. "Someone else."

Ajay humphed and got back to work. Several more drones crashed and fell. Their trip across the basin was a slow one. Ponderous due to their stealth programming. Ajay remembered his stealth drone and how it had always operated on its own unique programming. Maybe these were similar. Their quirks of proprietary software bent them into strange constraints. Either way, it appeared he had some time.

Not enough time.

Another drone crashed into an assassin, but the impact wasn't hard enough to bring either down.

Far away, Ajay saw the gathering around the Great Lakes Aquarium. Long limousines lined up in front of the building and festival lights lit the entire space. Men and women in formal wear made their way across the open courtyard to gawk at the slow catastrophe across the water. They were exposed. Even inside the building, the windows wouldn't be proof against this onslaught, but on the edge of the water? They were doomed. The first drones were almost in range to fire their weapons. How long would their programming tell them to wait?

Without looking away, Ajay said, "I need binoculars."

Kate placed something cumbersome and heavy into his outstretched hands.

It took him a moment to realize what it was. "A sniper rifle?"

"It has a scope."

It was a good scope, too. Looking through the glass, Ajay could see all the way across the basin to the aquarium. He zoomed in on the faces there. Grim, scarred men and women with cruel sneers on their painted faces gathered in conversation. These were not the idle elite that they appeared to be from far away. These were dangerous people. The top tier of mercenaries from around the country, all gathered in one place.

This was the top leadership of Frontier Arms.

And, smiling and friendly, right in the middle of the crowd, stood Isabelle Garver.

"My granddaughter is there," he muttered.

"Kylie?"

"Isabelle." Ajay didn't know how to describe the girl. "It's complicated. I need to warn her."

"How?"

How? Ajay's eyes went wide. Over the water, another impact sank an assassin, but it wasn't enough. Not even close. The tower shook from another impact. The Edmund's momentum carried it forward, even as it scraped the bottom of the canal.

Austin pulled himself over the rail and hauled a girl over behind him. Not Kylie. Someone else. The girl collapsed to the metal floor. Her blonde hair spilled out across the floor.

"Hanna," Austin said, trying to shake her awake. When she didn't move, he checked her vital signs and put her into a recovery position on her side. To Ajay, he said, "She's been hit by the neurotoxin pellets."

"Friend of yours?" Ajay asked.

"She was awful to us at camp, but she probably doesn't deserve this."

"Can you get the rest of them?" Kate asked, peering over the edge.

"Silver's down there now," Austin said, gasping for breath. "She grabbed Brian."

"Silver?" Ajay asked, turning back to the display. "Sonya Silver? What's she doing there?"

"I don't know." Austin ran his fingers through his hair. "I don't *know*. We were supposed to infiltrate the ship for her, but it's *her* ship. We were supposed to find a guy, but nobody cares about the guy. There's just a bunch of crazy people running around down there and assassin drones are flying toward the ambassador meeting."

"Ambassadors?" Ajay asked. "Is that who we're saying those people are?"

"I. Don't. Know." Austin stalked away, turned on his heel, and returned. "It doesn't make any sense. She's created a situation where there are a dozen things pulling us in a dozen different directions. I don't even know what our mission is supposed to be anymore."

Ajay thought about it. Too many variables. Chaos. This couldn't all be planned. Silver couldn't have known her ship would get hit by a torpedo. She couldn't have known the prisoners would get free.

Then what had she expected? If she wanted Kylie's team to infiltrate the ship, she must have expected them to find the prisoners.

"I don't know." Austin's voice tense with frustration. "It was supposed to be an easy infiltration job. Our plan was to pretend to be the band. Get in, deliver the warning, then leave."

"Does she have the codes?" Ajay snapped.

"Ajay," said Kate in warning.

"How much of this was a setup?" Austin said. "Was it broken from the start? If Silver was in on it, then she must have known all this was going to happen. Why did she want us here?"

The display showed the locations of the few remaining police drones. Surveillance drones zipped through the air at top speeds, hoping to randomly strike one of the camouflaged assassin drones. It was a bad solution—one Ajay was a little bit ashamed to use. There were better options out there, but the best would be the abort codes.

Even with the right keys, he didn't know if he could stop the drones.

"Austin," he said, tearing himself away from the screen. "Austin, I need to know. Does Silver know the keys?"

He blinked and met Ajay's gaze. "Yes. Absolutely. That's the only way it makes sense. She was in charge of the thing all along and now she's the one launching this attack."

"Then we need to talk to her. Can you patch us in?"

Austin thought for a long breath before saying, "I can boost the tower signal to push through the noise. It'll make it so everyone can talk. No secure channels."

"Do it," said Ajay. "Let's see if we can have a chat here."

The display showed another impact, and two more drones splashed down into the basin. Ajay selected a drone from his fleet—a police drone with flashing lights and an integrated taser—and used it to bounce a signal toward Isabelle.

"Isabelle," he said through the comm. "Isabelle, can you read me?"

No response. Figures. She had a different relationship with her tech from her sister. Isabelle had used it to reshape herself. She'd been working on closing herself off in ways that even Ajay hadn't discovered. If she had been open, this would be easy. But there still had to be a way to initiate the communication. He didn't know a zero-day to sneak into a back door for her. She had closed everything, and he didn't have the tools necessary to find anything else. There had to be another way.

There *was* another way. There was one thing that would always be able to reach Isabelle Garver.

But for that, Ajay needed something else.

"Isabelle," he said, recording the signal. "This is your grandfather. I'm sending comm info. Please contact me through this. There's an incoming attack, and you need to get to safety." Ajay set the signal on repeat, varying the frequency of the signal. It would blast out on a hundred channels, but maybe one of them would find its way into Isabelle's feed.

"Got it," said Austin. "All channels open."

There was a click on Ajay's comm, and a background roar of noise reverberated through his skull.

"Kylie dear," crackled a woman's voice with a cruel sneer. "I'm so disappointed. You were supposed to be something special." It was the infamous Sonya Silver.

Anger bubbled up in Ajay's gut. "You'll shut your mouth, young lady. Kylie *is* special, and I'll hear nothing more from you to the contrary."

"Papa?" said Kylie over the line.

"This isn't the plan," gasped Tenen over the comm.

The plan. Kate was supposed to cover them using the rifle. Ajay was supposed to hack the drones and stop the assassination. There was a lot that he'd promised the big man that probably wasn't going to happen.

One thing Ajay *could* do was defend his granddaughter from this awful woman. He snatched the rifle up from where it leaned against the railing. Through its scope, he saw the woman standing with a gun to a boy's head. Kylie was a short distance away with both her hands raised.

"We're all going to wait a minute," said Silver through the comm. "Things will resolve themselves."

"Bullshit," said Ajay. "You just want your assassin drones to kill everyone over there, but it's not going to happen." Ajay poked his head over the railing and saw Silver not far down on the ship. She held a boy in her arms and pressed a gun to his head. "Don't think that kid's life matters to me, Silver. I don't know him."

She barked a laugh. "Oh, what kind of example are you setting for your granddaughter, Ajay Andersen?"

"The same kind I've always set," Ajay said. "The kind I hope she doesn't follow."

He looked at the sniper rifle, but while he could pick up any strange computer and instinctively know how to use it, guns were a complete mystery. He cast a pleading look at Kate, but it was Austin who stepped up to help.

The boy took the rifle, expertly locked it into position, and aimed it at Silver down below. "It fires neuropellets," he said. "Non-lethal, high velocity, neuropellets." He breathed deep and slow. "I can do this."

"That won't save the kid," Ajay said. "They're too slow."

Austin checked his range. "We're too close. It might kill her at this range." His hands shook. A look of panic flashed across his face. He wasn't a killer. Ajay doubted he was the kind of kid who could hurt anyone, even in a pinch. No, Austin wasn't cut out for this.

Ajay glanced at Kate. Her nerves were catching up with her. He could see it in her red-rimmed eyes. This needed to end, and soon.

He clipped the harness around himself and stepped over the railing onto the narrow ledge. Sonya Silver was stalling. That much was clear. She wanted to wait until the assassin drones did their business. How long that would be, Ajay didn't know. Minutes, maybe. Every second that passed put Isabelle in more danger.

"Silver," he said through the comm as he lowered himself to the still-moving ship. "It's time we made a deal."

Chapter Fifty-One

Papa stepped onto the slanted deck of the superyacht and stood in that way he did when he was pretending to know what he was doing. Kylie reflexively puffed herself up. If he could pretend, then so could she.

"This ship was going to be your new base of operations," Papa said to Silver. "I was wondering why you were moving this gigantic thing into the basin, but that's it, isn't it? It's supposed to be a place to run your unethical experiments in the center of a base of power that you control."

Silver fixed him with her cold eyes. "We'll crack the code to that tech in your granddaughter's head. We were making progress out in international waters, but not enough."

"So you brought the whole thing to Minnesota."

"It's the biotech capital of the world, Mr. Andersen. Where else would I want to be?"

"Isabelle is across the harbor basin," Papa said. His voice rang out both over the comm and through the cold wind coming off the great lake. "But if you call off the attack and take me instead of that kid, then we can all walk away today."

Silver's lips twisted up in a sneer. "If I call off the attack, the leadership of Frontier Arms survives. You and I both know it's better if they don't."

"You're killing the whole organization."

"Only its redundant leadership."

"So, this is a power grab," said Ajay. "You're going to use your shares in the company to take full control."

She took a step back, dragging Brian with her. "With the leadership out of the way, I'll easily gain control of the organization."

"You're not afraid of police interference?"

"Digital forensics isn't what it used to be," she said. "Nothing here points to me."

"Except that you're here. Your students are here."

"Sometimes students go rogue, especially when they're led astray by a teacher."

"Go rogue?" Ajay asked. "Or are you just playing both sides like you did with Olexie Sokolov?"

Recognition sparked in her eyes. "The old Russian."

"You hired him to bring workers across the border, then had kids from your school take him down when he wasn't convenient anymore."

Her red lips parted in a smile. "Guilty."

A realization dawned on Kylie, and she saw that Papa came to the same conclusion. Silver wouldn't tell them this unless she either trusted them or planned on killing them. Kylie didn't feel very trusted.

"Leave Isabelle alive," said Papa. "That's all I ask."

Kylie couldn't believe what she was hearing. "You're just going to let all those people die?" She stepped forward. "Papa, what are you doing?"

Silver regarded Papa with a gaze that could have frozen the lake itself.

Mr. Lang emerged from below deck, and Silver's crowd of prisoners moved to block him. He looked terrible, with fresh bruises on his neck and face.

"Isabelle Garver is the worst of them all," said Silver. "Why would I let her live?"

"You mean she's the greatest threat," said Papa.

"Same thing."

"Who are these people?" Papa asked, indicating the prisoners.

Silver's hand went to a black box clipped to her belt. "Volunteers," she said. "Every one of them."

"Isabelle is my granddaughter," Papa said. "You know that, though, don't you? You probably planned it to have Kylie here because of it."

"How do you figure?" Silver asked.

"It's why you wanted Kylie so badly. You wanted to test her abilities so that you knew what Isabelle was capable of. You also wanted Kylie here because you thought it would protect you from retaliation, but the ship sank anyway."

"Proof of how dangerous your granddaughter is."

"She didn't bring the sub, though, did she?"

"No," said Silver. She blinked, and Ajay got the impression she didn't know the answer to that one.

Lang handed the cane to Kylie but nudged her another step back. She stood stupidly with the hefty cane, wondering what she could do to make things better. Her gun was gone. She was too far away to hit anyone with the cane and the taser probably didn't work anymore. It was useless—

No. It wasn't useless. She saw the program flickering on what remained of its holographic display. The migraine in the back of her skull pulsed in response to the hazy lights.

"I don't want to do this," she whispered to herself.

"Just point the gun at me, and let that kid walk away. Let Kylie leave," Ajay said. "And stop delaying."

"And what if I don't?" asked Silver.

Papa pointed up to the bridge. "There's a rifle up there that might help you come to a decision faster."

Silver sneered at Papa. "A neuropellet rifle. Do you know that there is a counteragent to the neurotoxin? It's not pleasant. Your granddaughter shot me earlier today and I'm still under the effect of the cure. The neuropellets shut down most of a person's extraneous neurological systems, but the counteragent keeps every nerve ending awake by making it fire full strength." She glanced down at the gun that she held to Brian's head. "It doesn't put a person in a good mood."

"Neither does chronic hip pain, but you don't see me let it affect my charm." Papa fixed her with a serious look. "You're still stalling."

"Fine." Silver pointed her gun at Papa. She shoved Brian away. "Now, let's chat."

The flickering hologram danced before Kylie's eyes. It was proof of what her grandfather thought of her. It showed that he knew the tech in her head was the extent of her usefulness. He left open the one program that would unlock everything for her. It would make her the ultimate hacker again because—because she had failed.

But he couldn't know the noise she felt coming from the prisoners. They still forced a wave of static through the bridge of her nose. Her head still ached from their interference. How much worse would it be if she opened herself up?

"How long have you turned children into killers?" Papa asked.

Silver scoffed, "I separate wheat from the chaff."

The ship drifted forward under the bridge. Papa probably couldn't see from his position, but Austin would soon lose his angle with the rifle. He was so close. Dangerously close with the high-powered rifle. The ship rumbled beneath them. Smoke belched from the decks below.

If Kylie was going to act, then she needed to do it soon.

"Call off the attack," said Papa. "Now."

"That wasn't the deal, was it?" Silver flicked a holographic image out of the fidget on her left hand. It showed a drone's-eye view of the cluster of limousines outside the aquarium. "You wanted me to spare Isabelle Garver." In the center of the image, Isabelle stood alone in a sleek white dress.

"Call off the attack, or I signal my shooter," said Papa.

But it only seemed to amuse Silver.

Kylie had to act. "Fine," she whispered to herself. She pressed the head of the cane against her forehead. Papa was right. She was nothing without her abilities, and this was their one chance to save Isabelle. She activated the program.

Silver glanced up to the bridge. "The boy won't shoot," she said to Papa. "And even if he did, he couldn't hit me, not even from this range. I watch my students. I know what each is capable of."

Then, she moved. Her hand touched the box on her belt.

The prisoners launched themselves at Kylie, but Lang blocked their way. He lashed out at the first one to touch him and slammed the guy to the floor with a sickening crack. The effort must have ruined his tenuous sense of balance, because he fell as the next attacker slammed a fist into his side. Another prisoner piled on. And another. They pounded brutal fists into his big body.

Tenen Lang took it all. He heaved up, met Kylie's gaze, and rasped, "Do it."

But she was already there. Kylie unlocked all the constraints on her abilities. Her mind opened like a flower. Like a satellite dish, signals washed over her mind like a cold waterfall.

She took them. Accepted them. Redirected them.

The migraine exploded like a string of fireworks.

She was vaguely aware of the gunshots. Papa dove across the deck for cover. Silver shot at him with her huge pistol.

Halos around the bridge lights blotted out her vision. Blind, she stumbled backward until the felt the cold solidness of the railing in her hand.

The halos weren't from light but people. From the attackers. Kylie pointed herself at them and selected each. They were transmitting, but it was a nonsensical white noise of transmission. As her whole mind came online, nothing was how she remembered it. She had more available now that she had never noticed before. Maybe it was the time disconnected, or maybe it was access to these differently modified people, but she felt their presence like a weight on her soul.

And yet, not everything was there. Papa's program *hadn't* unlocked everything. He'd only activated one single function, and everything she now sensed blossomed from that one singular ability.

"You have to warn your sister, Kylie," Papa said through the comm. What did he mean? "You're her zero-day, dear."

Zero-day. The undiscovered flaw. The chink in the armor. Kylie blinked. The pressure was so much. It crushed her. Those prisoners. The ragged attackers, still pounding, clawing, gouging Lang. They were so horrible, like repulsive angry balls of hate spitting agony into the back of her skull.

There was more to their abilities, though. She could sense it. There was anger, but it wasn't directed at her. She might not have grasped it before, but now... now she understood it all. There was still so much she couldn't do. She had limitations in how her brain worked, but she could see that these people, though they were dangerous, had wants and desires of their own. They were people. They had feelings—but those feelings were being suppressed. Supplanted.

Papa had unlocked in her an ability to connect her innate empathy to her signals, and it gave her so much more than he expected.

"Stop," she said, pushing her command through the signal.

The attackers stopped.

Silver swung her pistol to point it at Kylie. "What are you doing?" Her eyes brightened. "It's true. Like they said. It's true what you can do."

Kylie saw it. The plastic comm in the unit clipped to Silver's belt was emitting a faint signal. That was the clumsy method she used to control her prisoners.

Kylie dove to one side. She ignored the gunshots, knowing how hard it must be to hit anything on the shaking, sinking ship.

"Be free," Kylie commanded because it was the best thing she could think of. Let the people decide for themselves what to do with their hate. Maybe they would attack Silver.

But they didn't. The surviving prisoners ran, jumping over the side of the ship toward the land. She heard them hit below, but the fall wasn't far. Most fled into the night.

Crap. Crap, crap, crap.

"Zero-day," Papa repeated, gasping.

Isabelle. Kylie needed to help Isabelle. The assassin drones were making their way across the basin undetected by Isabelle and the horrible leaders of Frontier Arms. If Kylie could warn her, maybe Isabelle could escape to safety.

Silver ran toward Kylie, but Kylie was fast. She kept the flaming wreckage of a drone car between herself and the woman, moving as another car slid across the increasingly tilting deck. She would need to leave the ship soon. If she didn't, she'd end up falling into the canal, and she didn't know if she could swim free through the frigid waves.

Kylie reached the front of the ship, barely able to stand as the deck shook from another impact. There was a crash, and the last drone car slid away.

Sis. Kylie reached as far as she could with her signal. The sensation felt strange to her, and when she pushed, the migraine in the back of her skull eased a little bit. Something about this felt familiar. *Sis, are you there?*

Tenen Lang mopped blood from his face. He might as well have been miles away from Silver. No way could he help. Papa was nowhere to be seen, but she couldn't always expect him to save her, could she? She needed to do some things herself.

Isabelle, where are you? She remembered their days together and how they often communicated without words. Isabelle was her big sister. There was something special about that relationship. Something that transcended the need for a solid connection, a spoken word, or even a normal non-verbal signal. Maybe that's what Kylie had been missing these last couple of years. Connection that didn't need words.

She remembered her times with Austin—how they often knew what the other was thinking without saying anything. She thought of her time with Papa, how she always knew what he wanted for supper. Pizza. It was always pizza. Maybe she didn't need her abilities to make connections with other people.

But she had something special with her sister. She always would.

Silver steadied herself. She wasn't far now, and she still had the gun. "Work for me, Kylie," she said. "I can teach you so much. In a few seconds, we'll be in charge of every operation in the Midwest. We'll have decapitated all the criminal and mercenary operations from here to Chicago. With my help, you could be amazing, child. Amazing."

"I'm already amazing," said Kylie.

Then, she felt. She *felt*. Not the migraine. Not the grief or pain of her life. Not the emptiness of being alone and strange every single day of her life.

She allowed herself to feel the longing brought out by the loss of her sister.

Because she missed her so much it hurt.

Silver leveled her pistol at Kylie. "I don't have time for negotiations, dear." Her perfectly manicured finger touched the trigger. "Join my cause or get out of my way."

Kylie met the woman's gaze and saw her cold cruelty. This was it. This was the moment Lang had talked about where Kylie either needed to kill or be killed, but she didn't have a way to kill Silver. She had never had a way to kill the woman. That was part of Silver's genius. She made people dangerous but never gave them the tools to actually *be* dangerous. She made them survivors, but she never let them have all the tools for survival.

Then, Kylie looked up at the bridge. Papa was helping Brian over the railing. They were safe. Next to them was Austin, but Austin no longer held the sniper rifle.

Someone else did. It was the woman who was with Papa. Kate.

"Kate?" Kylie said through the comm.

"I've got you, kid," said Papa's friend. More than a friend? Kylie didn't know. She'd probably want to figure that out.

Kylie reached out to Isabelle one last time, trying her best to simply sense her sister's presence. "Thank you," she said through the comm. "I appreciate that." She closed her eyes. "Take the shot."

The double crack of gunfire echoed across the canal, but Kylie felt no pain. She felt only the rumbling shift of the ship under her feet as it struck the canal wall one more time. She felt the spray of blood on the wind as Silver staggered from the too-close shot from the sniper rifle.

She felt the connection as her sister reached back to her. *Kylie?*

A surge of anger boiled up in Kylie's chest. *I hate you,* she pushed through their strengthening connection. *You left me!*

It was for your own safety.

I have never *been safe.*

There was a long pause, and the connection wavered. Kylie remembered playing together with her sister for long hours in the lab where they grew up. They had always been able to communicate, and while she interpreted the thoughts as words, in truth it was their own customized communication developed even before she ever truly had language. It was a raw sense of emotion and image that flowed between them.

Isabelle finally responded, *You've infiltrated Silver's organization.*

I didn't do that for you.

No, Isabelle's message came with a hint of regret. *But I'm proud of you, sis.*

Go fuck yourself. The anger in Kylie's fists dissipated into steam in the cool night. *They're coming for you.*

Her sister's feed wavered again, almost dropping completely.

Assassin drones, she added. *Over the basin.*

There was a wave of signal chatter. She felt the tiny halos of dozens of drones flare to life as Isabelle grabbed control. Her sister had always had a talent for drones that were supposed to be unhackable. Kylie felt a little rush of pride for her big sister.

Thanks, sis, said Isabelle, and the signal faded into the background.

The sound of metal tearing vibrated through the ship, pitching Kylie to one side. She landed next to Silver, whose eyes were still open, staring up at the sky.

Blood pulsed from her shoulder, but she still drew breath. The pellet had pierced her skin, sending neurotoxin directly into her bloodstream. Kylie didn't want to know what the stuff was doing to the woman's nerves.

Kylie kicked the gun away, and it twirled over the railing into the water. Then, she took Silver in a half-carry, just like they had been taught. She heaved the woman down the tilting deck, staggering under the dead weight.

Deadweight, but not *dead.* Kylie ran. The *Edmund* was so close to land. She could almost step across the small gap, but farther up the deck, she could drop directly onto the concrete wall. If she could make it that far.

"Kylie, drop her," said Papa from above. "I'll help you up."

"No," Kylie said in a way that she hoped would sever all argument.

"You won't make it. The ship is splitting in two."

Kylie doubled her efforts. She wrenched herself up and onto the railing. The ground was a long jump away. Too far for her while carrying Silver. Above, she saw Papa descending on the climbing rope. He was too slow.

"You have to let her go!" Papa shouted down.

Kylie's voice was a ragged rasp. "I won't kill her."

"Sonya Silver made her choice," Papa said. "She took her risks. It's not your fault she tried to kill people. It's not your fault she failed in her bid to take over the region. She knew the risks."

"I'm. Not. A. Killer." Kylie heaved herself forward, dragging the woman farther along the rail. The ship shuddered, and now she would need to step up in addition to crossing the gap between the ship and ledge.

"You're not," Papa gasped. His feet hit the deck, but he was struggling to detach from the harness. "You're not a killer. You never have to be. But that doesn't mean you have to die for that woman."

Tears blurred Kylie's vision. Every step she took, land grew farther away. Higher up. There was no way she could get there fast enough.

Still, she wouldn't stop. Her lungs burned. Muscles ached.

"I'm sorry," she whispered into her comm, not sure what she was sorry for. The top of the wall was now higher than her head. The water rushed below, frigid and black as doom. "I'm sorry."

A voice came not through her comm, but from above. "Nothing to be sorry about, kid."

Tenen Lang lay on his belly on the wall and reached a strong hand down. He grasped Silver's arm and pulled, but his angle was bad. Kylie pushed, but Silver went limp under her grasp.

Her foot slipped. "I can't—"

"You can," said Tenen, perfectly calm. "You can do whatever you put your mind to, kid."

She looked up to see two silhouettes above him. Prisoners. Her eyes went wide.

But they didn't attack. They got down next to him. Was she controlling them? One grasped Silver and helped heave her up onto the wall, where Tenen immediately started tending to her wounds. The other took Kylie's hand and hauled her up.

She crouched on the wall for a long time, breathing cool air and trying her very best to calm the furious adrenaline burning through her veins. Finally, she said through the comm, "I'm okay, Papa. You can go back up. I'm okay. We stopped it. I talked to Isabelle and we stopped it all."

Across the dark waters of the Harbor Basin, in the warm lights that suffused the summer night, the drones commenced their attack in an explosion of gunfire, and people started to die.

Chapter
Fifty-Two

By the time Ajay found Kylie on the smoky shores of the canal, the ship had settled and ambulance drones had carried away the badly injured Sonya Silver and a dozen others.

"The medic said the neuropellet entered her bloodstream," Kylie said. Her eyes glistened with unshed tears. "He said something about the possibility of permanent neurological damage."

Police drones lit up the skies with lightning flashes of blue and red. Ajay limped across the wet grass, leaning on Kate for as little support as he could manage, which was actually quite a bit of support. Behind him, Hanna, Brian, and Austin followed, ragged but alive.

"Jess?" Kylie asked.

"She finally checked in. She wasn't in the water by the time the torpedoes hit."

"Good."

"She basically did her job and got out."

"Oh, is that what we were supposed to do?"

Then, she was hugging Papa, nearly toppling him over. She pulled Kate in as well, then Austin and Brian, and finally, after a tense but silent negotiation, Hanna.

Ajay had never known Kylie to be so warm. Affectionate. There was probably a lot he didn't know about the kid.

An enormous figure stepped from the shadow, leaning hard on a cane. Tenen Lang.

"Papa," Kylie said, "You know Mr. Lang. He helped me."

Ajay looked up at the big man, not sure what form his punishment would take. Even injured as he was, Tenen Lang was terrifying.

All Tenen said was, "Thanks for letting me use the cane."

"Keep it," Ajay said, turning to Kylie. "As long as you'll make me a new one."

A grin spread across her face. "Of course."

The group made their way across the grass to the water's edge. Far away across the basin, the Great Lakes Aquarium still glowed in the night. Ajay squinted at the view. Tiny flashes of light sparkled like glitter around the bright building.

"Austin," he said. "Do you have that scope?"

"Sure." Austin handed him the scope from the sniper rifle. He had left it detached when he had packed up the team's gear.

Looking through the scope, Ajay saw what was happening. "The assassin drones are still attacking, and there's nothing we can do about it."

"I warned Isabelle," Kylie said. "You were right that I could contact her when nobody else could. We've always been able to sense each other. Turns out she was using me to infiltrate Silver's camp."

Sure enough, Ajay spotted Isabelle walking from the aquarium, untouched, as everyone else around her died. Her white dress was spattered with red. She bent down and plucked something from the suit coat of one of the men and tucked it into her tiny clutch purse.

Then, the girl looked directly at Ajay and smiled. It was a cruel smile—the smile of victory over unworthy opponents. A fist unclenched in Ajay's chest. She wasn't in danger. He wasn't sure if she had ever been in danger.

She *was* the danger, and he would need to deal with her sooner or later. But not tonight.

"Papa?" Kylie asked. Her voice sounded small.

"Yes, dear?"

"Do you think it was Isabelle who told Silver about me?"

Ajay had to admit that it fit. If Isabelle wanted Kylie in the camp, then the best way to get her there was to drop hints about her abilities. It hinted at a dangerous path that Isabelle was walking down, and he didn't like it.

He put an arm around Kylie's shoulders, and the kid melted into him. "We'll get her back. Sometimes family relationships are complicated."

"She's a horrible person, isn't she?"

Ajay considered his answer carefully, and then simply blurted out the first answer he could manage. "Yes, but we love her anyway. That's why families are complicated."

It was time to take Kylie home and finally, hopefully, relax. With the dangers of the assassins taken care of, he could think about returning to his house. After months away, it wouldn't feel much like home, but he would manage. For Kylie's sake, he would manage.

"Is it true you have a camper now?" Kylie asked.

It was Kate who answered. "He's been on the move all summer."

Kylie looked to Kate, then back at Ajay. "Both of you?"

Ajay pulled Kate closer and fought to keep the goofy grin from his lips. "We're still working things out."

"Can we keep traveling?" Kylie said as they stepped onto the first of many streets. "I mean, at least until school starts again."

Ajay thought about it. "We should drop Austin off at home," he said. "And make sure everyone is safe."

After a moment's consideration, she said, "Can I get a guitar?"

"Acoustic?"

"Electric."

Ajay considered it. "Only if you take lessons."

A bright grin spread across her face. "Deal."

Tenen spoke up. "With Silver out of commission, the camp is going to need leadership, but I think I can manage until things go back to normal. I'll get the rest of the kids home safe."

"Is that how it works?" Ajay asked. "The boss is hurt, so the next in charge gets to own it all?"

"It's the American way," said Tenen.

"I don't think that sounds right," said Ajay, finding himself oddly comfortable in the big man's presence. He still remembered the day he had almost killed Tenen Lang. At the time he'd doubted his decision. He had thought the world would probably be better off with the big man dead. Now, he wasn't sure. Tenen seemed to have changed.

Tenen continued, "I'll tell them I'm in charge. If anyone disagrees, I'll get violent."

Kate laughed. "That *does* sound pretty American."

"Great." Ajay squeezed Kate's hand and pulled her away from the group. "Kate—"

"I'm sticking with you," Kate said.

"I wasn't going to—"

"You were going to suggest I lay low and get away for a while. For my safety. You were going to suggest that I stay home and recover. Maybe wait for your call when it's safe."

Ajay pressed his lips together. She was right, but he didn't want to admit it. He desperately wanted her to stay with him, even though he didn't know where things were going. When he finally opened his mouth to talk, she kissed him.

Oh, *that* was where it was going.

And he kissed back, the heat scattering the last remains of cold from the evening air. They lost themselves in each other for an eternity, absorbing all the tension and danger and insecurity they had felt over the summer.

Now was when they were safe. *Now* was when they could be together, at least for a time. Kylie was right. They could go on the move. They'd return to Bemidji when it felt right to do so, but for now, they could go anywhere.

"This is going to be an adventure," he said when they separated.

"Yeah," she murmured. "It's going to be fun."

They walked hand in hand for a while, and Ajay started to wonder why he had parked the Winnebago so far away. Then, he realized that the camper wasn't where he left it. It was stranded at the scene of a crash.

When they reached the camper in the parking lot, Ajay made sure Kylie didn't see the wreckage. There wasn't any significant damage to the camper itself, but he didn't want her to see what they had done. He needn't have bothered. Someone had already cleaned up the ruined car and the body next to it.

Kylie spent forever greeting Garrison, who would have been thrilled to see anyone, but was doubly so to find Kylie outside his little home. The others piled into his vehicle, but Ajay pulled Kate aside one last time before climbing into the driver's seat. He kissed her gently and gazed into her eyes.

"You took the shot," he said.

"I did what I had to do."

"How did you know how to use that sniper rifle?"

A smile sparkled in her eyes. "I told you, my husband was a little bit of a gun nut. Once you've used enough guns, they pretty much all make sense."

"It's just," Ajay said, "it was a really good shot. An inch left and you would have killed Silver. A little to the right and you risked hitting Kylie."

The smile disappeared from Kate's eyes but stayed on her lips. She flung an arm around Ajay's shoulders and led him to the camper. "You're sounding paranoid, Ajay."

"Yeah." He searched her eyes for a long breath. "I am, but I want you to know, there's nobody I would rather have had on that bridge. Nobody at all."

That actually seemed to affect her. Her blush was a warm glow in the cool night. "One thing I know about these last few months."

"What's that?"

"Retirement hasn't been dull." She flashed another smile, and Ajay was lost in the crinkles at the corners of her eyes. "Not for one second."

They climbed into the camper, and Ajay pulled away into the night. Behind them, the flash of red and blue spread across the Harbor Basin, enveloping the aquarium, the bridge, and all the chaos left in their wake. The authorities had a lot to sort out, and the residents of Duluth weren't going to be happy with their bridge out of commission and a superyacht stuck in their canal.

But Kylie was safe. Isabelle was alive. In that, Ajay decided to declare victory.

"Another day," he said as he pulled onto Interstate 35 driving south. "Another day."

The moment Kate stepped into her farmhouse, she knew something was wrong. Outside, her truck cooled in the first cold wind of the evening. Fireflies lit the too-tall grasses of her lawn.

"You might as well come out," Kate called into the dark house. "Don't make me come find you."

The man moved in the shadows of the living room. He sat in Bill's favorite recliner—the one she hadn't sat in since the day he died.

"Well, are you here to kill me?" Kate tried to sound casual, but there was a tightness in her voice.

The shadow steepled his fingers. He was a tall man with dark skin, and he wore the black suit that only government men made look good. His voice was rich and deep. "It got messy."

The old farmhouse creaked in the wind.

"I've been retired thirty years," Kate finally said. "You want modern skills, hire someone younger."

"You sell yourself short."

Kate felt her anger rising. "My job was to keep him safe, and he's *safe*."

"By some measurements." The man stood, unfolding in the darkness like a Swiss Army knife.

"It would help if you didn't send people to kill him," Kate snapped.

"They were hired to keep him from getting involved," said the man. "Sometimes the contractors we hire get a little overzealous." His eyes narrowed. "It's easy for them to get personally involved. I'm sure you understand."

Kate ignored the dig. She *had* gotten personally involved. She would *stay* personally involved as long as she could. "They followed me, didn't they? To find his house?"

"Not everyone is as gifted at locating a target as you. It's what you were always known for back when we worked together, wasn't it?"

Kate remembered training the tall boy when he had first started. She remembered, too, the long years in witness protection after everything had blown up. "I never missed the CIA," she said. "Not one single day for all those years."

He shrugged. "The CIA has missed you, Kate. There have been a lot of changes, but we're still trying to do the right things."

She wasn't so sure. "I'm sorry things didn't turn out the way you wanted."

A flicker in the corners of his eyes told her that maybe there was something more to his goals than she understood. "The goal was to prevent the total decapitation of the largest private standing army in the United States. As it turns out, all we've done is consolidate that power under the leadership of a single player."

"Isabelle Garver," Kate said. She saw now that this was probably a better outcome than the man had ever dreamed. "And you want me to influence her through Ajay."

This time his smile was large and genuine. "See," he said, "you *do* still understand how the game is played."

Kate sat at the kitchen table. Suddenly, she felt more exhausted than she had after all those years working the farm with Bill. "What do they call you these days, Alvin?"

"Black," said the man. "They call me Mr. Black."

Patreon

It can all be yours. Become a Patron now and gain access to raw chapters from future books, short stories, and even early copies of every Anthony W. Eichenlaub book before it's released. Every tier gets access to the private Oak Leaf Collective Discord—the perfect hangout for readers and writers alike.

Not everyone wants to chip in a few dollars to ensure the future will be written, and that's fine. Joining the newsletter will get you updates when new books come out. It'll also get you progress updates, book recs, and pictures of my dog.

But becoming a Patron is an incredible opportunity to not only support the work you love, but to also gain access to exclusives not available anywhere else. Want to be the first to get finished copies of the next book? Support today and you'll be first in line.

Some are content to wait and see what the future brings. Others prefer to nudge fate in the right direction.

If that's you, come join me and help write the future.

patreon.com/AWEichenlaub

Also by Anthony W. Eichenlaub

Old Code
Grandfather Anonymous
Grandfather Ghost
Grandfather Guardian
Grandfather Zero

Colony of Edge
Of a Strange World Made
Upon Another Edge Broken
On a Forsaken Land Found
From a Barren Seed Grown
Above a Distant Sky Seen

Metal and Men
Justice in an Age of Metal and Men
Peace in an Age of Metal and Men
Honor in an Age of Metal and Men